Teresa

ROALD DAHL

Charlie and the Great Glass Elevator

Illustrated by
Michael Foreman

Collins
An Imprint of HarperCollins*Publishers*

Roald Dahl was born in 1916 in Wales of Norwegian parents. He was educated in England before starting work for an oil company in Africa when he was eighteen. He began writing after a 'monumental bash on the head' sustained as an RAF fighter pilot during the Second World War. His books are read by children the world over, and his popularity is unequalled by any other children's writer. Roald Dahl died in 1990.

For my daughters
Tessa   Ophelia   Lucy
and for my godson
Edmund Pollinger

First published in Great Britain by George Allen & Unwin
(Publishers) Ltd 1973
This edition published by HarperCollins Publishers Ltd 1991
Text copyright © Roald Dahl 1973, 1986
Illustrations copyright © Michael Foreman 1986
ISBN 0 00 185431-3

A CIP record for this book is available from the British Library

Printed in Great Britain by The Bath Press, Avon

Contents

I

Mr Wonka Goes Too Far

The last time we saw Charlie, he was riding high above his home town in the Great Glass Lift. Only a short while before, Mr Wonka had told him that the whole gigantic fabulous Chocolate Factory was his, and now our small friend was returning in triumph with his entire family to take over. The passengers in the Lift (just to remind you) were:

Charlie Bucket, our hero.

Mr Willy Wonka, chocolate-maker extraordinary.

Mr and Mrs Bucket, Charlie's father and mother.

Grandpa Joe and Grandma Josephine, Mr Bucket's father and mother.

Grandpa George and Grandma Georgina, Mrs Bucket's father and mother.

Grandma Josephine, Grandma Georgina and Grandpa George were still in bed, the bed having been pushed on board just before take-off. Grandpa Joe, as you remember, had got out of bed to go around the Chocolate Factory with Charlie.

The Great Glass Lift was a thousand feet up and cruising nicely. The sky was brilliant blue. Everybody on board was wildly excited at the thought of going to live in the famous

Chocolate Factory. Grandpa Joe was singing. Charlie was jumping up and down. Mr and Mrs Bucket were smiling for the first time in years, and the three old ones in the bed were grinning at one another with pink toothless gums.

'What in the world keeps this crazy thing up in the air?' croaked Grandma Josephine.

'Madam,' said Mr Wonka, 'it is not a lift any longer. Lifts only go up and down *inside* buildings. But now that it has taken us up into the sky, it has become an ELEVATOR. It is THE GREAT GLASS ELEVATOR.'

'And what keeps it up?' said Grandma Josephine.

'Skyhooks,' said Mr Wonka.

'You amaze me,' said Grandma Josephine.

'Dear lady,' said Mr Wonka, 'you are new to the scene. When you have been with us a little longer, nothing will amaze you.'

'These skyhooks,' said Grandma Josephine. 'I assume one end is hooked on to this contraption we're riding in. Right?'

'Right,' said Mr Wonka.

'What's the other end hooked on to?' said Grandma Josephine.

'Every day,' said Mr Wonka, 'I get deafer and deafer. Remind me, please, to call up my ear doctor the moment we get back.'

'Charlie,' said Grandma Josephine. 'I don't think I trust this gentleman very much.'

'Nor do I,' said Grandma Georgina. 'He footles around.'

Charlie leaned over the bed and whispered to the two old women. 'Please,' he said, 'don't spoil everything. Mr Wonka is a fantastic man. He's my friend. I love him.'

'Charlie's right,' whispered Grandpa Joe, joining the group. 'Now you be quiet, Josie, and don't make trouble.'

Mr Wonka Goes Too Far

'We must hurry!' said Mr Wonka. 'We have so much time and so little to do! No! Wait! Cross that out! Reverse it! Thank you! Now back to the factory!' he cried, clapping his hands once and springing two feet in the air with two feet. 'Back we fly to the factory! But we must go *up* before we can come down. We must go *higher and higher!*'

'What did I tell you,' said Grandma Josephine. 'The man's cracked!'

'Be quiet, Josie,' said Grandpa Joe. 'Mr Wonka knows exactly what he's doing.'

'He's cracked as a crab!' said Grandma Georgina.

'We must go higher!' said Mr Wonka. 'We must go tremendously high! Hold on to your stomach!' He pressed a brown button. The Elevator shuddered, and then with a

fearful whooshing noise it shot vertically upward like a rocket. Everybody clutched hold of everybody else and as the great machine gathered speed, the rushing whooshing sound of the wind outside grew louder and louder and shriller and shriller until it became a piercing shriek and you had to yell to make yourself heard.

'Stop!' yelled Grandma Josephine. 'Joe, you make him stop! I want to get off!'

'Save us!' yelled Grandma Georgina.

'Go down!' yelled Grandpa George.

'No, no!' Mr Wonka yelled back. 'We've got to go up!'

'But why?' they all shouted at once. 'Why up and not down?'

'Because the higher we are when we start coming down, the faster we'll all be going when we hit,' said Mr Wonka. 'We've got to be going at an absolutely sizzling speed when we hit.'

'When we hit *what?*' they cried.

'The factory, of course,' answered Mr Wonka.

'You must be whackers,' said Grandma Josephine. 'We'll all be pulpified!'

'We'll be scrambled like eggs!' said Grandma Georgina.

'That,' said Mr Wonka, 'is a chance we shall have to take.'

'You're joking,' said Grandma Josephine. 'Tell us you're joking.'

'Madam,' said Mr Wonka, 'I never joke.'

'Oh, my dears!' cried Grandma Georgina. 'We'll be *lixivated*, every one of us!'

'More than likely,' said Mr Wonka.

Grandma Josephine screamed and disappeared under the bedclothes, Grandma Georgina clutched Grandpa George so tight he changed shape. Mr and Mrs Bucket stood hugging each other, speechless with fright. Only Charlie and Grandpa Joe kept moderately cool. They had travelled a long way with Mr Wonka and had grown accustomed to surprises. But as the Great Elevator continued to streak upward further and further away from the earth, even Charlie began to feel a trifle nervous. 'Mr Wonka!' he yelled above the noise, 'what I don't understand is *why* we've got to come down at such a terrific speed.'

'My dear boy,' Mr Wonka answered, 'if we don't come down at a terrific speed, we'll never burst our way back in through the roof of the factory. It's not easy to punch a hole in a roof as strong as that.'

'But there's a hole in it already,' said Charlie. 'We made it when we came out.'

'Then we shall make another,' said Mr Wonka. 'Two holes are better than one. Any mouse will tell you that.'

Higher and higher rushed the Great Glass Elevator until soon they could see the countries and oceans of the Earth spread out below them like a map. It was all very beautiful, but when you are standing on a glass floor looking down, it gives you a nasty feeling. Even Charlie was beginning to feel frightened now. He hung on tightly to Grandpa Joe's hand and looked up anxiously into the old man's face. 'I'm scared, Grandpa,' he said.

Grandpa Joe put an arm around Charlie's shoulders and held him close. 'So am I, Charlie,' he said.

'Mr Wonka!' Charlie shouted. 'Don't you think this is about high enough?'

'Very nearly,' Mr Wonka answered. 'But not quite. Don't talk to me now, please. Don't disturb me. I must watch things very carefully at this stage. Split-second timing, my

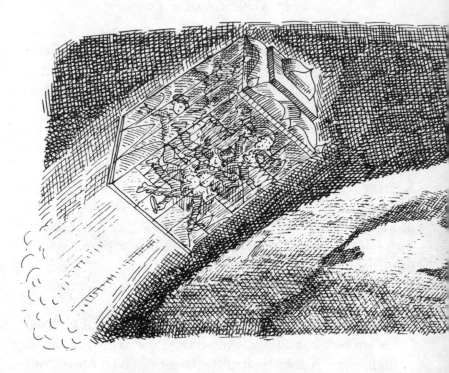

boy, that's what it's got to be. You see this green button. I
must press it at exactly the right instant. If I'm just half a
second late, then we'll go *too high!*'

'What happens if we go too high?' asked Grandpa Joe.

'Do please stop talking and let me concentrate!' Mr
Wonka said.

At that precise moment, Grandma Josephine poked her
head out from under the sheets and peered over the edge of
the bed. Through the glass floor she saw the entire continent
of North America nearly two hundred miles below and
looking no bigger than a bar of chocolate. '*Someone*'s got to
stop this maniac!' she screeched and she shot out a wrinkled
old hand and grabbed Mr Wonka by the coat-tails and
yanked him backwards on to the bed.

'No, no!' cried Mr Wonka, struggling to free himself. 'Let me go! I have things to see to! Don't disturb the pilot!'

'You madman!' shrieked Grandma Josephine, shaking Mr Wonka so fast his head became a blur. 'You get us back home this instant!'

'Let me go!' cried Mr Wonka, 'I've got to press that button or we'll go too high! Let me go! Let me go!' But Grandma Josephine hung on. 'Charlie!' shouted Mr Wonka. 'Press the button! The green one! Quick, quick, quick!'

Charlie leaped across the Elevator and banged his thumb down on the green button. But as he did so, the Elevator gave a mighty groan and rolled over on to its side and the rushing whooshing noise stopped altogether. There was an eerie silence.

'Too late!' cried Mr Wonka. 'Oh, my goodness me, we're cooked!' As he spoke, the bed with the three old ones in it and Mr Wonka on top lifted gently off the floor and hung suspended in mid-air. Charlie and Grandpa Joe and Mr and Mrs Bucket also floated upwards so that in a twink the entire company, as well as the bed, were floating around like balloons inside the Great Glass Elevator.

'*Now* look what you've done!' said Mr Wonka, floating about.

'What happened?' Grandma Josephine called out. She

had floated clear of the bed and was hovering near the ceiling in her nightshirt.

'Did we go too far?' Charlie asked.

'Too *far?*' cried Mr Wonka. 'Of course we went too far! You know where we've gone, my friends? We've gone into orbit!'

They gaped, they gasped, they stared. They were too flabbergasted to speak.

'We are now rushing around the Earth at seventeen thousand miles an hour,' Mr Wonka said. 'How does that grab you?'

'I'm choking!' gasped Grandma Georgina. 'I can't breathe!'

'Of course you can't,' said Mr Wonka. 'There's no air up here.' He sort of swam across under the ceiling to a button marked OXYGEN. He pressed it. 'You'll be all right now,' he said. 'Breathe away.'

'This is the queerest feeling,' Charlie said, swimming about. 'I feel like a bubble.'

'It's great,' said Grandpa Joe. 'It feels as though I don't weigh anything at all.'

'You don't,' said Mr Wonka. 'None of us weighs anything – not even one ounce.'

'What piffle!' said Grandma Georgina. 'I weigh one hundred and thirty-seven pounds exactly.'

'Not now you don't,' said Mr Wonka. 'You are completely weightless.'

The three old ones, Grandpa George, Grandma Georgina and Grandma Josephine, were trying frantically to get back into bed, but without success. The bed was floating about in mid-air. They, of course, were also floating, and every time they got above the bed and tried to lie down, they simply floated up out of it. Charlie and Grandpa Joe were hooting with laughter. 'What's so funny?' said Grandma Josephine.

'We've got you out of bed at last,' said Grandpa Joe.

'Shut up and help us back!' snapped Grandma Josephine.

'Forget it,' said Mr Wonka. 'You'll never stay down. Just keep floating around and be happy.'

'The man's a madman!' cried Grandma Georgina. 'Watch out, I say, or he'll lixivate the lot of us!'

2

Space Hotel 'U.S.A.'

Mr Wonka's Great Glass Elevator was not the only thing orbiting the Earth at that particular time. Two days before, the United States of America had successfully launched its first Space Hotel, a gigantic sausage-shaped capsule no less than one thousand feet long. It was called Space Hotel

'U.S.A.' and it was the marvel of the space age. It had inside it a tennis-court, a swimming pool, a gymnasium, a children's playroom and five hundred luxury bedrooms, each with a private bath. It was fully air-conditioned. It was also equipped with a gravity-making machine so that you didn't float about inside it. You walked normally.

This extraordinary object was now speeding round and round the earth at a height of 240 miles. Guests were to be taken up and down by a taxi-service of small capsules blasting off from Cape Kennedy every hour on the hour, Mondays to Fridays. But as yet there was nobody on board at all, not even an astronaut. The reason for this was that no one had really believed such an enormous thing would ever get off the ground without blowing up.

But the launching had been a great success and now that the Space Hotel was safely in orbit, there was a tremendous hustle and bustle to send up the first guests. It was rumoured that the President of the United States himself was going to be among the first to stay in the hotel, and of course there was a mad rush by all sorts of other people across the world to book rooms. Several kings and queens had cabled the White House in Washington for reservations, and a Texas millionaire called Orson Cart, who was about to marry a Hollywood starlet called Helen Highwater, was offering one hundred thousand dollars a day for the honeymoon suite.

But you cannot send guests to an hotel unless there are lots of people there to look after them, and that explains why there was yet another interesting object orbiting the earth at that moment. This was the large Transport Capsule containing the entire staff for Space Hotel 'U.S.A.' There were managers, assistant managers, desk-clerks, waitresses, bell-boys, chambermaids, pastry chefs and hall porters. The capsule they were travelling in was manned by the three famous astronauts, Shuckworth, Shanks and Showler, all of them handsome, clever and brave.

'In exactly one hour,' said Shuckworth, speaking to the passengers over the loudspeaker, 'we shall link up with

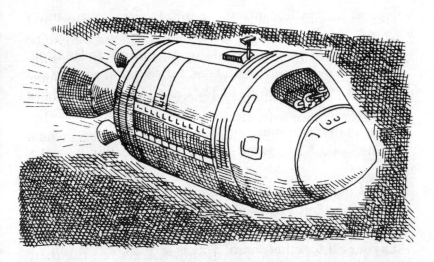

Space Hotel "U.S.A.", your happy home for the next ten years. And any moment now, if you look straight ahead, you should catch your first glimpse of this magnificent space-ship. Ah-ha! I see something there! That must be it, folks! There's definitely something up there ahead of us!'

Shuckworth, Shanks and Showler, as well as the managers, assistant managers, desk-clerks, waitresses, bell-boys, chambermaids, pastry chefs and hall porters, all stared excitedly through the windows. Shuckworth fired a couple of small rockets to make the capsule go faster, and they began to catch up very quickly.

'Hey!' yelled Showler. 'That isn't our space hotel!'

'Holy rats!' cried Shanks. 'What in the name of Nebuchadnezzar is it!'

'Quick! Give me the telescope!' yelled Shuckworth. With one hand he focused the telescope and with the other he flipped the switch connecting him to Ground Control.

'Hello, Houston!' he cried into the mike. 'There's something crazy going on up here! There's a thing orbiting ahead of us and it's not like any space-ship I've ever seen, that's for sure!'

'Describe it at once,' ordered Ground Control in Houston.

'It's . . . it's all made of glass and it's kind of square and it's got lots of people inside it! They're all floating about like fish in a tank!'

'How many astronauts on board?'

'None,' said Shuckworth. 'They can't possibly be astronauts.'

'What makes you say that?'

'Because at least three of them are in nightshirts!'

'Don't be a fool, Shuckworth!' snapped Ground Control. 'Pull yourself together, man! This is serious!'

'I swear it!' cried poor Shuckworth. 'There's three of them in nightshirts! Two old women and one old man! I can see them clearly! I can even see their faces! Jeepers, they're older than Moses! They're about ninety years old!'

'You've gone mad, Shuckworth!' shouted Ground Control. 'You're fired! Give mc Shanks!'

'Shanks speaking,' said Shanks. 'Now listen here, Houston. There's these three old birds in nightshirts floating around in this crazy glass box and there's a funny little guy with a pointed beard wearing a black top-hat and a plum-coloured velvet tail-coat and bottle-green trousers . . .'

'Stop!' screamed Ground Control.

'That's not all,' said Shanks. 'There's also a little boy about ten years old . . .'

'That's no boy, you idiot!' shouted Ground Control. 'That's an astronaut in disguise! It's a midget astronaut dressed up as a little boy! Those old people are astronauts too! They're all in disguise!'

'But who *are* they?' cried Shanks.

'How the heck would I know?' said Ground Control. 'Are they heading for our Space Hotel?'

'That's exactly where they are heading!' cried Shanks. 'I can see the Space Hotel now about a mile ahead.'

'They're going to blow it up!' yelled Ground Control. 'This is desperate! This is . . .' Suddenly his voice was cut off and Shanks heard another quite different voice in his earphones. It was deep and rasping.

'I'll take charge of this,' said the deep rasping voice. 'Are you there, Shanks?'

'Of course I'm here,' said Shanks. 'But how dare you butt in. Keep your big nose out of this. Who are you anyway?'

'This is the President of the United States,' said the voice.

'And this is the Wizard of Oz,' said Shanks. 'Who are you kidding?'

'Cut the piffle, Shanks,' snapped the President. 'This is a national emergency!'

'Good grief!' said Shanks, turning to Shuckworth and Showler. 'It really *is* the President. It's President Gilligrass himself . . . Well, *hello there*, Mr President, sir. How are *you* today?'

'How many people are there in that glass capsule?' rasped the President.

'Eight,' said Shanks. 'All floating.'

'Floating?'

'We're outside the pull of gravity up here, Mr President. Everything floats. We'd be floating ourselves if we weren't strapped down. Didn't you know that?'

'Of course I knew it,' said the President. 'What else can you tell me about that glass capsule?'

'There's a bed in it,' said Shanks. 'A big double bed and that's floating too.'

'A bed!' barked the President. 'Whoever heard of a bed in a spacecraft!'

'I swear it's a bed,' said Shanks.

'You must be loopy, Shanks,' declared the President. 'You're dotty as a doughnut! Let me talk to Showler!'

'Showler here, Mr President,' said Showler, taking the mike from Shanks. 'It is a great honour to talk to you Mr President, sir.'

'Oh, shut up!' said the President. 'Just tell me what you see.'

'It's a bed all right, Mr President. I can see it through my telescope. It's got sheets and blankets and a mattress . . .'

'That's not a bed, you drivelling thickwit!' yelled the President. 'Can't you understand it's a trick! It's a bomb. It's a bomb disguised as a bed! They're going to blow up our magnificent Space Hotel!'

'Who's *they*, Mr President, sir?' said Showler.

'Don't talk so much and let me think,' said the President.

There were a few moments of silence. Showler waited tensely. So did Shanks and Shuckworth. So did the managers and assistant managers and desk-clerks and waitresses and bell-boys and chambermaids and pastry chefs and hall porters. And down in the huge Control Room at Houston, one hundred controllers sat motionless in front of their dials and monitors, waiting to see what orders the President would give next to the astronauts.

'I've just thought of something,' said the President. 'Don't you have a television camera up there on the front of your spacecraft, Showler?'

'Sure do, Mr President.'

'Then switch it on, you nit, and let all of us down here get a look at this object!'

'I never thought of that,' said Showler. 'No *wonder* you're the President. Here goes . . .' He reached out and switched on the TV camera in the nose of the spacecraft, and at that moment, five hundred million people all over the world who had been listening in on their radios rushed to their television sets.

On their screens they saw exactly what Shuckworth and Shanks and Showler were seeing – a weird glass box in splendid orbit around the earth, and inside the box, seen not too clearly but seen nonetheless, were seven grown-ups and one small boy and a big double bed, all floating. Three of the grown-ups were barelegged and wearing nightshirts. And far off in the distance, beyond the glass box, the TV watchers could see the enormous, glistening, silvery shape of Space Hotel 'U.S.A.'

But it was the sinister glass box itself that everyone was staring at, and the cargo of sinister creatures inside it – eight astronauts so tough and strong they didn't even bother to wear space-suits. Who were these people and where did they come from? And what in heaven's name was that big evil-looking thing disguised as a double bed? The President had said it was a bomb and he was probably right. But what were they going to do with it? All across America and Canada and Russia and Japan and India and China and Africa and England and France and Germany and everywhere else in the world a kind of panic began to take hold of the television watchers.

'Keep well clear of them, Showler!' ordered the President over the radio link.

'Sure will, Mr President!' Showler answered. 'I *sure will!*'

3

The Link-Up

Inside the Great Glass Elevator there was also a good deal of excitement. Charlie and Mr Wonka and all the others could see clearly the huge silvery shape of Space Hotel 'U.S.A.' about a mile ahead of them. And behind them was the smaller (but still pretty enormous) Transport Capsule. The Great Glass Elevator (not looking at all great now beside these two monsters) was in the middle. And of course everybody, even Grandma Josephine, knew very well what was going on. They even knew that the three astronauts in charge of the Transport Capsule were called Shuckworth, Shanks and Showler. The whole world knew about these things. Newspapers and television had been shouting about almost nothing else for the past six months. Operation Space Hotel was the event of the century.

'What a load of luck!' cried Mr Wonka. 'We've landed ourselves slap in the middle of the biggest space operation of all time!'

'We've landed ourselves in the middle of a nasty mess,' said Grandma Josephine. 'Turn back at once!'

'No, Grandma,' said Charlie. 'We've *got* to watch it now. We *must* see the Transport Capsule linking up with the Space Hotel.'

Mr Wonka floated right up close to Charlie. 'Let's beat them to it, Charlie,' he whispered. 'Let's get there first and go aboard the Space Hotel ourselves!'

Charlie gaped. Then he gulped. Then he said softly, 'It's impossible. You've got to have all sorts of special gadgets to link up with another spacecraft, Mr Wonka.'

'My Elevator could link up with a crocodile if it had to,' said Mr Wonka. 'Just leave it to me, my boy!'

'Grandpa Joe!' cried Charlie. 'Did you hear that? We're going to link up with the Space Hotel and go on board!'

'Yippeeeeee!' shouted Grandpa Joe. 'What a brilliant thought, sir! What a staggering idea!' He grabbed Mr Wonka's hand and started shaking it like a thermometer.

'Be quiet, you balmy old bat!' said Grandma Josephine. 'We're in a hot enough stew already. I want to go home.'

'Me, too!' said Grandma Georgina.

'What if they come after us?' said Mr Bucket, speaking for the first time.

'What if they capture us?' said Mrs Bucket.

'What if they shoot us?' said Grandma Georgina.

'What if my beard were made of green spinach?' cried Mr Wonka. 'Bunkum and tummyrot! You'll never get anywhere if you go about what-iffing like that. Would Columbus have discovered America if he'd said "What if I sink on the way over? What if I meet pirates? What if I never come back?" He wouldn't even have started. We want no what-iffers around here, right Charlie? Off we go, then. But wait . . . this is a very tricky manoeuvre and I'm going to need help. There are three lots of buttons we have to press all in different parts of the Elevator. I shall take those two over there, the white and the black.' Mr Wonka made a funny blowing noise with his mouth and glided effortlessly, like a huge bird, across the Elevator to the white and black buttons, and there he hovered. 'Grandpa Joe, sir, kindly station yourself beside that silver button there . . . yes, that's the one . . . And you, Charlie, go up and stay floating beside that little golden button near the ceiling. I must tell you that each of these buttons fires booster rockets from different places outside the Elevator. That's how we change direction. Grandpa Joe's rockets turn us to starboard, to the right. Charlie's turn us to port, to the left. Mine make us go higher or lower or faster or slower. All ready?'

'No! Wait!' cried Charlie, who was floating exactly midway between the floor and the ceiling. 'How do I get up? I can't get up to the ceiling!' He was thrashing his arms and legs violently, like a drowning swimmer, but getting nowhere.

'My dear boy,' said Mr Wonka. 'You can't *swim* in this stuff. It isn't water, you know. It's air and very thin air at that. There's nothing to push against. So you have to use jet propulsion. Watch me. First, you take a deep breath, then you make a small round hole with your mouth and you blow as hard as you can. If you blow downward, you jet-propel yourself up. If you blow to the left, you shoot off to the right and so on. You manoeuvre yourself like a spacecraft, but using your mouth as a booster rocket.'

Suddenly everyone began practising this business of flying about, and the whole Elevator was filled with the blowings and snortings of the passengers. Grandma Georgina, in her red flannel nightgown with two skinny bare legs sticking out of the bottom, was trumpeting and spitting like a rhinoceros and flying from one side of the Elevator to the other, shouting 'Out of my way! Out of my way!' and crashing into poor Mr and Mrs Bucket with terrible speed.

The Link-Up

Grandpa George and Grandma Josephine were doing the same. And well may you wonder what the millions of people down on earth were thinking as they watched these crazy happenings on their television screens. You must realize they couldn't see things very clearly. The Great Glass Elevator was only about the size of a grapefruit on their screens, and the people inside, slightly blurred through the glass, were no bigger than the pips of the grapefruit. Even so, the watchers below could see them buzzing about wildly like insects in a glass box.

'What in the world are they doing?' shouted the President of the United States, staring at the screen.

'Looks like some kind of a war-dance, Mr President,' answered astronaut Showler over the radio.

'You mean they're Red Indians!' said the President.

'I didn't say that, sir.'

'Oh, yes you did, Showler.'

'Oh, no I didn't, Mr President.'

'Silence!' said the President. 'You're muddling me up.'

Back in the Elevator, Mr Wonka was saying, *'Please! Please!* Do stop flying about! Keep still everybody so we can get on with the docking!'

'You miserable old mackerel!' said Grandma Georgina, sailing past him. 'Just when we start having a bit of fun, you want to stop it!'

'Look at me, everybody!' shouted Grandma Josephine. 'I'm flying! I'm a golden eagle!'

'I can fly faster than any of you!' cried Grandpa George, whizzing round and round, his nightgown billowing out behind him like the tail of a parrot.

'Grandpa George!' cried Charlie. 'Do please calm down. If we don't hurry, those astronauts will get there before us.

Don't you want to see inside the Space Hotel, any of you?'

'Out of my way!' shouted Grandma Georgina, blowing herself back and forth. 'I'm a jumbo jet!'

'You're a balmy old bat!' said Mr Wonka.

In the end, the old people grew tired and out of breath, and everyone settled quietly into a floating position.

'All set, Charlie and Grandpa Joe, sir?' said Mr Wonka.

'All set, Mr Wonka,' Charlie answered, hovering near the ceiling.

'I'll give the orders,' said Mr Wonka. 'I'm the pilot. Don't fire your rockets until I tell you. And don't forget who is who. Charlie, you're port. Grandpa Joe, you're starboard.' Mr Wonka pressed one of his own two buttons and immediately booster rockets began firing underneath the Great Glass Elevator. The Elevator leaped forward, but swerved violently to the right. 'Hard a-port!' yelled Mr Wonka.

Charlie pressed his button. His rockets fired. The Elevator swung back into line. 'Steady as you go!' cried Mr Wonka. 'Starboard ten degrees! . . . Steady! . . . Steady! . . . Keep her there! . . .'

Soon they were hovering directly underneath the tail of the enormous silvery Space Hotel. 'You see that little square door with the bolts on it?' said Mr Wonka. 'That's the docking entrance. It won't be long now . . . Port a fraction! . . . Steady! . . . Starboard a bit! . . . Good . . . Good . . . Easy does it . . . we're nearly there . . .'

To Charlie, it felt rather as though he were in a tiny rowboat underneath the stern of the biggest ship in the world. The Space Hotel towered over them. It was enormous. 'I can't wait,' thought Charlie, 'to get inside and see what it's like.'

4

The President

Half a mile back, Shuckworth, Shanks and Showler were keeping the television camera aimed all the time at the Glass Elevator. And across the world, millions and millions of people were clustered around their TV screens, watching tensely the drama being acted out two hundred and forty miles above the earth. In his study in the White House sat Lancelot R. Gilligrass, President of the United States of America, the most powerful man on Earth. In this moment of crisis, all his most important advisers had been summoned urgently to his presence, and there they all were now, following closely on the giant television screen every move made by this dangerous-looking glass capsule and its eight desperate-looking astronauts. The entire Cabinet was present. The Chief of the Army was there, together with four other generals. There was the Chief of the Navy and the Chief of the Air Force and a sword-swallower from Afghanistan, who was the President's best friend. There was the President's Chief Financial Adviser, who was standing in the middle of the room trying to balance the budget on top of his head, but it kept falling off. Standing nearest of all to the President was the Vice-President, a huge lady of eighty-nine with a whiskery chin. She had been the President's nurse when he was a baby and her name was Miss Tibbs. Miss Tibbs was the power behind the throne. She stood no nonsense from anyone. Some people said she was as strict with the President now as when he was a little boy. She was the terror of the White House and even the Head of the Secret Service broke into a sweat when summoned to her presence. Only the President was allowed to call her Nanny. The President's famous cat, Mrs Taubsypuss, was also in the room.

There was absolute silence now in the Presidential study. All eyes were riveted on the TV screen as the small glass object, with its booster-rockets firing, slid smoothly up behind the giant Space Hotel.

'They're going to link up!' shouted the President. 'They're going on board our Space Hotel!'

'They're going to blow it up!' cried the Chief of the Army. 'Let's blow *them* up first, crash bang wallop bang-bang-

bang-bang.' The Chief of the Army was wearing so many medal-ribbons they covered the entire front of his tunic on both sides and spread down on to his trousers as well. 'Come on, Mr P.,' he said. 'Let's have some really super-duper explosions!'

'Silence, you silly boy!' said Miss Tibbs, and the Chief of the Army slunk into a corner.

'Listen,' said the President. 'The point is this. *Who are they? And where do they come from?* Where's my Chief Spy?'

'Here, sir, Mr President, sir!' said the Chief Spy.

He had a false moustache, a false beard, false eyelashes, false teeth and a falsetto voice.

'Knock-Knock,' said the President.

'Who's there?' said the Chief Spy.

'Courteney.'

'Courteney who?'

'Courteney one yet?' said the President.

There was a brief silence. 'The President asked you a question,' said Miss Tibbs in an icy voice. 'Have you Courteney one yet?'

'No, ma'am, not yet,' said the Chief Spy, beginning to twitch.

'Well, here's your chance,' snarled Miss Tibbs.

'Quite right,' said the President. 'Tell me immediately who those people are in that glass capsule!'

'Ah-ha,' said the Chief Spy, twirling his false moustache. 'That is a very difficult question.'

'You mean you don't know?'

'I mean I do know, Mr President. At least I think I know. Listen. We have just launched the finest hotel in the world. Right?'

'Right!'

'And who is so madly jealous of this wonderful hotel of ours that he wants to blow it up?'

'Miss Tibbs,' said the President.

'Wrong,' said the Chief Spy. 'Try again.'

'Well,' said the President, thinking deeply. 'In that case, could it not perhaps be some other hotel owner who is envious of our lovely hotel?'

'Brilliant!' cried the Chief Spy. 'Go on, sir! You're getting warm!'

'It's Mr Savoy!' said the President.

'Warmer and warmer, Mr President!'

'Mr Ritz!'

'You're hot, sir! You're boiling hot! Go on!'

'I've got it!' cried the President. 'It's Mr Hilton!'

'Well done, sir!' said the Chief Spy.

'Are you sure it's him?'

'Not sure, but it's certainly a warm possibility, Mr President. After all, Mr Hilton's got hotels in just about every country in the world but he hasn't got one in space. And we have. He must be madder than a maggot!'

'By gum, we'll soon fix this!' snapped the President, grabbing one of the eleven telephones on his desk. 'Hello!' he said into the phone. 'Hello hello hello! Where's the operator?' He jiggled furiously on the little thing you jiggle when you want the operator. 'Operator, where are you?'

'They won't answer you now,' said Miss Tibbs. 'They're all watching television.'

'Well, *this* one'll answer!' said the President, snatching up a bright red telephone. This was the hot line direct to the Premier of Soviet Russia in Moscow. It was always open and only used in terrible emergencies. 'It's just as likely to be the Russians as Mr Hilton,' the President went on. 'Don't you agree, Nanny?'

'It's bound to be the Russians,' said Miss Tibbs.

'Premier Yugetoff speaking,' said the voice from Moscow. 'What's on your mind, Mr President?'

'Knock-Knock,' said the President.

'Who's there?' said the Soviet Premier.

'Warren.'

'Warren who?'

'Warren Peace by Leo Tolstoy,' said the President. 'Now see here, Yugetoff! You get those astronauts of yours off that Space Hotel of ours this instant! Otherwise, I'm afraid we're going to have to show you just where you get off, Yugetoff!'

'Those astronauts are not Russians, Mr President.'

'He's lying,' said Miss Tibbs.

'You're lying,' said the President.

'Not lying, sir,' said Premier Yugetoff. 'Have you looked closely at those astronauts in the glass box? I myself cannot

36

see them too clearly on my TV screen, but one of them, the little one with the pointed beard and the top hat, has a distinctly Chinese look about him. In fact, he reminds me very much of my friend the Prime Minister of China . . .'

'Great garbage!' cried the President, slamming down the rod phone and picking up a porcelain one. The porcelain phone went direct to the Head of the Chinese Republic in Peking.

'Hello hello hello!' said the President.

'Wing's Fish and Vegetable Store in Shanghai,' said a small distant voice. 'Mr Wing speaking.'

'Nanny!' cried the President, banging down the phone. 'I thought this was a direct line to the Premier!'

'It is,' said Miss Tibbs. 'Try again.'

The President picked up the receiver. 'Hello!' he yelled.

'Mr Wong speaking,' said a voice at the other end.

'Mister Who?' screamed the President.

'Mr Wong, assistant stationmaster, Chungking, and if you asking about ten o'clock tlain, ten o'clock tlain no lunning today. Boiler burst.'

The President threw the phone across the room at the Postmaster General. It hit him in the stomach. 'What's the matter with this thing?' shouted the President.

'It is very difficult to phone people in China, Mr President,' said the Postmaster General. 'The country's so full of Wings and Wongs, every time you wing you get the wong number.'

'You're not kidding,' said the President.

The Postmaster General replaced the telephone on the desk. 'Try it just once more, Mr President, please,' he said. 'I've tightened the screws underneath.'

The President again picked up the receiver.

'Gleetings, honourable Mr Plesident,' said a soft faraway voice. 'Here is Assistant-Plemier Chu-On-Dat speaking. How can I do for you?'

'Knock-Knock,' said the President.

'Who der?'

'Ginger.'

'Ginger who?'

'Ginger yourself much when you fell off the Great Wall of China?' said the President. 'Okay, Chu-On-Dat. Let me speak to Premier How-Yu-Bin.'

'Much regret Plemier How-Yu-Bin not here just this second, Mr Plesident.'

'Where is he?'

'He outside mending a puncture on his bicycle.'

'Oh no he isn't,' said the President. 'You can't fool me, you crafty old mandarin! At this very minute he's boarding our magnificent Space Hotel with seven other rascals to blow it up!'

'Excuse pleese, Mr Plesident. You make big mistake . . .'

'No mistake!' barked the President. 'And if you don't call them off right away I'm going to tell my Chief of the Army to blow them all sky high! So chew on that, Chu-On-Dat!'

'Hooray!' said the Chief of the Army. 'Let's blow everyone up! Bang-bang! Bang-bang!'

'Silence!' barked Miss Tibbs.

'I've done it!' cried the Chief Financial Adviser. 'Look at me, everybody! I've balanced the budget!' And indeed he had. He stood proudly in the middle of the room with the enormous 200 billion dollar budget balanced beautifully on the top of his bald head. Everyone clapped. Then suddenly the voice of astronaut Shuckworth cut in urgently on the radio loudspeaker in the President's study. 'They've linked

up and gone on board!' shouted Shuckworth. 'And they've taken in the bed . . . I mean the bomb!'

The President sucked in his breath sharply. He also sucked in a big fly that happened to be passing at the time. He choked. Miss Tibbs thumped him on the back. He swallowed the fly and felt better. But he was very angry. He seized pencil and paper and began to draw a picture. As he drew, he kept muttering, 'I won't have flies in my office! I won't put up with them!' His advisers waited eagerly. They knew that the great man was about to give the world yet another of his brilliant inventions. The last had been the Gilligrass Left-handed Corkscrew which had been hailed by left-handers across the nation as one of the greatest blessings of the century.

'There you are!' said the President, holding up the paper.

'This is the Gilligrass Patent Fly-Trap!' They all crowded round to look.

'The fly climbs up the ladder on the left,' said the President. 'He walks along the plank. He stops. He sniffs. He smells something good. He peers over the edge and sees the sugar-lump. "Ah-ha!" he cries. "Sugar!" He is just about to climb down the string to reach it when he sees the basin of water below. "Ho-ho!" he says. "It's a trap! They want me to fall in!" So he walks on, thinking what a clever fly he is. But as you see, I have left out one of the rungs in the ladder he goes down by, so he falls and breaks his neck.'

'Tremendous, Mr President!' they all exclaimed. 'Fantastic! A stroke of genius!'

'I wish to order one hundred thousand for the Army immediately,' said the Chief of the Army.

'Thank you,' said the President, making a careful note of the order.

'I repeat,' said the frantic voice of Shuckworth over the loudspeaker. 'They've gone on board and taken the bomb with them!'

'Stay well clear of them, Shuckworth,' ordered the President. 'There's no point in getting your boys blown up as well.'

And now, all over the world, the millions of watchers waited more tensely than ever in front of their television sets. The picture on their screens, in vivid colour, showed the sinister little glass box securely linked up to the underbelly of the gigantic Space Hotel. It looked like some tiny baby animal clinging to its mother. And when the camera zoomed closer, it was clear for all to see that the glass box was completely empty. All eight of the desperadoes had climbed into the Space Hotel and they had taken their bomb with them.

5

Men from Mars

There was no floating inside the Space Hotel. The gravity-making machine saw to that. So once the docking had been triumphantly achieved, Mr Wonka, Charlie, Grandpa Joe and Mr and Mrs Bucket were able to walk out of the Great Glass Elevator into the lobby of the Hotel. As for Grandpa George, Grandma Georgina and Grandma Josephine, none of them had had their feet on the ground for over twenty years and they certainly weren't going to change their habits now. So when the floating stopped, they all three plopped right back into bed again and insisted that the bed, with them in it, be pushed into the Space Hotel.

Charlie gazed around the huge lobby. On the floor there was a thick green carpet. Twenty tremendous chandeliers hung shimmering from the ceiling. The walls were covered with valuable pictures and there were big soft armchairs all over the place. At the far end of the room there were the doors of five lifts. The group stared in silence at all this luxury. Nobody dared speak. Mr Wonka had warned them that every word they uttered would be picked up by Space Control in Houston, so they had better be careful. A faint humming noise came from somewhere below the floor, but

that only made the silence more spooky. Charlie took hold
of Grandpa Joe's hand and held it tight. He wasn't sure he
liked this very much. They had broken into the greatest
machine ever built by man, the property of the United States
Government, and if they were discovered and captured as
they surely must be in the end, what would happen to them
then? Jail for life? Yes, or something worse.

Mr Wonka was writing on a little pad. He held up the
pad. It said: ANYBODY HUNGRY?

The three old ones in the bed began waving their arms
and nodding and opening and shutting their mouths. Mr
Wonka turned the paper over. On the other side it said:
THE KITCHENS OF THIS HOTEL ARE LOADED

WITH LUSCIOUS FOOD, LOBSTERS, STEAKS, ICE-CREAM. WE SHALL HAVE A FEAST TO END ALL FEASTS.

Suddenly, a tremendous booming voice came out of a loudspeaker hidden somewhere in the room. *'ATTENTION!'* boomed the voice and Charlie jumped. So did Grandpa Joe. Everybody jumped, even Mr Wonka. 'ATTENTION THE EIGHT FOREIGN ASTRONAUTS! THIS IS SPACE CONTROL IN HOUSTON, TEXAS, U.S.A.! YOU ARE TRESPASSING ON AMERICAN PROPERTY! YOU ARE ORDERED TO IDENTIFY YOURSELVES IMMEDIATELY! SPEAK NOW!'

'Ssshhh!' whispered Mr Wonka, finger to lips.

There followed a few seconds of awful silence. Nobody moved except Mr Wonka who kept saying 'Ssshhh! Ssshhh!'

'WHO ... ARE ... YOU?' boomed the voice from Houston, and the whole world heard it. 'I REPEAT ... WHO ... ARE ... YOU?' shouted the urgent angry voice, and five hundred million people crouched in front of their television sets waiting for an answer to come from the mysterious strangers inside the Space Hotel. The television was not able to show a picture of these mysterious strangers. There was no camera in there to record the scene. Only the words came through. The TV watchers saw nothing but the outside of the giant hotel in orbit, photographed of course by Shuckworth, Shanks and Showler who were following behind. For half a minute the world waited for a reply.

But no reply came.

'SPEAK!' boomed the voice, getting louder and louder and ending in a fearful frightening shout that rattled Charlie's eardrums. '*SPEAK! SPEAK! SPEAK!*' Grandma Georgina shot under the sheet. Grandma Josephine stuck her fingers in her ears. Grandpa George buried his head in the pillow. Mr and Mrs Bucket, both petrified, were once again in each other's arms. Charlie was clutching Grandpa Joe's hand, and the two of them were staring at Mr Wonka and begging him with their eyes to do something. Mr Wonka stood very still, and although his face looked calm, you can be quite sure his clever inventive brain was spinning like a dynamo.

'THIS IS YOUR LAST CHANCE!' boomed the voice. 'WE ARE ASKING YOU ONCE MORE ... WHO ... ARE ... YOU? REPLY IMMEDIATELY! IF YOU DO NOT REPLY WE SHALL BE FORCED TO REGARD

44

YOU AS DANGEROUS ENEMIES. WE SHALL THEN PRESS THE EMERGENCY FREEZER SWITCH AND THE TEMPERATURE IN THE SPACE HOTEL WILL DROP TO MINUS ONE HUNDRED DEGREES CENTIGRADE. ALL OF YOU WILL BE INSTANTLY DEEP FROZEN. YOU HAVE FIFTEEN SECONDS TO SPEAK. AFTER THAT YOU WILL TURN INTO ICICLES ... ONE ... TWO ... THREE ...'

'Grandpa!' whispered Charlie as the counting continued, 'we *must do* something! We *must*! Quick!'

'SIX!' said the voice. 'SEVEN! ... EIGHT! ... NINE! ...'

Mr Wonka had not moved. He was still gazing straight ahead, still quite cool, perfectly expressionless. Charlie and Grandpa Joe were staring at him in horror. Then, all at once, they saw the tiny twinkling wrinkles of a smile appear around the corners of his eyes. He sprang to life. He spun round on his toes, skipped a few paces across the floor and then, in a frenzied unearthly sort of scream he cried, *'FIMBO FEEZ!'*

The loudspeaker stopped counting. There was silence. All over the world there was silence.

Charlie's eyes were riveted on Mr Wonka. He was going to speak again. He was taking a deep breath. *'BUNGO BUNI!'* he screamed. He put so much force into his voice that the effort lifted him right up on to the tips of his toes.

    'BUNGO BUNI
    DAFU DUNI
    YUBEE LUNI!'

Again the silence.

The next time Mr Wonka spoke, the words came out

45

so fast and sharp and loud they were like bullets from a machine-gun. 'ZOONK-ZOONK-ZOONK-ZOONK-ZOONK!' he barked. The noise echoed around and around the lobby of the Space Hotel. It echoed around the world.

Mr Wonka now turned and faced the far end of the lobby where the loudspeaker voice had come from. He walked a few paces forward as a man would, perhaps, who wanted a more intimate conversation with his audience. And this time, the tone was much quieter, the words came more slowly, but there was a touch of steel in every syllable:

'KIRASUKU MALIBUKU,
WEEBEE WIZE UN YUBEE KUKU!

ALIPENDA KAKAMENDA,
PANTZ FORLDUN IFNO SUSPENDA!

FUIKIKA KANDERIKA,
WEEBE STRONGA YUBEE WEEKA!

POPOKOTA BORUMOKA
VERI RISKI YU PROVOKA!

KATIKATI MOONS UN STARS
FANFANISHA VENUS MARS!'

Mr Wonka paused dramatically for a few seconds. Then he took an enormous deep breath and in a wild and fearsome voice, he yelled out:

'KITIMBIBI ZOONK!
FUMBOLEEZI ZOONK!
GUGUMIZA ZOONK!
FUMIKAKA ZOONK!
ANAPOLALA ZOONK ZOONK ZOONK!'

Men from Mars

The effect of all this on the world below was electric. In the Control Room in Houston, in the White House in Washington, in palaces and city buildings and mountain shacks from America to China to Peru, the five hundred million people who heard that wild and fearsome voice yelling out these strange and mystic words all shivered with fear before their television sets. Everybody began turning to everybody else and saying, 'Who are they? What language was that? Where do they come from?'

In the President's study in the White House, Vice-President Tibbs, the members of the Cabinet, the Chiefs of the Army and the Navy and the Air Force, the sword-swallower from Afghanistan, the Chief Financial Adviser and Mrs Taubsypuss the cat, all stood tense and rigid. They were very much afraid. But the President himself kept a cool head and a clear brain. 'Nanny!' he cried. 'Oh, Nanny, what on earth do we do now?'

'I'll get you a nice warm glass of milk,' said Miss Tibbs.

'I hate the stuff,' said the President. 'Please don't make me drink it!'

'Summon the Chief Interpreter,' said Miss Tibbs.

'Summon the Chief Interpreter!' said the President. 'Where is he?'

'Right here, Mr President,' said the Chief Interpreter.

'What language was that creature spouting up there in the Space Hotel? Be quick! Was it Eskimo?'

'Not Eskimo, Mr President.'

'Ha! Then it was Tagalog! Either Tagalog or Ugro!'

'Not Tagalog, Mr President. Not Ugro, either.'

'Was it Tulu, then? Or Tungus or Tupi?'

'Definitely not Tulu, Mr President. And I'm quite sure it wasn't Tungus or Tupi.'

'Don't stand there telling him what it *wasn't*, you idiot!' said Miss Tibbs. 'Tell him what it *was*!'

'Yes, ma'am, Miss Vice-President, ma'am,' said the Chief Interpreter, beginning to shake. 'Believe me, Mr President,' he went on, 'it was not a language I have ever heard before.'

'But I thought you knew every language in the world?'

'I do, Mr President.'

'Don't lie to me, Chief Interpreter. How can you possibly know every language in the world when you don't know this one?'

'It is not a language of this world, Mr President.'

'Nonsense, man!' barked Miss Tibbs. 'I understood some of it myself!'

'These people, Miss Vice-President, ma'am, have obviously tried to learn just a few of our easier words, but the rest of it is a language that has never been heard before on this Earth!'

'Screaming scorpions!' cried the President. 'You mean to tell me they could be coming from ... from ... from *somewhere else?*'

'Precisely, Mr President.'

'Like where?' said the President.

'Who knows?' said the Chief Interpreter. 'But did you not notice, Mr President, how they used the words Venus and Mars?'

'Of course I noticed it,' said the President. 'But what's that got to do with it? ... Ah-ha! I see what you're driving at! Good gracious me! Men from Mars!'

'And Venus,' said the Chief Interpreter.

'That,' said the President, 'could make for trouble.'

'I'll say it could!' said the Chief Interpreter.

'He wasn't talking to you,' said Miss Tibbs.

'What do we do now, General?' said the President.

'Blow 'em up!' cried the General.

'You're always wanting to blow things up,' said the President crossly. 'Can't you think of something *else?*'

'I like blowing things up,' said the General. 'It makes such a lovely noise. *Woomph-woomph!*'

'Don't be a fool!' said Miss Tibbs. 'If you blow these people up, Mars will declare war on us! So will Venus!'

'Quite right, Nanny,' said the President. 'We'd be troculated like turkeys, every one of us! We'd be mashed like potatoes!'

'I'll take 'em on!' shouted the Chief of the Army.

'Shut up!' snapped Miss Tibbs. 'You're fired!'

'Hooray!' said all the other generals. 'Well done, Miss Vice-President, ma'am!'

Miss Tibbs said, 'We've *got* to treat these fellows gently. The one who spoke just now sounded extremely cross.

We've got to be polite to them, butter them up, make them happy. The last thing we want is to be invaded by men from Mars! You've got to talk to them, Mr President. Tell Houston we want another direct radio link with the Space Hotel. And hurry!'

6

Invitation to the White House

'The President of the United States will now address you!' announced the loudspeaker voice in the lobby of the Space Hotel.

Grandma Georgina's head peeped cautiously out from under the sheets. Grandma Josephine took her fingers out of her ears and Grandpa George lifted his face out of the pillow.

'You mean he's actually going to speak to us?' whispered Charlie.

'Ssshhh!' said Mr Wonka. 'Listen!'

'Dear friends!' said the well-known Presidential voice over the loudspeaker. 'Dear, *dear* friends! Welcome to Space Hotel "U.S.A." Greetings to the brave astronauts from Mars and Venus . . .'

'Mars and Venus!' whispered Charlie. 'You mean he thinks we're from . . .'

'Ssshh-ssshh-ssshh!' said Mr Wonka. He was doubled up with silent laughter, shaking all over and hopping from one foot to the other.

'You have come a long way,' the President continued, 'so why don't you come just a tiny bit farther and pay *us* a visit down here on our humble little Earth? I invite all eight of you to stay with me here in Washington as my honoured guests. You could land that wonderful glass air-machine of yours on the lawn in back of the White House. We shall have the red carpet out and ready. I do hope you know enough of our language to understand me. I shall wait most anxiously for your reply . . .'

There was a click and the President went off the air.

'What a fantastic thing!' whispered Grandpa Joe. 'The White House, Charlie! We're invited to the White House as honoured guests!'

Charlie caught hold of Grandpa Joe's hands and the two of them started dancing round and round the lobby of the hotel. Mr Wonka, still shaking with laughter, went and sat down on the bed and signalled everyone to gather round close so they could whisper without being heard by the hidden microphones.

'They're scared to death,' he whispered. 'They won't bother us any more now. So let's have that feast we were talking about and afterward we can explore the hotel.'

'Aren't we going to the White House?' whispered Grandma Josephine. 'I want to go to the White House and stay with the President.'

'My dear old dotty dumpling,' said Mr Wonka. 'You look as much like a man from Mars as a bedbug! They'd know at once they'd been fooled. We'd be arrested before we could say how d'you do.'

Mr Wonka was right. There could be no question of accepting the President's invitation and they all knew it.

'But we've got to say *something* to him,' Charlie whispered. 'He must be sitting down there in the White House this very minute waiting for an answer.'

'Make an excuse,' said Mr Bucket.

'Tell him we're otherwise engaged,' said Mrs Buckct.

'You are right,' whispered Mr Wonka. 'It is rude to ignore an invitation.' He stood up and walked a few paces from the group. For a moment or two he remained quite still, gathering his thoughts. Then once again Charlie saw those tiny twinkling smiling wrinkles around the corners of the eyes, and when he began to speak, his voice this time was like the voice of a giant, deep and devilish, very loud and very slow:

> *'In the quelchy quaggy sogmire,*
> *In the mashy mideous harshland,*
> *At the witchy hour of gloomness,*
> *All the grobes come oozing home.*
>
> *You can hear them softly slimeing,*
> *Glissing hissing o'er the slubber,*
> *All those oily boily bodies*
> *Oozing onward in the gloam.*
>
> *So start to run! Oh, skid and daddle*
> *Through the slubber slush and sossel!*
> *Skip jump hop and try to skaddle!*
> *All the grobes are on the roam!'*

In his study two hundred and forty miles below, the President turned white as the White House, 'Jumping jackrabbits!' he cried. 'I think they're after us!'

'Oh, *please* let me blow them up!' said the Ex-Chief of the Army.

'Silence!' said Miss Tibbs. 'Go stand in the corner!'

In the lobby of the Space Hotel, Mr Wonka had merely

paused in order to think up another verse, and he was just about to start off again when a frightful piercing scream stopped him cold. The screamer was Grandma Josephine. She was sitting up in bed and pointing with shaking finger at the lifts at the far end of the lobby. She screamed a second time, still pointing, and all eyes turned toward the lifts. The door of the one on the left was sliding slowly open and the watchers could clearly see that there was something . . . something thick . . . something brown . . . something not exactly brown, but greenish-brown . . . something with slimy skin and large eyes . . . squatting inside the lift!

7

Something Nasty in the Lifts

Grandma Josephine had stopped screaming now. She had gone rigid with shock. The rest of the group by the bed, including Charlie and Grandpa Joe, had become as still as stone. They dared not move. They dared hardly breathe. And Mr Wonka, who had swung quickly around to look when the first scream came, was as dumbstruck as the rest. He stood motionless, gaping at the thing in the lift, his mouth slightly open, his eyes stretched wide as two wheels. What he saw, what they all saw, was this:

It looked more than anything like an enormous egg balanced on its pointed end. It was as tall as a big boy and wider than the fattest man. The greenish-brown skin had a shiny wettish appearance and there were wrinkles in it. About three-quarters of the way up, in the widest part, there were two large round eyes as big as tea-cups. The eyes were white, but each had a brilliant red pupil in the centre. The red pupils were resting on Mr Wonka. But now they began travelling slowly across to Charlie and Grandpa Joe and the others by the bed, settling upon them and gazing at them with a cold malevolent stare. The eyes were everything. There were no other features, no nose or mouth or ears, but the entire egg-shaped body was itself moving very very slightly, pulsing and bulging gently here and there as though the skin were filled with some thick fluid.

At this point, Charlie suddenly noticed that the next lift was coming down. The indicator numbers above the door were flashing . . . 6 . . . 5 . . . 4 . . . 3 . . . 2 . . . 1 . . . L (for lobby). There was a slight pause. The door slid open and there, inside the second lift, was another enormous slimy wrinkled greenish-brown egg with eyes!

Now the numbers were flashing above all three of the remaining lifts. Down they came . . . down . . . down . . . down . . . And soon, at precisely the same time, they reached the lobby floor and the doors slid open . . . five open doors now . . . one creature in each . . . five in all . . . and five pairs of eyes with brilliant red centres all watching Mr Wonka and watching Charlie and Grandpa Joe and the others.

There were slight differences in size and shape between the five, but all had the same greenish-brown wrinkled skin and the skin was rippling and pulsing.

For about thirty seconds nothing happened. Nobody

stirred, nobody made a sound. The silence was terrible. So was the suspense. Charlie was so frightened he felt himself shrinking inside his skin. Then he saw the creature in the left-hand lift suddenly starting to change shape! Its body was slowly becoming longer and longer, and thinner and thinner, going up and up towards the roof of the lift, not straight up, but curving a little to the left, making a snake-like curve that was curiously graceful, up to the left and then curling over the top to the right and coming down again in a half-circle . . . and then the bottom end began to grow out as well, like a tail . . . creeping along the floor . . . creeping along the floor to the left . . . until at last the creature, which had originally looked like a huge egg, now looked like a long curvy serpent standing up on its tail.

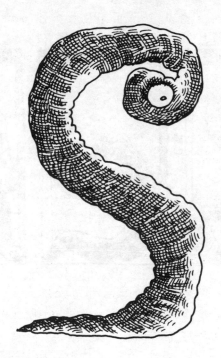

Then the one in the next lift began stretching itself in much the same way, and what a weird and oozy thing it was to watch! It was twisting itself into a shape that was a bit different from the first, balancing itself almost but not quite on the tip of its tail.

Then the three remaining creatures began stretching themselves all at the same time, each one elongating itself slowly upward, growing taller and taller, thinner and thinner, curving and twisting, stretching and stretching, curling and bending, balancing either on the tail or the head or both, and turned sideways now so that only one eye was visible. When they had all stopped stretching and bending, this was how they finished up:

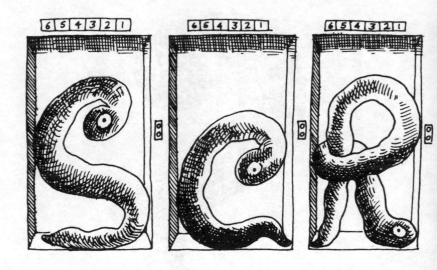

Something Nasty in the Lifts

'*Scram!*' shouted Mr Wonka. 'Get out quick!'

People have never moved faster than Grandpa Joe and Charlie and Mr and Mrs Bucket at that moment. They all got behind the bed and started pushing like crazy. Mr Wonka ran in front of them shouting 'Scram! Scram! Scram!' and in ten seconds flat all of them were out of the lobby and back inside the Great Glass Elevator. Frantically, Mr Wonka began undoing bolts and pressing buttons. The door of the Great Glass Elevator snapped shut and the whole thing leaped sideways. They were away! And of course all of them, including the three old ones in the bed, floated up again into the air.

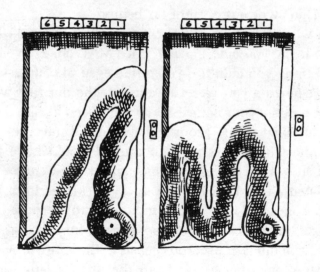

8

The Vermicious Knids

'Oh, my goodness me!' gasped Mr Wonka. 'Oh, my sainted pants! Oh, my painted ants! Oh, my crawling cats! I hope never to see anything like *that* again!' He floated over to the white button and pressed it. The booster-rockets fired. The Elevator shot forward at such a speed that soon the Space Hotel was out of sight far behind.

'But who *were* those awful creatures?' Charlie asked.

'You mean you didn't *know*?' cried Mr Wonka. 'Well, it's a good thing you didn't! If you'd had even the faintest idea of what horrors you were up against, the marrow would have run out of your bones! You'd have been fossilized with fear and glued to the ground! Then they'd have got you! You'd have been a cooked cucumber! You'd have been rasped into a thousand tiny bits, grated like cheese and flocculated alive! They'd have made necklaces from your knucklebones and bracelets from your teeth! Because those creatures, my dear ignorant boy, are the most brutal, vindictive, venomous, murderous beasts in the entire universe!' Here Mr Wonka paused and ran the tip of a pink tongue all the way around his lips. 'VERMICIOUS KNIDS!' he cried. 'That's what they were!' He sounded the K . . . K'NIDS, like that.

'I thought they were grobes,' Charlie said. 'Those oozy-woozy grobes you were telling the President about.'

'Oh, no, I just made those up to scare the White House,' Mr Wonka answered. 'But there is nothing made-up about Vermicious Knids, believe you me. They live, as everybody knows, on the planet Vermes, which is eighteen thousand four hundred and twenty-seven million miles away and they are very, very clever brutes indeed. The Vermicious Knid can turn itself into any shape it wants. It has no bones. Its body is really one huge muscle, enormously strong, but very stretchy and squishy, like a mixture of rubber and putty with steel wires inside. Normally it is egg-shaped, but it can just as easily give itself two legs like a human or four legs like a horse. It can become as round as a ball or as long as a kite-string. From fifty yards away, a fully-grown Vermicious Knid could stretch out its neck and bite your head off without even getting up!'

'Bite off your head with what?' said Grandma Georgina. 'I didn't see any mouth.'

'They have other things to bite with,' said Mr Wonka darkly.

'Such as what?' said Grandma Georgina.

'Ring off,' said Mr Wonka. 'Your time's up. But listen, everybody. I've just had a funny thought. There I was fooling around with the President and pretending we were creatures from some other planet and, by golly, there actually *were* creatures from some other planet on board!'

'Do you think there were many?' Charlie asked. 'More than the five we saw?'

'Thousands!' said Mr Wonka. 'There are five hundred rooms in that Space Hotel and there's probably a family of them in every room!'

'Somebody's going to get a nasty shock when they go on board!' said Grandpa Joe.

'They'll be eaten like peanuts,' said Mr Wonka. 'Every one of them.'

'You don't really mean that, do you, Mr Wonka?' Charlie said.

'Of course I mean it,' said Mr Wonka. 'These Vermicious Knids are the terror of the Universe. They travel through space in great swarms, landing on other stars and planets and destroying everything they find. There used to be some rather nice creatures living on the moon a long time ago. They were called Poozas. But the Vermicious Knids ate the lot. They did the same on Venus and Mars and any other planets.'

'Why haven't they come down to our Earth and eaten us?' Charlie asked.

'They've tried to, Charlie, many times, but they've never made it. You see, all around our Earth there is a vast envelope of air and gas, and anything hitting *that* at high speed gets red hot. Space capsules are made of special heat-proof metal, and when they make a re-entry, their speeds are reduced right down to about 2,000 miles an hour, first by retro-rockets and then by something called "friction". But even so, they get badly scorched. Knids, which are not heat-proof at all, and don't have any retro-rockets, get sizzled up completely before they're half-way through. Have you ever seen a shooting star?'

'Lots of them,' Charlie said.

'Actually, they're not shooting stars at all,' said Mr Wonka. 'They're Shooting Knids. They're Knids trying to enter the Earth's atmosphere at high speed and going up in flames.'

'What rubbish,' said Grandma Georgina.

'You wait,' said Mr Wonka. 'You may see it happening before the day is done.'

'But if they're so fierce and dangerous,' Charlie said, 'why didn't they eat us up right away in the Space Hotel? Why did they waste time twisting their bodies into letters and writing SCRAM?'

'Because they're show-offs,' Mr Wonka replied. 'They're tremendously proud of being able to write like that.'

'But why say *scram* when they wanted to catch us and eat us?'

'It's the only word they know,' Mr Wonka said.

'*Look!*' screamed Grandma Josephine, pointing through the glass. 'Over there!'

Before he even looked, Charlie knew exactly what he was going to see. So did the others. They could tell by the high hysterical note in the old lady's voice.

And there it was, cruising effortlessly alongside them, a simply colossal Vermicious Knid, as thick as a whale, as long as a lorry, with the most brutal vermicious look in its eye! It was no more than a dozen yards away, egg-shaped, slimy, greenish-brown, with one malevolent red eye (the only one visible) fixed intently upon the people floating inside the Great Glass Elevator!

'The end has come!' screamed Grandma Georgina.

'He'll eat us all!' cried Mrs Bucket.

'In one gulp!' said Mr Bucket.

'We're done for, Charlie,' said Grandpa Joe. Charlie nodded. He couldn't speak or make a sound. His throat was seized up with fright.

But this time Mr Wonka didn't panic. He remained perfectly calm. 'We'll soon get rid of *that*!' he said and he

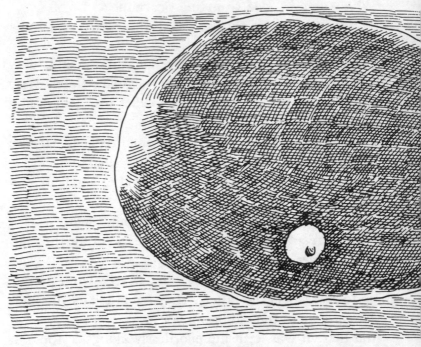

pressed six buttons all at once and six booster-rockets went off simultaneously under the Elevator. The Elevator leaped forward like a stung horse, faster and faster, but the great green greasy Knid kept pace alongside it with no trouble at all.

'Make it go away!' yelled Grandma Georgina. 'I can't stand it looking at me!'

'Dear lady,' said Mr Wonka, 'it can't possibly get in here. I don't mind admitting I was a trifle alarmed back there in the Space Hotel. And with good reason. But here we have nothing to fear. The Great Glass Elevator is shockproof, waterproof, bombproof, bulletproof and Knidproof! So just relax and enjoy it.'

64

'Oh you Knid, you are vile and vermicious!'

cried Mr Wonka.

'You are slimy and soggy and squishous!
But what do we care
'Cause you can't get in here,
So hop it and don't get ambitious!'

At this point, the massive Knid outside turned and started cruising away from the Elevator. 'There you are,' cried Mr Wonka, triumphant. 'It heard me! It's going home!' But Mr Wonka was wrong. When the creature was about a hundred yards off, it stopped, hovered for a moment, then went smoothly into reverse, coming back toward the Elevator with its rear-end (which was the pointed end of the egg) now in front. Even going backwards, its acceleration was unbelievable. It was like some monstrous bullet coming at them and it came so fast nobody had time even to cry out.

CRASH! It struck the Glass Elevator with the most enormous bang and the whole thing shivered and shook but the glass held and the Knid bounced off like a rubber ball.

'What did I tell you!' shouted Mr Wonka, triumphant. 'We're safe as sausages in here!'

'He'll have a nasty headache after that,' said Grandpa Joe.

'It's not his head, it's his bottom!' said Charlie. 'Look Grandpa, there's a big bump coming up on the pointed end where he hit! It's going black and blue!'

And so it was. A purple bruisy bump the size of a small car was appearing on the pointed rear-end of the giant Knid. 'Hello, you dirty great beast!' cried Mr Wonka.

'Hello, you great Knid! Tell us, how do you do?
You're a rather strange colour today.
Your bottom is purple and lavender blue.
Should it really be looking that way?

Are you not feeling well? Are you going to faint?
Is it something we cannot discuss?
It must be a very unpleasant complaint,
For your backside's as big as a bus!

Let me get you a doctor. I know just the man
For a Knid with a nasty disease.
He's a butcher by trade which is not a bad plan,
And he charges quite reasonable fees.

66

The Vermicious Knids

Ah, here he is now! "Doc, you really are kind
To travel so far into space.
There's your patient, the Knid with the purple behind!
Do you think it's a desperate case?"

"Great heavens above! It's no wonder he's pale!"
Said the doc with a horrible grin.
"There's a sort of balloon on the end of his tail!
I must prick it at once with a pin!"

So he got out a thing like an Indian spear,
With feathers all over the top,
And he lunged and he caught the Knid smack in the rear,
But alas, the balloon didn't pop!

Cried the Knid, "What on earth am I going to do
With this painful preposterous lump?
I can't remain standing the whole summer through!
And I cannot sit down on my rump!"

"It's a bad case of rear-ache," the medico said,
"And it's something I cannot repair.
If you want to sit down, you must sit on your head,
With your bottom high up in the air!" '

9

Gobbled Up

On the day when all this was happening, no factories opened anywhere in the world. All offices and schools were closed. Nobody moved away from the television screens, not even for a couple of minutes to get a Coke or to feed the baby. The tension was unbearable. Everybody heard the American President's invitation to the men from Mars to visit him in the White House. And they heard the weird rhyming reply, which sounded rather threatening. They also heard a piercing scream (Grandma Josephine), and a little later on, they heard someone shouting, 'Scram! Scram! Scram!' (Mr Wonka). Nobody could make head or tail of the shouting. They took it to be some kind of Martian language. But when the eight mysterious astronauts suddenly rushed back into their glass capsule and broke away from the Space Hotel, you could almost hear the great sigh of relief that rose up from the peoples of the earth. Telegrams and messages poured into the White House congratulating the President upon his brilliant handling of a frightening situation.

The President himself remained calm and thoughtful. He sat at his desk rolling a small piece of wet chewing-gum between his finger and thumb. He was waiting for the moment when he could flick it at Miss Tibbs without her seeing him. He flicked it and missed Miss Tibbs but hit the Chief of the Air Force on the tip of his nose.

'Do you think the men from Mars have accepted my invitation to the White House?' the President asked.

'Of course they have,' said the Foreign Secretary. 'It was a brilliant speech, sir.'

'They're probably on their way down here right now,' said Miss Tibbs. 'Go and wash that nasty sticky chewing-gum off your fingers quickly. They could be here any minute.'

'Let's have a song first,' said the President. 'Sing another one about me, Nanny . . . please.'

THE NURSE'S SONG

This mighty man of whom I sing,
The greatest of them all,
Was once a teeny little thing,
Just eighteen inches tall.

I knew him as a tiny tot.
I nursed him on my knee.
I used to sit him on the pot
And wait for him to wee.

I always washed between his toes,
And cut his little nails.
I brushed his hair and wiped his nose
And weighed him on the scales.

Through happy childhood days he strayed,
As all nice children should.
I smacked him when he disobeyed,
And stopped when he was good.

It soon began to dawn on me
He wasn't very bright,
Because when he was twenty-three
He couldn't read or write.

'What shall we do?' his parents sob.
'The boy has got the vapours!
He couldn't even get a job
Delivering the papers!'

'Ah-ha,' I said. 'This little clot
Could be a politician.'
'Nanny,' he cried. 'Oh Nanny, what
A super proposition!'

'Okay,' I said. 'Let's learn and note
The art of politics.
Let's teach you how to miss the boat
And how to drop some bricks,
And how to win the people's vote
And lots of other tricks.

Let's learn to make a speech a day
Upon the TV screen,
In which you never never say
Exactly what you mean.

Gobbled Up

And most important, by the way,
Is not to let your teeth decay,
And keep your fingers clean.'

And now that I am eighty-nine,
It's too late to repent.
The fault was mine the little swine
Became the President.

'Bravo Nanny!' cried the President, clapping his hands. 'Hooray!' shouted the others. 'Well done, Miss Vice-President, ma'am! Brilliant! Tremendous!'

'My goodness!' said the President. 'Those men from Mars will be here any moment! What on earth are we going to give them for lunch? Where's my Chief Cook?'

The Chief Cook was a Frenchman. He was also a French spy and at this moment he was listening at the keyhole of the President's study. 'Ici, Monsieur le President!' he said, bursting in.

'Chief Cook,' said the President. 'What do men from Mars eat for lunch?'

'Mars Bars,' said the Chief Cook.

'Baked or boiled?' asked the President.

'Oh, *baked*, of course, Monsieur le President. You will ruin a Mars Bar by boiling!'

The voice of astronaut Shuckworth cut in over the loudspeaker in the President's study. 'Request permission to link up and go aboard Space Hotel?' he said.

'Permission granted,' said the President. 'Go right ahead, Shuckworth. It's all clear now . . . Thanks to me.'

And so the large Transport Capsule, piloted by Shuckworth, Shanks and Showler, with all the hotel managers and assistant managers and hall porters and pastry chefs and bell-boys and waitresses and chambermaids on board, moved in smoothly and linked up with the giant Space Hotel.

'Hey there! We've lost our television picture,' called the President.

'I'm afraid the camera got smashed against the side of the Space Hotel, Mr President,' Shuckworth replied. The President said a very rude word into the microphone and ten million children across the nation began repeating it gleefully and got smacked by their parents.

'All astronauts and one hundred and fifty hotel staff safely aboard Space Hotel!' Shuckworth reported over the radio. 'We are now standing in the lobby!'

'And what do you think of it all?' asked the President. He knew the whole world was listening in and he wanted Shuckworth to say how wonderful it was. Shuckworth didn't let him down.

'Gee, Mr President, it's just *great!*' he said. 'It's *unbelievable!* It's so *enormous!* And so . . . it's kind of hard to find words to describe it, it's so truly grand, especially the chandeliers and the carpets and all! I have the Chief Hotel Manager, Mr Walter W. Wall, beside me now. He would like the honour of a word with you, sir.'

'Put him on,' said the President.

'Mr President, sir, this is Walter Wall. What a sumptuous hotel this is! The decorations are superb!'

'Have you noticed that all the carpets are wall-to-wall, Mr Walter Wall?' said the President.

'I have indeed, Mr President.'

'All the wallpaper is all wall-to-wall, too, Mr Walter Wall.'

'Yes, sir, Mr President! Isn't that something! It's going to be a real pleasure running a beautiful hotel like this! ... *Hey! What's going on over there? Something's coming out of the lifts! Help!'* Suddenly the loudspeaker in the President's study gave out a series of the most ghastly screams and yells. *'Ayeeeee! Owwwwww! Ayeeeee! Hel-l-l-lp! Hel-l-l-l-l-lp! Hel-l-l-l-l-l-l-l-lp!'*

'What on earth's going on?' said the President. *'Shuckworth! Are you there, Shuckworth? ... Shanks! Showler! Mr Walter Wall! Where are you all! What's happening?'*

The screams continued. They were so loud the President had to put his fingers in his ears. Every house in the world that had a television or radio receiver heard those awful screams. There were other noises, too. Loud grunts and snortings and crunching sounds. Then there was silence.

Frantically the President called the Space Hotel on the radio. Houston called the Space Hotel. The President called Houston. Houston called the President. Then both of them called the Space Hotel again. But answer came there none. Up there in space all was silent.

'Something nasty's happened,' said the President.

'It's those men from Mars,' said the Ex-Chief of the Army. 'I *told* you to let me blow them up.'

'Silence!' snapped the President. 'I've got to think.'

The loudspeaker began to crackle. 'Hello!' it said. 'Hello hello hello! Are you receiving me, Space Control in Houston?'

The President grabbed the mike on his desk. 'Leave this to me, Houston!' he shouted, 'President Gilligrass here receiving you loud and clear! Go ahead!'

'Astronaut Shuckworth here, Mr President, back aboard the Transport Capsule ... *thank heavens!'*

'What happened, Shuckworth? Who's with you?'

'We're most of us here, Mr President, I'm glad to say. Shanks and Showler are with me, and a whole bunch of other folks. I guess we lost maybe a couple of dozen people altogether, pastry chefs, hall porters, that sort of thing. It sure was a scramble getting out of that place alive!'

'What do you mean you *lost* two dozen people?' shouted the President. 'How did you lose them?'

'Gobbled up!' replied Shuckworth. 'One gulp and that was it! I saw a big six-foot-tall assistant-manager being swallowed up just like you'd swallow a lump of ice-cream, Mr President! No chewing – nothing! Just down the hatch!'

'But *who*?' yelled the President. 'Who are you talking about? Who did the swallowing?'

'*Hold it!*' cried Shuckworth. 'Oh, my lord, here they all come now! They're coming after us! They're swarming out of the Space Hotel! They're coming out in swarms! You'll have to excuse me a moment, Mr President. No time to talk right now!'

10

Transport Capsule in Trouble –
Attack No. 1

While Shuckworth, Shanks and Showler were being chased out of the Space Hotel by the Knids, Mr Wonka's Great Glass Elevator was orbiting the Earth at tremendous speed. Mr Wonka had all his booster-rockets firing and the Elevator was reaching speeds of thirty-four thousand miles an hour instead of the normal seventeen thousand. They were trying, you see, to get away from that huge angry Vermicious Knid with the purple behind. Mr Wonka wasn't afraid of it, but Grandma Josephine was petrified. Every time she looked at it, she let out a piercing scream and clapped her hands over her eyes. But of course thirty-four thousand miles an hour is dawdling to a Knid. Healthy young Knids think nothing of travelling a million miles between lunch and supper, and then another million before breakfast the next day. How else could they travel between the planet Vermes and other stars? Mr Wonka should have known this and saved his rocket-power, but he kept right on going and the giant Knid kept right on cruising effortlessly alongside, glaring into the Elevator with its wicked red eye. 'You people have bruised my backside,' the Knid seemed to be saying, 'and in the end I'm going to *get* you for that.'

They had been streaking around the Earth like this for about forty-five minutes when Charlie, who was floating comfortably beside Grandpa Joe near the ceiling, said suddenly, 'There's something ahead! Can you see it, Grandpa? Straight in front of us!'

'I can, Charlie, I can ... Good heavens, it's the Space Hotel!'

'It can't be, Grandpa. We left it miles behind us long ago.'

'Ah-ha,' said Mr Wonka. 'We've been going so fast we've gone all the way around the Earth and caught up with it again! A splendid effort!'

'And there's the Transport Capsule! Can you see it, Grandpa? It's just behind the Space Hotel!'

'There's something else there, too, Charlie, if I'm not mistaken!'

'*I know what those are!*' screamed Grandma Josephine. 'They're Vermicious Knids! Turn back at once!'

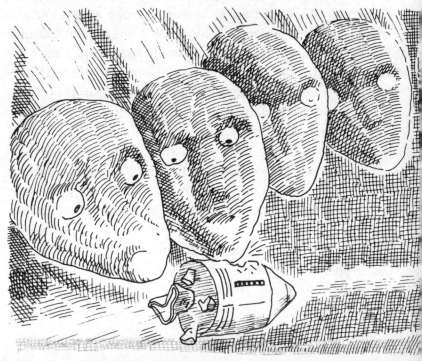

'Reverse!' yelled Grandma Georgina. 'Go the other way!'

'Dear lady,' said Mr Wonka. 'This isn't a car on the motorway. When you are in orbit, you cannot stop and you cannot go backwards.'

'I don't care about that!' shouted Grandma Josephine. 'Put on the brakes! Stop! Back-pedal! The Knids'll get us!'

'Now let's for heaven's sake *stop* this nonsense once and for all,' Mr Wonka said sternly. 'You know very well my Elevator is completely Knidproof. You have nothing to fear.'

They were closer now and they could see the Knids pouring out from the tail of the Space Hotel and swarming like wasps around the Transport Capsule.

'They're attacking it!' cried Charlie. 'They're after the Transport Capsule!'

It was a fearsome sight. The huge green egg-shaped Knids were grouping themselves into squadrons with about twenty Knids to a squadron. Then each squadron formed

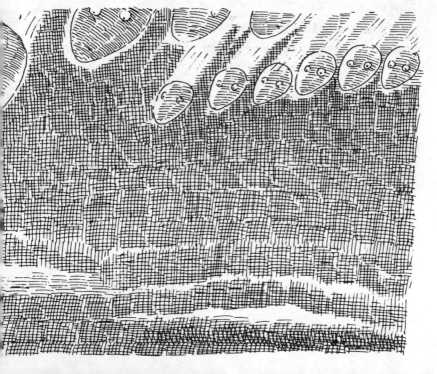

itself into a line abreast, with one yard between Knids. Then, one after another, the squadrons began attacking the Transport Capsule. They attacked in reverse with their pointed rear-ends in front and they came in at a fantastic speed.

WHAM! One squadron attacked, bounced off and wheeled away.

CRASH! Another squadron smashed against the side of the Transport Capsule.

'Get us out of here, you madman!' screamed Grandma Josephine. 'What are you waiting for?'

'They'll be coming after *us* next!' yelled Grandma Georgina. 'For heaven's sake, man, turn back!'

'I doubt very much if that capsule of theirs is Knidproof,' said Mr Wonka.

'Then we must help them!' cried Charlie. 'We've got to do something! There are a hundred and fifty people inside that thing!'

Down on the Earth, in the White House study, the President and his advisers were listening in horror to the voices of the astronauts over the radio.

'They're coming at us in droves!' Shuckworth was shouting. 'They're bashing us to bits!'

'But *who?*' yelled the President. 'You haven't even told us who's attacking you!'

'These dirty great greenish-brown brutes with red eyes!' shouted Shanks, butting in. 'They're shaped like enormous eggs and they're coming at us backwards!'

'Backwards?' cried the President. 'Why backwards?'

'Because their bottoms are even more pointy than their tops!' shouted Shuckworth. 'Look out! Here comes another lot!' *BANG!* 'We won't be able to stand this much longer, Mr President! The waitresses are screaming and the chambermaids are all hysterical and the bell-boys are being sick and the hall porters are saying their prayers so what shall we do, Mr President, sir, what on earth shall we do?'

'Fire your rockets, you idiot, and make a re-entry!' shouted the President. 'Come back to Earth immediately!'

'That's impossible!' cried Showler. 'They've busted our rockets! They've smashed them to smithereens!'

'We're cooked, Mr President!' shouted Shanks. 'We're done for! Because even if they don't succeed in destroying the capsule, we'll have to stay up here in orbit for the rest of our lives! We can't make a re-entry without rockets!'

The President was sweating and the sweat ran all the way down the back of his neck and inside his collar.

'Any moment now, Mr President,' Shanks went on, 'we're going to lose contact with you altogether! There's another lot coming at us from the left and they're aiming straight for our radio aerial! Here they come! I don't think we'll be able to . . .' The voice cut. The radio went dead.

'Shanks!' cried the President. 'Where are you, Shanks? . . . Shuckworth! Shanks! Showler! . . . Showlworth! Shucks! Shankler! . . . Shankworth! Show! Shuckler! Why don't you answer me?!'

Up in the Great Glass Elevator where they had no radio and could hear nothing of these conversations, Charlie was saying, 'Surely their only hope is to make a re-entry and dive back to Earth quickly!'

'Yes,' said Mr Wonka. 'But in order to re-enter the Earth's atmosphere they've got to kick themselves out of orbit. They've got to change course and head downwards and to

79

do that they need rockets! But their rocket tubes are all dented and bent! You can see that from here! They're crippled!'

'Why can't we tow them down?' Charlie asked.

Mr Wonka jumped. Even though he was floating, he somehow jumped. He was so excited he shot upwards and hit his head on the ceiling. Then he spun round three times in the air and cried, 'Charlie! You've got it! That's it! We'll tow them out of orbit! To the buttons, quick!'

'What do we tow them with?' asked Grandpa Joe. 'Our neckties?'

'Don't you worry about a little thing like that!' cried Mr Wonka. 'My Great Glass Elevator is ready for anything! In we go! Into the breach, dear friends, into the breach!'

'Stop him!' screamed Grandma Josephine.

'You be quiet, Josie,' said Grandpa Joe. 'There's someone over there needs a helping hand and it's our job to give it. If you're frightened, you'd better just close your eyes tight and stick your fingers in your ears.'

II

The Battle of the Knids

'Grandpa Joe, sir!' shouted Mr Wonka. 'Kindly jet yourself over to the far corner of the Elevator there and turn that handle! It lowers the rope!'

'A rope's no good, Mr Wonka! The Knids will bite through a rope in one second!'

'It's a steel rope,' said Mr Wonka. 'It's made of re-inscorched steel. If they try to bite through *that* their teeth will splinter like spillikins! To your buttons, Charlie! You've got to help me manoeuvre! We're going right over the top of the Transport Capsule and then we'll try to hook on to it somewhere and get a firm hold!'

Like a battleship going into action, the Great Glass Elevator with booster rockets firing moved smoothly in over the top of the enormous Transport Capsule. The Knids immediately stopped attacking the Capsule and went for the Elevator. Squadron after squadron of giant Vermicious Knids flung themselves furiously against Mr Wonka's marvellous machine! WHAM! CRASH! BANG! The noise was thunderous and terrible. The Elevator was tossed about the sky like a leaf, and inside it, Grandma Josephine, Grandma Georgina and Grandpa George, floating in their nightshirts, were all yowling and screeching and flapping their arms and calling for help. Mrs Bucket had wrapped her arms around Mr Bucket and was clasping him so tightly that one of his shirt buttons punctured his skin. Charlie and Mr Wonka, as cool as two cubes of ice, were up near the ceiling working the booster-rocket controls, and Grandpa Joe, shouting war-cries and throwing curses at the Knids, was down below turning the handle that unwound the steel rope. At the same time, he was watching the rope through the glass floor of the Elevator.

'Starboard a bit, Charlie!' shouted Grandpa Joe. 'We're right on top of her now! . . . Forward a couple of yards, Mr Wonka! . . . I'm trying to get the hook hooked around that stumpy thing sticking out in front there! . . . Hold it! . . . I've got it . . . That's it! . . . Forward a little now and see if it holds! . . . More! . . . More! . . .' The big steel rope tightened. It held! And now, wonder of wonders, with her booster-

rockets blazing, the Elevator began to tow the huge Transport Capsule forward and away!

'Full speed ahead!' shouted Grandpa Joe. 'She's going to hold! She's holding! She's holding fine!'

'All boosters firing!' cried Mr Wonka, and the Elevator leaped ahead. Still the rope held. Mr Wonka jetted himself down to Grandpa Joe and shook him warmly by the hand. 'Well done, sir,' he said. 'You did a brilliant job under heavy fire!'

Charlie looked back at the Transport Capsule some thirty yards behind them on the end of the tow-line. It had little windows up front, and in the windows he could clearly see the flabbergasted faces of Shuckworth, Shanks and Showler. Charlie waved to them and gave them the thumbs up signal. They didn't wave back. They simply gaped. They couldn't believe what was happening.

Grandpa Joe blew himself upward and hovered beside Charlie, bubbling with excitement. 'Charlie, my boy,' he said. 'We've been through a few funny things together lately, but never anything like this!'

'Grandpa, where are the Knids? They've suddenly vanished!'

Everyone looked round. The only Knid in sight was their old friend with the purple behind, still cruising alongside in its usual place, still glaring into the Elevator.

'*Just* a minute!' cried Grandma Josephine. 'What's *that* I see over there?' Again they looked, and this time, sure enough, away in the distance, in the deep blue sky of outer space, they saw a massive cloud of Vermicious Knids wheeling and circling like a fleet of bombers.

'If you think we're out of the woods yet, you're crazy!' shouted Grandma Georgina.

'I fear no Knids!' said Mr Wonka. 'We've got them beaten now!'

'Poppyrot and pigwash!' said Grandma Josephine. 'Any moment now they'll be at us again! Look at them! They're coming in! They're coming closer!'

This was true. The huge fleet of Knids had moved in at incredible speed and was now flying level with the Great Glass Elevator, a couple of hundred yards away on the right hand side. The one with the bump on its rear-end was much closer, only twenty yards away on the same side.

'It's changing shape!' cried Charlie. 'That nearest one! What's it going to do? It's getting longer and longer!' And indeed it was. The mammoth egg-shaped body was slowly stretching itself out like chewing-gum, becoming longer and longer and thinner and thinner, until in the end it looked exactly like a long slimy-green serpent as thick as a thick tree and as long as a football pitch. At the front end were the eyes, big and white with red centres, at the back a kind of tapering tail and at the very end of the tail was the enormous round swollen bump it had got when it crashed against the glass.

The people floating inside the Elevator watched and waited. Then they saw the long rope-like Knid turning and coming straight but quite slowly toward the Great Glass Elevator. Now it began actually wrapping its ropy body around the Elevator itself. Once around it went . . . then twice around, and very horrifying it was to be inside and to see the soft green body squishing against the outside of the glass no more than a few inches away.

'It's tying us up like a parcel!' yelled Grandma Josephine.

'Bunkum!' said Mr Wonka.

'It's going to crush us in its coils!' wailed Grandma Georgina.

'Never!' said Mr Wonka.

Charlie glanced quickly back at the Transport Capsule. The sheet-white faces of Shuckworth, Shanks and Showler were pressed against the glass of the little windows, terror-struck, stupefied, stunned, their mouths open, their expressions frozen like fishfingers. Once again, Charlie gave them the thumbs up signal. Showler acknowledged it with a sickly grin, but that was all.

'Oh, oh, oh!' screamed Grandma Josephine. 'Get that beastly squishy thing away from here!'

Having curled its body twice around the Elevator, the Knid now proceeded to tie a knot with its two ends, a good strong knot, left over right, then right over left. When it had pulled the knot tight, there remained about five yards of one end hanging loose. This was the end with the eyes on it. But it didn't hang loose for long. It quickly curled itself into the shape of a huge hook and the hook stuck straight out sideways from the Elevator as though waiting for something else to hook itself on to it.

While all this was going on, nobody had noticed what the other Knids were up to. 'Mr Wonka!' Charlie cried. 'Look at the others! What *are* they doing?'

What indeed?

These, too, had all changed shape and had become longer, but not nearly so long or so thin as the first one. Each of them had turned itself into a kind of thick rod and the rod was curled around at both ends – at the tail end and at the head end – so that it made a double-ended hook. And now all the hooks were linking up into one long chain . . . one thousand Knids . . . all joining together and curving around in the sky to make a chain of Knids half a mile long or more! And the Knid at the very front of the chain (whose front hook was not, of course, hooked up to anything) was leading them in a wide circle and sweeping in toward the Great Glass Elevator.

'Hey!' shouted Grandpa Joe. 'They're going to hook up with this brute who's tied himself around us!'

'And tow us away!' cried Charlie.

'To the planet Vermes,' gasped Grandma Josephine. 'Eighteen thousand four hundred and twenty-seven million miles from here!'

The Battle of the Knids

'They can't do that!' cried Mr Wonka. '*We're* doing the towing around here!'

'They're going to link up, Mr Wonka!' Charlie said. 'They really are! Can't we stop them? They're going to tow us away and they're going to tow the people we're towing away as well!'

'Do something, you old fool!' shrieked Grandma Georgina. 'Don't just float about looking at them!'

'I must admit,' said Mr Wonka, 'that for the first time in my life I find myself at a bit of a loss.'

They all stared in horror through the glass at the long chain of Vermicious Knids. The leader of the chain was

coming closer and closer. The hook, with two big angry eyes on it, was out and ready. In thirty seconds it would link up with the hook of the Knid wrapped around the Elevator.

'I want to go home!' wailed Grandma Josephine. 'Why can't we all go home?'

'Great thundering tomcats!' cried Mr Wonka. '*Home* is right! What on earth am I thinking of! Come on, Charlie! Quick! *Re-entry!* You take the yellow button! Press it for all you're worth! I'll handle this lot!' Charlie and Mr Wonka literally flew to the buttons. 'Hold your hats!' shouted Mr Wonka. 'Grab your gizzards! We're going down!'

Rockets started firing out of the Elevator from all sides. It tilted and gave a sickening lurch and then plunged downward into the Earth's atmosphere at a simply colossal speed. '*Retro-rockets!*' bellowed Mr Wonka. 'I mustn't forget to fire the retro-rockets!' He flew over to another series of buttons and started playing on them like a piano.

The Elevator was now streaking downward head first, upside down, and all the passengers found themselves floating upside down as well. 'Help!' screamed Grandma Georgina. 'All the blood's going to my head!'

'Then turn yourself the other way up,' said Mr Wonka. 'That's easy enough, isn't it?'

Everyone blew and puffed and turned somersaults in the air until at last they were all the right way up. 'How's the tow-rope holding, Grandpa?' Mr Wonka called out.

'They're still with us, Mr Wonka, sir! The rope's holding fine!'

It was an amazing sight – the Glass Elevator streaking down toward the Earth with the huge Transport Capsule in tow behind it. But the long chain of Knids was coming after them, following them down, keeping pace with them easily, and now the hook of the leading Knid in the chain was actually reaching out and grasping for the hook made by the Knid on the Elevator!

'We're too late!' screamed Grandma Georgina. 'They're going to link up and haul us back!'

'I think not,' said Mr Wonka. 'Don't you remember what happens when a Knid enters the Earth's atmosphere at high speed? He gets red-hot. He burns away in a long fiery trail. He becomes a shooting Knid. Soon these dirty beasts will start popping like popcorn!'

As they streaked on downward, sparks began to fly off the sides of the Elevator. The glass glowed pink, then red, then scarlet. Sparks also began to fly on the long chain of Knids, and the leading Knid in the chain started to shine like a red-hot poker. So did all the others. So did the great slimy brute coiled around the Elevator itself. This one, in fact, was trying frantically to uncoil itself and get away, but it was having trouble untying the knot, and in another ten seconds it began to sizzle. Inside the Elevator they could actually hear it sizzling. It made a noise like bacon frying. And exactly the same sort of thing was happening to the other one thousand Knids in the chain. The tremendous heat was simply sizzling them up. They were red-hot, every one of them. Then suddenly, they became white-hot and they gave out a dazzling white light.

'They're shooting Knids!' cried Charlie.

'What a splendid sight,' said Mr Wonka. 'It's better than fireworks.'

In a few seconds more, the Knids had blown away in a

cloud of ashes and it was all over. 'We've done it!' cried Mr
Wonka. 'They've been roasted to a crisp! They've been
frizzled to a fritter! We're saved!'

'What do you mean saved?' said Grandma Josephine.
'We'll all be frizzled ourselves if this goes on any longer!
We'll be barbecued like beefsteaks! Look at that glass! It's
hotter than a fizzgig!'

'Have no fears, dear lady,' answered Mr Wonka. 'My Elevator is air-conditioned, ventilated, aerated and automated
in every possible way. We're going to be all right now.'

'I haven't the faintest idea what's been going on,' said
Mrs Bucket, making one of her rare speeches. 'But whatever
it is, I don't like it.'

'Aren't you enjoying it, mother?' Charlie asked her.

'No,' she said. 'I'm not. Nor is your father.'

'What a great sight it is!' said Mr Wonka. 'Just look at the
Earth down there, Charlie, getting bigger and bigger!'

'And us going to meet it at two thousand miles an hour!'
groaned Grandma Georgina. 'How are you going to slow
down, for heaven's sake? You didn't think of that, did you!'

'He's got parachutes,' Charlie told her. 'I'll bet he's got
great big parachutes that open just before we hit.'

'*Parachutes!*' said Mr Wonka with contempt. 'Parachutes
are only for astronauts and sissies! And anyway, we don't
want to *slow down*. We want to *speed up*. I've told you
already we've got to be going at an absolutely tremendous
speed when we hit. Otherwise we'll never punch our way in
through the roof of the Chocolate Factory.'

'How about the Transport Capsule?' Charlie asked anxiously.

'We'll be letting them go in a few seconds now,' Mr

Wonka answered. 'They *do* have parachutes, three of them, to slow them down on the last bit.'

'How do you know we won't land in the Pacific Ocean?' said Grandma Josephine.

'I don't,' said Mr Wonka. 'But we all know how to swim, do we not?'

'This man,' shouted Grandma Josephine, 'is crazy as a crumpet!'

'He's cracked as a crayfish!' cried Grandma Georgina.

Down and down plunged the Great Glass Elevator. Nearer and nearer came the Earth below. Oceans and continents rushed up to meet them, getting bigger every second . . .

'Grandpa Joe, sir! Throw out the rope! Let it go!' ordered Mr Wonka. 'They'll be all right now so long as their parachutes are working.'

'Rope gone!' called out Grandpa Joe, and the huge Transport Capsule, on its own now, began to swing away to one side. Charlie waved to the three astronauts in the front window. None of them waved back. They were still sitting there in a kind of shocked daze, gaping at the old ladies and the old men and the small boy floating about in the Glass Elevator.

'It won't be long now,' said Mr Wonka, reaching for a row of tiny pale blue buttons in one corner. 'We shall soon know whether we are alive or dead. Keep very quiet please for this final bit. I have to concentrate awfully hard, otherwise we'll come down in the wrong place.'

They plunged into a thick bank of cloud and for ten seconds they could see nothing. When they came out of the cloud, the Transport Capsule had disappeared, and the Earth was very close, and there was only a great spread of land beneath them with mountains and forests . . . then fields and trees . . . then a small town.

'There it is!' shouted Mr Wonka. 'My Chocolate Factory! My beloved Chocolate Factory!'

'You mean *Charlie's* Chocolate Factory,' said Grandpa Joe.

'That's *right*!' said Mr Wonka, addressing Charlie. 'I'd clean forgotten! I do apologize to you, my dear boy! Of course it's yours! And here we go!'

Through the glass floor of the Elevator, Charlie caught a quick glimpse of the huge red roof and the tall chimneys of the giant factory. They were plunging straight down on to it.

'Hold your breath!' shouted Mr Wonka. 'Hold your nose! Fasten your seat-belts and say your prayers! We're going through the roof!'

12

Back to the Chocolate Factory

And then the noise of splintering wood and broken glass and absolute darkness and the most awful crunching sounds as the Elevator rushed on and on, smashing everything before it.

All at once, the crashing noises stopped and the ride became smoother and the Elevator seemed to be travelling on guides or rails, twisting and turning like a roller-coaster. And when the lights came on, Charlie suddenly realized that for the last few seconds he hadn't been floating at all. He had been standing normally on the floor. Mr Wonka was on the floor, too, and so was Grandpa Joe and Mr and Mrs Bucket and also the big bed. As for Grandma Josephine, Grandma Georgina and Grandpa George, they must have fallen right back on to the bed because they were now all three on top of it and scrabbling to get under the blanket.

'We're through!' yelled Mr Wonka. 'We've done it! We're in!' Grandpa Joe grabbed him by the hand and said, 'Well done, sir! How splendid! What a magnificent job!'

'Where in the world are we now?' said Mrs Bucket.

93

'We're back, mother!' Charlie cried. 'We're in the Chocolate Factory!'

'I'm very glad to hear it,' said Mrs Bucket. 'But didn't we come rather a long way round?'

'We had to,' said Mr Wonka, 'to avoid the traffic.'

'I have never met a man,' said Grandma Georgina, 'who talks so much absolute nonsense!'

'A little nonsense now and then, is relished by the wisest men,' Mr Wonka said.

'Why don't you pay some attention to where this crazy Elevator's going!' shouted Grandma Josephine. 'And stop footling about!'

'A little footling round about, will stop you going up the spout,' said Mr Wonka.

Back to the Chocolate Factory

'What did I tell you!' cried Grandma Georgina. 'He's round the twist! He's bogged as a beetle! He's dotty as a dingbat! He's got rats in the roof! I want to go home!'

'Too late,' said Mr Wonka. 'We're there!' The Elevator stopped. The doors opened and Charlie found himself looking out once again at the great Chocolate Room with the chocolate river and the chcocolate waterfall, where everything was eatable – the trees, the leaves, the grass, the pebbles and even the rocks. And there to meet them were hundreds and hundreds of tiny Oompa-Loompas, all waving and cheering. It was a sight that took one's breath away. Even Grandma Georgina was stunned into silence for a few seconds. But not for long. 'Who in the world are all those peculiar little men?' she said.

'They're Oompa-Loompas,' Charlie told her. 'They're wonderful. You'll love them.'

'Ssshh!' said Grandpa Joe. 'Listen, Charlie! The drums are starting up! They're going to sing.'

> *'Alleluia!'* sang the Oompa-Loompas.
> *'Oh alleluia and hooray!*
> *Our Willy Wonka's back today!*
> *We thought you'd never make it home!*
> *We thought you'd left us all alone!*
> *We knew that you would have to face*
> *Some frightful creatures up in space.*
> *We even thought we heard the crunch*
> *Of someone eating you for lunch . . .'*

'All right!' shouted Mr Wonka, laughing and raising both hands. 'Thank you for your welcome! Will some of you please help to get this bed out of here!'

Fifty Oompa-Loompas ran forward and pushed the bed with the three old ones in it out of the Elevator. Mr and Mrs Bucket, both looking completely overwhelmed by it all, followed the bed out. Then came Grandpa Joe, Charlie and Mr Wonka.

'Now,' said Mr Wonka, addressing Grandpa George, Grandma Georgina and Grandma Josephine. 'Up you hop out of that bed and let's get cracking. I'm sure you'll all want to lend a hand running the factory.'

'Who, us?' said Grandma Josephine.

'Yes, you,' said Mr Wonka.

'You must be joking,' said Grandma Georgina.

'I never joke,' said Mr Wonka.

'Now just you listen to me, sir!' said old Grandpa George,

sitting up straight in bed. 'You've got us into quite enough tubbles and trumbles for one day!'

'I've got you out of them, too,' said Mr Wonka proudly. 'And I'm going to get you out of that bed as well, you see if I don't!'

13

How Wonka-Vite Was Invented

'I haven't been out of this bed in twenty years and I'm not getting out now for anybody!' said Grandma Josephine firmly.

'Nor me,' said Grandma Georgina.

'You were out of it just now, every one of you,' said Mr Wonka.

'That was floating,' said Grandpa George. 'We couldn't help it.'

'We never put our feet on the floor,' said Grandma Josephine.

'Try it,' said Mr Wonka. 'You might surprise yourself.'

'Go on, Josie,' said Grandpa Joe. 'Give it a try. I did. It was easy.'

'We're perfectly comfortable where we are, thank you very much,' said Grandma Josephine.

Mr Wonka sighed and shook his head very slowly and very sadly. 'Oh well,' he said, 'so that's that.' He laid his head on one side and gazed thoughtfully at the three old people in the bed, and Charlie, watching him closely, saw those bright little eyes of his beginning to spark and twinkle once again.

Ha-ha, thought Charlie. What's coming now?

'I suppose,' said Mr Wonka, placing the tip of one finger on the point of his nose and pressing gently, 'I suppose . . . because this is a very special case . . . I suppose I *could* spare you just a tiny little bit of . . .' He stopped and shook his head.

'A tiny little bit of what?' said Grandma Josephine sharply.

'No,' said Mr Wonka. 'It's pointless. You seem to have decided to stay in that bed whatever happens. And anyway, the stuff is much too precious to waste. I'm sorry I mentioned it.' He started to walk away.

'Hey!' shouted Grandma Georgina. 'You can't begin something and not go on with it! *What* is too precious to waste?'

Mr Wonka stopped. Slowly he turned around. He looked long and hard at the three old people in the bed. They looked back at him, waiting. He kept silent a little longer, allowing their curiosity to grow. The Oompa-Loompas stood absolutely still behind him, watching.

'What is this thing you're talking about?' said Grandma Georgina.

'Get on with it, for heaven's sake!' said Grandma Josephine.

'Very well,' Mr Wonka said at last. 'I'll tell you. And listen carefully because this could change your whole lives. It could even change *you*.'

'I don't want to be *changed*!' shouted Grandma Georgina.

'May I go on, madam? Thank you. Not long ago, I was fooling about in my Inventing Room, stirring stuff around and mixing things up the way I do every afternoon at four o'clock, when suddenly I found I had made something that seemed very unusual. This thing I had made kept changing colour as I looked at it, and now and again it gave a little jump, it actually jumped up in the air, as though it were alive. *"What have we here?"* I cried, and I rushed it quickly to the Testing Room and gave some to the Oompa-Loompa who was on duty there at the time. The result was immediate! It was flabbergasting! It was unbelievable! It was also rather unfortunate.'

'What happened?' said Grandma Georgina, sitting up.

'What indeed,' said Mr Wonka.

'Answer her question,' said Grandma Josephine. 'What happened to the Oompa-Loompa?'

'Ah,' said Mr Wonka, 'yes . . . well . . . there's no point in crying over spilled milk, is there? I realized, you see, that I had stumbled upon a new and tremendously powerful vitamin, and I also knew that if only I could make it safe, if only I could stop it doing to others what it did to that Oompa-Loompa . . .'

'What *did* it do to that Oompa-Loompa?' said Grandma Georgina sternly.

'The older I get, the deafer I become,' said Mr Wonka. 'Do please raise your voice a trifle next time. Thank you so much. Now then. I simply *had* to find a way of making this stuff safe, so that people could take it without . . . er . . .'

'Without *what*?' snapped Grandma Georgina.

'Without a leg to stand on,' said Mr Wonka. 'So I rolled up my sleeves and set to work once more in the Inventing Room. I mixed and I mixed. I must have tried just about every mixture under the moon. By the way, there is a little hole in one wall of the Inventing Room which connects directly with the Testing Room next door, so I was able all the time to keep passing stuff through for testing to whichever brave volunteer happened to be on duty. Well, the first few weeks were pretty depressing and we won't talk about them. Let me tell you instead what happened on the one hundred and thirty-second day of my labours. That morning, I had changed the mixture drastically, and this time the little pill I produced at the end of it all was not nearly so active or alive as the others had been. It kept changing colour, yes, but only from lemon-yellow to blue, then back to yellow again. And when I placed it on the palm of my hand, it didn't jump about like a grasshopper. It only quivered, and then ever so slightly.

'I ran to the hole in the wall that led to the Testing Room. A very old Oompa-Loompa was on duty there that morning. He was a bald, wrinkled, toothless old fellow. He was in a wheel-chair. He had been in the wheel-chair for at least fifteen years.

'"This is test number one hundred and thirty-two!" I said, chalking it up on the board.

'I handed him the pill. He looked at it nervously. I couldn't blame him for being a bit jittery after what had happened to the other one hundred and thirty-one volunteers.'

'What *had* happened to them?' shouted Grandma Georgina. 'Why don't you answer the question instead of skidding around it on two wheels?'

'Who knows the way out of a rose?' said Mr Wonka. 'So this brave old Oompa-Loompa took the pill and, with the help of a little water, he gulped it down. And then, suddenly, the most amazing thing happened. Before my very eyes, queer little changes began taking place in the way he looked. A moment earlier, he had been practically bald, with just a fringe of snowy white hair around the sides and the back of his head. But now the fringe of white hair was turning gold and all over the top of his head new gold hair was beginning to sprout, like grass. In less than half a minute, he had grown a splendid new crop of long golden hair. At the same time, many of the wrinkles started disappearing from his face, not all of them, but about half, enough to make him look a good deal younger, and all of this must have given him a nice tickly feeling because he started grinning at me, then laughing, and as soon as he opened his mouth, I saw the strangest sight of all. Teeth were growing up out from those old toothless gums, good white teeth, and they were coming up so fast I could actually see them getting bigger and bigger.

'I was too flabbergasted to speak. I just stood there with my head poking through the hole in the wall, staring at the little Oompa-Loompa. I saw him slowly lifting himself out of his wheel-chair. He tested his legs on the ground. He stood up. He walked a few paces. Then he looked up at me and his face was bright. His eyes were huge and bright as two stars.

'"Look at me," he said softly. "I'm walking! It's a miracle!"

'"It's Wonka-Vite!" I said. "The great rejuvenator. It makes you young again. How old do you feel now?"

'He thought carefully about this question, then he said, "I feel almost exactly how I felt when I was fifty years old."

'"How old were you just now, before you took the Wonka-Vite?" I asked him.

'"Seventy last birthday," he answered.

' "That means," I said, "it has made you twenty years younger."

'"It has, it has!" he cried, delighted. "I feel as frisky as a froghopper!"

'"Not frisky enough," I told him. "Fifty is still pretty old. Let us see if I can't help you a bit more. Stay right where you are. I'll be back in a twink."

'I ran to my work-bench and began to make one more pill of Wonka-Vite, using exactly the same mixture as before.

'"Swallow this," I said, passing the second pill through the hatch. There was no hesitating this time. Eagerly, he popped it into his mouth and chased it down with a drink of water. And behold, within half a minute, another twenty years had fallen away from his face and body and he was now a slim and sprightly young Oompa-Loompa of thirty. He gave a whoop of joy and started dancing around the room, leaping high in the air and coming down on his toes. "Are you happy?" I asked him.

'"I'm ecstatic!" he cried, jumping up and down. "I'm

happy as a horse in a hay-field!" He ran out of the Testing Room to show himself off to his family and friends.

'Thus was Wonka-Vite invented!' said Mr Wonka. 'And thus was it made safe for all to use!'

'Why don't you use it yourself, then?' said Grandma Georgina. 'You told Charlie you were getting too old to run the factory, so why don't you just take a couple of pills and get forty years younger? Tell me that?'

'Anyone can ask questions,' said Mr Wonka. 'It's the answers that count. Now then, if the three of you in the bed would care to try a dose . . .'

'Just one minute!' said Grandma Josephine, sitting up straight. 'First I'd like to take a look at this seventy-year-old Oompa-Loompa who is now back to thirty!'

Mr Wonka flicked his fingers. A tiny Oompa-Loompa, looking young and perky, ran forward out of the crowd and did a marvellous little dance in front of the three old people in the big bed. 'Two weeks ago, he was seventy years old and in a wheel-chair!' Mr Wonka said proudly. 'And look at him now!'

'The drums, Charlie!' said Grandpa Joe. 'Listen! They're starting up again!'

Far away down on the bank of the chocolate river, Charlie could see the Oompa-Loompa band striking up once more. There were twenty Oompa-Loompas in the band, each with an enormous drum twice as tall as himself, and they were beating a slow mysterious rhythm that soon had all the other hundreds of Oompa-Loompas swinging and swaying from side to side in a kind of trance. They then began to chant:

How Wonka-Vite Was Invented

'If you are old and have the shakes,
If all your bones are full of aches,
If you can hardly walk at all,
If living drives you up the wall,
If you're a grump and full of spite,
If you're a human parasite,
THEN WHAT YOU NEED IS WONKA-VITE!
Your eyes will shine, your hair will grow,
Your face and skin will start to glow,
Your rotten teeth will all drop out
And in their place new teeth will sprout.
Those rolls of fat around your hips
Will vanish, and your wrinkled lips
Will get so soft and rosy-pink
That all the boys will smile and wink
And whisper secretly that this
Is just the girl they want to kiss!
But wait! For that is not the most
Important thing of which to boast.
Good looks you'll have, we've told you so,
But looks aren't everything, you know.
Each pill, as well, to you will give
AN EXTRA TWENTY YEARS TO LIVE!
So come, old friends, and do what's right!
Let's make your lives as bright as bright!
Let's take a dose of this delight!
This heavenly magic dynamite!
You can't go wrong, you must go right!
IT'S WILLY WONKA'S WONKA-VITE!'

14

Recipe for Wonka-Vite

'Here it is!' cried Mr Wonka, standing at the end of the bed and holding high in one hand a little bottle. 'The most valuable bottle of pills in the world! And that, by the way,' he said, giving Grandma Georgina a saucy glance, 'is why I haven't taken any myself. They are far too valuable to waste on me.'

He held the bottle out over the bed. The three old ones sat up and stretched their scrawny necks, trying to catch a glimpse of the pills inside. Charlie and Grandpa Joe also came forward to look. So did Mr and Mrs Bucket. The label said:

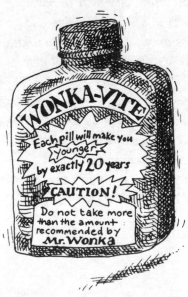

WONKA-VITE

Each pill will make you
younger
by exactly 20 years

CAUTION!

Do not take more
than the amount
recommended by
Mr. Wonka

Recipe for Wonka-Vite

They could all see the pills through the glass. They were brilliant yellow, shimmering and quivering inside the bottle. Vibrating is perhaps a better word. They were vibrating so rapidly that each pill became a blur and you couldn't see its shape. You could only see its colour. You got the impression that there was something very small but incredibly powerful, something not quite of this world, locked up inside them and fighting to get out.

'They're wriggling,' said Grandma Georgina. 'I don't like things that wriggle. How do we know they won't go on wriggling inside us after we've swallowed them? Like those Mexican jumping beans of Charlie's I swallowed a couple of years back. You remember that, Charlie?'

'I told you not to eat them, Grandma.'

'They went on jumping about inside me for a month,' said Grandma Georgina. 'I couldn't sit still!'

'If I'm going to eat one of those pills, I jolly well want to know what's in it first,' said Grandma Josephine.

'I don't blame you,' said Mr Wonka. 'But the recipe is extremely complicated. Wait a minute . . . I've got it written down somewhere . . .' He started digging around in the pockets of his coat-tails. 'I know it's here somewhere,' he said. 'I can't have lost it. I keep all my most valuable and important things in these pockets. The trouble is, there's such a lot of them . . .' He started emptying the pockets and placing the contents on the bed – a homemade catapult . . . a yo-yo . . . a trick fried-egg made of rubber . . . a slice of salami . . . a tooth with a filling in it . . . a stinkbomb . . . a packet of itching-powder . . . 'It must be here, it *must* be, it must,' he kept muttering. 'I put it away so carefully . . . Ah! *Here* it is!' He unfolded a crumpled piece of paper, smoothed it out, held it up and began to read as follows:

RECIPE FOR MAKING WONKA-VITE

Take a block of finest chocolate weighing one ton (or twenty sackfuls of broken chocolate, whichever is the easier). Place chocolate in very large cauldron and melt over red-hot furnace. When melted, lower the heat slightly so as not to burn the chocolate, but keep it boiling. Now add the following, in precisely the order given, stirring well all the time and allowing each item to dissolve before adding the next:

THE HOOF OF A MANTICORE
THE TRUNK (AND THE SUITCASE) OF AN
   ELEPHANT
THE YOLKS OF THREE EGGS FROM A
   WHIFFLE-BIRD
A WART FROM A WART-HOG
THE HORN OF A COW (IT MUST BE A LOUD
   HORN)
THE FRONT TAIL OF A COCKATRICE
SIX OUNCES OF SPRUNGE FROM A YOUNG
   SLIMESCRAPER
TWO HAIRS (AND ONE RABBIT) FROM THE
   HEAD OF A HIPPOCAMPUS
THE BEAK OF A RED-BREASTED
   WILBATROSS
A CORN FROM THE TOE OF A UNICORN
THE FOUR TENTACLES OF A QUADROPUS
THE HIP(AND THE PO AND THE POT) OF A
   HIPPOPOTAMUS
THE SNOUT OF A PROGHOPPER
A MOLE FROM A MOLE
THE HIDE (AND THE SEEK) OF A
   SPOTTED WHANGDOODLE

Recipe for Wonka-Vite

THE WHITES OF TWELVE EGGS FROM A
    TREE-SQUEAK
THE THREE FEET OF A SNOZZWANGER (IF
    YOU CAN'T GET THREE FEET, ONE YARD
    WILL DO)
THE SQUARE-ROOT OF A SOUTH AMERICAN
    ABACUS
THE FANGS OF A VIPER (IT MUST BE A
    VINDSCREEN VIPER)
THE CHEST (AND THE DRAWERS) OF A
    WILD GROUT

When all the above are thoroughly dissolved, boil for a further twenty-seven days but do not stir. At the end of this time, all liquid will have evaporated and there will be left in the bottom of the cauldron only a hard brown lump about the size of a football. Break this open with a hammer and in the very centre of it you will find a small round pill. This pill is WONKA-VITE.

15

Good-bye Georgina

When Mr Wonka had finished reading the recipe, he carefully folded the paper and put it back into his pocket. 'A very, *very* complicated mixture,' he said. 'So can you wonder it took me so long to get it just right?' He held the bottle up high and gave it a little shake and the pills rattled loudly inside it, like glass beads. 'Now, sir,' he said, offering the bottle first to Grandpa George. 'Will you take one pill or two?'

'Will you solemnly swear,' said Grandpa George, 'that it will do what you say it will and nothing else?'

Mr Wonka placed his free hand on his heart. 'I swear it,' he said.

Charlie edged forward. Grandpa Joe came with him. The two of them always stayed close together. 'Please excuse me for asking,' Charlie said, 'but are you really absolutely sure you've got it *quite right?*'

'Whatever makes you ask a funny question like that?' said Mr Wonka.

'I was thinking of the gum you gave to Violet Beauregarde,' Charlie said.

'So *that's* what's bothering you!' cried Mr Wonka. 'But

don't you understand, my dear boy, that I never did give that gum to Violet? She snatched it without permission. And I shouted, "Stop! Don't! Spit it out!" But the silly girl took no notice of me. Now Wonka-Vite is altogether different. I am *offering* these pills to your grandparents. I am recommending them. And when taken according to my instructions, they are as safe as sugar-candy!'

'Of course they are!' cried Mr Bucket. 'What are you waiting for, all of you!' An extraordinary change had come over Mr Bucket since he had entered the Chocolate Room. Normally he was a pretty timid sort of person. A lifetime devoted to screwing caps on to the tops of toothpaste tubes in a toothpaste factory had turned him into a rather shy and quiet man. But the sight of the marvellous Chocolate Factory had made his spirits soar. What is more, this business of the pills seemed to have given him a terrific kick. 'Listen!' he cried, going up to the edge of the bed. 'Mr Wonka's offering you a new life! Grab it while you can!'

'It's a delicious sensation,' Mr Wonka said. 'And it's very quick. You lose a year a second. Exactly one year falls away from you every second that goes by!' He stepped forward and placed the bottle of pills gently in the middle of the bed. 'So here you are, my dears,' he said. 'Help yourselves!'

'Come on!' cried all the Oompa-Loompas together.

> *'Come on, old friends, and do what's right!*
> *Come make your lives as bright as bright!*
> *Just take a dose of this delight!*
> *This heavenly magic dynamite!*
> *You can't go wrong, you must go right!*
> *IT'S WILLY WONKA'S WONKA-VITE!'*

This was too much for the old people in the bed. All three

of them made a dive for the bottle. Six scrawny hands shot out and started scrabbling to get hold of it. Grandma Georgina got it. She gave a grunt of triumph and unscrewed the cap and tipped all the little brilliant yellow pills on to the blanket on her lap. She cupped her hands around them so the others couldn't reach out and snatch them. 'All right!' she shouted excitedly, counting them quickly. 'There's twelve pills here! That's six for me and three each for you!'

'Hey! That's not fair!' shrilled Grandma Josephine. 'It's four for each of us!'

'Four each is right!' cried Grandpa George. 'Come on, Georgina! Hand over my share!'

Mr Wonka shrugged his shoulders and turned his back on them. He hated squabbles. He hated it when people got grabby and selfish. Let them fight it out among themselves, he thought, and he walked away. He walked slowly down toward the chocolate waterfall. It was an unhappy truth, he told himself, that nearly all people in the world behave badly when there is something really big at stake. Money is the thing they fight over most. But these pills were bigger than money. They could do things for you no amount of money could ever do. They were worth at least a million dollars a pill. He knew plenty of very rich men who would gladly pay that much in order to become twenty years younger. He reached the river-bank below the waterfall and he stood there gazing at the great gush and splash of melted chocolate pouring down. He had hoped the noise of the waterfall would drown the arguing voices of the old grandparents in the bed, but it didn't. Even with his back to them, he still couldn't help hearing most of what they were saying.

'I got them first!' Grandma Georgina was shouting. 'So they're mine to share out!'

'Oh no they're not!' shrilled Grandma Josephine. 'He didn't give them to you! He gave them to all three of us!'

'I want my share and no one's going to stop me getting it!' yelled Grandpa George. 'Come on, woman! Hand them over!'

Then came the voice of Grandpa Joe, cutting in sternly through the rabble. 'Stop this at once!' he ordered. 'All three of you! You're behaving like savages!'

'You keep out of this, Joe, and mind your own business!' said Grandma Josephine.

'Now you be careful, Josie,' Grandpa Joe went on. 'Four is too many for one person anyway.'

'That's right,' Charlie said. '*Please* Grandma, why don't you just take one or two each like Mr Wonka said, and that'll leave some for Grandpa Joe and mother and father.'

'Yes!' cried Mr Bucket. 'I'd love one!'

'Oh, wouldn't it be wonderful,' said Mrs Bucket, 'to be twenty years younger and not have aching feet any more! Couldn't you spare just one for each of us, mother?'

'I'm afraid not,' said Grandma Georgina. 'These pills are specially reserved for us three in the bed. Mr Wonka said so!'

'I want my share!' shouted Grandpa George. 'Come on, Georgina! Dish them out!'

'Hey, let me go, you brute!' cried Grandma Georgina. 'You're hurting me! Ow! . . . ALL RIGHT! *All right! I'll* share them out if you'll stop twisting my arm . . . That's better . . . Here's four for Josephine . . . and four for George . . . and four for me.'

'Good,' said Grandpa George. 'Now who's got some water?'

Without looking around, Mr Wonka knew that three Oompa-Loompas would be running to the bed with three glasses of water. Oompa-Loompas were always ready to help. There was a brief pause, and then:

'Well, here goes!' cried Grandpa George.

'Young and beautiful, that's what I'll be!' shouted Grandma Josephine.

'Farewell, old age!' cried Grandma Georgina. 'All together now! Down the hatch!'

Then there was silence. Mr Wonka was itching to turn around and look, but he forced himself to wait. Out of the corner of one eye he could see a group of Oompa-Loompas, all motionless, their eyes fixed intently in the direction of the big bed over by the Elevator. Then Charlie's voice broke the silence. '*Wow!*' he was shouting. 'Just look at *that*! It's . . . it's incredible!'

'I can't believe it!' Grandpa Joe was yelling. 'They're getting younger and younger! They really are! Just *look* at Grandpa George's hair!'

'And his teeth!' cried Charlie. 'Hey, Grandpa! You're getting lovely white teeth all over again!'

'Mother!' shouted Mrs Bucket to Grandma Georgina. 'Oh, mother! You're beautiful! You're so young! And just *look* at dad!' she went on, pointing at Grandpa George. 'Isn't he handsome!'

'What's it feel like, Josie?' asked Grandpa Joe excitedly. 'Tell us what it feels like to be back to thirty again! . . . Wait a minute! You look younger than thirty! You can't be a day more than twenty now! . . . But that's enough, isn't it! . . . I should stop there if I were you! Twenty's quite young enough! . . .'

Mr Wonka shook his head sadly and passed a hand over his eyes. Had you been standing very close to him you would have heard him murmuring softly under his breath, 'Oh, deary deary me, here we go again . . .'

'*Mother!*' cried Mrs Bucket, and now there was a shrill note of alarm in her voice. 'Why don't you stop, mother! You're going too far! You're way under twenty! You can't be more than fifteen! . . . You're . . . you're . . . you're ten . . . *you're getting smaller, mother!*'

'Josie!' shouted Grandpa Joe. 'Hey Josie! Don't do it, Josie! You're shrinking! You're a little girl! Stop her, somebody! Quick!'

'They're *all* going too far!' cried Charlie.

'They took too much,' said Mr Bucket.

'Mother's shrinking faster than any of them!' wailed Mrs Bucket. '*Mother! Can't you hear me, mother? Can't you stop?*'

'My heavens, isn't it quick!' said Mr Bucket, who seemed to be the only one enjoying it. 'It really is a year a second!'

'But they've hardly got any more years left!' wailed Grandpa Joe.

'Mother's no more than four now!' Mrs Bucket cried out. 'She's three . . . two . . . one . . . *Gracious me!* What's happening to her! Where's she gone? Mother? Georgina! Where are you? Mr Wonka! Come quickly! Come here, Mr Wonka! Something frightful's happened! Something's gone wrong! My old mother's disappeared!'

Mr Wonka sighed and turned around and walked slowly and quite calmly back toward the bed.

'*Where's my mother?*' bawled Mrs Bucket.

'Look at Josephine!' cried Grandpa Joe. 'Just look at her! I ask you!'

Mr Wonka looked first at Grandma Josephine. She was sitting in the middle of the huge bed, bawling her head off 'Wa! Wa! Wa!' she said. 'Wa! Wa! Wa! Wa! Wa!'

'She's a screaming baby!' cried Grandpa Joe. 'I've got a screaming baby for a wife!'

'The other one's Grandpa George!' Mr Bucket said, smiling happily. 'The slightly bigger one there crawling around. He's my wife's father.'

'That's right! He's my father!' wailed Mrs Bucket. 'And where's Georgina, my old mother? She's vanished! She's nowhere Mr Wonka! She's absolutely nowhere! I saw her getting smaller and smaller and in the end she got so small she just disappeared into thin air! What I want to know is where's she *gone* to! And how in the world are we going to get her back!'

'Ladies and gentlemen!' said Mr Wonka, coming up close and raising both hands for silence. '*Please*, I beg you, do not ruffle yourselves! There's nothing to worry about . . .'

'You call it nothing!' cried poor Mrs Bucket. 'When my old mother's gone down the drain and my father's a howling baby . . .'

'A lovely baby,' said Mr Wonka.

'I quite agree,' said Mr Bucket.

'What about my Josie?' cried Grandpa Joe.

'What *about* her?' said Mr Wonka.

'Well . . .'

'A great improvement, sir,' said Mr Wonka, 'don't you agree?'

'Oh, yes!' said Grandpa Joe. 'I mean *NO!* What am I saying. She's a howling baby!'

'But in perfect health,' said Mr Wonka. 'May I ask you, sir, how many pills she took?'

'Four,' said Grandpa Joe glumly. 'They all took four.'

Mr Wonka made a wheezing noise in his throat and a look of great sorrow came over his face. 'Why oh why can't people be more sensible?' he said sadly. 'Why don't they *listen* to me when I tell them something? I explained very carefully beforehand that each pill makes the taker exactly twenty years younger. So if Grandma Josephine took four of them, she automatically became younger by four times twenty, which is . . . wait a minute now . . . four twos are eight . . . add a nought . . . that's eighty . . . so she automatically became younger by eighty years. How old, sir, was your wife, if I may ask, before this happened?'

'She was eighty last birthday,' Grandpa Joe answered. 'She was eighty and three months.'

'There you are, then!' cried Mr Wonka, flashing a happy smile. 'The Wonka-Vite worked perfectly! She is now precisely three months old! And a plumper rosier infant I've never set eyes on!'

'Nor me,' said Mr Bucket. 'She'd win a prize in any baby competition.'

'*First* prize,' said Mr Wonka.

'Cheer up, Grandpa,' said Charlie, taking the old man's hand in his. 'Don't be sad. She's a beautiful baby.'

'Madam,' said Mr Wonka, turning to Mrs Bucket. 'How old, may I ask, was Grandpa George, your father?'

'Eighty-one,' wailed Mrs Bucket. 'He was eighty-one exactly.'

'Which makes him a great big bouncing one-year-old boy now,' said Mr Wonka happily.

'How splendid!' said Mr Bucket to his wife. 'You'll be the first person in the world to change her father's nappies!'

'He can change his own rotten nappies!' said Mrs Bucket. 'What I want to know is *where's my mother? Where's* Grandma *Georgina?*'

'Ah-ha,' said Mr Wonka. 'Oh-ho . . . Yes, indeed . . . Where oh where has Georgina gone? How old, please, was the lady in question?'

'Seventy-eight,' Mrs Bucket told him.

'Well, of *course!*' laughed Mr Wonka. 'That explains it!'

'What explains what?' snapped Mrs Bucket.

'My dear madam,' said Mr Wonka. 'If she was only seventy-eight and she took enough Wonka-Vite to make her eighty years younger, then naturally she's vanished. She's bitten off more than she could chew! She's taken off more years than she had!'

'Explain yourself,' said Mrs Bucket.

'Simple arithmetic,' said Mr Wonka. 'Subtract eighty from seventy-eight and what do you get?'

'Minus two!' said Charlie.

'Hooray!' said Mr Bucket. 'My mother-in-law's minus two years old!'

'Impossible!' said Mrs Bucket.

'It's true,' said Mr Wonka.

'And where is she now, may I ask?' said Mrs Bucket.

'That's a good question,' said Mr Wonka. 'A very good question. Yes, indeed. Where is she now?'

'You don't have the foggiest idea, do you?'

'Of course I do,' said Mr Wonka. 'I know exactly where she is.'

'Then tell me!'

'You must try to understand,' said Mr Wonka, 'that if she is now minus two, she's got to add two more years before she can start again from nought. She's got to wait it out.'

'Where does she wait?' said Mrs Bucket.

'In the Waiting Room, of course,' said Mr Wonka.

BOOM!-BOOM! said the drums of the Oompa-Loompa band. *BOOM-BOOM! BOOM-BOOM!* And all the Oompa-Loompas, all the hundreds of them standing there in the Chocolate Room began to sway and hop and dance to the rhythm of the music. 'Attention, please!' they sang.

> *'Attention, please! Attention, please!*
> *Don't dare to talk! Don't dare to sneeze!*
> *Don't doze or daydream! Stay awake!*
> *Your health, your very life's at stake!*
> *Ho-ho, you say, they can't mean me.*
> *Ha-ha, we answer, wait and see.*
>
> *Did any of you ever meet*
> *A child called Goldie Pinklesweet?*
> *Who on her seventh birthday went*
> *To stay with Granny down in Kent.*
> *At lunchtime on the second day*
> *Of dearest little Goldie's stay,*

Granny announced, "I'm going down
To do some shopping in the town."
(D'you know why Granny didn't tell
The child to come along as well?
She's going to the nearest inn
To buy herself a double gin.)

So out she creeps. She shuts the door.
And Goldie, after making sure
That she is really by herself,
Goes quickly to the medicine shelf,
And there, her little greedy eyes
See pills of every shape and size,
Such fascinating colours too –
Some green, some pink, some brown, some blue.
'All right,' she says, 'let's try the brown.'
She takes one pill and gulps it down.
'Yum-yum!' she cries. 'Hooray! What fun!
They're chocolate-coated, every one!'
She gobbles five, she gobbles ten,
She stops her gobbling only when
The last pill's gone. There are no more.
Slowly she rises from the floor.
She stops. She hiccups. Dear, oh dear,
She starts to feel a trifle queer.

You see, how could young Goldie know,
For nobody had told her so,
That Grandmama, her old relation,
Suffered from frightful constipation.
This meant that every night she'd give
Herself a powerful laxative,

And all the medicines that she'd bought
Were naturally of this sort.
The pink and red and blue and green
Were all extremely strong and mean.
But far more fierce and meaner still,
Was Granny's little chocolate pill.
Its blast effect was quite uncanny.
It used to shake up even Granny.
In point of fact she did not dare
To use them more than twice a year.
So can you wonder little Goldie
Began to feel a wee bit mouldy?

Inside her tummy, something stirred.
A funny gurgling sound was heard,
And then, oh dear, from deep within,
The ghastly rumbling sounds begin!
They rumbilate and roar and boom!
They bounce and echo round the room!
The floorboards shake and from the wall
Some bits of paint and plaster fall.
Explosions, whistles, awful bangs
Were followed by the loudest clangs.
(A man next door was heard to say,
'A thunderstorm is on the way.')
But on and on the rumbling goes.
A window cracks, a lamp-bulb blows.
Young Goldie clutched herself and cried,
'There's something wrong with my inside!'
This was, we very greatly fear,
The understatement of the year.
For wouldn't any child feel crummy,
With loud explosions in her tummy?

Granny, at half past two, came in,
Weaving a little from the gin,
But even so she quickly saw
The empty bottle on the floor.
'My precious laxatives!' she cried.
'I don't feel well,' the girl replied.
Angrily Grandma shook her head.
'I'm really not surprised,' she said.
'Why can't you leave my pills alone?'
With that, she grabbed the telephone
And shouted, 'Listen, send us quick
An ambulance! A child is sick!
It's number fifty, Fontwell Road!
Come fast! I think she might explode!'

We're sure you do not wish to hear
About the hospital and where
They did a lot of horrid things
With stomach-pumps and rubber rings.
Let's answer what you want to know;
Did Goldie live or did she go?
The doctors gathered round her bed,
'There's really not much hope' they said.
'She's going, going, gone!' they cried.
'She's had her chips! She's dead! She's dead!'
'I'm not so sure,' the child replied.
And all at once she opened wide
Her great big bluish eyes and sighed,
And gave the anxious docs a wink,
And said, 'I'll be okay, I think.'

So Goldie lived and back she went
At first to Granny's place in Kent.
Her father came the second day
And fetched her in a Chevrolet,
And drove her to their home in Dover.
But Goldie's troubles were not over.
You see, if someone takes enough
Of any highly dangerous stuff,
One will invariably find
Some traces of it left behind.
It pains us greatly to relate
That Goldie suffered from this fate.
She'd taken such a massive fill
Of this unpleasant kind of pill,
It got into her blood and bones,
It messed up all her chromosomes,
It made her constantly upset,
And she could never really get
The beastly stuff to go away.
And so the girl was forced to stay
For seven hours every day
Within the everlasting gloom
Of what we call The Ladies Room.
And after all, the W.C.
Is not the gayest place to be.
So now, before it is too late,
Take heed of Goldie's dreadful fate.
And seriously, all jokes apart,
Do promise us across your heart
That you will never help yourself
To medicine from the medicine shelf.'

16

Vita-Wonk and Minusland

'It's up to you, Charlie my boy,' said Mr Wonka. 'It's your factory. Shall we let your Grandma Georgina wait it out for the next two years or shall we try to bring her back right now?'

'You don't really mean you might be able to bring her back?' cried Charlie.

'There's no harm in trying, is there . . . if that's the way you want it?'

'Oh yes! Of course I do! For mother's sake especially! Can't you see how sad she is!'

Mrs Bucket was sitting on the edge of the big bed, dabbing her eyes with a hanky. 'My poor old mum,' she kept saying. 'She's minus two and I won't see her again for months and months and months – if ever at all!' Behind her, Grandpa Joe, with the help of an Oompa-Loompa, was feeding his three-months-old wife, Grandma Josephine, from a bottle. Alongside them, Mr Bucket was spooning something called 'Wonka's Squdgemallow Baby Food' into one-year-old Grandpa George's mouth but mostly all over his chin and chest. 'Big deal!' he was muttering angrily. 'What a lousy rotten rotten this is! They tell me I'm going to the Chocolate

Factory to have a good time and I finish up being a mother to my father-in-law.'

'Everything's under control, Charlie,' said Mr Wonka, surveying the scene, 'They're doing fine. They don't need us here. Come along! We're off to hunt for Grandma!' He caught Charlie by the arm and went dancing towards the open door of the Great Glass Elevator. 'Hurry up, my dear boy, hurry up!' he cried. 'We've got to hustle if we're going to get there before!'

'Before *what*, Mr Wonka?'

'Before she gets subtracted of course! All Minuses are subtracted! Don't you know any arithmetic at all?'

They were in the Elevator now and Mr Wonka was searching among the hundreds of buttons for the one he wanted. '*Here* we are!' he said, placing his finger delicately upon a tiny ivory button on which it said 'MINUSLAND'.

The doors slid shut. And then, with a fearful whistling whirring sound the great machine leaped away to the right. Charlie grabbed Mr Wonka's legs and held on for dear life. Mr Wonka pulled a jump-seat out of the wall and said, 'Sit down Charlie, quick, and strap yourself in tight! This journey's going to be rough and choppy!' There were straps on either side of the seat and Charlie buckled himself firmly in. Mr Wonka pulled out a second seat for himself and did the same.

'We are going a long way down,' he said. 'Oh, such a long way down we are going.'

The Elevator was gathering speed. It twisted and swerved. It swung sharply to the left, then it went right, then left again, and it was heading downward all the time – down and down and down. 'I only hope,' said Mr Wonka, 'the Oompa-Loompas aren't using the other Elevator today.'

'What other Elevator?' asked Charlie.

'The one that goes the opposite way on the same track as this.'

'Holy snakes, Mr Wonka! You mean we might have a collision?'

'I've always been lucky so far, my boy . . . Hey! Take a look out there! Quick!'

Through the window, Charlie caught a glimpse of what seemed like an enormous quarry with a steep craggy-brown rock-face, and all over the rock-face there were hundreds of Oompa-Loompas working with picks and pneumatic drills.

Vita-Wonk and Minusland

'Rock-candy,' said Mr Wonk. 'That's the richest deposit of rock-candy in the world.'

The Elevator sped on. 'We're going deeper, Charlie. Deeper and deeper. We're about two hundred thousand feet down already.' Strange sights were flashing by outside, but the Elevator was travelling at such a terrific speed that only occasionally was Charlie able to recognize anything at all. Once, he thought he saw in the distance a cluster of tiny houses shaped like upside-down cups, and there were streets in between the houses and Oompa-Loompas walking in the streets. Another time, as they were passing some sort of a vast red plain dotted with things that looked like oil derricks, he saw a great spout of brown liquid spurting out of the ground high into the air. 'A gusher!' cried Mr Wonka, clapping his hands. 'A whacking great gusher! How splendid! Just when we needed it!'

'A what?' said Charlie.

'We've struck chocolate again, my boy. That'll be a rich new field. Oh, what a beautiful gusher! Just look at it go!'

On they roared, heading downward more steeply than ever now, and hundreds, literally hundreds of astonishing sights kept flashing by outside. There were giant cog-wheels turning and mixers mixing and bubbles bubbling and vast orchards of toffee-apple trees and lakes the size of football grounds filled with blue and gold and green liquid, and everywhere there were Oompa-Loompas!

'You realize,' said Mr Wonka, 'that what you saw earlier on when you went round the factory with all those naughty little children was only a tiny corner of the establishment. It goes down for miles and miles. And as soon as possible I shall show you all the way around slowly and properly. But that will take three weeks. Right now we have other things to think about and I have important things to tell you. Listen carefully to me, Charlie. I must talk fast, for we'll be there in a couple of minutes.

'I suppose you guessed,' Mr Wonka went on, 'what happened to all those Oompa-Loompas in the Testing Room when I was experimenting with Wonka-Vite. Of course you did. They disappeared and became Minuses just like your Grandma Georgina. The recipe was miles too strong. One of them actually became Minus eighty-seven! Imagine that!'

'You mean he's got to wait eighty-seven years before he can come back?' Charlie asked.

'That's what kept bugging me, my boy. After all, one can't allow one's best friends to wait around as miserable Minuses for eighty-seven years . . .'

'And get subtracted as well,' said Charlie. 'That would be frightful.'

'Of course it would, Charlie. So what did I do? "Willy Wonka," I said to myself, "if you can invent Wonka-Vite to make people younger, then surely to goodness you can also invent something else to make people older!"'

'Ah-ha!' cried Charlie. 'I see what you're getting at. Then you could turn the Minuses quickly back into Pluses and bring them home again.'

'Precisely, my dear boy, precisely – always supposing, of course, that I could *find out* where the Minuses had gone to!'

The Elevator plunged on, diving steeply toward the centre of the Earth. All was blackness outside now. There was nothing to be seen.

'So once again,' Mr Wonka went on, 'I rolled up my sleeves and set to work. Once again I squeezed my brain, searching for the new recipe . . . I had to create *age* . . . to make people *old . . . old, older, oldest . . .* "Ha-ha!" I cried, for now the ideas were beginning to come. "What is the oldest living thing in the world? What lives longer than anything else?" '

'A tree,' Charlie said.

'Right you are, Charlie! But what kind of a tree? Not the Douglas Fir. Not the Oak. Not the Cedar. No no, my boy. It is a tree called the Bristlecone Pine that grows upon the slopes of Wheeler Peak in Nevada, U.S.A. You can find Bristlecone Pines on Wheeler Peak today that are over 4000 years old! This is fact, Charlie. Ask any dendrochronologist you like (and look that word up in the dictionary when you get home, will you please?). So that started me off. I jumped into the Great Glass Elevator and rushed all over the world collecting special items from the oldest living things . . .

A PINT OF SAP FROM A 4000 YEAR OLD
    BRISTLECONE PINE

THE TOE-NAIL CLIPPINGS FROM A 168 YEAR
    OLD RUSSIAN FARMER CALLED PETRO-
    VITCH GREGOROVITCH

AN EGG LAID BY A 200 YEAR OLD TORTOISE
    BELONGING TO THE KING OF TONGA

THE TAIL OF A 51 YEAR OLD HORSE IN
    ARABIA

THE WHISKERS OF A 36 YEAR OLD CAT
    CALLED CRUMPETS

AN OLD FLEA WHICH HAD LIVED ON CRUM-
    PETS FOR 36 YEARS

THE TAIL OF A 207 YEAR OLD GIANT RAT
    FROM TIBET

THE BLACK TEETH OF A 97 YEAR OLD GRIM-
ALKIN LIVING IN A CAVE ON MOUNT
POPOCATEPETL
THE KNUCKLEBONES OF A 700 YEAR OLD
CATTALOO FROM PERU . . .

. . . All over the world, Charlie, I tracked down very old and
ancient animals and took an important little bit of something from each one of them – a hair or an eyebrow or
sometimes it was no more than an ounce or two of the jam
scraped from between its toes while it was sleeping. I tracked
down THE WHISTLE-PIG, THE BOBOLINK, THE
SKROCK, THE POLLYFROG, THE GIANT
CURLICUE, THE STINGING SLUG AND THE
VENOMOUS SQUERKLE who can spit poison right into
your eye from fifty yards away. But there's no time to tell
you about them all now, Charlie. Let me just say quickly
that in the end, after lots of boiling and bubbling and mixing
and testing in my Inventing Room, I produced one tiny
cupful of oily black liquid and gave four drops of it to a
brave twenty-year-old Oompa-Loompa volunteer to see
what happened.'

'What did happen?' Charlie asked.

'It was fantastic!' cried Mr Wonka. 'The moment he
swallowed it, he began wrinkling and shrivelling up all over
and his hair started dropping off and his teeth started falling
out and, before I knew it, he had suddenly become an old
fellow of seventy-five! And thus, my dear Charlie, was Vita-
Wonk invented!'

'Did you rescue all the Oompa-Loompa Minuses, Mr
Wonka?'

'Every single one of them, my boy! One hundred and

thirty-one all told! Mind you, it wasn't quite as easy as all that. There were lots of snags and complications along the way . . . Good heavens! We're nearly there! I *must* stop talking now and watch where we're going.'

Charlie realized that the Elevator was no longer rushing and roaring. It was hardly moving at all now. It seemed to be drifting. 'Undo your straps,' Mr Wonka said. 'We must get ready for action.' Charlie undid his straps and stood up and peered out. It was an eerie sight. They were drifting in a heavy grey mist and the mist was swirling and swishing around them as though driven by winds from many sides. In the distance, the mist was darker and almost black and it seemed to be swirling more fiercely than ever over there. Mr Wonka slid open the doors. 'Stand back!' he said. 'Don't fall out, Charlie, whatever you do!'

The mist came into the Elevator. It had the fusty reeky smell of an old underground dungeon. The silence was overpowering. There was no sound at all, no whisper of wind, no voice of creature or insect, and it gave Charlie a queer frightening feeling to be standing there in the middle of this grey inhuman nothingness – as though he were in another world altogether, in some place where man should never be.

'Minusland!' whispered Mr Wonka. 'This is it, Charlie! The problem now is to find her. We may be lucky . . . and there again, we may not!'

17

Rescue in Minusland

'I don't like it here at all,' Charlie whispered. 'It gives me the willies.'

'Me, too,' Mr Wonka whispered back. 'But we've got a job to do, Charlie, and we must go through with it.'

The mist was condensing now on the glass walls of the Elevator making it difficult to see out except through the open doors.

'Do any other creatures live here, Mr Wonka?'

'Plenty of Gnoolies.'

'Are they dangerous?'

'If they bite you, they are. You're a gonner, my boy, if you're bitten by a Gnooly.'

The Elevator drifted on, rocking gently from side to side. The grey-black oily fog swirled around them.

'What does a Gnooly look like, Mr Wonka?'

'They don't *look* like anything, Charlie. They can't.'

'You mean you've never seen one?'

'You can't *see* Gnoolies, my boy. You can't even feel them ... until they puncture your skin ... then it's too late. They've got you.'

'You mean . . . There might be swarms of them all around us this very moment?' Charlie asked.

'There might,' said Mr Wonka.

Charlie felt his skin beginning to creep. 'Do you die at once?' he asked.

'First you become subtracted . . . a little later you are divided . . . but very slowly . . . it takes a long time . . . it's long division and it's very painful. After that, you become one of them.'

'Couldn't we shut the door?' Charlie asked.

'I'm afraid not, my boy. We'd never see her through the glass. There's too much mist and moisture. She's not going to be easy to pick out anyway.'

Charlie stood at the open door of the Elevator and stared into the swirling vapours. This, he thought, is what hell must be like . . . hell without heat . . . there was something unholy about it all, something unbelievably diabolical . . . It was all so deathly quiet, so desolate and empty . . . At the same time, the constant movement, the twisting and swirling of the misty vapours, gave one the feeling that some very powerful force, evil and malignant, was at work all around . . . Charlie felt a jab on his arm! He jumped! He almost jumped out of the Elevator! 'Sorry,' said Mr Wonka. 'It's only me.'

'Oh-h-h!' Charlie gasped. 'For a second, I thought . . .'

'I know what you thought, Charlie . . . And by the way, I'm awfully glad you're with me. How would you like to come here alone . . . as I did . . . as I had to . . . many times?'

'I wouldn't,' said Charlie.

'There she is!' said Mr Wonka, pointing. 'No, she isn't! . . . Oh, dear! I could have sworn I saw her for a moment right over there on the edge of that dark patch. Keep watching, Charlie.'

'*There!*' said Charlie. '*Over there. Look!*'

'Where?' said Mr Wonka. 'Point to her, Charlie!'

'She's ... she's gone again. She sort of faded away,' Charlie said.

They stood at the open door of the Elevator, peering into the swirly grey vapours.

'*There! Quick! Right there!*' Charlie cried. '*Can't you see her?*'

'*Yes, Charlie! I see her!*' I'm moving up close now!'

Mr Wonka reached behind him and began touching a number of buttons.

'Grandma!' Charlie cried out. 'We've come to get you, Grandma!'

They could see her faintly through the mist, but oh so

faintly. And they could see the mist through *her* as well. She was transparent. She was hardly there at all. She was no more than a shadow. They could see her face and just the faintest outline of her body swathed in a sort of gown. But she wasn't upright. She was floating lengthwise in the swirling vapour.

'Why is she lying down?' Charlie whispered.

'Because she's a Minus, Charlie. Surely you know what a minus sign looks like ... Like that ...' Mr Wonka drew a horizontal line in the air with his finger.

The Elevator glided close. The ghostly shadow of Grandma Georgina's face was no more than a yard away now. Charlie reached out through the door to touch her but there was nothing there to touch. His hand went right through her skin. 'Grandma!' he gasped. She began to drift away.

'Stand back!' ordered Mr Wonka, and suddenly, from some secret place inside his coat-tails he whisked out a spray-gun. It was one of those old-fashioned things people used to use for spraying fly-spray around the room before aerosols came along. He aimed the spray-gun straight at the shadow of Grandma Georgina and he pumped the handle hard ONCE . . . TWICE . . . THREE TIMES! Each time, a fine black spray spurted out from the nozzle of the gun. Instantly, Grandma Georgina disappeared.

'A bull's eye!' cried Mr Wonka, jumping up and down with excitement. 'I got her with both barrels! I plussed her good and proper! That's Vita-Wonk for you!'

'Where's she gone?' Charlie asked.

'Back where she came from, of course! To the factory! She's a Minus no longer, my boy! She's a one hundred per cent red-blooded Plus! Come along now! Let's get out of here quickly before the Gnoolies find us!' Mr Wonka jabbed a button. The doors closed and the Great Glass Elevator shot upwards for home.

'Sit down and strap yourself in again, Charlie!' said Mr Wonka. 'We're going flat out this time!'

The Elevator roared and rocketed up toward the surface of the Earth. Mr Wonka and Charlie sat side by side on their little jump-seats, strapped in tight. Mr Wonka started tucking the spray-gun back into that enormous pocket somewhere in his coat-tails. 'It's such a pity one has to use a clumsy old thing like this,' he said. 'But there's simply no other way of doing it. Ideally, of course, one would measure out exactly the right number of drops into a teaspoon and feed it carefully into the mouth. But it's impossible to feed anything into a Minus. It's like trying to feed one's own shadow. That's why I've got to use a spray-gun. Spray 'em all over, my boy! That's the only way!'

'It worked fine, though, didn't it?' Charlie said.

'Oh, it worked all right, Charlie! It worked beautifully! All I'm saying is that there's bound to be a slight overdose . . .'

'I don't quite know what you mean, Mr Wonka '

'My dear boy, if it only takes *four drops* of Vita-Wonk to turn a young Oompa-Loompa into an old man . . .' Mr Wonka lifted his hands and let them fall limply on to his lap.

'You mean Grandma may have got too much?' asked Charlie, turning slightly pale.

'I'm afraid that's putting it rather mildly,' said Mr Wonka.

'But . . . but why did you give her such a lot of it, then?' said Charlie, getting more and more worried. 'Why did you spray her *three times?* She must have got pints and pints of it!'

'*Gallons!*' cried Mr Wonka, slapping his thighs. 'Gallons and gallons! But don't let a little thing like that bother you, my dear Charlie! The important part of it is we've got her back! She's a Minus no longer! She's a lovely Plus!

> '*She's as plussy as plussy can be!*
> *She's more plussy than you or than me!*
> *The question is how,*
> *Just how old is she now?*
> *Is she more than a hundred and three?*'

18

The Oldest Person in the World

'We return in triumph, Charlie!' cried Mr Wonka as the Great Glass Elevator began to slow down. 'Once more your dear family will all be together again!'

The Elevator stopped. The doors slid open. And there was the Chocolate Room and the chocolate river and the Oompa-Loompas and in the middle of it all the great bed belonging to the old grandparents. 'Charlie!' said Grandpa Joe, rushing forward. 'Thank heavens you're back!' Charlie hugged him. Then he hugged his mother and his father. 'Is she here?' he said. 'Grandma Georgina?'

Nobody answered. Nobody did anything except Grandpa Joe, who pointed to the bed. He pointed but he didn't look where he was pointing. None of them looked at the bed – except Charlie. He walked past them all to get a better view, and he saw at one end the two babies, Grandma Josephine and Grandpa George, both tucked in and sleeping peacefully. At the other end . . .

'Don't be alarmed,' said Mr Wonka, running up and placing a hand on Charlie's arm. 'She's bound to be just a teeny bit over-plussed. I warned you about that.'

'*What have you done to her?*' cried Mrs Bucket. 'My poor old mother!'

The Oldest Person in the World

Propped up against the pillows at the other end of the bed was the most extraordinary-looking thing Charlie had ever seen! Was it some ancient fossil? It couldn't be that because it was moving slightly! And now it was making sounds! Croaking sounds – the kind of sounds a very old frog might make if it knew a few words. 'Well well well,' it croaked. 'If it isn't dear Charlie.'

'Grandma!' cried Charlie. 'Grandma Georgina! Oh . . . Oh . . . Oh!'

Her tiny face was like a pickled walnut. There were such masses of creases and wrinkles that the mouth and eyes and even the nose were sunken almost out of sight. Her hair was pure white and her hands, which were resting on top of the blanket, were just little lumps of wrinkly skin.

The presence of this ancient creature seemed to have terrified not only Mr and Mrs Bucket, but Grandpa Joe as well. They stood well back, away from the bed. Mr Wonka, on the other hand, was as happy as ever. 'My dear lady!' he cried, advancing to the edge of the bed and clasping one of those tiny wrinkled hands in both of his. 'Welcome home! And how are you feeling on this bright and glorious day?'

'Not too bad,' croaked Grandma Georgina. 'Not too bad at all . . . considering my age.'

'Good for you!' said Mr Wonka. 'Atta girl! All we've got to do now is find out exactly how old you are! Then we shall be able to take further action!'

'You're taking no further action around here,' said Mrs Bucket, tight-lipped. 'You've done enough damage already!'

'But my dear old muddleheaded mugwump,' said Mr Wonka, turning to Mrs Bucket. 'What does it matter that the old girl has become a trifle too old? We can put that right in a jiffy! Have you forgotten Wonka-Vite and how every tablet makes you twenty years younger? We shall bring her back! We shall transform her into a blossoming blushing maiden in the twink of an eye!'

'What good is that when her husband's not even out of his nappies yet?' wailed Mrs Bucket, pointing a finger at the one-year-old Grandpa George, so peacefully sleeping.

'Madam,' said Mr Wonka, 'let us do one thing at a time . . .'

'I forbid you to give her that beastly Wonka-Vite!' said Mrs Bucket. 'You'll turn her into a Minus again just as sure as I'm standing here!'

'I don't want to be a Minus!' croaked Grandma Georgina. 'If I ever have to go back to that beastly Minusland again, the Gnoolies will knickle me!'

'Fear not!' said Mr Wonka. 'This time I *myself* will supervise the giving of the medicine. I shall personally see to it that you get the correct dosage. But listen very carefully now! I cannot work out how many pills to give you until I know exactly how old you are! That's obvious, isn't it?'

'It is not obvious at all,' said Mrs Bucket. 'Why can't you give her one pill at a time and play it safe?'

'Impossible, madam. In very serious cases such as this one, Wonka-Vite doesn't work at all when given in small doses. You've got to throw everything at her in one go. You've got to hit her with it hard. A single pill wouldn't even begin to shift her. She's too far gone for that. It's all or nothing.'

'No,' said Mrs Bucket firmly.

'Yes,' said Mr Wonka. 'Dear lady, please listen to me. If you have a very severe headache and you need *three* aspirins to cure it, it's no good taking only one at a time and waiting four hours between each. You'll never cure yourself that way. You've got to gulp them all down in one go. It's the same with Wonka-Vite. May I proceed?'

'Oh, all *right*, I suppose you'll have to,' said Mrs Bucket.

'Good,' said Mr Wonka, giving a little jump and twirling his feet in the air. 'Now then, how old are you, my dear Grandma Georgina?'

'I don't know,' she croaked. 'I lost count of that years and years ago.'

'Don't you have *any* idea?' said Mr Wonka.

'Of course I don't,' gibbered the old woman. 'Nor would you if you were as old as I am.'

'Think!' said Mr Wonka. 'You've *got* to think!'

The tiny old wrinkled brown walnut face wrinkled itself up more than ever. The others stood waiting. The Oompa-Loompas, enthralled by the sight of this ancient object, were all edging closer and closer to the bed. The two babies slept on.

'Are you, for example, a hundred?' said Mr Wonka. 'Or a hundred and ten? Or a hundred and twenty?'

'It's no good,' she croaked. 'I never did have a head for numbers.'

'This is a *catastrophe!*' cried Mr Wonka. 'If you can't tell me how old you are, I can't help you! I dare not risk an overdose!'

Gloom settled upon the entire company, including for once Mr Wonka himself. 'You've messed it up good and proper this time, haven't you?' said Mrs Bucket.

'Grandma,' Charlie said, moving forward to the bed. 'Listen, Grandma. Don't worry about exactly how old you might be. Try to think of a *happening* instead . . . think of something that *happened* to you . . . anything you like . . . as far back as you can . . . it may help us . . .'

'Lots of things happened to me, Charlie . . . so many many things happened to me . . .'

'But can you *remember* any of them, Grandma?'

'Oh, I don't know, my darling . . . I suppose I could remember one or two if I thought hard enough . . .'

'Good, Grandma, good!' said Charlie eagerly. 'Now what is the very earliest thing you can remember in your whole life?'

'Oh, my dear boy, that really would be going back a few years, wouldn't it?'

'When you were little, Grandma, like me. Can't you remember anything you did when you were little?'

The tiny sunken black eyes glimmered faintly and a sort of smile touched the corners of the almost invisible little slit of a mouth. 'There was a ship,' she said. 'I can remember a ship . . . I couldn't ever forget that ship . . .'

'Go on, Grandma! A ship! What sort of a ship? Did you sail on her?'

'Of course I sailed on her, my darling . . . we all sailed on her . . .'

'Where from? Where to?' Charlie went on eagerly.

'Oh no, I couldn't tell you that . . . I was just a tiny little girl . . .' She lay back on the pillow and closed her eyes. Charlie watched her, waiting for something more. Everybody waited. No one moved.

'. . . It had a lovely name, that ship . . . there was something beautiful . . . something so beautiful about that name . . . but of course I couldn't possibly remember it . . .'

Charlie, who had been sitting on the edge of the bed, suddenly jumped up. His face was shining with excitement. 'If I said the name, Grandma, would you remember it then?'

'I might, Charlie . . . yes . . . I think I might . . .'

'THE MAYFLOWER!' cried Charlie.

The old woman's head jerked up off the pillow. '*That's it!*' she croaked. 'You've *got* it, Charlie! The *Mayflower* . . . Such a lovely name . . .'

'Grandpa!' Charlie called out, dancing with excitement. 'What year did the *Mayflower* sail for America?'

'The *Mayflower* sailed out of Plymouth Harbour on September the sixth, sixteen hundred and twenty,' said Grandpa Joe.

'Plymouth . . .' croaked the old woman. 'That rings a bell, too . . . Yes, it might easily have been Plymouth . . .'

'Sixteen hundred and twenty!' cried Charlie. 'Oh, my heavens above! That means you're . . . you do it, Grandpa!'

'Well now,' said Grandpa Joe. 'Take sixteen hundred and twenty away from nineteen hundred and seventy-two . . . that leaves . . . don't rush me now, Charlie . . . That leaves three hundred . . . and . . . and fifty-two.'

'Jumping jackrabbits!' yelled Mr Bucket. 'She's three hundred and fifty-two years old!'

'She's more,' said Charlie. 'How old did you say you were, Grandma, when you sailed on the *Mayflower*? Were you about eight?'

'I think I was even younger than that, my darling . . . I was only a bitty little girl . . . probably no more than six . . .'

'Then she's *three hundred and fifty-eight!*' gasped Charlie.

'That's Vita-Wonk for you,' said Mr Wonka proudly. 'I told you it was powerful stuff.'

'Three hundred and fifty-eight!' said Mr Bucket. 'It's unbelievable!'

'Just imagine the things she must have seen in her lifetime!' said Grandpa Joe.

'My poor old mother!' wailed Mrs Bucket. 'What on earth . . .'

'Patience, dear lady,' said Mr Wonka. 'Now comes the interesting part. Bring on the Wonka-Vite!'

An Oompa-Loompa ran forward with a large bottle and gave it to Mr Wonka. He put it on the bed. 'How young does she want to be?' he asked.

'Seventy-eight,' said Mrs Bucket firmly. 'Exactly where she was before all this nonsense started!'

'Surely she'd like to be a bit younger than that?' said Mr Wonka.

'Certainly not!' said Mrs Bucket. 'It's too risky!'

'Too risky, too risky!' croaked Grandma Georgina. 'You'll only Minus me again if you try to be clever!'

'Have it your own way,' said Mr Wonka. 'Now then, I've got to do a few sums.' Another Oompa-Loompa trotted forward, holding up a blackboard. Mr Wonka took a piece of chalk from his pocket and wrote:

Present age of person... 358
Age she wants to be
(subtract this) _____ 78
Number of years younger = 280
she must become
If each pill of Wonka-Vite makes
you 20 years younger, we must
divide 280 by 20 to find out   14
how many pills to give: _____
                              20) 280

'Fourteen pills of Wonka-Vite exactly,' said Mr Wonka. The Oompa-Loompa took the blackboard away. Mr Wonka picked up the bottle from the bed and opened it and counted out fourteen of the little brilliant yellow pills. 'Water!' he said. Yet another Oompa-Loompa ran forward with a glass of water. Mr Wonka tipped all fourteen pills into the glass. The water bubbled and frothed. 'Drink it while it's fizzing,' he said, holding the glass up to Grandma Georgina's lips. 'All in one gulp!'

She drank it.

Mr Wonka sprang back and took a large brass clock from his pocket. 'Don't forget,' he cried, 'it's a year a second! She's got two hundred and eighty years to lose! That'll take her four minutes and forty seconds! Watch the centuries fall away!'

The room was so silent they could hear the ticking of Mr Wonka's clock. At first nothing much happened to the ancient person lying on the bed. She closed her eyes and lay back. Now and again, the puckered skin of her face gave a twitch and her little hands jerked up and down, but that was all . . .

'One minute gone!' called Mr Wonka. 'She's sixty years younger.'

'She looks just the same to me,' said Mr Bucket.

'Of course she does,' said Mr Wonka. 'What's a mere sixty years when you're over three hundred to start with!'

'Are you all right, mother?' said Mrs Bucket anxiously. 'Talk to me, mother!'

'Two minutes gone!' called Mr Wonka. 'She's one hundred and twenty years younger!'

And now definite changes were beginning to show in the old woman's face. The skin was quivering all over and some of the deepest wrinkles were becoming less and less deep, the mouth less sunken, the nose more prominent.

'Mother!' cried Mrs Bucket. 'Are you all right? Speak to me, mother, please!'

Suddenly, with a suddenness that made everyone jump, the old woman sat bolt upright in bed and shouted, *'Did you hear the news! Admiral Nelson has beaten the French at Trafalgar!'*

'She's going crazy!' said Mr Bucket.

'Not at all,' said Mr Wonka. 'She's going through the nineteenth century.'

'Three minutes gone!' said Mr Wonka.

Every second now she was growing slightly less and less shrivelled, becoming more and more lively. It was a marvellous thing to watch.

'Gettysburg!' she cried. *'General Lee is on the run!'*

And a few seconds later she let out a great wail of anguish and said, 'He's dead, he's dead, he's dead!'

'Who's dead?' said Mr Bucket, craning forward.

'*Lincoln!*' she wailed. '*There goes the train . . .*'

'She must have seen it!' said Charlie. 'She must have been there!'

'She *is* there,' said Mr Wonka. 'At least she was a few seconds ago.'

'Will someone please explain to me,' said Mrs Bucket, 'what on earth . . .'

'Four minutes gone!' said Mr Wonka. 'Only forty seconds left! Only forty more years to lose!'

'Grandma!' cried Charlie, running forward. 'You're looking almost exactly like you used to! Oh, I'm so glad!'

'Just as long as it all stops when it's meant to,' said Mrs Bucket.

'I'll bet it doesn't,' said Mr Bucket. 'Something always goes wrong.'

'Not when *I'm* in charge of it, sir,' said Mr Wonka. 'Time's up! She is now seventy-eight years old! How do you feel, dear lady? Is everything all right?'

'I feel tolerable,' she said. 'Just tolerable. But that's no thanks to you, you meddling old mackerel!'

There she was again, the same cantankerous grumbling old Grandma Georgina that Charlie had known so well before it all started. Mrs Bucket flung her arms around her and began weeping with joy. The old woman pushed her aside and said, 'What, may I ask, are those two silly babies doing at the other end of the bed?'

'One of them's your husband,' said Mr Bucket.

'Rubbish!' she said. 'Where *is* George?'

'I'm afraid it's true, mother,' said Mrs Bucket. 'That's him on the left. The other one's Josephine . . .'

'You . . . you chiselling old cheeseburger!' she shouted, pointing a fierce finger at Mr Wonka. 'What in the name of . . .'

'Now now now now now!' said Mr Wonka. 'Let us not for mercy's sake have another row so late in the day. If everyone will keep their hair on and leave this to Charlie and me, we shall have them exactly where they used to be in the flick of a fly's wing!'

19

The Babies Grow Up

'Bring on the Vita-Wonk!' said Mr Wonka. 'We'll soon fix these two babies.'

An Oompa-Loompa ran forward with a small bottle and a couple of silver teaspoons.

'Wait just one minute!' snapped Grandma Georgina. 'What sort of devilish dumpery are you up to now?'

'It's all right, Grandma,' said Charlie. 'I promise you it's all right. Vita-Wonk does the opposite to Wonka-Vite. It makes you older. It's what we gave *you* when you were a Minus. It saved you!'

'You gave me too much!' snapped the old woman.

'We had to, Grandma.'

'And now you want to do the same to Grandpa George!'

'Of course we don't,' said Charlie.

'I finished up three hundred and fifty-eight years old!' she went on. 'What's to stop you making another little mistake and giving him *fifty times more than you gave me?* Then I'd suddenly have a twenty-thousand-year-old caveman in bed beside me! *Imagine that*, and him with a big knobby club in one hand and dragging me around by my hair with the other! No, thank you!'

'Grandma,' Charlie said patiently. 'With you we had to use a spray because you were a Minus. You were a ghost. But here Mr Wonka can . . .'

'Don't talk to me about that man!' she cried. 'He's batty as a bullfrog!'

'No, Grandma, he is *not*. And here he can measure it out exactly right, drop by drop, and feed it into their mouths. That's true isn't it, Mr Wonka?'

'Charlie,' said Mr Wonka. 'I can see that the factory is going to be in good hands when I retire. You learn very fast. I am so pleased I chose you, my dear boy, so very pleased. Now then, what's the verdict? Do we leave them as babies or do we grow them up with Vita-Wonk?'

'You go ahead, Mr Wonka,' said Grandpa Joe. 'I'd like you to grow my Josie up so she's just the same as before – eighty years old.'

'Thank you, sir,' said Mr Wonka. 'I appreciate the confidence you place in me. But what about the other one, Grandpa George?'

'Oh, all *right*, then,' said Grandma Georgina. 'But if he ends up a caveman I don't want him in *this* bed any more!'

'That's settled then!' said Mr Wonka. 'Come along, Charlie! We'll do them both together. You hold one spoon and I'll hold the other. I shall measure out four drops and four drops only into each spoon and we'll wake them up and pop it into their mouths.'

'Which one shall I do, Mr Wonka?'

'You do Grandma Josephine, the tiny one. I'll do Grandpa George, the one-year-old. Here's your spoon.'

Charlie took the spoon and held it out. Mr Wonka opened the bottle and dripped four drops of oily black liquid into

Charlie's spoon. Then he did the same to his own. He handed
the bottle back to the Oompa-Loompa.

'Shouldn't someone hold the babies while you give it?'
said Grandpa Joe. 'I'll hold Grandma Josephine.'

'Are you mad!' said Mr Wonka. 'Don't you realize that
Vita-Wonk acts instantly? It's not one year a second like
Wonka-Vite. Vita-Wonk is as quick as lightning! The
moment the medicine is swallowed – ping! – and it all
happens! The getting bigger and the growing older and
everything else *all happens in one second!* So don't you see,
my dear sir,' he said to Grandpa Joe, 'that one moment
you'd be holding a tiny baby in your arms and just one
second later you'd find yourself staggering about with an
eighty-year-old woman and you'd drop her like a ton of
bricks on the floor!'

'I see what you mean,' said Grandpa Joe.

'All set, Charlie?'

'All set, Mr Wonka.' Charlie moved around the bed to where the tiny sleeping baby lay. He placed one hand behind her head and lifted it. The baby awoke and started yelling. Mr Wonka was on the other side of the bed doing the same to the one-year-old George. 'Both together now, Charlie!' said Mr Wonka. 'Ready, steady, *go*! Pop it in!' Charlie pushed his spoon into the open mouth of the baby and tipped the drops down her throat.

'Make sure she swallows it!' cried Mr Wonka. 'It won't work until it gets into their tummies!'

It is difficult to explain what happened next, and whatever it was, it only lasted for one second. A second is about as long as it takes you to say aloud and quickly, 'one-two-three-four-five'. And that is how long it took, with Charlie watching closely, for the tiny baby to grow and swell and wrinkle into the eighty-year-old Grandma Josephine. It was a frightening thing to see. It was like an explosion. A small baby suddenly exploded into an old woman, and Charlie all at once found himself staring straight into the well-known and much-loved wrinkly old face of his Grandma Josephine. '*Hello*, my darling,' she said. 'Where have *you* come from?'

'Josie!' cried Grandpa Joe, rushing forward. 'How marvellous! You're back!'

'I didn't know I'd been away,' she said.

Grandpa George had also made a successful comeback. 'You were better-looking as a baby,' Grandma Georgina said to him. 'But I'm glad you've grown up again, George . . . for one reason.'

'What's that?' asked Grandpa George.

'You won't wet the bed any more.'

20

How to Get Someone out of Bed

'I am sure,' said Mr Wonka, addressing Grandpa George, Grandma Georgina and Grandma Josephine, 'I am quite sure the three of you, after all *that*, will now want to jump out of bed and lend a hand in running the Chocolate Factory.'

'Who, us?' said Grandma Josephine.

'Yes, you,' said Mr Wonka.

'Are you crazy?' said Grandma Georgina. 'I'm staying right here where I am in this nice comfortable bed, thank you very much!'

'Me, too!' said Grandpa George.

At that moment, there was a sudden commotion among the Oompa-Loompas at the far end of the Chocolate Room. There was a buzz of excited chatter and a lot of running about and waving of arms, and out of all this a single Oompa-Loompa emerged and came rushing toward Mr Wonka, carrying a huge envelope in his hands. He came up close to Mr Wonka. He started whispering. Mr Wonka bent down low to listen.

'*Outside the factory gates?*' cried Mr Wonka. '*Men!... What sort of men?... Yes, but do they look dangerous?... Are they*

ACTING dangerously? ... And a what? ... A HELICOP-TER! ... And these men came out of it? ... They gave you this? ...'

Mr Wonka grabbed the huge envelope and quickly slit it open and pulled out the folded letter inside. There was absolute silence as he skimmed swiftly over what was written on the paper. Nobody moved. Charlie began to feel cold. He knew something dreadful was going to happen. There was a very definite smell of danger in the air. The men outside the gates, the helicopter, the nervousness of the Oompa-Loompas ... He was watching Mr Wonka's face, searching for a clue, for some change in expression that would tell him how bad the news was.

'Great whistling whangdoodles!' cried Mr Wonka, leaping so high in the air that when he landed his legs gave way and he crashed on to his backside.

'Snorting snozzwangers!' he yelled, picking himself up and waving the letter about as though he were swatting

mosquitoes. 'Listen to this, all of you! Just you listen to this!'
He began to read aloud:

                        THE WHITE HOUSE
                        WASHINGTON D.C.

TO MR WILLY WONKA.
SIR
     TODAY THE ENTIRE NATION, INDEED THE
WHOLE WORLD IS REJOICING AT THE SAFE
RETURN OF OUR TRANSPORT CAPSULE
FROM SPACE WITH 136 SOULS ON BOARD.
HAD IT NOT BEEN FOR THE HELP THEY
RECEIVED FROM AN UNKNOWN SPACESHIP,
THESE 136 PEOPLE WOULD NEVER HAVE
COME BACK. IT HAS BEEN REPORTED TO ME
THAT THE COURAGE SHOWN BY THE EIGHT
ASTRONAUTS ABOARD THIS UNKNOWN
SPACESHIP WAS EXTRAORDINARY. OUR
RADAR STATIONS, BY TRACKING THIS
SPACESHIP ON ITS RETURN TO EARTH, HAVE
DISCOVERED THAT IT SPLASHED DOWN IN
A PLACE KNOWN AS WONKA'S CHOCOLATE
FACTORY. THAT, SIR, IS WHY THIS LETTER
IS BEING DELIVERED TO YOU.
     I WISH NOW TO SHOW THE GRATITUDE OF
THE NATION BY INVITING ALL EIGHT OF
THOSE INCREDIBLY BRAVE ASTRONAUTS
TO COME AND STAY IN THE WHITE HOUSE
FOR A FEW DAYS AS MY HONOURED GUESTS.
     I AM ARRANGING A SPECIAL CELEBRA-
TION PARTY IN THE BLUE ROOM THIS EVEN-

ING AT WHICH I MYSELF WILL PIN MEDALS FOR BRAVERY UPON ALL EIGHT OF THESE GALLANT FLIERS. THE MOST IMPORTANT PERSONS IN THE LAND WILL BE PRESENT AT THIS GATHERING TO SALUTE THE HEROES WHOSE DAZZLING DEEDS WILL BE WRITTEN FOR EVER IN THE HISTORY OF OUR NATION. AMONG THOSE ATTENDING WILL BE THE VICE-PRESIDENT (MISS ELVIRA TIBBS), ALL THE MEMBERS OF MY CABINET, THE CHIEFS OF THE ARMY, THE NAVY AND THE AIR FORCE, ALL MEMBERS OF THE CONGRESS. A FAMOUS SWORD-SWALLOWER FROM AFGHANISTAN WHO IS NOW TEACHING ME TO EAT MY WORDS (WHAT YOU DO IS YOU TAKE THE S OFF THE BEGINNING OF THE SWORD AND PUT IT ON THE END BEFORE YOU SWALLOW IT). AND WHO ELSE IS COMING? OH YES, MY CHIEF INTERPRETER, AND THE GOVERNORS OF EVERY STATE IN THE UNION, AND OF COURSE MY CAT, MRS TAUBSYPUSS.

A HELICOPTER AWAITS ALL EIGHT OF YOU OUTSIDE THE FACTORY GATES. I MYSELF AWAIT YOUR ARRIVAL AT THE WHITE HOUSE WITH THE VERY GREATEST PLEASURE AND IMPATIENCE.

I BEG TO REMAIN, SIR,

MOST SINCERELY YOURS

Lancelot R. Gilligrass.

LANCELOT R. GILLIGRASS
President of the United States

P.S. COULD YOU PLEASE BRING ME A FEW
WONKA FUDGEMALLOW DELIGHTS. I LOVE
THEM SO MUCH BUT EVERYBODY AROUND
HERE KEEPS STEALING MINE OUT OF THE
DRAWER IN MY DESK. AND DON'T TELL
NANNY.

Mr Wonka stopped reading. And in the stillness that
followed Charlie could hear people breathing. He could hear
them breathing in and out much faster than usual. And
there were other things, too. There were so many feelings
and passions and there was so much sudden happiness
swirling around in the air it made his head spin. Grandpa
Joe was the first to say something . . . *'Yippeeeeeeeeeeee!'* he
yelled out, and he flew across the room and caught Charlie
by the hands and the two of them started dancing away
along the bank of the chocolate river. 'We're going, Charlie!'
sang Grandpa Joe. 'We're going to the White House after
all!' Mr and Mrs Bucket were also dancing and laughing
and singing, and Mr Wonka ran all over the room proudly
showing the President's letter to the Oompa-Loompas. After
a minute or so, Mr Wonka clapped his hands for attention.
'Come along, come along!' he called out. 'We mustn't dilly!
We mustn't dally! Come on, Charlie! And you, sir, Grandpa
Joe! And Mr and Mrs Bucket! The helicopter is outside the
gates! We can't keep it waiting!' He began hustling the four
of them toward the door.

'*Hey!*' screamed Grandma Georgina from the bed. 'What
about us? We were invited too, don't you forget that!'

'It said *all eight of us* were invited!' cried Grandma Josephine.

'And that includes *me*!' said Grandpa George.

Mr Wonka turned and looked at them. 'Of course it includes you,' he said. 'But we can't possibly get that bed into a helicopter. It won't go through the door.'

'You mean ... you mean if we don't get out of bed we can't come?' said Grandma Georgina.

'That's exactly what I mean,' said Mr Wonka. 'Keep going, Charlie,' he whispered, giving Charlie a little nudge. 'Keep walking toward the door.'

Suddenly, behind them, there was a great *SWOOSH* of blankets and sheets and a pinging of bedsprings as the three old people all exploded out of the bed together. They came sprinting after Mr Wonka, shouting, 'Wait for us! Wait for us!' It was amazing how fast they were running across the floor of the great Chocolate Room. Mr Wonka and Charlie and the others stood staring at them in wonder. They leaped across paths and over little bushes like gazelles in springtime, with their bare legs flashing and their nightshirts flying out behind them.

Suddenly Grandma Josephine put the brakes on so hard she skidded five yards before coming to a stop. 'Wait!' she screamed. 'We must be mad! We can't go to a famous party in the White House in our nightshirts! We can't stand there practically naked in front of all those people while the President pins medals all over us!'

'Oh-h-h-h!' wailed Grandma Georgina. 'Oh, what *are* we going to do?'

'Don't you have any clothes with you at all?' asked Mr Wonka.

'Of course we don't!' said Grandma Josephine. 'We haven't been out of that bed for twenty years!'

'We can't go!' wailed Grandma Georgina. 'We'll have to stay behind!'

How to Get Someone out of Bed

'Couldn't we buy something from a store?' said Grandpa George.

'What with?' said Grandma Josephine. 'We don't have any money!'

'*Money!*' cried Mr Wonka. 'Good gracious me, don't you go worrying about money! I've got plenty of *that!*'

'Listen,' said Charlie. 'Why couldn't we ask the helicopter to land on the roof of a big shop on the way over. Then you can all pop downstairs and buy exactly what you want!'

'Charlie!' cried Mr Wonka, grasping him by the hand. 'What *would* we do without you? You're brilliant! Come along everybody! We're off to stay in the White House!'

They all linked arms and went dancing out of the Chocolate Room and along the corridors and out through the front door into the open where the big helicopter was waiting near the factory gates. A group of extremely important-looking gentlemen came toward them and bowed.

'Well, Charlie,' said Grandpa Joe. 'It's certainly been a busy day.'

'It's not over yet,' Charlie said, laughing. 'It hasn't even begun.'

THE BEST OF ROALD DAHL

available in hardback from HarperCollins

Stevens has
thick fair
hair

<u>PLOT</u>

* Brother involved in shady dealings.

Reporter suspects ~~for~~ Rebus (does reporter perhaps know of
brother's shady dealings?).

Everything is revealed during Rebus's dark night of the
soul. But instead of actual hypnosis, have Rebus doing
self-hypnosis (a concept explained to him by Michael).

* Maybe have Reeve/Knott involved with Michael in
drug-pushing. And through Michael, Reeve learns about
Rebus.

READER MADE TO SUSPECT REBUS AS MURDERER.
OTHER SUSPECTS: ALL POLICE, MICHAEL, REPORTER.

McGregor Campbell ('Mac') will tell the reporter
about Rebus. (string & 'There are clues everywhere').
(Maxwell von the big light.)

CLIMAX ~~&~~   If Rebus arrests Reeve, then
Reeve will 'shop' Michael for the drugs.

NEAR CLIMAX — Rebus & reporter fight. Reporter
says, okay, you're not involved. Involved with
what?, asks Rebus. Your brother & that librarian.
⟹ Drugs. (Rebus already suspecting a librarian as
being a possible murderer.) Rebus goes to library.

FLASHBACKS — leading up to & in confinement.
But making out that everything was rosy
between Rebus & Reeve, that they survived
as brothers.

dawns on
Rebus that
coffee-
apple
smell in
Mickey's
house was
smell of
drugs.

The very first Inspe
reissued in a collectors' editio

'And in Edinburgh of all places. I mea
thing happening in Edinburgh, do yo

That sort of thing is the brutal ab
young girls. And now a third is mis
same sad end. Detective Sergeant
drinking too much, his own young (
by his disenchanted wife, is one of n
killer. And then messages begin to
matchstick crosses – taunting Rebus
he can solve.

Now reissued here with notes and r
publication, *Knots & Crosses* is a landma
absorbing mystery and the genesis of o
detectives around.

THE NAMING OF THE DEAD

'One has come to take his extraordinary ability to construct a compelling plot, and pace his narrative, almost for granted, and that itself is a high compliment. He is a story-teller of genius . . . Here he is at his best . . . *The Naming of the Dead* is Ian Rankin's finest novel. It is more than a crime novel, or rather, Rankin's achievement is to show, convincingly, how crime permeates society.' *Scotsman*

'Rebus may seem always to be running on something very near empty, but there is no sign that Rankin has lost any of the energy to continue this consistently impressive series.' *The Sunday Times*

FLESHMARKET CLOSE

'As always, Rankin proves himself the master of his own milieu. He brings the dark underside of Edinburgh deliciously to life . . . Rankin never puts a foot wrong.' *Daily Mail*

'No one writes more gripping stories than Rankin; his imagination peoples Edinburgh the way Balzac's fantasy did Paris. The scenes which emerge . . . are the product of a troubling imagination and a probing intellect which uses the crime genre to examine aspects of life, especially contemporary Scottish life, that politicians prefer to ignore.' *Times Literary Supplement*

'Another year and another surefire bestseller for Britain's No.1 crime writer, Ian Rankin.' *Daily Mirror*

A QUESTION OF BLOOD

'He writes with a natural rhythm which exerts an almost hypnotic effect.' *Independent*

'Exemplifies the enhanced craftsmanship of the author's recent work; the sheer number of handicaps Rebus overcomes and of the puzzles he solves evinces a relishable virtuosity.' *The Sunday Times*

'An exceptionally well-plotted book, which is guaranteed to hook you and keep you hooked.' *Sunday Telegraph*

RESURRECTION MEN

'What is impressive in *Resurrection Men* is not just the deftness of the links between disparate crimes, but the fluency of the fugue-like counterpoint between investigations ... On this form, nothing is beyond him.' *The Sunday Times*

'Rankin's Rebus novels should be required reading for anyone whose knowledge of Edinburgh has been derived from visits to the festival ... Rankin conveys the visceral fears and hatreds lurking just below the smart Georgian surface of the "you'll have your tea" New Town.' *Sunday Telegraph*

'Bears all the qualities that have established Rankin as one of the Britain's leading novelists in any genre: a powerful sense of place; a redefinition of Scotland and its past; persuasive characters and a growing compassion among its characters.'
New Statesman

THE FALLS

'Rankin masterfully pulls his fascinating plot together, and his sense of place casts a powerful shadow over this subtle tale of the recurrence of evil.' *Guardian*

'*The Falls* pulses with vitality. Suspense vigorously propels you through its pages. Rankin's prose is crisp, laconic and witty. So is his tangy dialogue.' *The Sunday Times*

'An extraordinarily rich addition to crime literature.'
Independent on Sunday

SET IN DARKNESS

'Rankin is a master of his craft, handling each twist and turn of the plot with consummate skill as he takes us by the hand and leads us from the sparkling edifices of New Labour-controlled Scotland to the misty, mysterious Edinburgh alleyways, and from hip and trendy restaurants to dank pubs and bars without missing a step . . . Rankin is streets ahead in the British procedural writing field . . . our top crime writer.'
Independent on Sunday

'This is, astonishingly, the eleventh Inspector Rebus novel by a writer who is still not yet 40, but whose consistent level of excellence is unmatched in the field of British crime fiction.'
The Times

'Rankin's particular skill is in producing a highly complex plot whose different strands cleverly come together at the end, a setting which brings to life the grim back streets of Edinburgh and a well-drawn cast of characters.' *Sunday Telegraph*

DEAD SOULS

'Rankin weaves his plot with a menacing ease . . . His prose is understated, yet his canvas of Scotland's criminal underclass has a panoramic breadth. His ear for dialogue is as sharp as a switchblade. This is, quite simply, crime writing of the highest order.' *Daily Express*

'An atmospheric and cleverly plotted tale well up to Rankin's CWA Gold Dagger standard.' *Books Magazine*

'Rankin strips Edinburgh's polite façade to its gritty skeleton.'
The Times

By Ian Rankin

The Inspector Rebus Series
Knots & Crosses
Hide & Seek
Tooth & Nail
(previously published as Wolfman)
Strip Jack
The Black Book
Mortal Causes
Let It Bleed
Black and Blue
The Hanging Garden
Death is Not the End (a novella)
Dead Souls
Set in Darkness
The Falls
Resurrection Men
A Question of Blood
Fleshmarket Close
The Naming of the Dead

Other Novels
The Flood
Watchman
Westwind

Writing as Jack Harvey
Witch Hunt
Bleeding Hearts
Blood Hunt

Short Stories
A Good Hanging and Other Stories
Beggars Banquet

Non-fiction
Rebus's Scotland

IAN RANKIN

Knots & Crosses

COLLECTORS' EDITION

First published in Great Britain in 1987 by The Bodley Head
This collectors' edition published in 2007 by
Orion Books, an imprint of The Orion Publishing Group Ltd
Orion House, 5 Upper St Martin's Lane,
London WC2H 9EA

1 3 5 7 9 10 8 6 4 2

A CIP catalogue record for this book
is available from the British Library.

Hardback ISBN 978 0 7528 8622 0
Limited edition hardback ISBN 978 0 7528 8875 0

Typeset by Deltatype Ltd, Birkenhead, Merseyside
Printed and bound in Great Britain by
Clays Ltd, St Ives plc

The Orion Publishing Group's policy is to use papers
that are natural, renewable and recyclable products and
made from wood grown in sustainable forests. The logging
and manufacturing processes are expected to conform to
the environmental regulations of the country of origin.

To Miranda
without whom
nothing is worth finishing

INTRODUCTION

The nineteenth of March 1985 was a big day for me. I was a postgraduate student at the University of Edinburgh, studying the novels of Muriel Spark. My thesis, however, was proving less important to me than my own writing. I'd started with poetry, then found some minor success with short stories. A first novel had failed to find a publisher, but my second attempt had just been given the thumbs-up by a small Edinburgh-based outfit called Polygon. That novel was titled *The Flood*, and on 19 March I went to the Polygon offices to sign my first ever book contract. I recorded the event in my diary, where, however, it was reduced to second billing after the following: 'It's happened. An idea for a novel (crime thriller) which started as one situation and has blossomed into a whole plot. I've not written any of it yet, but it's all there in my head, from page one to circa page 250.'

By 22 March I was working on this new story, and two days later recorded that 'it needs a working title; I'm going to give it *Knots & Crosses*'. I certainly remember sitting in a chair in my bedsit, directly in front of the gas fire, and toying with the pun of noughts/knots and crosses. Rebus, it seems to me now, entered as a fully formed character, complete with estranged wife, young daughter and fragile sanity. When I started writing, I did so on an electric typewriter, at the table by the window. I stared from that window at the tenement opposite, and decided that Rebus would live there, directly aross from my own digs at 24 Arden Street, Marchmont, Edinburgh.

By late October, I had finished the second draught of the book: 'two hundred and ten pages of sixty per cent satisfactory

xiii

prose'. I had an agent by this time, and she suggested some changes, the most substantial of which involved cutting a large part of the central flashback section. This I did, making the book leaner, but no less potent.

Knots & Crosses is a pretty nasty book, dealing as it does with a serial killer who preys on children. I'm fairly sure I meant it to be a contemporary reworking of *Dr Jekyll and Mr Hyde*. Having studied Stevenson's masterpiece as part of my thesis, I was intrigued that he chose to set the story in London. Yet it remains a very Scottish novel, based as it is (at least partially) on the real-life Edinburgh character Deacon William Brodie, who was gentleman by day, criminal by night.

At the time, I had no interest in reading detective fiction, and no knowledge of police procedure. I also had no notion that *Knots* would be the first book of a series. This led me blithely to give Rebus a complex personal history and a name which was one of many in-jokes in the book (a rebus being a pictorial puzzle). In fact, rereading the book now, I find myself blushing at the number of literary puns and references (including nods to Spark, Mailer, Anthony Burgess and Thomas Pynchon). Rebus himself is too well-read, quoting from Shakespeare and passionate about Dostoevsky. He thinks like the student/novelist who created him, rather than as a real cop. The sky is described as being 'dark as Wagnerian opera', while the phrase 'the manumission of dreams' sent me (in 2005) to a dictionary. I'm guessing it was a word I'd only just learned in 1985, and I was keen to show it off. I was a young man in love with language, striving for a voice and sometimes overreaching.

The story is set in 1985. At that time, most of the shops on Princes Street closed on a Sunday. There was an ABC cinema (now an Odeon) on Lothian Road and a Mr Boni's ice-cream parlour (now defunct) at Tollcross. People used telex machines, but no one had a mobile phone. And when Rebus sought out a bar, he tended to choose one with larger quarter-gill measures (since replaced by their metric equivalent). Already, *Knots & Crosses* feels like a historical document, written in and about an

Edinburgh that no longer exists. As for the book's hero, well, he's changed in time as well. In this, his first outing, he listens to jazz mainly, using a Nakamichi cassette deck, probably the same one my girlfriend Miranda had bought for me. Later on, I would switch his preference to rock music. And though I've never really described him physically in any of the novels, here we learn that he has brown hair and green eyes (same as me). He's also meant to be a possible suspect, which is why I make him so troubled, suffering weird flashbacks and with a spare bedroom in his flat that's kept permanently locked.

Some of the secondary characters in *Knots* would become useful to me in future books. The Journalist Jim Stevens would play a role in a non-Rebus novel (*Watchman*) before reappearing in the series. Rebus's brother would return, as would his fellow detective Jack Morton. And Gill Templer is still around, her relationship with Rebus coloured, even after all these years, by the events of this first novel. In later books, of course, I take Rebus into real police stations and real pubs. But the Edinburgh of *Knots* is altogether more fictive: Rebus's police station is sited on a non-existent street, and bars such as the Sutherland remain figments of my imagination.

One other thing about Rebus: he dies at the end. Not in the final draft, obviously, but that was my original plan. If I'd stuck to it, I don't know what I'd be doing now. The book climaxes in some tunnels beneath the Central Library on George IV Bridge. There may or may not be tunnels there. However, beneath the National Library (right across the street from the Central) there are certainly tunnels – I know because we postgraduate students were given a tour of them . . . and, as Muriel Spark says, nothing is ever lost to an author.

Since I had no idea how the police went about investigating a murder, I did what any good research student would have done: wrote to the Chief Constable. He took pity on me and directed me to Leith police station, where two wary detectives answered my questions, and added my name to their database, just in case I had some darker ulterior motive. In my duffel coat and Doc Marten boots, a Dr Who scarf wrapped around me, I probably wasn't their idea of a novelist. Sometimes even now I look in the mirror and am forced to agree.

Knots was finally published in London by The Bodley Head (now also defunct) on 19 March 1987, exactly two years to the day since I'd had the initial idea. The cover was a drawing of a game of noughts and crosses, played with knotted pieces of twine and crosses made from matchsticks. As for the author photo, the less said the better. By this time, I was married, living in London, and working at Middlesex Polytechnic. I went into work as usual, and saw no reviews of the book in any of the day's newspapers. Forty-eight hours later, I headed to Edinburgh to spend some weeks at a writers' retreat. There seemed no great fuss about the book. Sales would continue to be poor, with few reviews. I said as much in my diary: 'Knots has had less publicity than *Flood*.' So much for my fledgling career as a crime writer. I was by this time working on a London-based spy novel called *Watchman*, and had plans to be the next Le Carré. Rebus was history, as far as I was concerned.

But that would change.

Between 1990 and 1996 I lived full-time in south-west France, but in the summer of 1996 we moved back to Edinburgh. However, many of our worldly possessions stayed in a spare bedroom at the French farmhouse – we simply didn't have space for them in the flat we'd bought. Then, in the autumn of 2005, we sold the farmhouse and were forced into action. Renting a Ford Transit, we headed across the Channel, loaded boxes, rugs, an old bed-frame, and my collection of vinyl LPs into the back of the van, and returned to Edinburgh, where the garage (by now we had a nice detached house with grounds) soon filled with French artefacts. One by one, I brought the musty cardboard boxes into my office and started going through them, discovering what to me were treasures – forgotten, never-published short stories; pamphlets and photographs; and drafts of early novels.

Including *Knots & Crosses*.

The manuscript had been kept in a brown A4 envelope, marked on its front with the words 'Middlesex Polytechnic'. My first job after moving to London in 1986 had been as an assistant at the National Folktale Centre, housed within the confines of the Middlesex Poly campus on White Hart Lane. Obviously, I'd purloined the envelope from my office. But it didn't just contain the earliest existing typed draft of *Knots* – there were also some pages of notes, including my very first night's musings. The hero of the novel 'might' be a cop, I wrote to myself. But the actual plot seemed to have formed very quickly – pretty much over the course of that first evening as I sat in my digs. Along with the notes were some lined sheets – my first attempt at beginning the novel, written longhand (a novelty for me). A few sheets are missing, though I suppose they may turn up in another of the garaged boxes . . . I haven't had time to go through all of them yet. That first draft of the novel was typed on a portable typewriter I'd bought from my sister Linda's mail-order catalogue (paid off at something like fifty pence a week), with amendments made in pencil. The excised section of the flashback to Rebus's SAS training is now reproduced at the end of this edition, but looking back, what amazes me is that the idea of the book came so quickly and fluently, and that even those first few hand-written pages of text show few changes from the version which would see eventual publication.

2007 sees the twentieth anniversary of *Knots & Crosses*. Thanks to all those cardboard boxes I've been gifted the ability to travel back through time. It's been quite a ride.

PROLOGUE

1

The girl screamed once, only the once.

Even that, however, was a minor slip on his part. That might have been the end of everything, almost before it had begun. Neighbours inquisitive, the police called in to investigate. No, that would not do at all. Next time he would tie the gag a little tighter, just a little tighter, just that little bit more secure.

Afterwards, he went to the drawer and took from it a ball of string. He used a pair of sharp nail-scissors, the kind girls always seem to use, to snip off a length of about six inches, then he put the ball of string and the scissors back into the drawer. A car revved up outside, and he went to the window, upsetting a pile of books on the floor as he did so. The car, however, had vanished, and he smiled to himself. He tied a knot in the string, not any special kind of knot, just a knot. There was an envelope lying ready on the sideboard.

2

It was 28th April. Wet, naturally, the grass percolating water as John Rebus walked to the grave of his father, dead five years to the day. He placed a wreath so that it lay, yellow and red, the colours of remembrance, against the still shining marble. He paused for a moment, trying to think of things to say, but there seemed nothing to say, nothing to think. He had been a good enough father and that was that. The old man wouldn't have wanted him to waste his words in any case. So he stood there, hands respectfully behind his back, crows laughing on the walls around him, until the water seeping into his shoes told him that there was a warm car waiting for him at the cemetery gates.

He drove quietly, hating to be back here in Fife, back where the old days had never been 'good old days,' where ghosts rustled in the shells of empty houses and the shutters went up every evening on a handful of desultory shops, those metal shutters that gave the vandals somewhere to write their names. How Rebus hated it all, this singular lack of an environment. It stank the way it had always done: of misuse, of disuse, of the sheer wastage of life.

He drove the eight miles towards the open sea, to where his brother Michael still lived. The rain eased off as he approached the skull-grey coast, the car throwing up splashings of water from a thousand crevasses in the road. Why was it, he wondered, that they never seemed to fix the roads here, while in Edinburgh they worked on the surfaces so often that things were made even worse? And why, above all, had he made the maniacal decision to come all the way through to Fife, just because it was the anniversary of the old man's death? He tried to focus his mind on something else, and found himself fantasising about his next cigarette.

Through the rain, falling as drizzle now, Rebus saw a girl about his daughter's age walking along the grass verge. He slowed the car, examined her in his mirror as he passed her, and stopped. He motioned for her to come to his window.

Her short breaths were visible in the cool, still air, and her dark hair fell in rats-tails down her forehead. She looked at him apprehensively.

'Where are you going, love?'

'Kirkcaldy.'

'Do you want a lift?'

She shook her head, drops of water flying from her coiled hair.

'My mum said I should never accept lifts from strangers.'

'Well,' said Rebus, smiling, 'your mum is quite right. I've got a daughter about your age and I tell her the same thing. But it is raining, and I *am* a policeman, so you can trust me. You've still got a fair way to go, you know.'

She looked up and down the silent road, then shook her head again.

'Okay,' said Rebus, 'but take care. Your mum was quite right.'

He wound his window up again and drove off, watching her in his mirror as she watched him. Clever kid. It was good to know that parents still had a little sense of responsibility left. If only the same could be said of his ex-wife. The way she had brought up their daughter was a disgrace. Michael, too, had given his daughter too long a leash. Who was to blame?

Rebus's brother owned a respectable house. He had followed in the old man's footsteps and become a stage hypnotist. He seemed to be quite good at it, too, from all accounts. Rebus had never asked Michael how it was done, just as he had never shown any interest or curiosity in the old man's act. He had observed that this still puzzled Michael, who would drop hints and red herrings as to the authenticity of his own stage act for him to chase up if he so wished.

But then John Rebus had too many things to chase up, and that had been the position during all of his fifteen years on the force. Fifteen years, and all he had to show were an amount of self-pity and a busted marriage with an innocent daughter hanging between them. It was more disgusting than sad. And meantime Michael was happily married with two kids and a larger house than Rebus could ever afford. He headlined at hotels, clubs, and even theatres as far away as Newcastle and Wick. Occasionally he would make six-hundred quid from a single show. Outrageous. He drove an expensive car, wore good clothes, and would never have been caught dead standing in the pissing rain in a graveyard in Fife on the dullest April day for many a year. No, Michael was too clever for that. And too stupid.

'John! Christ, what's up? I mean, it's great to see you. Why didn't you phone to warn me you were coming? Come on inside.'

It was the welcome Rebus had expected: embarrassed surprise, as though it were painful to be reminded that one still had some family left alive. And Rebus had noted the use of the word 'warn' where 'tell' would have sufficed. He was a policeman. He noticed such things.

Michael Rebus bounded through to the living-room and turned down the wailing stereo.

'Come on in, John,' he called. 'Do you want a drink? Coffee perhaps? Or something stronger? What brings you here?'

Rebus sat down as though he were in a stranger's house, his back straight and professional. He examined the panelled walls of the room – a new feature – and the framed photographs of his niece and nephew.

'I was just in the neighbourhood,' he said.

Michael, turning from the drinks cabinet with the glasses

ready, suddenly remembered, or did a good impersonation of just having remembered.

'Oh, John, I forgot all about it. Why didn't you tell me? Shit, I hate forgetting about Dad.'

'Just as well you're a hypnotist then and not Mickey the Memory Man, isn't it? Give me that drink, or are you two getting engaged?'

Michael, smiling, absolved, handed over the glass of whisky.

'Is that your car outside?' asked Rebus, taking the glass. 'I mean the big BMW?'

Michael, still smiling, nodded.

'Christ,' said Rebus. 'You treat yourself well.'

'As well as I treat Chrissie and the kids. We're building an extension onto the back of the house. Somewhere to put a jacuzzi or a sauna. They're the in thing just now, and Chrissie's desperate to keep ahead of the field.'

Rebus took a swallow of whisky. It turned out to be a malt. Nothing in the room was cheap, but none of it was exactly desirable either. Glass ornaments, a crystal decanter on a silver salver, the TV and video, the inscrutably miniature hi-fi system, the onyx lamp. Rebus felt a little guilty about that lamp. Rhona and he had given it to Michael and Chrissie as a wedding present. Chrissie no longer spoke to him. Who could blame her?

'Where is Chrissie, by the way?'

'Oh, she's out doing some shopping. She has her own car now. The kids will still be at school. She'll pick them up on the way home. Are you staying for something to eat?'

Rebus shrugged his shoulders.

'You'd be welcome to stay,' said Michael, meaning that Rebus wouldn't. 'So how's the cop-shop? Still muddling along?'

'We lose a few, but they don't get the publicity. We catch a few, and they do. It's the same as always, I suppose.'

The room, Rebus was noticing, smelled of toffee-apples, of penny arcades.

Michael was speaking:

'This is a terrible business about those girls being kidnapped.'
Rebus nodded.

'Yes,' he said, 'yes, it is. But we can't strictly call it kidnapping, not yet. There hasn't been a demand note or anything. It's more likely to be a straightforward case of sexual assault.'

Michael started up from his chair.

'Straightforward? What's straightforward about that?'

'It's just the terminology we use, Mickey, that's all.' Rebus shrugged again and finished his drink.

'Well, John,' said Michael, sitting, 'I mean, we've both got daughters, too. You're so casual about the whole thing. I mean, it's frightening to think of it.' He shook his head slowly in the world-wide expression of shared grief, and relief, too, that the horror was someone else's for the moment. 'It's frightening,' he repeated. 'And in Edinburgh of all places. I mean, you never think of that sort of thing happening in Edinburgh, do you?'

'There's more happening in Edinburgh than anyone knows.'

'Yes.' Michael paused. 'I was across there just last week playing at one of the hotels.'

'You didn't tell me.'

It was Michael's turn to shrug his shoulders.

'Would you have been interested?' he said.

'Maybe not,' said Rebus, smiling, 'but I would have come along anyway.'

Michael laughed. It was the laughter of birthdays, of money found in an old pocket.

'Another whisky, sir?' he said.

'I thought you were never going to ask.'

Rebus returned to his study of the room while Michael went to the cabinet.

'How's the act going?' he asked. 'And I really *am* interested.'

'It's going fine,' said Michael. 'In fact, it's going very well indeed. There's talk of a television spot, but I'll believe that when I see it.'

'Great.'

7

Another drink reached Rebus's willing hand.

'Yes, and I'm working on a new slot. It's a bit scary though.' An inch of gold flashed on Michael's wrist as he tipped the glass to his lips. The watch was expensive: it had no numbers on its face. It seemed to Rebus that the more expensive something was, the less of it there always seemed to be: tiny little hi-fi systems, watches without numbers, the translucent Dior ankle-socks on Michael's feet.

'Tell me about it,' he said, taking his brother's bait.

'Well,' said Michael, sitting forward in his chair, 'I take members of the audience back into their past lives.'

'Past lives?'

Rebus was staring at the floor as if admiring the design of the dark and light green carpet.

'Yes,' Michael continued, 'Reincarnation, born again, that sort of thing. Well, I shouldn't have to spell it out to you, John. After all, *you're* the Christian.'

'Christians don't believe in past lives, Mickey. Only future ones.'

Michael stared at Rebus, demanding silence.

'Sorry,' said Rebus.

'As I was saying, I tried the act out in public for the first time last week, though I've been practising it for a while with my private consultees.'

'Private consultees?'

'Yes. They pay me money for private hypnotherapy. I stop them smoking, or make them more confident, or stop them from wetting the bed. Some are convinced that they have past lives, and they ask me to put them under so that they can prove it. Don't worry though. Financially, it's all above board. The tax-man gets his cut.'

'And do you prove it? Do they have past lives?'

Michael rubbed a finger around the rim of his glass, now empty.

'You'd be surprised,' he said.

'Give me an example.'

Rebus was following the lines of the carpet with his eyes. Past lives, he thought to himself. Now there was a thing. There was plenty of life in *his* past.

'Well,' said Michael, 'remember I told you about my show in Edinburgh last week? Well,' he leaned further forward in his chair, 'I got this woman up from the audience. She was a small woman, middle-aged. She'd come in with an office-party. She went under pretty easily, probably because she hadn't been drinking as heavily as her friends. Once she was under, I told her that we were going to take a trip into her past, way, way back before she was born. I told her to think back to the earliest memory she had . . .'

Michael's voice had taken on a professional but easy mellifluence. He spread his hands before him as if playing to an audience. Rebus, nursing his glass, felt himself relax a little. He thought back to a childhood episode, a game of football, one brother pitted against the other. The warm mud of a July shower, and their mother, her sleeves rolled up, stripping them both and putting them, giggling knots of arms and legs, into the bath . . .

'. . . well,' Michael was saying, 'she started to speak, and in a voice not quite her own. It was weird, John. I wish you *had* been there to see it. The audience were silent, and I was feeling all cold and then hot and then cold again, and it had nothing to do with the hotel's heating-system by the way. I'd done it, you see. I'd taken that woman into a past life. She was a nun. Do you believe that? A *nun*. And she said that she was alone in her cell. She described the convent and everything, and then she started to recite something in Latin, and some people in the audience actually *crossed* themselves. I was bloody well petrified. My hair was probably standing on end. I brought her out of it as quickly as I could, and there was a long pause before the crowd started to applaud. Then, maybe out of sheer relief, her friends started to cheer and laugh, and that broke the ice. At the end of the show, I found out that this woman was a staunch Protestant, a Rangers supporter no less, and she swore blind that she knew no Latin at all. Well, *somebody* inside her did. I'll tell you that.'

Rebus was smiling.

'It's a nice story, Mickey,' he said.

'It's the truth.' Michael opened his arms wide in supplication. 'Don't you believe me?'

'Maybe.'

Michael shook his head.

'You must make a pretty bad copper, John. I had around a hundred and fifty witnesses. Iron-clad.'

Rebus could not pull his attention away from the design in the carpet.

'Plenty of people believe in past lives, John.'

Past lives . . . Yes, he believed in some things . . . In God, certainly . . . But past lives . . . Without warning, a face screamed up at him from the carpet, trapped in its cell.

He dropped his glass.

'John? Is anything wrong? Christ, you look as if you've seen . . .'

'No, no, nothing's the matter.' Rebus retrieved the glass and stood up. 'I just . . . I'm fine. It's just that,' he checked his watch, a watch with numbers, 'well, I'd better be going. I'm on duty this evening.'

Michael was smiling weakly, glad that his brother was not going to stay, but embarrassed at his relief.

'We'll have to meet again soon,' he said, 'on neutral territory.'

'Yes,' said Rebus, tasting once again the tang of toffee-apples. He felt a little pale, a little shaky, as though he were too far out of his territory. 'Let's do that.'

Once or twice or three times a year, at weddings, funerals, or over the telephone at Christmas, they promised themselves this get-together. The mere promise now was a ritual in itself, and so could be safely proffered and just as safely ignored.

'Let's do that.'

*

Rebus shook hands with Michael at the door. Escaping past the BMW to his own car, he wondered how alike they were, his brother and him. Uncles and aunts in their funeral-cold rooms occasionally commented, 'Ah, you're both the spitting image of your mother.' That was as far as it went. John Rebus knew that his own hair was a shade of brown lighter than Michael's, and that his eyes were a shade of green darker. He knew also, however, that the differences between them were such that any similarities were made to look unutterably superficial. They were brothers without any sense of brotherhood. Brotherhood belonged to the past.

He waved once from the car and was gone. He would be back in Edinburgh within the hour, and on duty another half-hour after that. He knew that the reason he could never feel comfortable in Michael's house was Chrissie's hatred of him, her unshakeable belief that he alone had been responsible for the break-up of his marriage. Maybe she was right at that. He tried ticking off in his mind the definite chores of the next seven or eight hours. He had to tidy up a case of burglary and serious assault. A nasty one that. The CID was undermanned as it was, and now these abductions would stretch them even more. Those two young girls, girls his own daughter's age. It was best not to think about it. By now they would be dead, or would wish that they were dead. God have mercy on them. In Edinburgh of all places, in his own dear city.

A maniac was on the loose.

People were staying in their homes.

And a screaming in his memory.

Rebus shrugged, feeling a slight sensation of attrition in one of his shoulders. It was not his business after all. Not yet.

Back in his living-room, Michael Rebus poured himself another whisky. He went to the stereo and turned it all the way up, then reached underneath his chair and, after a little fumbling, pulled out an ashtray that was hidden there.

PART ONE

'There are Clues
Everywhere'

1

On the steps of the Great London Road police station in Edinburgh, John Rebus lit his last legitimate cigarette of the day before pushing open the imposing door and stepping inside.

The station was old, its floor dark and marbled. It had about it the fading grandeur of a dead aristocracy. It had character.

Rebus waved to the duty sergeant, who was tearing old pictures from the notice-board and pinning up new ones in their place. He climbed the great curving staircase to his office. Campbell was just leaving.

'Hello, John.'

McGregor Campbell, a Detective Sergeant like Rebus, was donning coat and hat.

'What's the word, Mac? Is it going to be a busy night?' Rebus began checking the messages on his desk.

'I don't know about that, John, but I can tell you that it's been pandemonium in here today. There's a letter there for you from the man himself.'

'Oh yes?' Rebus seemed preoccupied with another letter which he had just opened.

'Yes, John. Brace yourself. I think you're going to be transferred to that abduction case. Good luck to you. Well, I'm off to the pub. I want to catch the boxing on the BBC. I should be in time.' Campbell checked his watch. 'Yes, plenty of time. Is anything wrong, John?'

Rebus waved the now empty envelope at him.

'Who brought this in, Mac?'

'I haven't the faintest, John. What is it?'

'Another crank letter.'

15

'Oh yes?' Campbell sidled over to Rebus's shoulder. He examined the typed note. 'Looks like the same bloke, doesn't it?'

'Clever of you to notice that, Mac, seeing as it's the exact same message.'

'What about the string?'

'Oh, it's here too.' Rebus lifted a small piece of string from his desk. There was a simple knot tied in its middle.

'Queer bloody business.' Campbell walked to the doorway. 'See you tomorrow, John.'

'Yes, yes, see you, Mac.' Rebus paused until his friend had made his exit. 'Oh, Mac!' Campbell came back into the doorway.

'Yes?'

'Maxwell won the big fight,' said Rebus, smiling.

'God, you're a bastard, Rebus.' Gritting his teeth, Campbell stalked out of the station.

'One of the old school,' Rebus said to himself. 'Now, what possible enemies could I have?'

He studied the letter again, then checked the envelope. It was blank, save for his own name, unevenly typed. The note had been handed in, just like the other one. It was a queer bloody business right enough.

He walked back downstairs and headed for the desk.

'Jimmy?'

'Yes, John.'

'Have you seen this?' He showed the envelope to the desk sergeant.

'That?' The sergeant wrinkled not only his brow but, it seemed to Rebus, his whole face. Only forty years in the force could do that to a man, forty years of questions and puzzles and crosses to bear. 'It must have been put through the door, John. I found it myself on the floor just there.' He pointed vaguely in the direction of the station's front door. 'Is anything up?'

'Oh no, it's nothing really. Thanks, Jimmy.'

But Rebus knew that he would be niggled all night by the

arrival of this note, only days after he had received the first anonymous message. He studied the two letters at his desk. The work of an old typewriter, probably portable. The letter S about a millimetre higher than the other letters. The paper cheap, no water-mark. The piece of string, tied in the middle, cut with a sharp knife or scissors. The message. The same typewritten message:

THERE ARE CLUES EVERYWHERE.

Fair enough; perhaps there were. It was the work of a crank, a kind of practical joke. But why him? It made no sense. Then the phone rang.

'Detective Sergeant Rebus?'

'Speaking.'

'Rebus, it's Chief Inspector Anderson here. Have you received my note?'

Anderson. Bloody Anderson. That was all he needed. From one crank to another.

'Yes, sir,' said Rebus, holding the receiver under his chin and tearing open the letter on his desk.

'Good. Can you be here in twenty minutes? The briefing will be in the Waverley Road Incident Room.'

'I'll be there, sir.'

The phone went dead on Rebus as he read. It was true then, it was official. He was being transferred to the abduction case. God, what a life. He pushed the messages, envelopes and string into his jacket pocket, looking around the office in frustration. Who was kidding who? It would take an act of God to get him to Waverley Road inside of half an hour. And when was he supposed to get round to finishing all his work? He had three cases coming to court and another dozen or so crying out for some paperwork before his memory of them faded entirely. That would be nice, actually, nice to just erase the lot of them. Wipe-out. He closed his eyes. He opened them again. The paperwork was still there, large as life. Useless. Always incomplete. No sooner had he finished with a case than another two or three appeared in its place. What was the name of that creature? The Hydra, was it? That was what he was fighting. Every time he cut off a head, more popped into his in-tray. Coming back from a holiday was a nightmare.

And now they were giving him rocks to push up hills as well.

He looked to the ceiling.

'With God's grace,' he whispered. Then he headed out to his car.

2

The Sutherland Bar was a popular watering-hole. It contained no jukebox, no video machines, no bandits. The decor was spartan, and the TV usually flickered and jumped. Ladies had not been welcome until well into the 1960s. There had, it seemed, been something to hide: the best pint of draught beer in Edinburgh. McGregor Campbell supped from his heavy glass, his eyes intent on the television set above the bar.

'Who wins?' asked a voice beside him.

'I don't know,' he said, turning to the voice. 'Oh, hello, Jim.'

A stocky man was sitting beside him, money in hand, waiting to be served. His eyes, too, were on the TV.

'Looks like a cracker of a fight,' he said. 'I fancy Mailer to win.'

Mac Campbell had an idea.

'No, I reckon Maxwell will walk it, win by a mile. Fancy a bet?'

The stocky man fished into his pocket for his cigarettes, eyeing the policeman.

'How much?' he asked.

'A fiver?' said Campbell.

'You're on. Tom, give me a pint over here, please. Do you want one yourself, Mac?'

'Same again, thanks.'

They sat in silence for a while, supping the beer and watching the fight. A few muffled roars went up occasionally from behind them as a punch landed or was dodged.

'It's looking good for your man if it goes the distance,' said Campbell, ordering more drinks.

'Aye. But let's wait and see, eh? How's work, by the way?'

'Fine, how's yours?'

'A pure bloody slog at the moment, if you must ask.' Some ash dropped onto his tie as he talked, the cigarette never leaving his mouth, though it wobbled precariously from time to time. 'A pure slog.'

'Are you still chasing up that drugs story?'

'Not really. I've landed on this kidnapping thing.'

'Oh? So has Rebus. You'd better not get into *his* hair.'

'Newspapermen get in *everybody's* hair, Mac. It goes with the etcetera.'

Mac Campbell, though wary of Jim Stevens, was grateful for a friendship, however tenuous and strained it had sometimes been, which had given him some information useful to his career. Stevens kept much of the juiciest tidbits to himself, of course. That's what 'exclusives' were made of. But he was always willing to trade, and it seemed to Campbell that the most innocuous pieces of gossip and information often seemed adequate for Stevens' needs. He was a kind of magpie, collecting everything without prejudice, storing much more of it than, surely, he would ever use. But with reporters you never could tell. Certainly, Campbell was happier with Stevens as a friend than as an enemy.

'So what's happening about your drugs dossier?'

Jim Stevens shrugged his creased shoulders.

'There's nothing in there just now that could be of much use to you boys anyway. I'm not about to let the whole thing drop though, if that's what you mean. No, that's too big a nest of vipers to be allowed to go free. I'll still be keeping my eyes open.'

A bell rang for the last round of the fight. Two sweating, dog-tired bodies converged on one another, becoming a single knot of limbs.

'Still looks good for Mailer,' said Campbell, an uneasy feeling coming over him. It couldn't be true. Rebus wouldn't have done that to him. Suddenly, Maxwell, the heavier and slower-moving of the two fighters, was hit by a blow to the face and staggered back. The bar erupted, sensing blood and victory. Campbell stared into his glass. Maxwell was taking a standing count. It was all over. A sensation in the final seconds of the contest, according to the commentator.

Jim Stevens held out his hand.

I'll kill bloody Rebus, thought Campbell. So help me, I'll kill him.

Later, over drinks bought with Campbell's money, Jim Stevens asked about Rebus.

'So it looks as if I'll be meeting him at last?'

'Maybe, maybe not. He's not exactly friendly with Anderson, so he may well get the shitty end of the stick, sitting at a desk all day. But then John Rebus isn't exactly friendly with anybody.'

'Oh?'

'Ach, he's not that bad, I suppose, but he's not the easiest of men to like.' Campbell, ducking from his friend's interrogative eyes, studied the reporter's tie. The recent layer of cigarette-ash had merely formed a veil over much older stains. Egg, perhaps, fat, alcohol. The scruffiest reporters were always the sharp ones, and Stevens was sharp, as sharp as ten years on the local newspaper could make a man. It was said that he had turned down jobs with London papers, just because he liked to live in Edinburgh. And what he liked best about his job was the opportunity it gave him to uncover the city's murkier depths, the crime, the corruption, the gangs and the drugs. He was a better detective than anyone Campbell knew, and, because of that very fact perhaps, the high-ups in the police both disliked and distrusted him. That seemed proof enough that he was doing his job well. Campbell watched as a little beer escaped from Stevens' glass and dripped onto his trousers.

'This Rebus,' said Stevens, wiping his mouth, 'he's the brother of the hypnotist, isn't he?'

'Must be. I've never asked him, but there can't be too many people about with a name like that, can there?'

'That's what I was thinking.' He nodded to himself as though confirming something of great importance.

'So what?'

'Oh, nothing. Just something. And he's not a popular man, you say?'

'I didn't say that exactly. I feel sorry for him really. The poor bugger has a lot on his plate. He's even started getting crank letters.'

'Crank letters?' Smoke enveloped Stevens for a moment as he puffed on another cigarette. Between the two men lay a thin blue pub-haze.

'I shouldn't have told you that. That was *strictly* off the record.'

Stevens nodded.

'Absolutely. No, it's just that I was interested. That sort of thing does happen though, doesn't it?'

'Not often. And not nearly as queer as the ones he's getting. I mean, they're not abusive or anything. They're just . . . queer.'

'Go on. How so?'

'Well, there's a bit of string in each one, tied into a knot, and there's a message that reads something like "clues are every-where".'

'Bloody hell. That is strange. They're a strange family. One a bloody hypnotist and the other getting anonymous notes. He was in the Army, wasn't he?'

'John was, yes. How did you know?'

'I know everything, Mac. That's the job.'

'Another funny thing is that he won't speak about it.'

The reporter looked interested again. When he was interested in something, his shoulders shivered slightly. He stared at the television.

'Won't speak about the Army?'

'Not a word. I've asked him about it a couple of times.'

'Like I said, Mac, it's a funny family that one. Drink up, I've got lots of your money left to spend.'

'You're a bastard, Jim.'

'Born and bred,' said the reporter, smiling for only the second time that evening.

3

'Gentlemen, and, of course, ladies, thank you for being so quick to gather here. This will remain the centre of operations during the inquiry. Now, as you all know . . .'

Detective Chief Superintendent Wallace froze in mid-speech as the Inquiry Room door pushed itself open abruptly and John Rebus, all eyes turned towards him, entered the room. He looked about in embarrassment, smiled a hopeful but wasted apology towards the senior officer, and sat himself down on a chair nearest to the door.

'As I was saying,' continued the superintendent.

Rebus, rubbing at his forehead, studied the roomful of officers. He knew what the old boy would be saying, and right now the last thing he needed was a pep-talk of the old school. The room was packed. Many of them looked tired, as if they'd been on the case for a while. The fresher, more attentive faces belonged to the new boys, some of them brought in from stations outwith the city. Two or three had notebooks and pencils at the ready, almost as if they were back in the school classroom. And at the front of the group, legs crossed, sat two women, peering up at Wallace, who was in full flight now, parading before the blackboard like some Shakespearean hero in a bad school play.

'Two deaths, then. Yes, deaths I'm afraid.' The room shivered expectantly. 'The body of Sandra Adams, aged eleven, was found on a piece of waste ground adjacent to Haymarket Station at six o'clock this evening, and that of Mary Andrews at six-fifty on an allotment in the Oxgangs district. There are officers at both locations, and at the end of this briefing more of you will be selected to join them.'

Rebus was noticing that the usual pecking-order was in play: inspectors near the front of the room, sergeants and the rest to the back. Even in the midst of murder, there is a pecking-order. The British Disease. And he was at the bottom of the pile, because he had arrived late. Another black mark against him on someone's mental sheet.

He had always been one of the top men while he had been in the Army. He had been a Para. He had trained for the SAS and come out top of his class. He had been chosen for a crack Special Assignments group. He had his medal and his commendations. It had been a good time, and yet it had been the worst of times, too, a time of stress and deprivation, of deceit and brutality. And when he had left, the police had been reluctant to take him. He understood now that it was something to do with the pressure applied by the Army to get him the job that he wanted. Some people resented that, and they had thrown down banana skins ever since for him to slide on. But he had sidestepped their traps, had performed the job, and had grudgingly been given his commendations here also. But there was precious little promotion, and that had caused him to say a few things out of line, a few things that were always to be held against him. And then he had cuffed an unruly bastard one night in the cells. God forgive him, he had simply lost his head for a minute. There had been more trouble over that. Ah, but it was not a nice world this, not a nice world at all. It was an Old Testament land that he found himself in, a land of barbarity and retribution.

'We will, of course, have more information for you to work on come tomorrow, after the post-mortems. But for the moment I think that will do. I'm going to hand you over to Chief Inspector Anderson, who will assign you to your tasks for the present.'

Rebus noticed that Jack Morton had nodded off in the corner and, if left unattended, would begin snoring soon. Rebus smiled, but the smile was short-lived, killed by a voice at the front of the room, the voice of Anderson. This was all Rebus needed. Anderson, the man at the centre of his out-of-line remarks. It felt for one sickening moment like predestination. Anderson was in charge. Anderson was doling out their tasks. Rebus reminded himself to stop praying. Perhaps if he stopped praying, God would take the hint and stop being such a bastard to one of his few believers on this near-godforsaken planet.

'Gemmill and Hartley will be assigned to door-to-door.'

Well, thank God he'd not been landed with that one. There was only one thing worse than door-to-door . . .

'And for an initial check on the MO files, Detective Sergeants Morton and Rebus.'

. . . and that was it.

Thank you, God, oh, thank you. That's just what I wanted to do with my evening: read through the case histories of all the bloody perverts and sex-offenders in east central Scotland. You must really hate my guts. Am I Job or something? Is that it?

But there was no ethereal voice to be heard, no voice at all save that of the satanic, leering Anderson, whose fingers slowly turned the pages of the roster, his lips moist and full, his wife a known adulteress and his son – of all things – an itinerant poet. Rebus heaped curse after curse upon the shoulders of that priggish, stick-thin superior officer, then kicked Jack Morton's leg and brought him snorting and chaffing into consciousness.

One of those nights.

4

'One of those nights,' said Jack Morton. He sucked luxuriously on his short, tipped cigarette, coughed loudly, brought his handkerchief from his pocket and deposited something into it from his mouth. He studied the contents of the handkerchief. 'Ah ha, some vital new evidence,' he said. All the same, he looked rather worried.

Rebus smiled. 'Time to stop smoking, Jack,' he said.

They were seated together at a desk upon which were piled about a hundred and fifty files on known sex-offenders in central Scotland. A smart young secretary, doubtless relishing the overtime that came with a murder inquiry, kept bringing more files into the office, and Rebus stared at her in mock outrage every time she entered. He was hoping to scare her away, and if she came back again, the outrage would become real.

'No, John, it's these tipped bastards. I can't take to them, really I can't. Sod that bloody doctor.'

So saying, Morton took the cigarette from his lips, broke off the filter, and replaced the cigarette, now ridiculously short, between thin, bloodless lips.

'That's better. That's more like a fag.'

Rebus had always found two things remarkable. One was that he liked, and in return was liked by, Jack Morton. The other was that Morton could pull so hard on a cigarette and yet release so little smoke. Where did all that smoke go? He could not figure it out.

'I see you're abstaining this evening, John.'

'Limiting myself to ten a day, Jack.'

27

Morton shook his head.

'Ten, twenty, thirty a day. Take it from me, John, it makes no difference in the end. What it comes down to is this: you either stop or you don't, and if you can't stop, then you're as well smoking as many as you like. That's been proven. I read about it in a magazine.'

'Aye, but we all know the magazines *you* read, Jack.'

Morton chuckled, gave another tremendous cough, and searched for his handkerchief.

'What a bloody job,' said Rebus, picking up the first of the files.

The two men sat in silence for twenty minutes, flicking through the facts and fantasies of rapists, exhibitionists, peder-asts, paedophiles, and procurers. Rebus felt his mouth filling with silt. It was as if he saw himself there, time after time after time, the self that lurked behind his everyday consciousness. His Mister Hyde by Robert Louis Stevenson, Edinburgh-born. He felt ashamed of his occasional erection: doubtless Jack Morton had one too. It came with the territory, as did the revulsion, the loathing and the fascination.

Around them, the station whirled in the business of the night. Men in shirtsleeves walked purposefully past their open door, the door of their assigned office, cut off from everyone else so that no one would be contaminated by their thoughts. Rebus paused for a moment to reflect that his own office back in Great London Road was in need of much of this equipment: the modern desk (unwobbly, with drawers that could be opened easily), the filing-cabinets (ditto), the drinks-dispenser just outside. There were carpets even, rather than his own liver-red linoleum with its curled, dangerous edges. It was a very palatable environment this in which to track down the odd pervert or killer.

'What exactly are we looking for, Jack?'

Morton snorted, threw down a slender brown file, looked at Rebus, shrugged his shoulders, and lit a cigarette.

'Garbage,' he said, picking up another folder, and whether or not it was meant as an answer Rebus was never to know.

'Detective Sergeant Rebus?'

A young constable, acne on his throat, cleanly-shaven, stood at the open door.

'Yes.'

'Message from the Chief, sir.'

He handed Rebus a folded piece of blue notepaper.

'Good news?' asked Morton.

'Oh, the best news, Jack, the very best news. Our boss sends us the following fraternal message: "Any leads from the files?" End of message.'

'Will there be any reply, sir?' asked the constable.

Rebus crumpled the note and tossed it into a new aluminium bin.

'Yes, son, there will be,' he said, 'but I very much doubt whether you'd want to deliver it.'

Jack Morton, wiping ash from his tie, laughed.

It was one of those nights. Jim Stevens, walking home at long last, had not found anything interesting since his conversation with Mac Campbell all of four hours ago. He had told Mac then that he was not about to drop his own investigation into Edinburgh's burgeoning drugs racket, and that had been the whole truth. It was becoming a private obsession, and though his boss might move him on to a murder case, still he would follow up his old investigation in his free, spare and private time, time found late at night when the presses were rolling, time spent in lower and lower dives further and further out of town. For he was close, he knew, to a big fish, and yet not close enough to be able to enlist the help of the forces of law and order. He wanted the story to be watertight before he called for the cavalry.

He knew the dangers, too. The ground he walked upon was always likely to fall away beneath his feet, letting him slip into Leith docks of a dark and silent morning, finding him trussed and gagged in some motorway ditch outside Perth. He didn't mind all that. It was no more than a passing thought, brought on by tiredness and a need to lift his emotions out of the rather tawdry, unglamorous world of Edinburgh's dope scene, a scene carried out in the sprawling housing-schemes and after-hours drinking holes more than in the glittery discotheques and chintzy rooms of the New Town.

What he disliked, really disliked, was that the people ultimately behind it all were so silent and so secretive and so alien to it all. He liked his criminals to be involved, to live the life and stick close to the lifestyle. He liked the Glasgow gangsters of the 1950s and '60s, who lived in the Gorbals and operated from the Gorbals and loaned illicit money to neighbours, and who would slash those same neighbours eventually, when the need arose. It was like a family affair. Not like this, not at all like this. This was other, and he hated it for that reason.

His talk with Campbell had been interesting though, interesting for other reasons. Rebus sounded a fishy character. So was his brother. They might be in it together. If the police were involved in all of this, then his task would be all the harder, and all the more satisfying for that.

Now what he needed was a break, a nice break in the investigation. It couldn't be far off. He was supposed to have a nose for that sort of thing.

5

At one-thirty they took a break. There was a small canteen in the building, open even at this ungodly hour. Outside, the majority of the day's petty crime was being committed, but inside it was warm and cosy, and there was hot food to be had and endless cups of coffee for the vigilant policemen.

'This is a complete shambles,' said Morton, pouring coffee back from his saucer into the cup. 'Anderson hasn't a clue what he's up to.'

'Give me a cigarette, will you? I'm out.' Rebus patted his pockets convincingly.

'Christ, John,' said Morton, wheezing an old man's cough and passing across the cigarettes, 'the day you give up smoking is the day I change my underwear.'

Jack Morton was not an old man, despite the excesses that were leading him quickly and inexorably towards that early fate. He was thirty-five, six years younger than Rebus. He, too, had a broken marriage behind him, the four children now resident with their grandmother while their mother was off on a suspiciously long vacation with her present lover. Misery, he had told Rebus, surrounded the whole bloody set-up, and Rebus had agreed with him, having a daughter who troubled his own conscience.

Morton had been a policeman for two decades, and unlike Rebus had started at the extreme bottom of the heap, pulling himself up to his present rank through sheer hard slog alone. He had given Rebus his life story when the two of them had gone off for a day's fly-fishing near Berwick. It had been a glorious day, both of them landing fine catches, and over the course of the day they had become friends. Rebus, however, had not deigned to tell his own life story to Morton. It felt, to Jack Morton, as if the man were in a little prison-cell of his own construction. He seemed especially tight-lipped about his years in the Army. Morton knew that the Army could occasionally do that to a man, and he respected Rebus's silence. Perhaps there were a few skeletons in that particular closet. He knew all about those himself; some of his most noteworthy arrests had not exactly been conducted along 'correct procedural lines'.

Nowadays, Morton did not concern himself with headlines and high-profile arrests. He got on with the job, collected his salary, thought now and then of his pension and the fishing-years to come, and drank his wife and children out of his conscience.

'This is a nice canteen,' said Rebus, smoking, struggling to start a conversation.

'Yes, it is. I'm in here now and again. I know one of the guys who work in the computer room. Comes in handy, you know, having one of those terminal-operators in your pocket. They can track down a car, a name, an address quicker than you can blink. It only costs the occasional drink.'

'Get them to sort out this lot of ours then.'

'Give them time, John. Then *all* the files will be on computer. And a little while after that, they'll find that they don't need the work-horses like us any more. There'll just be a couple of DIs and a desk console.'

'I'll bear that in mind,' said Rebus.

'It's progress, John. Where would we be without it? We'd still be out there with our pipes and our guess-work and our magnifying glasses.'

'I suppose you're right, Jack. But remember what the Super says: "Give me a dozen good men every time, and send your machines back to their makers." '

Rebus looked around him as he spoke. He saw that one of the two women from the briefing room had settled at a table by herself.

'And besides,' said Rebus, 'there'll always be a place for people like us, Jack. Society couldn't do without us. Computers can never have inspired guesses. That's where we've got them beat hands down.'

'Maybe, I don't know. Still, we better be getting back, eh?' Morton looked at his watch, drained his cup, and pushed back his chair.

'You go on ahead, Jack. I'll be with you in a minute. I want to check out an inspired guess.'

'Mind if I join you?'

Rebus, a fresh cup of coffee in his hand, pulled out the chair from opposite the woman officer, who had her head buried in the day's newspaper. He noted the garish headline on the front page. Someone had slipped out a little information to the local media.

'Not at all,' she said, not looking up.

Rebus smiled to himself and sat down. He began to sip the powdery, instant murk.

'Busy?' he asked.

'Yes. Shouldn't you be? Your friend left a few minutes ago.'

Sharp then, very sharp. Very, very sharp indeed. Rebus began to feel a mite uneasy. He disliked ballcrushers, and here were all the outward signs of one.

'Yes, he did, didn't he? But then he's a glutton for punishment. We're working on the Modus Operandi files. I'd do anything to defer that particular pleasure.'

She looked up at last, bitten by the potential insult.

'That's what I am, is it? A delaying tactic?'

Rebus smiled and shrugged.

'What else?' he said.

It was her turn to smile now. She closed the paper and folded it twice, placing it before her on the formica-topped table. She tapped the headline.

'Looks like we're in the news,' she said.

Rebus turned the paper towards him.

EDINBURGH ABDUCTIONS – NOW IT'S MURDER!

'A terrible bloody case,' he offered. 'Just terrible. And the newspapers don't make it any better.'

'Yes, well, we'll have the PM results in a couple of hours, and then we just might have something to go on.'

'I hope so. Just so long as I can put away those bloody files.'

'I thought policemen,' stressing the latter part of the word, 'got their kicks from reading that stuff?'

Rebus spread his hands before him, a gesture he seemed to have picked up from Michael.

'You have us to a T. How long have you been in the force?'

Rebus took her to be thirty, give or take two years. She had thick, short brown hair, and a long, straight ski-slope of a nose. There were no rings on her fingers, but these days that told him nothing.

'Long enough,' she said.

'I think I knew you would say that.'

She was smiling still: no ballcrusher then.

'Then you're cleverer than I took you for,' she said.

'You'd be surprised.'

He was growing tired, realising that the game was going nowhere. It was all midfield, a friendly rather than a cup-tie. He checked his watch conspicuously.

'Time I was getting back,' he said.

She picked up her newspaper.

'Are you doing anything this weekend?' she asked.

John Rebus sat down again.

6

He left the station at four o'clock. The birds were doing their best to persuade everyone that it was dawn, but no one seemed fooled. It was dark still, and the air was chilled.

He decided to leave his car and walk home, a distance of two miles. He needed it, needed to feel the cool, damp air, the expectancy of a morning shower. He breathed deep, trying to relax, to forget, but his mind was too full of those files, and little pieces of recollected fact and figure, pieces of horror no bigger than a paragraph, haunted his walk.

To indecently assault an eight-week old baby girl. The babysitter who had calmly admitted to the assault saying that she had done it 'for a kick'.

To rape a grandmother in front of her two grandchildren, then give the kids some sweets from a jar before leaving. The act premeditated; committed by a bachelor of fifty.

To burn with cigarettes the name of a street gang onto the breasts of a twelve-year old, leaving her for dead in a burning hut. Never caught.

And now the crux: to abduct two girls and then strangle them *without* having sexually abused them. That, Anderson had posited only thirty minutes before, was a perversion in itself, and in a funny way Rebus knew what he meant. It made the deaths even more arbitrary, more pointless – and more shocking.

Well, at least they were not dealing with a sex-offender; not right away. Which only, Rebus was forced to agree, made their task that much more difficult, for now they were confronted with something like a 'serial killer', striking at random and without clues, aiming at the record books rather than at any idea of 'kicks'. The question now was would he stop at two? It seemed unlikely.

Strangulation. It was a fearful way to go, wrestling, kicking your way towards oblivion, panic, the fretful sucking for air, and the killer behind you most likely, so that you faced the fear of something totally anonymous, a death without knowledge of who or why. Rebus had been taught methods of killing in the SAS. He knew what it felt like to have the garotte tighten on your neck, trusting to the opponent's prevailing sanity. A fearful way to go.

Edinburgh slept on, as it had slept on for hundreds of years. There were ghosts in the cobbled alleys and on the twisting stairways of the Old Town tenements, but they were Enlightenment ghosts, articulate and deferential. They were not about to leap from the darkness with a length of twine ready in their hands. Rebus paused and looked around him. Besides, it was morning now and any godfearing spirit would be tucked up in bed, as he, John Rebus, flesh and blood, would be soon.

Near his flat, he passed a little grocery shop outside which were stacked crates of milk and morning rolls. The owner had complained in private to Rebus about petty and occasional thefts, but would not submit a complaint proper. The shop was as dead as the street, the solitude of the moment disturbed only by the distant rumble of a taxi on cobblestones and the persistence of the dawn chorus. Rebus looked around him, examining the many curtained windows. Then, swiftly, he tore six rolls from a layer and stuffed them into his pockets, walking away a little too briskly. A moment later he hesitated, then walked on tiptoe back to the shop, the criminal returning to the scene of the crime, the dog to its vomit. Rebus had never actually seen dogs doing that, but he had it on the authority of Saint Peter.

Looking round again, he lifted a pint of milk out of its crate and made his getaway, whistling silently to himself.

Nothing in the world tasted as good for breakfast as stolen

rolls with some butter and jam and a mug of milky coffee. Nothing tasted better than a venial sin.

He sniffed the stairwell of his tenement, catching the faint odour of tom-cats, a persistent menace. He held his breath as he climbed the two flights of stairs, fumbling in his pocket beneath the squashed rolls, trying to liberate his door-key.

The interior of the flat felt damp and smelt damp. He checked the central heating and, sure enough, the pilot-light had gone out again. He cursed as he relit it, turning the heat up all the way, and went through to the living-room.

There were still spaces on the book-case, the wall-unit, the mantelpiece where Rhona's ornaments had once stood, but many of the gaps had already been filled by new mementoes of his own: bills, unanswered letters, old ring-pulls from tins of cheap beer, the occasional unread book. Rebus collected unread books. Once upon a time, he had actually read the books that he bought, but these days he seemed to have so little time. Also, he was more discriminating now than he had been then, back in the old days when he would read a book to its bitter end whether he liked it or not. These days, a book he disliked was unlikely to last ten pages of his concentration.

These were the books that lay around his living-room. His books for reading tended to congregate in the bedroom, lying in co-ordinated rows on the floor like patients in a doctor's waiting-room. One of these days he would take a holiday, would rent a cottage in the Highlands or on the Fife coast, and would take with him all of these waiting-to-be-read-or-reread books, all of that knowledge that could be his for the breaking open of a cover. His favourite book, a book he turned to at least once a year, was *Crime and Punishment*. If only, he thought, modern murderers would exhibit some show of conscience more often. But no, modern killers bragged of their crimes to their friends, then played pool in their local pub, chalking their cues with poise and certainty, knowing which balls would drop in which order . . .

While a police-car slept nearby, its occupants unable to do

anything save curse the mountains of rules and regulations and rue the deep chasms of crime. It was everywhere, crime. It was the life-force and the blood and the balls of life: to cheat, to edge; to take that body-swerve at authority, to kill. The higher up you climbed into crime, the more subtly you began to move back towards legitimacy, until a handful of lawyers only could crack open your system, and they were always affordable, always on hand to be bribed. Dostoevsky had known all that, clever old bastard. He had felt the stick burning from both ends.

But poor old Dostoevsky was dead and had not been invited to a party this weekend, while he, John Rebus, had. Often he declined invitations, because to accept meant that he had to dust off his brogues, iron a shirt, brush down his best suit, take a bath, and splash on some cologne. He had also to be affable, to drink and be merry, to talk to strangers with whom he had no inclination to talk and with whom he was not being paid to talk. In other words, he resented having to play the part of a normal human animal. But he had accepted the invitation given to him by Cathy Jackson in the Waverley Road canteen. Of course he had.

And he whistled at the thought of it, wandering through to the kitchen to make some breakfast, which he then took through to his bedroom. This was a ritual after a night duty. He stripped, climbed into bed, balanced the plate of rolls on his chest, and held a book to his nose. It was not a very good book. It was about a kidnapping. Rhona had taken away the bed proper, but had left him the mattress, so it was easy for him to reach down for his mug of coffee, easy for him to discard one book and find another.

He fell asleep soon enough, the lamp still burning, as cars began to pass by his window.

His alarm did the trick for a change, pulling him off the mattress as a magnet attracts filings. He had kicked off the duvet, and was drenched in sweat. He felt suffocated, and remembered suddenly that the central heating was still boiling away like a steamship. On his way to switching off the thermostat, he stooped at the front door to pick up the day's mail. One of the letters was unstamped and unfranked. It bore only his name in typescript across the front. Rebus's stomach squeezed hard on the paste of rolls and butter. He ripped the envelope open, pulling out the single sheet of paper.

FOR THOSE WHO READ BETWEEN THE TIMES.

So now the lunatic knew where he lived. Checking in the envelope, laconic now and expecting to find the knotted string, he found instead two matchsticks, tied together with thread into the shape of a cross.

PART TWO

'For those who read between the times'

7

Organized chaos: that summed up the newspaper office.
Organized chaos on the grandest of scales. Stevens rummaged
amongst the sheaf of paper in his tray, looking for a needle. Had
he perhaps filed it somewhere else? He opened one of the large,
heavy drawers of his desk, then shut it quickly, afraid that some
of the mess in there might escape. Controlling himself, he took
a deep breath and opened it again. He plunged a hand into the
jumble of paper inside the drawer, as if something in there
would bite. A huge dog-clip, springing loose from one particular
file, did bite. It nicked his thumb and he slammed the drawer
shut, the cigarette wobbling in his mouth as he cursed the
office, the journalistic profession, and trees, begetters of paper.
Sod it. He sat back and squeezed his eyes shut as the smoke
began to sting. It was eleven in the morning, and already the
office was a blue haze, as though everything were happening
on the set of a *Brigadoon* marsh-scene. He grabbed a sheet of
typescript, turned it over, and began to scribble with a nub of
pencil which he had lifted from a betting shop.

'X (Mr Big?) delivers to Rebus, M. How does the policeman
fit in? Answer – perhaps everywhere, perhaps nowhere.'

He paused, taking the cigarette from his mouth, replacing it
with a fresh one, and using the butt to light its successor.

'Now – anonymous letters. Threats? A code?'

Stevens found it unlikely that John Rebus could not know
about his brother's involvement in the Scottish drug-pushing
world, and knowing, the chances were that he was involved in
it too, perhaps leading the whole investigation the wrong way
to protect his flesh and blood. It would make a cracking good

story when it broke, but he knew that he would be treading on eggs from here on in. No one would go out of their way to help him nail a policeman, and if anyone found out what he was up to, he would be in very serious trouble indeed. He needed to do two things: check his life insurance policy, and tell nobody about this.

'Jim!'

The editor gestured for him to step into the torture chamber. He rose from his seat, as though tearing himself up from something organic, straightened his mauve and pink striped tie, and headed towards a presumed bawling-out.

'Yes, Tom?'

'Aren't you supposed to be at a press conference?'

'Plenty of time, Tom.'

'Which photographer are you taking?'

'Does it matter? I'd be better off taking my bloody instamatic. These young boys don't know the ropes, Tom. What about Andy Fleming? Can't I have him?'

'No chance, Jim. He's covering the royal tour.'

'What royal tour?'

Tom Jameson seemed about to rise again from his chair, which would have been an unprecedented move. He only straightened his back and shoulders however, and eyed his 'star' crime reporter suspiciously.

'You *are* a journalist, Jim, aren't you? I mean, you've not gone into early retirement, or become a recluse? No history of senile dementia in the family?'

'Listen, Tom, when the Royal Family commits a crime, I'll be the first on the scene. Otherwise, as far as I'm concerned, they don't exist. Not outside of my nightmares, anyway.'

Jameson pointedly examined his wristwatch.

'Okay, okay, I'm going.'

With that, Stevens turned on his heels with amazing speed and left the office, ignoring the cries of his boss at his back, asking which of the available photographers he wanted.

It wouldn't matter. He had yet to meet a policeman who was

photogenic. Then, leaving the building, he remembered who was Liaison Officer on this particular case, and he changed his mind, smiling.

' "There are clues everywhere, for those who read between the times." It's pure gobbledygook, isn't it, John?'

Morton was driving the car towards the Haymarket district of the city. It was another afternoon of consistent, wind-driven rain, the rain itself fine and cold, the kind that seeped into bones and marrow. The city had been dull all day, to a point where motorists were using their headlamps at noon. A great day for some outside work.

'I'm not so sure, Jack. The second part leads on from the first as if there was a logical connection.'

'Well, let's hope he sends you some more notes. Maybe that would make things clearer.'

'Maybe. I'd rather he'd just stop this shit altogether. It's not very nice knowing that a crank knows where you work and where you live.'

'Is your phone number in the telephone book?'

'No, unlisted.'

'That rules out that idea then. So how does he know your home address?'

'He *or* she,' said Rebus, tucking the notes back into his pocket. 'How should I know?'

He lit two cigarettes and passed one to Morton, breaking the filter off for him.

'Ta,' said Morton, placing the tiny cigarette in the corner of his mouth. The rain was easing. 'Floods in Glasgow,' he said, expecting no reply.

Both men were bleary-eyed from lack of sleep, but the case had taken possession of them, so they drove, minds numbed, towards the bleak heart of the inquiry. A portakabin had been set up on waste ground next to the spot where the girl's body had been found. From there, a door-to-door operation was being co-ordinated. Friends and family were also to be inter-viewed. Rebus foresaw much tedium in the day ahead.

'What worries me,' Morton had said, 'is that if the two murders are linked, then we're dealing with someone who probably didn't know either of the girls. *That* makes for a bastard of a job.'

Rebus had nodded. There was still the chance, however, either that both girls had known their murderer, or that the murderer had been someone in a position of trust. Otherwise, the girls being nearly twelve-years old and not daft, they would surely have struggled when abducted. Yet no one had come forward to say that they had witnessed any such thing. It was bloody strange.

The rain had stopped by the time they reached the cramped operations-room. The inspector in charge of outdoor operations was there to hand them lists of names and addresses. Rebus rejoiced to be away from the HQ, away from Anderson and his thirst for paperwork results. *This* was where the work really took place, where the contacts were made, where one slip by a suspect could tip a case one way or the other.

'Do you mind me asking, sir, who it was that suggested my colleague and me for this particular job?'

The DI, his eyes twinkling, studied Rebus for a second.

'Yes, I bloody well do mind, Rebus. It doesn't matter one way or the other, does it? Every single task in this case is as vital and as important as every other. Let's not forget that.'

'Yes, sir,' said Rebus.

'This must be a bit like working inside a shoebox, sir,' said Morton examining the cramped interior.

'Yes, son, I'm in the shoebox, but you lot are the shoes, so get bloody well moving.'

This particular inspector, thought Rebus, pocketing his list, seemed a nice bloke, his tongue just sharp enough for Rebus's taste.

'Don't worry, sir,' he said now, 'this won't take us long.'

He hoped that the inspector noted the irony in his voice.

'Last one back's a fairy,' said Morton.

They were doing this by the rule-book then, yet the case would seem to demand that new rules be drawn up. Anderson was sending them out to look for the usual suspects: family, acquaintances, people with records. Doubtless, back at HQ, groups such as the Paedophile Information Exchange were being investigated. Rebus hoped that there were plenty of crank calls for Anderson to sift through. There usually were: the callers who admitted to the crime, the callers who were psychic and could help by getting in touch with the deceased, the callers who pressed a red-herring to your nose so that you could have a sniff. They were all mastered by past guilt and present fantasies. Perhaps everyone was.

At his first house, Rebus battered on the door and waited. It was opened by a rank old woman, her feet bare, a cardigan comprised of ninety-percent hole to ten-percent wool hanging around her scarp-like shoulders.

'Whit is it?'

'Police, madam. It's about the murder.'

'Eh? Whitever it is, I dinnae want it. Away ye get afore I ca' for the coppers.'

'The murders,' shouted Rebus. 'I'm a policeman. I've come to ask you a few questions.'

'Eh?' She stood back a little to peer at him, and Rebus could swear that he saw the faint glow of a past intelligence in the dulled black of her pupils.

'Whit murders?' she said.

One of those days. To improve matters, the rain began again, heavy dollops of stinging water gripping to his neck and face, seeping into his shoes. Just like that day at the old man's grave . . . Only yesterday? A lot could happen in twenty-four hours, all of it to him.

By seven o'clock, Rebus had covered six of the fourteen individuals on his list. He walked back to the operations-shoebox, his feet sore, his stomach awash with tea and craving something stronger.

At the boggy waste ground, Jack Morton stood and stared out over the acres of clay, strewn with bricks and detritus: a child's heaven.

'What a hellish place to die in.'

'She didn't die here, Jack. Remember what forensic said.'

'Well, you know what I mean.'

Yes, Rebus knew what he meant.

'By the way,' said Morton, 'you're the fairy.'

'I'll drink to that,' said Rebus.

They drank in some of Edinburgh's seedier bars, bars the tourist never sees. They tried to shut the case out of their minds, but could not. It was like that with big murder inquiries; they got to you, physically and mentally, consuming you and making you work all the harder. There was a rush of pure adrenalin behind every murder. It kept them going past the point of no return.

'I'd better be getting back to the flat,' said Rebus.

'No, have another.'

Jack Morton weaved towards the bar, his empty glass in his hand.

Rebus, his mind foggy, thought more about his mysterious correspondent. He suspected Rhona, though it could not be said to be her style. He suspected his daughter Sammy, perhaps taking a delayed-action revenge for her father's dismissal of her from his life. Family and acquaintances were, initially at least, always the chief suspects. But it could be anyone, anyone who knew where he worked and where he lived. Someone in his own force was always a possibility to be feared.

The 10,000 dollar question, as ever, was why?

'Here we go, two lovely pints of beer, *gratis* from the management.'

'I call that very public-spirited,' said Rebus.

'Or publican-spirited, eh, John?' Morton chuckled at his joke, wiping froth from his top lip. He noticed that Rebus wasn't laughing. 'A penny for them,' he said.

'A serial killer,' said Rebus, 'It must be. In which case we've not seen the last of our friend's handiwork.'

Morton put down his glass, suddenly not very thirsty.

'Those girls went to different schools,' continued Rebus, 'lived in different areas of the city, had different tastes, different friends, were of different religions, and were killed by the same murderer in the same way and without noticeable abuse of any kind. We're dealing with a maniac. He could be anywhere.'

A fight was breaking out at the bar, apparently over a game of dominoes, which had gone very badly wrong. A glass fell to the floor, followed by a hush in the bar. Then everyone seemed to calm down a little. One man was led outside by his supporters in the argument. Another remained slumped against the bar, muttering to a woman beside him.

Morton took a gulp of beer.

'Thank God we're off duty,' he said. Then: 'Fancy a curry?'

Morton finished the chicken vindaloo and threw his fork down on to the plate.

'I reckon I ought to have a word with the Health Department boys,' he said, still chewing. 'Either that or the Trading Standards. Whatever that was, it wasn't chicken.'

They were in a small curry-house near Haymarket Station. Purple lighting, red flock wallpaper, a churning wall of sitar-music.

'You looked as if you were enjoying it,' said Rebus, finishing his beer.

'Oh yes, I enjoyed it, but it wasn't chicken.'

'Well, there's nothing to complain about if you enjoyed it.' Rebus sat slant-wise on his chair, his legs straight out before him, an arm along the chair's back while he smoked his umpteenth cigarette that day.

Morton leaned unsteadily towards his partner.

'John, there's *always* something to complain about, especially if you think you can get off with not paying the bill by doing so.'

He winked at Rebus, sat back, burped, and reached into his pocket for a cigarette.

'Garbage,' he said.

Rebus tried to count the number of cigarettes he himself had smoked that day, but his brain told him that such calculations were not to be attempted.

'I wonder what our friend the murderer is up to at this exact moment?' he said.

'Finishing a curry?' suggested Morton. 'Trouble is, John, he could be one of these Joe Normal types, clean on the surface, married with kids, your average suburban hard-working chap, but underneath a nutter, pure and simple.'

'There's nothing simple about our man.'

'True.'

'But you could well be right. You mean that he's a sort of Jekyll and Hyde, right?'

'Exactly.' Morton flicked ash onto the table-top, already splashed with curry sauce and beer. He was peering at his empty plate as though wondering where all the food had gone. 'Jekyll and Hyde. You've got it in a nutshell. I'll tell you, John, I'd lock these bastards up for a million years, a million years of solitary in a cell the size of a shoebox. That's what I'd do.'

Rebus was staring at the flock wallpaper. He thought back to his own days in solitary, days when the SAS were trying to crack him, days of the ultimate testing, of sighs and silence, starvation and filth. No, he wouldn't want that again. And yet they had not beaten him, not really beaten him. The others had not been so lucky.

Trapped in its cell, the face screaming
Let me out Let me out
Let me out . . .

'John? Are you okay there? If you're going to be sick, the toilet's behind the kitchen. Listen, when you're passing, do me a favour and see if you can notice what it is that they're chopping up and throwing into the pot . . .'

Rebus walked smartly to the toilet with the over-cautious gait of the tremendously drunk, yet he did not feel drunk, not *that* drunk. His nostrils filled with the smells of curry, disinfectant, shit. He washed his face. No, he was not going to be sick. It wasn't too much to drink, for he had felt the same shudder at Michael's, the same momentary horror. What was happening to him? It was as if his insides were concretizing, slowing him down, allowing the years to catch up on him. It felt a little like the nervous breakdown which he had been awaiting, yet it was no nervous breakdown. It was nothing. It had passed.

'Can I give you a lift, John?'

'No thanks, I'll walk. Clear my head.'

They parted at the door of the restaurant. An office-party, loosened neckties and strong, sickly perfume, made its way towards Haymarket Station. Haymarket was the last station into Edinburgh before the much grander Waverley. Rebus remembered that the premature withdrawal of the penis during intercourse for contraceptive reasons was often referred to as 'getting off at Haymarket.' Who said the people in Edinburgh were dour? A smile, a song, and a strangulation. Rebus wiped sweat from his forehead. He felt weak still, and leaned against a lamp-post. He knew vaguely what it was. It was a rejection by his whole being of the past, as though his vital organs were rejecting a donor heart. He had pushed the horror of the training so far to the back of his mind that any echo of it at all was now to be violently fought against. And yet it was in that same confinement that he had found friendship, brotherhood, camaraderie, call it what you like. And he had learned more about himself than human beings ever do. He had learned so much.

His spirit had not been broken. He had come out of the training on top. And then had come the nervous breakdown.

Enough. He began to walk, steadying himself with thoughts

of his day off tomorrow. He would spend the day reading and sleeping and readying himself for a party, Cathy Jackson's party.

And the day after that, Sunday, he would be spending a rare day with his daughter. Then, perhaps, he would find out who was behind the crank letters.

8

The girl woke up with a dry, salty taste in her mouth. She felt sleepy and numb and wondered where she was. She had fallen asleep in his car. She had not felt sleepy before then, before he had given her a piece of his chocolate-bar. Now she was awake, but not in her bedroom at home. This room had pictures on its walls, pictures cut out of colour magazines. Some were photographs of soldiers with fierce expressions on their faces, others were of girls and women. She looked closely at some self-developing photographs grouped together on one wall. There was a picture of her there, asleep on the bed with her arms spread wide. She opened her mouth in a slight gasp.

Outside, in the living-room, he heard her movements as he prepared the garotte.

That night, Rebus had one of his nightmarish dreams again. A long, lingering kiss was followed by an ejaculation, both in the dream and in reality. He woke up immediately afterwards and wiped himself down. The breath of the kiss was still around him, hanging to him like an aura. He shook his head clear of it. He needed a woman. Remembering the party to come, he relaxed a little. But his lips were dry. He padded into the kitchen and found a bottle of lemonade. It was flat, but served the purpose. Then he remembered that he was still drunk, and would have a hangover if he wasn't careful. He poured himself three glassfuls of water and forced them down.

He was pleased to find that the pilot-light was still on. It was like a good omen. When he slipped back into bed, he even remembered to say his prayers. That would surprise the Big

Man upstairs. He would note it in his muckle book: Rebus remembered me tonight. May give him a nice day tomorrow.

Amen.

9

Michael Rebus loved his BMW as dearly as he loved life itself, perhaps more so. As he sped down the motorway, the traffic to his left hardly appearing to move at all, he felt that his car *was* life in a strange, satisfying sort of way. He pointed its nose towards the bright point of the horizon and let it forge towards that future, revving it hard, making no concessions to anyone or anything.

That was the way he liked it; hard, fast luxury, push-button and on-hand. He drummed his fingers on the leather of the steering-wheel, toyed with the radio-cassette, eased his head back onto the padded headrest. He dreamed often of just taking off, leaving wife and children and house, just his car and him. Taking off towards that far point, never stopping except to eat and fill up the car, driving until he died. It seemed like paradise, and so he felt quite safe fantasising about it, knowing that he would never dare put paradise into practice.

When he had first owned a car, he had wakened in the middle of the night, opening his curtains to see if it was still waiting for him outside. Sometimes he would rise at four or five in the morning and take off for a few hours, astonished at the distance he could cover so quickly, glad to be out on the silent roads with only the rabbits and the crows for company, his hand on the horn scaring fluttering clouds of birds into the air. He had never lost that initial love-affair with cars, the manumission of dreams.

People stared at his car now. He would park it in the streets of Kirkcaldy and stand a little distance away, watching people envy that car. The younger men, full of bravado and expectancy, would peer inside, staring at leather and dials as though examining living things at the zoo. The older men, some with their wives in tow, would glance at the machine, sometimes spitting on the road afterwards, knowing that it represented everything they had wanted for themselves and failed to find. Michael Rebus had found his dream, and it was a dream he could watch any time he chose.

In Edinburgh, however, it depended where you parked as to whether your car would attract attention. He had parked on George Street one day, only to find a Rolls-Royce cruising to a stop behind him. He had keyed the ignition again, fuming, near-spitting. He had parked eventually outside a discotheque. He knew that parking an expensive car outside a restaurant or a discotheque would mean that a few people would mistake you for the owner of the particular set-up, and that thought pleased him immensely, erasing the memory of the Rolls-Royce and infusing him with new versions of the dream.

Stopping at traffic-lights, too, could be exciting, except when some half-arsed biker on a big machine roared to a standstill behind him or, even worse, beside him. Some of those bikes were made for initial acceleration. More than once he had been beaten mercilessly in a race from traffic-lights. He tried not to think about those times either.

Today he parked where he had been told to park: in the car park atop Calton Hill. He could see over to Fife from his front window, and from the back he could see Princes Street laid out before him like a toy-set. The hill was quiet; it was not quite the tourist season, and it was cold. He knew that things hotted up at night: car chases, girls and boys hoping for a ride, parties at Queensferry beach. Edinburgh's gay community would mix with those merely curious or lonely, and a couple, hand-in-hand, would now and again enter the graveyard at the bottom of the hill. When darkness fell, the east end of Princes Street became a territory all of its own, to be passed around, to be shared. But he was not about to share his car with anyone. His dream was a fragile entity.

He watched Fife across the Firth of Forth, looking quite splendid from this distance, until the man's car slowed and stopped beside him. Michael slid across to his passenger seat and wound down the window, just as the other man was winding down his.

'Got the stuff?' he said.

'Of course,' said the man. He checked in his mirror. Some people, a family of all things, had just come over the rise. 'We better wait for a minute.'

They paused, staring blankly at the scenery.

'No hassles across in Fife?' asked the man.

'None.'

'The word's going round that your brother was over seeing you. Is that correct?' The man's eyes were hard; his whole being was hard. But the car he drove was a heap. Michael felt safe for the moment.

'Yes, but it was nothing. It was just the anniversary of our dad's death. That was all.'

'He doesn't know anything?'

'Absolutely not. Do you think I'm thick or something?'

The man's glance silenced Michael. It was a mystery to him how this one man could invoke such fear in him. He hated these meetings.

'If anything happens,' the man was saying, 'if *anything* goes wrong, you'll be in for it. I really mean that. Keep well clear of that bastard in future.'

'It wasn't my fault. He just dropped in on me. He didn't even phone first. What could I do?'

His hands were gripping hard to the steering-wheel, cemented there. The man checked in his mirror again.

'All clear,' he said, reaching behind him. A small package slipped through Michael's window. He took a look inside it, brought an envelope out of his pocket, and reached for the ignition.

'Be seeing you around, Mister Rebus,' said the man, opening the envelope.

'Yes,' said Michael, thinking: not if I can help it. This work was getting a bit too hairy for him. These people seemed to know everything about his movements. He knew, however, that the fear always evaporated, to be replaced by euphoria when he had rid himself of another load, pocketing a nice profit on the deal. It was that moment when fear turned to euphoria that kept him in the game. It was like the fastest piece of acceleration from traffic-lights that you could experience – ever.

Jim Stevens, watching from the hill's Victorian folly, a ridiculous, never-completed copy of a Greek temple, saw Michael Rebus leave. That much was old news to him; he was more interested in the Edinburgh connection, a man he could not trace and did not know, a man who had lost him twice before and who could doubtless lose him again. Nobody seemed to know who this mysterious figure was, and nobody particularly wanted to know. He looked like trouble. Stevens, feeling suddenly impotent and old, could do nothing other than jot down the car registration number. He thought that perhaps McGregor Campbell could do something with it, but he was wary of being found out by Rebus. He felt trapped in the middle of something which was proving altogether a knottier problem than he had suspected.

Shivering, he tried to persuade himself that he liked it that way.

10

'Come in, come in, whoever you are.'

Rebus's coat, gloves, and bottle of wine were taken from him by complete strangers, and he was plunged into one of those packed, smoky, loud parties where it is easy to smile at people but near impossible to get to know anyone. He moved from the hall into the kitchen, and from there, through a connecting-door, into the living-room itself.

The chairs, table, settee had been pushed back to the walls, and the floor was filled with writhing, whooping couples, the men tieless, their shirts sticking to them.

The party, it appeared, had started earlier than he had anticipated.

He recognized a few faces around and beneath him, stepping over two inspectors as he waded into the room. He could see that the table at the far end had bottles and plastic cups heaped upon it, and it seemed as good a vantage point as any, and safer than some.

Getting to it was the problem however, and he was reminded of some of the assault courses of his Army days.

'Hi there!'

Cathy Jackson, doing a passable imitation of a rag-doll, reeled into his path for a second before being swept off her feet by the large – the very large – man with whom she was pretending to dance.

'Hello,' managed Rebus, his face twisting into a grimace rather than a smile. He achieved the relative safety of the drinks-table and helped himself to a whisky and a chaser. That would do for starters. Then he watched as Cathy Jackson (for whom he had bathed, polished, scraped, adjusted, and sprayed) pushed her tongue into the cavernous mouth of her dancing-partner. Rebus thought that he was going to be sick. His partner for the evening had done a bunk before the evening had begun! That would teach him to be optimistic. So what did he do now? Leave quietly, or try to pull a few words of introduction out of his hat?

A stocky man, not at all a policeman, came from the kitchen, and, cigarette in mouth, approached the table with a couple of empty glasses in his hand.

'Bloody hell,' he said to nobody in particular, rummaging amongst the bottles, 'this is all a bit fucking grim, isn't it? Excuse my language.'

'Yes, it is a bit.'

Rebus thought to himself, well, there it is, I've done it now, I've spoken to someone. The ice is broken, so I may as well leave while the going's good.

But he did not leave. He watched as the man weaved his way quite expertly back through the dancers, the drinks as safe as tiny animals in his hands. He watched as another record pounded out of the invisible stereo system, the dancers recommenced their war-dance, and a woman, looking every inch as uncomfortable as he did, squeezed her way into the room and was pointed in the direction of Rebus's table.

She was about his own age, a little ragged around the edges. She wore a reasonably fashionable dress, he supposed (who was he to talk about fashion? his suit looked downright funereal in the present company), and her hair had been styled recently, perhaps as recently as this afternoon. She wore a secretary's glasses, but she was no secretary. Rebus could see that much by looking at her, by examining the way she handled herself as she picked her way towards him.

He held a Bloody Mary, newly-prepared, towards her.

'Is this okay for you?' he shouted. 'Have I guessed right or wrong?'

She gulped the drink thankfully, pausing for breath as he refilled the tumbler.

'Thanks,' she said. 'I don't normally drink, but that was much appreciated.'

Great, Rebus thought to himself, the smile never leaving his eyes, Cathy Jackson's out of her head (and her morals) on alcohol, and I'm landed with a TT. Oh, but that thought was unworthy of him, and did no justice to his companion. He breathed a quick prayer of contrition.

'Would you like to dance?' he asked, for his sins.

'You're kidding!'

'I'm not. What's wrong?'

Rebus, guilty of a streak of chauvinism, could not believe it. She was a DI. Moreover, she was Press Liaison Officer on the murder case.

'Oh,' he said, 'it's just that I'm working that case, too.'

'Listen, John, if it keeps on like this, every policeman and policewoman in Scotland is going to be on the case. Believe me.'

'What do you mean?'

'There's been another abduction. The girl's mother reported her missing this evening.'

'Shit. Excuse my language.'

They had danced, drunk, separated, met again, and were now old friends for the evening, it seemed. They stood in the hallway, a little way from the noise and chaos of the dance-floor. A queue for the flat's only toilet was becoming unruly at the end of the corridor.

Rebus found himself staring past Gill Templer's glasses, past all that glass and plastic, to the emerald-green eyes beyond. He wanted to tell her that he had never seen eyes as lovely as hers, but was afraid of being accused of cliché. She was sticking to orange juice now, but he had loosened himself up with a few more whiskies, not expecting anything special from the evening.

'Hello, Gill.'

Rebus recognized the stocky man before them as the person he had spoken with at the drinks-table.

'Long time no see.'

The man attempted to peck Gill Templer's cheek, but succeeded only in falling past her and butting the wall.

'Had a drop too much to drink, Jim?' said Gill, coolly.

The man shrugged his shoulders. He was looking at Rebus.

'We all have our crosses to bear, eh?'

A hand was extended towards Rebus.

'Jim Stevens,' said the man.

'Oh, the reporter?'

Rebus accepted the man's warm, moist hand for a moment.

'This is Detective Sergeant John Rebus,' said Gill.

Rebus noticed the quick flushing in Stevens' face, the startled eyes of a hare. He recovered quickly though, expertly.

'Pleased to meet you,' he said. Then, motioning with his head, 'Gill and I go back a long way, don't we, Gill?'

'Not as far as you seem to think, Jim.'

He laughed then, glancing towards Rebus.

'She's just shy,' he said. 'Another girl murdered, I hear.'

'Jim has spies everywhere.'

Stevens tapped the side of his blood-red nose, grinning towards Rebus.

'Everywhere,' he said, 'and I *get* everywhere, too.'

'Yes, spreads himself a little thin, does our Jim,' said Gill, her voice sharp as a blade's edge, her eyes suddenly shrouded in glass and plastic, inviolable.

'Another press briefing tomorrow, Gill?' said Stevens, searching through his pockets for his cigarettes, lost long before.

'Yes.'

The reporter's hand found Rebus's shoulder.

'A long way, me and Gill.'

Then he was gone, his hand held back towards them as he retreated, waving without the necessity of acknowledgement, searching out his cigarettes, filing away John Rebus's face.

Gill Templer sighed, leaning against the wall where Stevens' failed kiss had landed.

'One of the best reporters in Scotland,' she said, matter-of-factly.

'And your job is dealing with the likes of him?'

'He's not so bad.'

An argument seemed to be starting in the living-room.

'Well,' said Rebus, all smiles, 'shall we phone for the police, or would you rather be taken to a little restaurant I know?'

'Is that a chat-up line?'

'Maybe. You tell me. After all, you're the detective.'

'Well, whatever it is, Detective Sergeant Rebus, you're in luck. I'm starving. I'll get my coat.'

Rebus, feeling pleased with himself, remembered that his own coat was lurking somewhere. He found it in one of the bedrooms, along with his gloves, and – a cracking surprise – his unopened bottle of wine. He pocketed this, seeing it as a divine sign that he would be needing it later.

Gill was in the other bedroom, rummaging through the pile of coats on the bed. Beneath the bedcovers, congress seemed to be taking place, and the whole mess of coats and bedclothes seethed and writhed like some gigantic amoeba. Gill, giggling through it all, found her coat at last and came towards Rebus, who smiled conspiratorially in the doorway.

'Goodbye, Cathy,' she shouted back into the room, 'thanks for the party.'

There was a muffled roar, perhaps an acknowledgement, from beneath the bedclothes. Rebus, his eyes wide, felt his moral fibre crumbling like a dry cheese-biscuit.

In the taxi, they sat a little distance apart.

'So, do you and this Stevens character go back a long way?'

'Only in his memory.' She stared past the driver at the sleek wet road beyond. 'Jim's memory can't be what it was. Seriously, we went out together once, and I do mean once.' She held up a finger. 'A Friday night, I think it was. A big mistake, it certainly was.'

Rebus was satisfied with that. He began to feel hungry again.

By the time they reached the restaurant, however, it was closed – even to Rebus – so they stayed in the taxi and Rebus directed the driver towards his flat.

'I'm a dab hand at bacon sandwiches,' he said.

'What a pity,' she said. 'I'm a vegetarian.'

'Good God, you mean you eat no vegetables at all?'

'Why is it,' acid seeping into her voice, 'that carnivores always have to make a joke out of it? It's the same with men and women's lib. Why is that?'

'It's because we're afraid of them,' said Rebus, quite sober now.

Gill looked at him, but he was watching from his window as the city's late-night drunks rolled their way up and down the obstacle-strewn hazard of Lothian Road, seeking alcohol, women, happiness. It was a never-ending search for some of them, staggering in and out of clubs and pubs and take-aways, gnawing on the packaged bones of existence. Lothian Road was Edinburgh's dustbin. It was also home to the Sheraton Hotel and the Usher Hall. Rebus had visited the Usher Hall once, sitting with Rhona and the other smug souls listening to Mozart's Requiem Mass. It was typical of Edinburgh to have a crumb of culture sited amidst the fast-food shops. A requiem mass and a bag of chips.

'So how is the old Press Liaison these days?'

They were seated in his rapidly tidied living-room. His pride and joy, a Nakamichi tape-deck, was tastefully broadcasting one of his collection of late-night-listening jazz tapes; Stan Getz or Coleman Hawkins.

He had rustled up a round of tuna fish and tomato sandwiches, Gill having admitted that she ate fish occasionally. The bottle of wine was open, and he had prepared a pot of freshly ground coffee (a treat usually reserved for Sunday breakfasts). He now sat across from his guest, watching her eat. He thought with a small start that this was his first female guest since Rhona had left him, but then recalled, very vaguely, a couple of other one-nighters.

'Press Liaison is fine. It's not really a complete waste of time, you know. It serves a useful purpose in this day and age.'

'Oh, I'm not knocking it.'

She looked at him, trying to gauge how serious he was being.

'Well,' she went on, 'it's just that I know a lot of our colleagues who think that a job like mine is a complete waste of time and manpower. Believe me, in a case like this one it's absolutely crucial that we keep the media on *our* side, and that we let them have the information that we want made public *when* it needs to be made public. It saves a lot of hassle.'

'Hear, hear.'

'Be serious, you rat.'

Rebus laughed.

'I'm never anything other than serious. A one-hundred percent policeman's policeman, that's me.'

Gill Templer stared at him again. She had a real inspector's eyes: they worked into your conscience, sniffing out guilt and guile and drive, seeking give.

'And being a Liaison Officer,' said Rebus, 'means that you have to . . . liaise with the press quite closely, right?'

'I know what you're getting at, Sergeant Rebus, and as your superior, I'm telling you to stop it.'

'Ma'am!' Rebus gave her a short salute.

He came back from the kitchen with another pot of coffee.

'Wasn't that a dreadful party?' said Gill.

'It was the finest party I have ever attended,' said Rebus. 'After all, without it, I might never have met you.'

She roared with laughter this time, her mouth filled with a paste of tuna and bread and tomato.

'You're a nutter,' she cried, 'you really are.'

Rebus raised his eyebrows, smiling. Had he lost his touch? He had not. It was miraculous.

Later, she needed to go to the bathroom. Rebus was changing a tape, and realising how limited his musical tastes were. Who were these groups that she kept referring to?

'It's in the hall,' he said. 'On the left.'

When she returned, more jazz was playing, the music at times almost too low to be heard, and Rebus was back in his chair.

'What's that room across from the bathroom, John?'

'Well,' he said, pouring coffee, 'it used to be my daughter's, but now it's just full of junk. I never use it.'

'When did your wife and you split up?'

'Not as long ago as we should have. I mean that seriously.'

'How old is your daughter?' She sounded maternal now, domestic; no longer the acid single woman or the professional.

'Nearly twelve,' he said. 'Nearly twelve.'

'It's a difficult age.'

'Aren't they all.'

When the wine was finished and the coffee was down to its last half-cup, one or the other of them suggested bed. They exchanged sheepish smiles and ritual promises about not promising anything, and, the contract agreed and signed without words, went to the bedroom.

It all started well enough. They were mature, had played this game before too often to let the little fumblings and apologies get to them. Rebus was impressed by her agility and invention, and hoped that she was being impressed by his. She arched her spine to meet him, seeking the ultimate and unobtainable ingress.

'John,' pushing at him now.

'What is it?'

'Nothing. I'm just going to turn over, okay?'

He knelt up, and she turned her back to him, sliding her knees down the bed, clawing at the smooth wall with her fingertips, waiting. Rebus, in the slight pause, looked around at the room, the pale blue light shading his books, the edges of the mattress.

'Oh, a futon,' she had said, pulling her clothes off quickly. He had smiled in the silence.

. . .

He was losing it.

'Come on, John. Come on.'

He bent towards her, resting his face on her back. He had talked about books with Gordon Reeve when they had been captured. Talked endlessly, it seemed, reading to him from his memory. In close confinement, torture a closed door away. But they had endured. It was a mark of the training.

'John, oh, John.'

Gill raised herself up and turned her head towards his, seeking a kiss. Gill, Gordon Reeve, seeking something from him, something he couldn't give. Despite the training, despite the years of practice, the years of work and persistence.

'John?'

But he was elsewhere now, back inside the training camp, back trudging across a muddy field, the Boss screaming at him to speed up, back in that cell, watching a cockroach pace the begrimed floor, back in the helicopter, a bag over his head, the spray of the sea salty in his ears . . .

'John?'

She turned round now, awkwardly, concerned. She saw the tears about to start from his eyes. She held his head to her.

'Oh, John. It doesn't matter. Really, it doesn't.'

And a little later: 'Don't you like it that way?'

They lay together afterwards, he guiltily, and cursing the facts of his confusion and the fact that he had run out of cigarettes, she drowsily, caring still, whispering bits and pieces of her life-story to him.

After a while, Rebus forgot to feel guilty: there was nothing, after all, to feel guilty about. He felt merely the distinct lack of nicotine. And he remembered that he was seeing Sammy in six hours' time, and that her mother would instinctively know what he, John Rebus, had been up to these past few hours. She was cursed with a witch-like ability to see into the soul, and she had seen his occasional bouts of crying at very close quarters indeed. Partly, he supposed, that had been responsible for their break-up.

'What time is it, John?'

'Four. Maybe a little after.'

He slid his arm from beneath her and rose to leave the room.

'Do you want anything to drink?' he said.

'What did you have in mind?'

'Coffee maybe. It's hardly worth going to sleep now, but if you feel sleepy, don't mind me.'

'No, I'll take a cup of coffee.'

Rebus knew from her voice, from its slurred growliness, that she would be fast asleep by the time he reached the kitchen.

'Okay,' he said.

He made himself a cup of dark, sweet coffee and slumped into a chair with it. He turned on the living-room's small gas fire and began to read one of his books. He was seeing Sammy today, and his mind wandered from the story in front of him, a tale of intrigue which he could not remember having started. Sammy was nearly twelve. She had survived many years of danger, and now, for her, other dangers were imminent. The perverts in watch, the ogling old men, the teenage cockfighters, would be supplemented by the new urges of boys her age, and boys she already knew as friends would become sudden and forceful hunters. How would she cope with it? If her mother had anything to do with it, she would cope admirably, biting in a clinch and ducking on the ropes. Yes, she would survive without her father's advice and protection.

The kids were harder these days. He thought back to his own youth. He had been Mickey's big brother, fighting battles for the two of them, going home to watch his brother coddled by his father. He had pushed himself further into the cushions on the settee, hoping to disappear one day. Then they'd be sorry. Then they'd be sorry . . .

At seven-thirty he went through to the musky bedroom,

which smelt two parts sex to one part animal lair, and kissed Gill awake.

'It's time,' he said. 'Get up, I'll run you a bath.'

She smelt good, like a baby on a fireside towel. He admired the shapes of her twisted body as they awoke to the thin, watery sunlight. She had a good body all right. No real stretch-marks. Her legs unscarred. Her hair just tousled enough to be inviting

'Thanks.'

She had to be at HQ by ten in order to co-ordinate the next press release. There could be no rest. The case was still growing like a cancer. Rebus filled the bath, wincing at the rim of grime around it. He needed a cleaning-lady. Perhaps he could get Gill to do it.

Another unworthy thought, forgive me.

Which brought him to think of church-going. It was another Sunday, after all, and for weeks he had been promising himself that he would try again, would find another church in the city and would try all over again.

He hated congregational religion. He hated the smiles and the manners of the Sunday-dressed Scottish Protestant, the empha-sis on a communion not with God but with your neighbours. He had tried seven churches of varying denominations in Edinburgh, and had found none to be to his liking. He had tried sitting for two hours at home of a Sunday, reading the Bible and saying a prayer, but somehow that did not work either. He was caught; a believer outwith his belief. Was a personal faith good enough for God? Perhaps, but not *his* personal faith, which seemed to depend upon guilt and his feelings of hypocrisy whenever he sinned, a guilt assuaged only by public show.

'Is my bath ready, John?'

She re-tousled her hair, naked and confident, her glasses left behind in the bedroom. John Rebus felt his soul to be imperilled. Sod it, he thought, catching her around the hips. Guilt could wait. Guilt could always wait.

*

He had to mop up the bathroom floor afterwards, empirical evidence that Archimedes' displacement of water had been proved once again. The bath-water had flowed like milk and honey, and Rebus had nearly drowned.

Still, he felt better now.

'Lord, I am a poor sinner,' he whispered, as Gill dressed. She looked stern and efficient when she opened the front-door, almost as if she had been on a twenty-minute official visit.

'Can we fix a date?' he suggested.

'We can,' she replied, looking through her bag. Rebus was curious to know why women always did that, especially in films and thrillers, after they had been sleeping with a man. Did women suspect their sleeping partners of rifling their purses?

'But it might be difficult,' she continued, 'the case going the way it is. Let's just promise to keep in touch, okay?'

'Okay.'

He hoped that she took note of the dismay in his voice, the disappointment of the small boy at having his request denied.

They pecked a final kiss, mouths brittle by now, and then she was gone. Her scent remained, however, and he breathed it in deeply as he prepared for the day ahead. He found a shirt and a pair of trousers that didn't reek of tobacco, and these he put on slowly, admiring himself in the bathroom mirror, the soles of his feet damp, while he hummed a hymn.

Sometimes it was good to be alive. Sometimes.

11

Jim Stevens poured another three aspirin into his mouth and drank his orange juice. The ignominy of it, being seen in a Leith bar sucking on fruit juice, yet the idea of drinking even a half-pint of the rich, frothing beer made him feel nauseous. He had drunk far too much at that party; too much too quickly, and in too many combinations.

Leith was trying to improve itself. Someone somewhere had decided to give it a bit of a dust and a wash. It boasted French-style cafés and wine bars, studio flats, delicatessen. But it was still Leith, still the old port, an echo of its roaring, bustling past when Bordeaux wines would be unloaded by the gallon and sold on the streets from a horse and cart. If Leith retained nothing else, it would retain a port's mentality, and a port's traditional drinking dens.

'By Christ,' roared a voice behind him, 'the man drinks everything in doubles, even his soft drinks!'

A heavy fist, twice the dimensions of his own, landed on Stevens' back. The swarthy figure landed on a stool beside him. The hand stayed firmly where it was.

'Hello, Podeen,' said Stevens. He was starting to sweat in the heavy atmosphere of the saloon, and his heart was pounding: terminal hangover symptoms; he could smell the alcohol squeezing itself out of his pores.

'Lordy, James me boy, what the hell's that you're supping? Barman, get this man a whisky quick. He's wasting away on kiddies' juice!'

With a roar, Podeen took his hand off the reporter's back just long enough to relieve the pressure, before bringing it back down again in a stinging back-slap. Stevens felt his insides shudder rebelliously.

'Anything I can do for you today?' said Podeen, his voice much lower.

Big Podeen had been a sailor for twenty years, with the scars and nicks of a thousand ports on his body. How he made his money these days, Stevens did not wish to know. He did some bouncing for pubs on Lothian Road and dubious drinking-dens around Leith, but that would be the tip of his earnings iceberg. Podeen's fingers were so encrusted with dirt that he might have carved out the black economy single-handedly from the rotten, fertile soil beneath him.

'Not really, Big Man. No, I'm just mulling things over.'

'Get me a breakfast, will you? Double helpings of everything.'

The barman, almost saluting, went off to give the order.

'See,' said Podeen, 'you're not the only man who orders everything in doubles, eh, Jimmy?'

The hand was lifted from Stevens' back again. He grimaced, waiting for the slap, but the arm flopped onto the bar beside him instead. He sighed, audibly.

'Rough night last night was it, Jimmy?'

'I wish I could remember.'

He had fallen asleep in one of the bedrooms, very late in the evening. Then a couple had come in, and they had lifted him into the bathroom, depositing him in the bath. There he had slept for two hours, maybe three. He had awakened with a terrific stiffness in his neck, back, and legs. He had drunk some coffee, but not enough, never enough.

And had walked in the chilled morning air, chatting in a newsagent's shop with some taxi-drivers, sitting in the porter's cubby-hole of one of the big hotels on Princes Street, supping sweet tea and talking football with the bleary nightporter. But he had known he would end up down here, for this was his morning off, and he was back on the drugs case, his own little baby.

'Is there much stuff around at the moment, Big?'

'Oh, now, that depends what you're looking for, Jimmy. Word's out that you're getting to be a bit too nosy in every department. Best if you were sticking to the safe drugs. Keep away from the big stuff.'

'Is this a timely warning or a threat or what?' Stevens wasn't in the mood to be threatened, not when he had a Sunday morning hangover to sort out.

'It's a *friendly* warning, a warning from a friend.'

'Who's the friend, Big?'

'Me, you silly sod. Don't be so suspicious all the time. Listen, there's a little cannabis around, but that's about it. Nobody brings the stuff into Leith any more. They land it on the Fife coast, or up by Dundee. Places the Customs men have all but disappeared from. And that's the truth.'

'I know, Big, I know. But there *is* a delivery going on around here. I've seen it. I don't know what it is. Whether it's big stuff or not. But I've seen a handover. Very recently.'

'How recent?'

'Yesterday.'

'Where?'

'Calton Hill.'

Big Podeen shook his head.

'Then it's nothing at all to do with anyone or anything I know, Jimmy.'

Stevens knew the Big Man, knew him well. He gave out good information, but it was only what was given to him by people who wanted Stevens to get to know about something. So the heroin boys would come across, via Big, with information about cannabis dealing. If Stevens took the story up, chances were the cannabis dealers would be caught. And that left the territory and the demand to the heroin boys. It was clever stuff, ploy and counter-ploy. The stakes were high, too. But Stevens was a clever player himself. He knew that there was a tacit understanding that he was never to aim for the really big players, for that would mean aiming for the city's businessmen and bureaucrats, the titled landowners, the New Town's Mercedes owners.

And that would never be allowed. So he was fed tidbits, enough to keep the presses rolling, the tongues wagging about what a terrible place Edinburgh was becoming. Always a little, never the lot. Stevens understood all that. He had been playing the game so long he hardly knew sometimes what side he was on. In the end, it hardly mattered.

'You don't know about it?'

'Nothing, Jimmy. But I'll nose around. See what's doing. Listen, though, there's a new bar opened up by the Mackay showroom. Know the one I mean?'

Stevens nodded.

'Well,' went on Podeen, 'it's a bar at the front, but it's a brothel at the back. There's a wee cracker of a barmaid does her stuff of an afternoon, if you're interested.'

Stevens smiled. So a new boy was trying to move in, and the old boys, Podeen's ultimate employers, didn't like it. And so he, Jim Stevens, was being given enough information to close down the new boy if he liked. There was a nice headline-catcher in it certainly, but it was a one-day wonder.

Why didn't they just telephone the police anonymously? He thought he knew the answer to that one, though once it had puzzled him: they were playing the game by its old-fashioned rules, which meant no snitching, no grassing to the enemy. He was left to play the part of messenger-boy, but a messenger-boy with power built into the system. Just a little power, but more power than lay in doing things along the straight and narrow.

'Thanks, Big. I'll bear that in mind.'

The food arrived then, great piles of curled, shining bacon, two soft, near-transparent eggs, mushrooms, fried bread, beans. Stevens kept his eyes to the bar, suddenly interested in one of the beer-mats, damp still from Saturday night.

'I'm going across to my table to eat this, okay, Jimmy?'

Stevens could not believe his good luck.

'Oh, fine, Big Man, fine.'

'Cheers, then.'

And with that he was left alone, only the ghost of a smell remaining. He noticed that the barman was standing opposite him. His hand, shiny with grease, was held out.

'Two pounds sixty,' he said.

Stevens sighed. Put that one down to experience, he thought to himself as he paid, or to the hangover. The party had been worth it, however, for he had met John Rebus. And Rebus was friendly with Gill Templer. It was all becoming just a little confusing. But interesting too. Rebus was certainly interesting, though physically he did not resemble his brother in the slightest. The man had looked honest enough, but how did you tell a bent copper from the outside? It was the inside that was rotten. So, Rebus was seeing Gill Templer. He remembered the night they had spent together, and shuddered. That, surely, had been his nadir.

He lit a cigarette, his second of the day. His head was still clotted, but his stomach felt a little more composed. He might even be getting hungry. Rebus looked a tough nut, but not as tough as he would have been ten years ago. At this moment he was probably in bed with Gill Templer. The bastard. The lucky bastard. His stomach turned a tiny somersault of chilled jealousy. The cigarette felt good. It poured life and strength back into him, or seemed to. Yet he knew that it was scooping him out, too, tearing his guts to shreds of darkened meat. The hell with it. He smoked because without cigarettes he couldn't think. And he was thinking now.

'Hey, give me a double here will you?'

The barman came over.

'Orange juice again?'

Stevens looked at him disbelievingly.

'Don't be daft,' he said – 'whisky, Grouse if that's what's in the Grouse bottle.'

'We don't play those sorts of game here.'

'I'm glad to hear it.'

He drank the whisky and felt better. Then he began to feel

worse again. He went to the toilet, but the smell in there made him feel even worse. He held himself over the sink and brought up a few bubbles of liquid, retching loudly but emptily. He had to get off the booze. He had to get off the ciggies. They were killing him, yet they were the only things keeping him alive.

He walked over to Big Podeen's table, sweating, feeling older than his years.

'That was a good breakfast, that was,' said the hulk of a man, his eyes gleaming like a child's.

Stevens sat down beside him.

'What's the word on bent coppers?' he asked.

12

'Hello, daddy.'

She was eleven, but looked and spoke and smiled older: eleven going on twenty-one. That was what living with Rhona had done to his daughter. He pecked her cheek, thinking back to Gill's leavetaking. There was perfume around her, and a hint of make-up on her eyes.

He could kill Rhona.

'Hello, Sammy,' he said.

'Mummy says that I'm to be called Samantha now that I'm growing up so quickly, but I suppose it's all right for *you* to call me Sammy.'

'Oh, well, mummy knows best, Samantha.'

He cast a look towards the retreating figure of his wife, her body pressed, pushed and prodded into a shape attainable only with the aid of some super-strong girdle. She was not, he was relieved to find, wearing as well as their occasional telephone conversations would have had him believe. She stepped into her car now, never looking back. It was a small and expensive model, but had a sizeable dent in one side. Rebus blessed that dent.

He recalled that, making love, he had gloried in her body, in the soft flesh – the padding, as she had called it – of her thighs and her back. Today she had looked at him with cold eyes, filled with a cloud of unknowing, and had seen in his eyes the gleam of sexual satisfaction. Then she had turned on her heels. So it was true: she could still see into his heart. Ah, but she had failed to see into his soul. She had missed that most vital organ completely.

'What do you want to do then?'

They were standing at the entrance to Princes Street Gardens, adjacent to the tourist haunts of Edinburgh. A few people wandered past the closed shops of a Princes Street Sunday, while others sat on benches in the gardens, feeding crumbs to the pigeons and the Canadian squirrels or else reading the heavy-printed Sunday papers. The Castle reared above them, its flag flying briskly in the all-too-typical breeze. The Gothic missile of the Scott Monument pointed religious believers in the right direction, but few of the tourists who snapped it with their expensive Japanese cameras seemed at all interested in the structure's symbolic connotations, never mind its reality, just so long as they had some snaps of it to show off to their friends back home. These tourists spent so much time photographing things that they never actually *saw* anything, unlike the young people milling around, who were too busy enjoying life to be bothered capturing false impressions of it.

'What do you want to do then?'

The tourist side of his capital city. They were never interested in the housing-estates around this central husk. They never ventured into Pilton or Niddrie or Oxgangs to make an arrest in a piss-drenched tenement; they were not moved by Leith's pushers and junkies, the deft-handed corruption of the city gents, the petty thefts of a society pushed so far into material-ism that stealing was the only answer to what they thought of as their needs. And they were almost certainly unaware (they were not, after all, here to read local newspapers and watch local TV) of Edinburgh's newest media star, the child murderer the police could not catch, the murderer who was leading the forces of law and order a merry dance without a clue or a lead or a cat in hell's chance of finding him until he slipped up. He pitied Gill her job. He pitied himself. He pitied the city, right down to its crooks and bandits, its whores and gamblers, its perpetual losers and winners.

'So what do you want to do?'

His daughter shrugged her shoulders.

'I don't know. Walk maybe? Go for a pizza? See a film?'
They walked.

John Rebus had met Rhona Phillips just after joining the police.
He had suffered a nervous breakdown just prior to his joining
the force (*why did you leave the Army, John?*) and had recuper-
ated in a fishing-village on the Fife coast, though he had never
told Michael of his presence in Fife during that time.

On his first holiday from police-work, his first proper *holiday*
in years, the others having been spent on courses or working
towards examinations, Rebus had returned to that fishing-
village, and there had met Rhona. She was a school-teacher,
already with a brutally short and unhappy marriage behind her.
In John Rebus she saw a strong and able husband, someone
who would not flinch in a fight; someone she could care for,
too, however, since his strength failed to conceal an inner
fragility. She saw that he was haunted still by his years in the
Army, and especially by his time in 'special services'. He would
awake crying some nights, and sometimes would weep as he
made love, weeping silently, the tears falling hard and slow on
her breasts. He would not speak about it much, and she had
never pushed him. She was aware that he had lost a friend
during his training days. She understood that much, and he
appealed to the child in her and to the mother. He seemed
perfect. Too, too perfect.

He was not. He should never have married. They lived
happily enough, she teaching English in Edinburgh until
Samantha was born. Then, however, niggling fights and power-
plays had turned into sourer, unabated periods of resentment
and suspicion. Was she seeing another man, a teacher at her
school? Was he seeing another woman when he claimed to be
involved in his numerous double-shifts? Was she taking drugs
without his knowledge? Was he taking bribes without hers? In
fact, the answer to all of these suspicions was no, but that did
not seem to be what was at stake in any case. Rather,
something larger was looming, yet neither could perceive the

inevitability of it until too late, and they would cuddle up and make things right between them over and over again, as though in some morality-tale or soap-opera. There was, they agreed, the child to think of.

The child, Samantha, had become the young woman, and Rebus felt his eyes straying appreciatively and guiltily (yet again) over her as they walked through the gardens, around the Castle, and up towards the ABC cinema on Lothian Road. She was not beautiful, for only women could be that, but she was growing towards beauty with a confident inevitability which was breathtaking in itself, and horrifying. He was, after all, her father. There had to be some feelings there. It went with the territory.

'Do you want me to tell you about Mummy's new boy-friend?'

'You know damn well I do.'

She giggled; still something of the girl left in her then, and yet even a giggle seemed different in her now, seemed more controlled, more womanly.

'He's a poet, supposedly, but really he hasn't had a book out or anything yet. His poems are crap, too, but Mummy won't tell him that. She thinks the sun shines out of his you-know-where.'

Was all this 'adult' talk supposed to impress him? He supposed so.

'How old is he?' Rebus asked, flinching at his suddenly revealed vanity.

'I don't know. Twenty maybe.'

He stopped flinching and started to reel. Twenty. She was cradle-snatching now. My God. What effect was all this having on Sammy? On Samantha, the pretend adult? He dreaded to think, but he was no psychoanalyst; that was Rhona's department, or once had been.

'Honest though, Dad, he's an *awful* poet. I've done better stuff than his in my essays at school. I go to the big school after the summer. It'll be funny to go to the school where Mum works.'

'Yes, won't it.' Rebus had found something niggling him. A poet, aged twenty. 'What's this boy's name?' he asked.

'Andrew,' she said, 'Andrew Anderson. Doesn't that sound funny? He's nice really, but he's a bit weird.'

Rebus cursed under his breath: Anderson's son, the dreaded Anderson's itinerant poet son was shacked up with Rebus's wife. What an irony! He didn't know whether to laugh or cry. Laughter seemed marginally more appropriate.

'What are you laughing at, Daddy?'

'Nothing, Samantha. I'm just happy, that's all. What were you saying?'

'I was saying that Mum met him at the library. We go there a lot. Mum likes the literature books, but I like books about romances and adventures. I can never understand the books Mum reads. Did you read the same books as her when you were . . . before you . . . ?'

'Yes, yes we did. But I could never understand them either, so don't worry about it. I'm glad that you read a lot. What's this library like?'

'It's really big, but a lot of tramps go there to sleep and spend a lot of time. They get a book and sit down and just fall asleep. They smell awful!'

'Well, you don't need to go near them, do you? Best to let them keep themselves to themselves.'

'Yes, Daddy.' Her tone was slightly reproachful, warning him that he was giving fatherly advice and that such advice was unnecessary.

'Fancy seeing a film then, do you?'

The cinema, however, was not open, so they went to an ice-cream parlour at Tollcross. Rebus watched Samantha scoop five colours of ice-cream from a Knickerbocker Glory. She was still at the stick-insect stage, eating without putting on an ounce of weight. Rebus was conscious of his sagging waistband, a stomach pampered and allowed to roam as it pleased. He sipped cappuccino (without sugar) and watched from the corner of his eye as a group of boys at another table looked towards his daughter and him, whispering and sniggering. They pushed back their hair and smoked their cigarettes as though sucking on life itself. He would have arrested them for self-afflicted growth-stunting had Sammy not been there.

Also, he envied them their cigarettes. He did not smoke when with Sammy: she did not like him smoking. Her mother also, once upon a time, had screamed at him to stop, and had hidden his cigarettes and lighter, so that he had made secret little nests of cigarettes and matches all around the house. He had smoked on regardless, laughing in victory when he sauntered into the room with another lit cigarette between his lips, Rhona screeching at him to put the bloody thing out, chasing him around the furniture, her hands flapping to knock the incendiary from his mouth.

Those had been happy times, times of loving conflict.

'How's school?'

'It's okay. Are you involved in the murder case?'

'Yes.' God, he could murder for a cigarette, could tear a young male head from its body.

'Will you catch him?'

'Yes.'

'What does he do to the girls, Daddy?' Her eyes, trying to seem casual, examined the near-empty ice-cream glass very scrupulously.

'He doesn't do anything to them.'

'Just murders them?' Her lips were pale. Suddenly she was very much his child, his daughter, very much in need of protection. Rebus wanted to put his arms around her, to comfort her, to tell her that the big bad world was out there, not in here, that she was safe.

'That's right,' he said instead.

'I'm glad that's all he does.'

The boys were whistling now, trying to attract her attention. Rebus felt his face growing red. On another day, any day other than this, he would march up to them and ram the law into their chilled little faces. But he was off-duty. He was enjoying an afternoon out with his daughter, the freakish result of a single grunted climax, that climax which had seen a lucky sperm, crawling through the ooze, make it all the way to the winning-post. Doubtless Rhona would already be reaching over for her book of the day, her literature. She would prise the still, spent body of her lover from her without a word being passed between them. Was her mind on her books all the time? Perhaps. And he, the lover, would feel deflated and empty, a vacant space, but suddenly as if no form of transference had taken place. That was her victory.

And then he would scream at her with a kiss. The scream of longing, of his solitary.

Let me out. Let me out . . .

'Come on, let's get out of here.'

'Okay.'

And as they passed the table of hankering boys, their faces full of barely restrained lust, jabbering like monkeys, Samantha smiled at one of them. *She smiled at one of them.*

Rebus, sucking in fresh air, wondered what his world was coming to. He wondered whether his reason for believing in another reality behind this one might not be because the everyday was so frightening and so very sad. If this were all there was, then life was the sorriest invention of all time. He could kill those boys, and he wanted to smother his daughter, to protect her from that which she wanted – and would get. He realised that he had nothing to say to her, and that those boys did; that he had nothing in common with her save blood, while they had everything in common with her. The skies were dark as Wagnerian opera, dark as a murderer's thoughts. Darkening like similes, while John Rebus's world fell apart.

'It's time,' she said, by his side yet so much bigger than him, so much more full of life. 'It's time.'

And indeed it was.

'We better hurry,' said Rebus, 'it's going to rain.'

*

He felt tired, and recalled that he had not slept, that he had been involved in strenuous labour throughout the short night. He took a taxi back to the flat – sod the expense – and crawled up the winding stairs to his front door. The smell of cats was overpowering. Inside his door, a letter, unstamped, awaited him. He swore out loud. The bastard was everywhere, everywhere and yet invisible. He ripped open the letter and read.

YOU'RE GETTING NOWHERE. NOWHERE. ARE YOU? SIGNED

But there was no signature, not in writing anyway. But inside the envelope, like some child's plaything, lay the piece of knotted twine.

'Why are you doing this, Mister Knot?' said Rebus, fingering the twine. 'And just what are you doing?'

Inside, the flat was like a fridge: the pilot-light had blown out again.

PART THREE

Knot

13

The media, sensing that the 'Edinburgh Strangler' was not about to vanish in the night, took the story by its horns and created a monster. TV crews moved into some of the better hotel rooms in the city, and the city was happy enough to have them, it being not quite the tourist season yet.

Tom Jameson was as astute an editor as any, and he had a team of four reporters working on the story. He could not help noticing, however, that Jim Stevens was not on his best form. He seemed uninterested – never a good sign in a journalist. Jameson was worried. Stevens was the best he had, a household name. He would speak to him about it soon.

As the case grew along with the interest in it, John Rebus and Gill Templer became confined to communicating by telephone and via the occasional chance meeting in or around HQ. Rebus hardly saw his old station now. He was strictly a murder-case victim himself, and was told to think about nothing else during his waking hours. He thought about everything else: about Gill, about the letters, about his car's inability to pass its MOT. And all the time he watched Anderson, father of Rhona's lover, watched him as he grew ever more frantic for a motive, a lead, anything. It was almost a pleasure to watch the man in action.

As to the letters, Rebus had pretty much discounted his wife and daughter. A slight mark on Knot's last missive had been checked by the forensic boys (for the price of a pint) and had turned out to be blood. Had the man nicked his finger while cutting the twine? It was yet another small mystery. Rebus's life was full of mysteries, not the least of which was where his ten legitimate daily cigarettes went. He would open his packet of a late afternoon, count the contents, and find that he was supposed to have smoked all ten of his ration already. It was absurd; he could hardly remember smoking one of the alloted ten, never mind all of them. Yet a count of the butts in his ashtray would produce empirical evidence enough to withstand any denials on his part. Bloody strange though. It was as though he were shutting out a part of his waking life.

He was stationed in the HQ's Incident Room at the moment, while Jack Morton, poor sod, was on door-to-door. From his vantage point he could see how Anderson was running the shambles. It was little wonder the man's son had turned out to be less than bright. Rebus also had to deal with the many phone-calls – from those of the trying-to-be-helpfuls to those of the psychic-cranks-who-want-to-confess – and with the interviews carried out in the building itself at all hours of the day and night. There were hundreds of these, all to be filed and put into some kind of order of importance. It was a huge task, but there was always the chance that a lead would come from it, so he was not allowed to slack.

In the hectic, sweaty canteen he smoked cigarette number eleven, lying to himself that it was from the next day's ration, and read the daily paper. They were straining for new, shocked adjectives now, having exhausted their thesauruses. The appalling, mad, evil crimes of The Strangler. This insane, evil, sex-crazed man. (They did not seem to mind that the killer had never sexually assaulted his victims.) Gymslip Maniac! 'What are our police doing? All the technology in the world cannot replace the reassurance offered by bobbies on the beat. WE NEED THEM NOW.' That was from James Stevens, our crime correspondent. Rebus remembered the stocky drunk man from the party. He recalled the look on Stevens' face when he had been told Rebus's name. That was strange. Everything was bloody strange. Rebus put down the newspaper. Reporters. Again, he wished Gill well in her job. He studied the blurred photograph on the front of the tabloid. It showed a crop-haired, unintelligent child. She was grinning nervously, as though snapped at a moment's notice. There was a slight, endearing gap between her front teeth. Poor Nicola Turner, aged twelve, a pupil at one of the southside's comprehensive schools. She had no attachments to either of the other dead girls. There were no visible links between them, and what was more, the killer had moved up a year, choosing a High School kid this time. So there was to be no regularity about his choice of age-groups. The randomness continued unabated. It was driving Anderson nuts.

But Anderson would never admit that the killer had his beloved police force tied in knots. Tied in absolute knots. Yet there *had* to be clues. There had to be. Rebus drank his coffee and felt his head spin. He was feeling like the detective in a cheap thriller, and wished that he could turn to the last page and stop all his confusion, all the death and the madness and the spinning in his ears.

Back in the Incident Room, he gathered together reports of phone-calls that had come in since he had left for his break. The telephonists were working flat out, and near them a telex-machine was almost constantly printing out some new piece of information thought useful to the case and sent on by other forces throughout the country.

Anderson pushed his way through the noise as if swimming in treacle.

'A car is what we need, Rebus. A car. I want all the sightings of men driving away with children collated and on my desk in an hour. I want that bastard's car.'

'Yes, sir.'

And he was off again, wading through treacle deep enough to drown any normal human being. But not Indestructible Anderson, impervious to any danger. That made him a liability, thought Rebus, sifting through the piles of paper on his desk, which were meant to be in some system of order.

Cars. Anderson wanted cars, and cars he would have. There were swear-on-a-Bible descriptions of a man in a blue Escort, a white Capri, a purple Mini, a yellow BMW, a silver TR7, a converted ambulance, an ice-cream van (the telephone-caller sounding Italian and wishing to remain anonymous), and a great big Rolls-Royce with personalized number plates. Yes, let's put them all into the computer and have it run a check of every blue Escort, white Capri, and Rolls-Royce in Britain. And with all that information at our fingertips . . . then what? More door-to-door, more gathering of telephone-calls and inter-views, more paperwork and bullshit. Never mind, Anderson would swim through it all, indomitable amidst all the craziness of his personal world, and at the end of it all he would come out looking clean and shiny and untouchable, like an advertise-ment for washing powder. Three cheers.

Hip hip

Rebus had not enjoyed bullshit during his Army days either, and there had been plenty of it then. But he had been a good soldier, a very good soldier, when finally they had got down to soldiering. But then, in a fit of madness, he had applied to join the Special Air Service, and there had been very little bullshit there, and an incredible amount of savagery. They had made him run from the railway station to the camp behind a sergeant in his jeep. They had tortured him with twenty-hour marches, brutal instructors, the works. And when Gordon Reeve and he had made the grade, the SAS had tested them just that little bit further, just that inch too far, confining them, interrogating them, starving them, poisoning them, and all for a little piece of worthless information, a few words that would show they had cracked. Two naked, shivering animals with sacks tied over their heads, lying together to keep warm.

'I want that list in an hour, Rebus,' called Anderson, walking past again. He would have his list. He would have his pound of flesh.

Jack Morton arrived back, looking foot-weary and not at all amused with life. He slouched across to Rebus, a sheaf of papers under his arm, a cigarette in the other hand.

'Look at this,' he said, lifting his leg. Rebus saw the foot-long gash in the material.

'What happened to you then?'

'What do you think? I got chased by a great fucking alsatian, that's what happened to me. Will I get a penny for this? Will I hell.'

'You could try claiming for it anyway.'

'What's the point? I'd just be made to look stupid.'

Morton dragged a chair across to the table.

'What are you working on?' he asked, seating himself with visible relief.

'Cars. Lots of them.'

'Fancy a drink later on?'

Rebus looked at his watch, considering.

'Might do, Jack. Thing is, I'm hoping to make a date for tonight.'

'With the ravishing Inspector Templer?'

'How did you know that?' Rebus was genuinely surprised.

'Come on, John. You can't keep that sort of thing a secret – not from policemen. Better watch your step, mind. Rules and regulations, you know.'

'Yes, I know. Does Anderson know about this?'

'Has he said anything?'

'No.'

'Then he can't, can he?'

'You'd make a good policeman, son. You're wasted in this job.'

'You're telling me, dad.'

Rebus busied himself with lighting cigarette number twelve. It was true, you couldn't keep anything secret in a police station, not from the lower ranks anyway. He hoped Anderson and the Chief wouldn't find out about it though.

'Any luck with the door-to-door?' he asked.

'What do you think?'

'Morton, you have an annoying habit of answering a question with another question.'

'Have I? It must be all this work then, spending my days asking questions, mustn't it?'

Rebus examined his cigarettes. He found he was smoking number thirteen. This was becoming ridiculous. Where had number twelve gone?

'I'll tell you, John, there's nothing to be had out there, not a sniff of a lead. No one's seen anything, no one knows anything. It's almost like a conspiracy.'

'Maybe that's what it is then, a conspiracy.'

'And has it been established that all three murders were the work of a single individual?'

'Yes.'

The Chief Inspector did not believe in wasting words, especially with the press. He sat like a rock behind the table, his hands clasped before him, Gill Templer on his right. Her glasses – an affectation really, her vision was near-perfect – were in her bag. She never wore them while on duty, unless the occasion demanded it. Why had she worn them to the party? They were like jewellery to her. She found it interesting, too, to gauge different reactions towards her when she was and was not wearing them. When she explained this to her friends, they looked at her askance as if she were joking. Perhaps it all went back to her first true love, who had told her that girls who wore glasses seemed, in his experience, to be the best fucks. That had been fifteen years ago, but she still saw the look on his face, the smile, the glint. She saw, too, her own reaction – shock at his use of the word 'fuck'. She could smile at that now. These days she swore as much as her male colleagues; again gauging their reaction. Everything was a game to Gill Templer, everything but the job. She had not become an Inspector through luck or looks, but through hard, efficient work and the will to climb as high as they would let her go. And now she sat with her Chief Inspector, who was a token presence at these gatherings. It was Gill who made up the handouts, who briefed the Chief Inspector, who handled the media afterwards, and they all knew it. A Chief Inspector might add weight of seniority to the proceedings, but Gill Templer it was who could give the journalists their 'extras', the useful snippets left unsaid.

Nobody knew that better than Jim Stevens. He sat to the back of the room, smoking without removing the cigarette from his mouth once. He took little of the Chief Inspector's words in. He could wait. Still, he jotted down a sentence or two for future use. He was still a newsman after all. Old habits never died. The photographer, a keen teenager, nervously changing lenses every few minutes, had departed with his roll of film. Stevens looked around for someone he might have a drink with later on. They were all here. All the old boys from the Scottish press, and the English correspondents too. Scottish, English, Greek – it didn't matter, pressmen always looked like nothing other than pressmen. Their faces were robust, they smoked, their shirts were a day or two old. They did not look well-paid, yet were extremely well-paid, and with more fringe benefits than most. But they worked for their money, worked hard at building up contacts, squeezing into nooks and crannies, stepping on toes. He watched Gill Templer. What would she know about John Rebus? And would she be willing to tell? They were still friends after all, her and him. Still friends.

Maybe not good friends, certainly not good friends – though he had tried. And now she and Rebus . . . Wait until he nailed that bastard, if there *was* anything there to nail. Of course there was something there to nail. He could sense it. Then her eyes would be opened, truly opened. Then they would see what they would see. He was already preparing the headline. Something to do with 'Brothers in Law – Brothers in Crime!' Yes, that had a nice ring to it. The Rebus brothers put behind bars, and all his own work. He turned his attention back to the murder case. But it was all too easy, too easy to sit down and write about police inefficiency, about the conjectured maniac. Still, it was bread and butter for the moment. And there was always Gill Templer to stare at.

*

'Gill!'

He caught her as she was getting into her car.

'Hello, Jim.' Cold, businesslike.

'Listen, I just wanted to apologise for my behaviour at the party.' He was out of breath after a brief jog across the car park, and the words came slowly from his burning chest. 'I mean, I was a bit pissed. Anyway, sorry.'

But Gill knew him too well, knew that this was merely a prelude to a question or request. Suddenly she felt a little sorry for him, sorry for his fair thick hair which needed a wash, sorry for his short, stocky – she had once thought it powerful – body, for the way he trembled now and again as though cold. But the pity soon wore off. It had been a hard day.

'Why wait till now to tell me? You could have said something at Sunday's briefing.'

He shook his head.

'I didn't make Sunday's briefing. I was a bit hungover. You must have noticed I wasn't there?'

'Why should I have noticed that? Plenty of other people were there, Jim.'

That cut him, but he let it pass.

'Well, anyway,' he said, 'sorry. Okay?'

'Fine.' She made to step into her car.

'Can I buy you a drink or something? To cement the apology, so to speak.'

'Sorry, Jim, I'm busy.'

'Meeting that man Rebus?'

'Maybe.'

'Look after yourself, Gill. That one might not be what he seems.'

She straightened up again.

'I mean,' said Stevens, 'just take care, all right?'

He wouldn't say any more just yet. Having planted a seed of suspicion, he would give it time to grow. Then he would question her closely, and perhaps then she would be willing to tell. He turned away from her and walked, hands in pockets, towards the Sutherland Bar.

14

At Edinburgh's Main Public Lending Library, a large, unstuffy old building sandwiched between a bookshop and a bank, the tramps were settling down for a day's snoozing. They came here, as though waiting out fate itself, to see through the few days of absolute poverty before their next amount of state benefit was due. This money they would then spend in a day (perhaps, if stretched, two days) of festivity: wine, women, and songs to an unappreciative public.

The attitudes of the library staff towards these down-and-outs ranged from the immensely intolerant (usually voiced by the older members of staff) to the sadly reflective (the youngest librarians). It was, however, a public library, and as long as the worldly-wise travellers picked up a book at the start of the day there was nothing that could be done about them, unless they became rowdy, in which case a security-man was quickly on the scene.

So they slept in the comfortable seats, sometimes frowned upon by those who could not help wondering if this was what Andrew Carnegie had in mind when he put up the finance for the first public libraries all those years ago. The sleepers did not mind these stares, and they dreamed on, though nobody bothered to inquire what it was they dreamed of, and no one thought them important.

They were not, however, allowed into the children's section of the library. Indeed, any browsing adult not dragging a child in tow was looked at askance in the children's section, and especially since the murders of those poor wee girls. The librarians talked about it amongst themselves. Hanging was the answer; they were agreed on that. And indeed, hanging was being discussed again in Parliament, as happens whenever a mass murderer emerges out of the shadows of civilized Britain. The most oft-repeated statement amongst the people of Edinburgh, however, did not concern hanging at all. It was put cogently by one of the librarians: 'But *here*, in Edinburgh! It's unthinkable.' Mass murderers belonged to the smoky back streets of the South and the Midlands, not to Scotland's picture-postcard city. Listeners nodded, horrified and sad that this was something they all had to face, each and every Morningside lady in her faded hat of gentility, every thug who roamed the streets of the housing-estates, every lawyer, banker, broker, shop-assistant and vendor of evening newspapers. Vigilante groups had been hastily set up and just as hastily disbanded by the swiftly reacting police. This was not, said the Chief Constable, the answer. Be vigilant by all means, but the law was never to be taken into one's own hands. He rubbed together his own gloved hands as he spoke, and some newspapermen wondered if his subconscious were not washing its Freudian hands of the whole affair. Jim Stevens' editor decided to put it thus: LOCK UP YOUR DAUGHTERS!, and left it pretty much at that.

Indeed, the daughters *were* being locked up. Some of them were being kept away from school by their parents, or were under heavy escort all the way there and all the way back home, with an additional check on their welfare at lunch-time. The children's section of the Main Lending Library had grown deathly quiet of late, so that the librarians there had little to do with their days except talk about hanging and read the lurid speculations in the British press.

The British press had cottoned onto the fact that Edinburgh had a rather less than genteel past. They ran reminders of Deacon Brodie (the inspiration, it was said, behind Stevenson's Jekyll & Hyde), Burke and Hare, and anything else that came to light in their researches, right down to the ghosts that haunted a suspicious number of the city's Georgian houses. These tales kept the imaginations of the librarians alive while there was a lull in their duties. They made sure each to buy a different paper, so that they could glean as many pieces of information as possible, but were disillusioned by how often journalists seemed to swap a central story between them, so that an identical piece would appear in two or three different papers. It was as if a conspiracy of writers was at work.

Some children, however, did still come to the library. The vast majority of these were accompanied by mother, father, or minder, but one or two still came alone. This evidence of the foolhardiness of some parents and their offspring further disturbed the faint-hearted librarians, who would ask the children, appalled, where their mothers and fathers were.

Samantha rarely came to the library's children's section, preferring older books, but she did so today to get away from her mother. A male librarian came over to her as she pored over the most childish stuff.

'Are you here on your own, dear?' he said.

Samantha recognised him. He'd been working here ever since she could remember.

'My mum's upstairs,' she said.

'I'm glad to hear it. Stick close to her, that's my advice.'

She nodded, inwardly fuming. Her mother had given her a similar lecture only five minutes before. She wasn't a child, but no one seemed prepared to accept that. When the librarian went over to talk with another girl, Samantha took out the book she wanted and gave her ticket to the old lady librarian with the dyed hair, whom the children called Mrs Slocum. Then she hurried up the steps to the library's reference section, where her mother was busy looking for a critical study of George Eliot. George Eliot, her mother had told her, was a woman who had written books of tremendous realism and psychological depth at a time when men were supposed to be the great realists and psychologists, and women were supposed to be for nothing but the housework. That was why she had been forced to call herself 'George' to get published.

To counter these attempts at indoctrination, Samantha had brought from the children's section an illustrated book about a boy who flies away on a giant cat and has adventures in a fantasy land beyond his dreams. That, she hoped, would piss her mother off. In the reference section, a lot of people sat at desks, coughing, their coughs echoing around the hushed hall. Her mother, glasses perched on her nose, looking very much like a schoolteacher, argued with a librarian about some book she had ordered. Samantha walked between the rows of desks, glancing at what people were reading and writing. She wondered why people spent so much time reading books when there were other things to be doing. She wanted to travel round the world. Perhaps then she would be ready to sit in dull rooms poring over these old books. But not until then.

He watched her as she moved up and down the rows of desks. He stood with his face half to her, looking as if he were studying a shelf of books on angling. She wasn't looking around her though. There was no danger. She was in her own little world, a world of her own design and her own rules. That was fine. All the girls were like that. But this one was with someone. He could see that. He took a book from the shelf and flicked through it. One chapter caught his eye, and turned his thoughts away from Samantha. It was a chapter dealing with fly-knotting. There were lots of designs for knots. Lots of them.

15

Another briefing. Rebus enjoyed the briefings now, for there was always the possibility that Gill would be present, and that afterwards they would be able to go for a cup of coffee together. Last night they had eaten late at a restaurant, but she had been tired and had looked at him strangely, quizzing him a little more even than usual with her eyes, not wearing her spectacles at first, but then slipping them on halfway through the meal.

'I want to see what I'm eating.'

But he knew she could see well enough. The glasses were a psychological strengthener. They protected her. Perhaps he was just being paranoid. Perhaps she had been tired merely. But he suspected something more, though he could not think what. Had he insulted her in some way? Snubbed her without realising? He was tired himself. They went to their separate flats and lay awake, wanting not to be alone. Then he dreamed the dream of the kiss, and awoke to the usual result, the sweat tainting his forehead, his lips moist. Would he awake to another letter? To another murder?

Now he felt lousy from lack of sleep. But still he enjoyed the briefing, and not just because of Gill. There was the inkling of a lead at long last, and Anderson was anxious to have it substantiated.

'A pale blue Ford Escort,' said Anderson. Behind him sat the Chief Superintendent, whose presence seemed to be unnerving the Chief Inspector. 'A pale blue Ford Escort.' Anderson wiped his brow. 'We have reports of such a car being seen in the Haymarket district on the evening when victim number one's body was found, and we have two sightings of a man and a girl, the girl apparently asleep, in such a car on the night that victim number three went missing.' Anderson's eyes came up from the document before him to gaze, it seemed, into the eyes of every officer present. 'I want this made top priority, or better. I want to know the ownership details of every blue Ford Escort in the Lothians, and I want that information *sooner* than possible. Now I know you've been working flat out as it is, but with a little extra push we can nail chummy before he does any more killing. To this end, Inspector Hartley has drawn up a roster. If your name's on it, drop what you're doing and get busy on tracing this car. Any questions?'

Gill Templer was scribbling notes in her tiny note-pad, perhaps concocting a story for the press. Would they want to release this? Probably not, not straight away. They would wait first to see if anything came of the initial search. If nothing did, then the public would be asked to help. Rebus didn't fancy this at all: gathering ownership details, trekking out to the suburbs, and mass-interviewing the suspects, trying to 'nose' whether they were probable or possible suspects, then perhaps a second interview. No, he did not fancy this at all. He fancied accompanying Gill Templer back to his cave and making love to her. Her back was all he could see of her from his present vantage point by the door. He had been last into the room yet again, having stayed at the pub a little longer than anticipated. It had been a prior appointment, lunch (liquid) with Jack Morton. Morton told him about the slow, steady progress of the outdoor inquiry: four-hundred people interviewed, whole families checked and rechecked, the usual cranks and amoral groups examined. And not a jot of actual light had been thrown on the case.

But now they had a car, or at least thought they did. The evidence was tenuous, but it was there, the likeness of a fact, and that was something. Rebus felt a little proud of his own part in the investigation, for it had been his painstaking cross-referencing of sightings which had thrown up this slender link. He wanted to tell Gill all about it, then arrange a rendezvous for later in the week. He wanted to see her again, to see anybody again, for his flat was becoming a prison-cell. He would slouch home of a late evening or early morning, tip onto his bed, and sleep, not bothering these days to tidy or to read or to buy (or even steal) any foodstuffs. He had neither the time nor the energy. Instead, he ate from kebab-houses and chip-shops, early-morning bakeries and chocolate-dispensers. His face was becoming paler than usual, and his stomach groaned as though there were no skin left to distend. He still shaved and put on a tie, as a matter of necessary propriety, but that was about it. Anderson had noticed that his shirts were not as clean as they might have been, but had said nothing so far. For one thing, Rebus was in his good books, begetter of the lead, and for another, anyone could see that in Rebus's present mood he was likely to take a swing at any detractor.

The meeting was breaking up. There were no questions in anyone's mind except the obvious one: when do we start cracking up? Rebus hovered just outside the door, waiting for Gill. She came out in the last group, in quiet conversation with Wallace and Anderson. The Superintendent had his arm around her waist playfully, gently ushering her out of the room. Rebus glared at the group, this motley crew of superior officers. He watched Gill's face, but she did not seem to notice him. Rebus felt himself slide back down the snake on the board, right down to the bottom line again, back into the heap. So this was love. Who was kidding who?

As the group of three walked up the corridor, Rebus stood there like a jilted teenager and cursed and cursed and cursed.

He'd been let down again. Let down.

Don't let me down, John. Please.

Please Please Please

And a screaming in his memory . . .

He felt dizzy, his ears ringing with the sea. Staggering a little, he caught hold of the wall, trying to take comfort in its solidity, but it seemed to be throbbing. He breathed hard, thinking back to his days on the rock-strewn beach, recovering from his breakdown. The sea had been in his ears then, too. The floor adjusted itself slowly. People walked by quizzically, but no one stopped to help. Sod them all. And sod Gill Templer too. He could manage on his own. He could manage on his own, God save him. He would be okay. All he needed was a cigarette and some coffee.

But really he needed their pats on the back, their congratulations on a job well done, their acceptance. He needed someone to assure him that it was all going to be all right.

That *he* would be all right.

That evening, a couple of after-duty drinks under his belt already, he decided to make a night of it. Morton had to go off on some errand, but that was okay, too. Rebus didn't need company. He walked along Princes Street, breathing in the evening's promise. He was a free man after all, just as free as any of the kids hanging about outside the hamburger bar. They preened and joked and waited, waiting for what? He knew that: waiting for the time to come when they could go home and sleep into tomorrow. He too was waiting, in his own way. Killing time.

In the Rutherford Arms he met a couple of drinkers whom he knew from evenings like this just after Rhona had left him. He drank with them for an hour, sucking at the beer as though it were mother's milk. They talked about football, about horse-racing, about their jobs, and the whole scene brought tranquillity to Rebus. It was a normal evening's conversation, and he embraced it greedily, throwing in his own snippets of news. But enough was as good as a feast, and he walked briskly, drunkenly out of the bar, leaving his friends with promises of another time, edging his way down the street towards Leith.

Jim Stevens, sitting at the bar, watched in the mirror as Michael Rebus left his drink on his table and went to the toilet. A few seconds later, the mystery man followed him inside, having been sitting at another table. It looked as though they were meeting to discuss the next swap-over, both seeming too casual actually to be carrying anything incriminating. Stevens smoked his cigarette, waiting. In less than a minute, Rebus reappeared, coming up to the bar for another drink.

John Rebus, pushing through the pub's swing-doors, could not believe his eyes. He slapped his brother on the shoulder.

'Mickey! What are you doing here?'

Michael Rebus nearly died at that moment. His heart leapt high into his throat, causing him to cough.

'Just having a drink, John.' But he looked guilty as hell, he was sure of that. 'You gave me a fright,' he went on, trying to smile, 'hitting me like that.'

'A brotherly slap, that's all it was. What are you drinking?'

While the brothers were in conversation, the man slipped out of the toilet and walked out of the bar, his eyes never glancing to left or right. Stevens watched him go, but had other things on his mind now. He could not let the policeman see him. He turned away from the bar, as if searching for a face amongst the people at the tables. Now he was sure. The policeman had to be in on it. The whole sequence of actions had been very slick indeed, but now he was sure.

'So you're doing a show down here?' John Rebus, cheered by his previous drinks, now felt that things were going right for a change. He was reunited with his brother for that drink they had always been promising themselves. He ordered whiskies with lager chasers. 'This is a quarter-gill pub,' he told Michael. 'That's a decent size of a measure.'

Michael smiled, smiled, smiled, as though his life depended upon it. His mind was racing and jumbled. The last thing he needed was another drink. If word of this got out, it would seem too unlikely to his Edinburgh connection, too unlikely. He, Michael, would have his legs broken for this if it ever was to get out. He had been warned. And what was John doing here anyway? He seemed complacent enough, drunk even, but what if it were all a set-up? What if his connection had already been arrested outside? He felt as he had when, as a child, he had stolen money from his father's wallet, denying the crime for weeks afterwards, his heart heavy with guilt.

Guilty, guilty, guilty.

John Rebus meantime drank on and chatted, unaware of the sudden change of atmosphere, the sudden interest in him. All he cared about was the whisky in front of him and the fact that Michael was about to go off and do a show at a local bingo hall.

'Mind if I come along?' he asked. 'I might as well see how my brother earns his crust.'

'Sure,' said Michael. He toyed with the whisky glass. 'I'd better not drink this, John. I've got to keep my mind clear.'

'Of course you have. Need to let the mysterious sensations flood over you.' Rebus made an action with his hands as though hypnotising Michael, his eyes wide, smiling.

And Jim Stevens picked up his cigarettes and, his back to them still, left the smoky, noisy public house. If only it had been quieter in there. If only he could have heard what they were saying. Rebus saw him go.

'I think I know him,' he told Michael, gesturing towards the door with his head. 'He's a reporter on the local rag.'

Michael Rebus tried to smile, smile, smile, but it seemed to him that his world was falling apart.

The Rio Grande Bingo Hall had been a cinema. The front twelve rows of seats had been taken out and bingo boards and stools put in their place, but to the back of these were still many rows of dusty, red seats, and the balcony seating was completely intact. John Rebus said that he preferred to sit upstairs, so that he would not distract Michael. He followed an elderly man and his wife upstairs. The seats looked comfortable, but as he eased himself into the second row, Rebus felt springs jar against his buttocks. He moved around a little, trying to get comfortable, and settled finally for a position where one cheek supported most of his weight.

There seemed a good enough crowd downstairs, but up here in the gloom of the neglected balcony there were only the old couple and himself. Then he heard shoes tapping on the aisle. They paused for a second, before a hefty woman slid into the second row. Rebus was forced to look up, and saw her smiling at him.

'Mind if I sit here?' she said. 'Not waiting for anyone, are you?'

Her look was hopeful. Rebus shook his head, smiling politely. 'Thought not,' she said, sitting down beside him. And he smiling. He had never seen Michael smile so much, or so uneasily. Was it so embarrassing for him to meet his elder brother? No, there had to be more to it than that. Michael's had been the smile of the small-time thief, caught yet again. They needed to talk.

'I come here a lot to the bingo. But I thought this might be a good laugh, you know. Ever since my husband died,' meaningful pause, 'well, it's not been the same. I like to get out now and again, you know. Everybody does, don't they? So I thought I'd come along. Don't know what made me come upstairs. Fate, I suppose.' Her smile broadened. Rebus smiled back.

She was in her early forties, a little too much make-up and scent, but quite well-preserved. She talked as if she had not spoken to anyone in days, as if it were important for her to establish that she could still speak and be listened to and understood. Rebus felt sorry for her. He saw a little of himself in her; not much, but almost enough.

'So what are you doing here?' She was forcing him to speak.

'Just here for the show, same as you are.' He didn't dare say that his brother was the hypnotist. That would have left too many avenues for a response.

'You like this sort of thing, do you?'

'I've never been before.'

'Neither have I.' She smiled again, conspiratorially this time. She had found that they had something in common. Thankfully, the lights were going down – what lighting there was – and a spot had come up on the stage. Someone was introducing the show. The woman opened her handbag and produced a noisy bag of boiled sweets. She offered one to Rebus.

Rebus found himself, to his own surprise, enjoying the show, but not half as much as the woman beside him was. She howled with laughter as one willing participant, his trousers left on the stage, pretended to swim up and down the aisles. Another guinea-pig was made to believe that he was ravenously hungry. Another that she was a professional striptease artiste at one of her bookings. Another that he was falling asleep.

Still enjoying the show, Rebus began to nod off himself. It was the effect of too much alcohol, too little sleep, and the warm, broody darkness of the theatre. Only the final applause of the audience awoke him. Michael, sweating in his glittery stage suit, took the applause as though addicted to it, coming back for another bow when most of the people were leaving their seats. He had told his brother that he had to get home quickly, that he would not see him after the show, that he would phone him sometime for his reaction.

And John Rebus had slept through much of it.

He felt refreshed, however, and could hear himself accepting the perfumed woman's offer of a 'one for the road' drink at a local bar. They left the theatre arm-in-arm, smiling at something. Rebus felt relaxed, a child again. This woman was treating him like her son, really, and he was happy enough to be coddled. A final drink, and then he'd go home. Just one drink.

Jim Stevens watched them leave the theatre. It was becoming very strange indeed. Rebus seemed to be ignoring his brother now, and he had a woman with him. What did it all mean? One thing it meant was that Gill should be told about it at some opportune moment. Stevens, smiling, added it to his collection of such moments. It had been a good night's work so far.

So where in the evening had mother-love changed into physical contact? In that pub, perhaps, where her reddened fingers had bitten into his thigh? Outside in the cooling air when he wrapped his arms around her neck in a fumbled attempt at a kiss? Or here in her musty flat, smelling still of her husband, where Rebus and she lie across an old settee and exchange tongues?

No matter. It's too late to regret anything, and too early. So he slouches after her when she retires to her bedroom. He tumbles into the huge double-bed, springy and covered in thick blankets and quilts. He watches her undress in darkness. The bed feels like one he had as a kid, when a hot-water-bottle was all he had to keep the chill off, and mounds of gritty blankets, puffed-out quilts. Heavy and suffocating, tiring in themselves.

No matter.

Rebus did not enjoy the particulars of her heavy body, and was forced to think of everything in the abstract. His hands on her well-suckled breasts reminded him of late nights with Rhona. Her calves were thick, unlike Gill's, and her face was worn with too much living. But she was a woman, and she was with him, so he squeezed her into an abstract and tried to make them both happy. But the heaviness of the bedding oppressed him, caging him, making him feel small and trapped and isolated from the world. He fought against it, fought against the memory of Gordon Reeve and he as they sat in solitary, listening to the screams of those around them, but enduring, always enduring, and reunited finally. Having won. Having lost. Lost everything. His heart was pounding to her grunts, now some distance away it seemed. He felt the first wave of that absolute repulsion hit him in the stomach like a truncheon, and his hands slid around the hanging, yielding throat beneath him. The moans were inhuman now, cat-like, keening. His hands pushed a little, the fingers finding their own purchase against skin and sheet. They locked him up and they threw away the key. They pushed him to his death and they poisoned him. He should not have been alive. He should have died back then, back in the rank, animal cells with their power-hoses and their constant questionings. But he had survived. He had survived. And he was coming.

He alone, all alone
And the screaming
Screaming

Rebus became aware of the gurgling sounds beneath him just before his head started to fry. He fell over onto the gasping figure and lost consciousness. It was like a switch being flipped.

16

He awoke in a white room. It reminded him very much of the hospital room in which he had awoken after his nervous breakdown all those years ago. There were muffled noises from outside. He sat up, his head throbbing. What had happened? Christ, that woman, that poor woman. He had tried to kill her! Drunk, way too drunk. Merciful God, he had tried to strangle her, hadn't he? Why in God's name had he done that? Why?

A doctor pushed open his door.

'Ah, Mister Rebus. Good, you're awake. We're about to move you into one of the wards. How do you feel?'

His pulse was taken.

'Simple exhaustion, we think. Simple nervous exhaustion. Your friend who called for the ambulance—'

'My friend?'

'Yes, she said that you just collapsed. And from what we can gather from your employers, you've been working pretty hard on this dreadful murder hunt. Simple exhaustion. What you need is a break.'

'Where's my . . . my friend?'

'No idea. At home, I expect.'

'And according to her, I just collapsed?'

'That's right.'

Rebus felt immediate relief flooding through him. She had not told them. She had not told them. Then his head began to pulse again. The doctor's wrists were hairy and scrubbed clean. He slipped a thermometer into Rebus's mouth, smiling. Did he know what Rebus had been doing prior to the blackout? Or had his friend dressed him before calling the ambulance? He had to contact the woman. He didn't know where she stayed, not exactly, but the ambulancemen would know, and he could check.

Exhaustion. Rebus did not feel exhausted. He was beginning to feel rested and, though slightly unnerved, quite unworried about life. Had they given him anything while he was asleep?

'Can I see a newspaper?' he muttered past the thermometer.

'I'll get an orderly to fetch you one. Is there anyone you wish us to contact? Any close relative or friend?'

Rebus thought of Michael.

'No,' he said, 'there's nobody to contact. All I want is a newspaper.'

'Fair enough.' The thermometer was removed, the details noted.

'How long do you want to keep me in here?'

'Two or three days. I may want you to see an analyst.'

'Forget the analyst. I'll need some books to read.'

'We'll see what we can do.'

Rebus settled back then, having decided to let things take their course. He would lie here, resting though he needed no rest, and would let the rest of them worry about the murder case. Sod them all. Sod Anderson. Sod Wallace. Sod Gill Templer.

But then he remembered his hands slipping around that ageing throat, and he shivered. It was as though his mind were not his own. Had he been about to kill that woman? Should he see the analyst after all? The questions made his headache worse. He tried not to think about anything at all, but three figures kept coming back to him: his old friend Gordon Reeve, his new lover Gill Templer, and the woman he had betrayed her for, and nearly strangled. They danced in his head until the dance became blurred. Then he fell asleep.

'John!'

She walked quickly to his bed, fruit and vitamin-drink in her hands. She had make-up on her face, and was wearing strictly off-duty clothes. She pecked his cheek, and he could smell her French perfume. He could also see down the front of her silk blouse. He felt a little guilty.

'Hello, D.I. Templer,' he said. 'Here,' lifting one edge of the bedcover, 'get in.'

She laughed, dragging across a stern-looking chair. Other visitors were entering the ward, their smiles and quiet voices redolent of illness, an illness Rebus did not feel.

'How are you, John?'

'Terrible. What have you brought me?'

'Grapes, bananas, diluting orange. Nothing very imaginative, I'm afraid.'

Rebus picked a grape from the bunch and popped it into his mouth, setting aside the trashy novel in which he had been painfully involved.

'I don't know, Inspector, the things I have to do to get a date with you.' Rebus shook his head wearily. Gill was smiling, but nervously.

'We were worried about you, John. What happened?'

'I fainted. In the home of a friend, by all accounts. It's nothing very serious. I have a few weeks to live.'

Gill's smile was warm.

'They say it's overwork.' Then she paused. 'What's all this "Inspector" stuff?'

Rebus shrugged, then looked sulky. His guilt was mixing with the remembrance of that snub he had been given, that snub which had started the whole ball rolling. He turned into a patient again, weakly slumping against his pillow.

'I'm a very ill man, Gill. Too ill to answer questions.'

'Well, in that case I won't bother to slip you the cigarettes sent by Jack Morton.'

Rebus sat up again.

'Bless that man. Where are they?'

She brought two packs from her jacket pocket and slipped them beneath the bedclothes. He gripped her hand.

'I missed you, Gill.' She smiled, and did not withdraw the hand.

Limitless visiting time being a prerogative of the police, Gill stayed for two hours, talking about her past, asking him about his own. She had been born on an air-force base in Wiltshire, just after the war. She told Rebus that her father had been an engineer in the RAF.

'My dad,' Rebus said, 'was in the Army during the war. I was conceived while he was on one of his last leaves. He was a stage hypnotist by profession.' People usually raised an eyebrow at that, but not Gill Templer. 'He used to work the music-halls and theatres, doing summer stints in Blackpool and Ayr and places like that, so we were always sure of a summer holiday away from Fife.'

She sat with her head cocked to one side, content to be told stories. The ward was quiet once the other visitors had obeyed the leaving-bell. A nurse pushed around a trolley with a huge battered pot of tea on it. Gill was given a cup, the nurse smiling at her in sisterhood.

'She's a nice kid, that nurse,' said Rebus, relaxed. He had been given two pills, one blue and one brown, and they were making him drowsy. 'She reminds me of a girl I knew when I was in the Paras.'

'How long were you in the Paras, John?'

'Six years. No, eight years it was.'

'What made you leave?'

What made him leave? Rhona had asked him the same question over and over, her curiosity piqued by the feeling that he had something to hide, some monstrous skeleton in his closet.

'I don't know really. It's hard to remember that far back. I was picked for special training and I didn't like it.'

And this was the truth. He had no use for memories of his training, the reek of fear and mistrust, the screaming, that screaming in his memory. *Let me out.* The echo of solitary.

'Well,' said Gill, 'if *my* memory serves me right, I've got a case waiting for me back at base-camp.'

'That reminds me,' he said, 'I think I saw your friend last night. The reporter. Stevens, wasn't it? He was in a pub the same time I was. Strange.'

'Not so very strange. That's his kind of hunting-ground. Funny, he's a bit like you in some ways. Not as sexy though.' She smiled and pecked his cheek again, rising from the metal chair. 'I'll try to drop in again before they let you out, but you know what it's like. I can't make any concrete promises, D.S. Rebus.'

Standing, she seemed taller than Rebus had imagined her. Her hair fell forward onto his face for another kiss, full on the lips this time, and he staring at the dark cleft between her breasts. He felt a little tired, so tired. He forced his eyes to remain open while she walked away, her heels clacking on the tiled floor while the nurses floated past like ghosts on their rubber-soled shoes. He pushed himself up so that he could watch her legs retreat. She had nice legs. He had remembered that much. He remembered them gripping his sides, the feet resting on his buttocks. He remembered her hair falling across the pillow like a Turner seascape. He remembered her voice hissing in his ears, that hissing. Oh yes, John, oh, John, yes, yes, yes.

Why did you leave the army?

As she turned over, turning into the woman with the choking cries of his climax.

Why did you?

Oh, oh, oh, oh.

Oh yes, the safety of dreams.

17

The editors loved what the Edinburgh Strangler was doing for the circulations of their newspapers. They loved the way his story grew almost organically, as though carefully nurtured. The *modus operandi* had altered ever so slightly for the killing of Nicola Turner. The Strangler had, it seemed, tied a knot in the cord prior to strangulation. This knot had pressed heavily on the girl's throat, bruising it. The police did not consider this of much significance. They were too busy checking through the records of blue Ford Escorts to be busy with a slight detail of technique. They were out there checking every blue Escort in the area, questioning every owner, every driver.

Gill Templer had released details of the car to the press, hoping for a huge public response. It came: neighbours reported their neighbours, fathers their sons, wives their husbands, and husbands their wives. There were over two-hundred blue Escorts to investigate, and if nothing came of that, they would be re-investigated, before moving on to other colours of Ford Escort, other makes of light-blue saloon car. It might take months; certainly it would take weeks.

Jack Morton, another xeroxed list folded in his hand, had consulted his doctor about swollen feet. The doctor had told him that he walked too much in cheap, unsupportive shoes. This Morton already knew. He had now interviewed so many suspects that it was all becoming a blur to him. They all looked the same and acted the same: nervous, deferential, innocent. If only the Strangler would make a mistake. There were no clues worth going on. Morton suspected the car to be a false trail. No clues worth going on. He remembered John Rebus's anonymous letters. *There are clues everywhere.* Could that be true of this case? Could the clues be too big to notice, or too abstract? Certainly it was a rare – an extraordinarily rare – murder case that did not have some bumper, extravagant clue lying about somewhere just waiting to be picked up. He was damned if he knew where this one was though, and that was why he had visited his doctor – hoping for some sympathy and a few days off. Rebus had landed on *his* feet again, lucky sod. Morton envied him his illness.

He parked his car on a double-yellow line outside the library and sauntered in. The great front hall reminded him of the days when he had used this library himself, clutching picture-books borrowed from the children's section. It used to be situated downstairs. He wondered if it still was. His mother would give him the bus-fare, and he would come into town, ostensibly to change his library books, but really so that he could wander the streets for an hour or two, savouring the taste of what it would be like to be grown up and free. He would trail American tourists, taking note of their swaggering self-confidence and their bulging wallets and waistbands. He would watch them as they photographed Greyfriars Bobby's statue across from the kirkyard. He had stared long and hard at the statue of the small dog, and had felt nothing. He had read of Covenanters, of Deacon Brodie, of public executions on the High Street, wondering what kind of city this was, and what kind of country. He shook his head now, past caring about fantasies, and went to the information desk.

'Hello, Mister Morton.'

He turned to find a girl, more a young lady really, standing before him, a book clasped to her small chest. He frowned.

'It's me, Samantha Rebus.'

His eyes went wide.

'Goodness, so it is. Well, well. You've certainly grown since I last saw you. Mind you, that must have been a year or two back. How are you?'

'I'm fine, thanks. I'm here with my mother. Are you here on police business?'

'Something like that, yes.' Morton could feel her eyes burning into him. God, she had her father's eyes all right. He had left his mark.

'How's dad keeping?'

To tell or not to tell. Why not tell her? Then again, was it his place to tell her?

'He's fine, so far as I know,' he said, knowing this to be seventy-per-cent truth.

'I'm just going down to the teenagers' section. Mum's in the Reference Room. It's dead boring in there.'

'I'll go with you. That's just where I was headed.'

She smiled at him, pleased about something that was going on in her adolescent head, and Jack Morton had the thought that she wasn't at all like her father. She was far too nice and polite.

A fourth girl was missing. The outcome seemed a foregone conclusion. No bookie would have given odds.

'We need special vigilance,' stressed Anderson. 'More officers are being drafted in tonight. Remember,' the officers present looked hollow-eyed and demoralized, 'if and when he kills this victim, he will attempt to dispose of the body, and if we can spot him doing that, or if any member of the public can spot him doing that, just once, then we've got him.' Anderson slapped a fist into his open hand. Nobody seemed very cheered. So far the Strangler had dumped three corpses, quite successfully, in different areas of the city: Oxgangs, Haymarket, Colinton. The police could not be everywhere (though these days it seemed to the public that they were), no matter how hard they tried.

'Again,' continued the Chief Inspector, consulting a file, 'the recent abduction seems to have little enough in common with the others. The victim's name is Helen Abbot. Eight years of age, a bit younger than the others you'll notice, light-brown shoulder-length hair. Last seen with her mother in a Princes Street store. The mother says that the girl simply disappeared. One minute there, the next minute gone, as was the case with the second victim.'

Gill Templer, thinking this over later, found it curious. The girls could not themselves have been abducted actually in the shops. That would have been impossible without screams, without witnesses. One member of the public had come forward to say that a girl resembling Mary Andrews – the second victim – had been seen by him climbing the steps from the National Gallery up towards The Mound. She had been alone, and had seemed happy enough. In which case, Gill mused, the girl had sneaked away from her mother. But why? For some secret rendezvous with someone she had known, someone who had turned out to be her killer? In that case, it seemed likely that *all* the girls had known their murderer, so they *had* to have something in common. Different schools, different friends, different ages. What was the common denominator?

She admitted defeat when her head started to hurt. Besides, she had reached John's street and had other things to think about. He had sent her here to collect some clean clothes for his release, and to see if there were any mail, as well as to check that the central heating was working still. He had given her his key, and as she climbed the stairs, pinching her nose against the pervasive smell of cats, she felt a bond between John Rebus and herself. She wondered if the relationship were about to turn serious. He was a nice man, but a little hung-up, a little secretive. Maybe that was what she liked.

She opened his door, scooped up the few letters lying on the hall-carpet, and made a quick tour of the flat. Standing by the bedroom door, she recalled the passion of that night, the odour of which seemed to cling in the air still.

The pilot-light was lit. He would be surprised to learn that. What a lot of books he had, but then his wife had been an English teacher. She lifted some of them off the floor and arranged them on the empty shelves of the wall-unit. In the kitchen, she made herself some coffee and sat down to drink it black, looking over the mail. One bill, one circular, and one typed letter, posted in Edinburgh and three days ago at that. She stuffed the letters into her bag and went to inspect the wardrobe. Samantha's room, she noted, was still locked. More memories pushed safely away. Poor John.

Jim Stevens had far too much work to do. The Edinburgh Strangler was proving himself a meaty individual. You couldn't ignore the bastard, even if you felt you had better things to do. Stevens had a staff of three working with him on the newspaper's daily reports and features. Child abuse in Britain today was the flavour of tomorrow's piece. The figures were horrifying enough, but more horrifying yet was the sense of biding time, waiting for the dead girl to turn up. Waiting for the next one to go missing. Edinburgh was a ghost town. Children were kept indoors, those allowed out scuttling through the streets like creatures under chase. Stevens wanted to turn his attentions to the drugs case, the mounting evidence, the police connection. He wanted to, but there simply was not the time. Tom Jameson was on his back every hour of the day, roaming through the office. Where's that copy, Jim? It's about time you earned your keep, Jim. When's the next briefing, Jim? Stevens was burned out by the end of each and every day. He decided that his work on the Rebus case had to stop for the moment. Which was a pity, because with the police at full stretch working on the murders, the field was left wide open for any and all other crimes, including pushing drugs. The Edinburgh Mafia must be having a field-day. He had used the story of the Leith 'bordello', hoping for some information in return, but the big boys appeared not to be playing. Well, sod them. His time would come.

When she arrived in the ward, Rebus was reading through a Bible, courtesy of the hospital. When the Sister had found out about his request, she had asked him if he wished to speak to a priest or a minister, but this offer he had declined strenuously. He was quite content – more than content – to flick through some of the better passages in the Old Testament, refreshing his memory of their power and their moral strength. He read the stories of Moses, Samson, and David, before coming to the Book of Job. Here he found a power he could not remember having encountered before:

> When an innocent man suddenly dies, God laughs.
> God gave the world to the wicked.
> He made all the judges blind,
> And if God didn't do it, who did?
>
> If I smile and try to forget my pain,
> All my suffering comes back to haunt me;
> I know that God does hold me guilty.
> Since I am held guilty, why should I bother?
> No soap can wash away my sins.

Rebus felt his spine shiver, though the ward itself was oppressively warm, and his throat cried out for water. As he poured some of the tepid liquid into a plastic beaker, he saw Gill coming towards him on quieter heels than previously. She was smiling, bringing what joy there was into the ward with her. A few of the men eyed her appreciatively. Rebus felt glad, all of a sudden, to be leaving this place today. He put the Bible aside and greeted her with a kiss on the nape of her neck.

'What have you got there?'

He took the parcel from her and found it to contain his change of clothes.

'Thanks,' he said. 'I didn't think this shirt was clean though.'

'It wasn't.' She laughed and pulled across a chair. 'Nothing was. I'd to wash and iron all your clothes. They constituted a health hazard.'

'You're an angel,' he said, putting the parcel aside.

'Speaking of which, what were you reading in the book?' She tapped the red, fake-leather binding of the Bible.

'Oh, nothing much. Job, actually. I read it once a long time ago. It seems more frightening now though. The man who begins to doubt, who shouts out against his God, looking for a response, and who gets one. "God gave the world to the wicked," he says at one point, and "Why should I bother?" at another.'

'It sounds interesting. But he goes on bothering?'

'Yes, that's the incredible thing.'

Tea arrived, the young nurse handing Gill her cup. There was a plate of biscuits for them.

'I've brought you some letters from the flat, and here's your key.' She held the small Yale key towards him, but he shook his head.

'Keep it,' he said, 'please. I've got a spare one.'

They studied one another.

'All right,' Gill said finally. 'I will. Thanks.' With that, she handed him the three letters. He sorted through them in a second.

'He's started sending them by mail, I see.' Rebus tore open the latest bulletin. 'This guy,' he said, 'is haunting me. Mister Knot, I call him. My own personal anonymous crank.'

Gill looked interested, as Rebus read through the letter. It was longer than usual.

YOU STILL HAVEN'T GUESSED, HAVE YOU? YOU'VE NO IDEAS. NOT AN IDEA IN YOUR HEAD. AND IT'S ALMOST OVER NOW, ALMOST OVER. DON'T SAY I'VE NOT GIVEN YOU A CHANCE. YOU CAN NEVER SAY THAT. SIGNED

Rebus pulled a small matchstick cross out of the envelope.

'Ah, Mister Cross today, I see. Well, thank God he's nearly finished. Getting bored, I suppose.'

'What is all this, John?'

'Haven't I told you about my anonymous letters? It's not a very exciting story.'

'How long has this been going on?' Gill, having studied the letter, was now examining the envelope.

'Six weeks. Maybe a little longer. Why?'

'Well, it's just that this letter was posted on the day Helen Abbot went missing.'

'Oh?' Rebus reached for the envelope and looked at its postmark. 'Edinburgh, Lothian, Fife, Borders,' it read. A big enough area. He thought again of Michael.

'I don't suppose you can remember when you received the other letters?'

'What are you getting at, Gill?' He looked up at her, and saw a professional policewoman suddenly staring back at him. 'For Christ's sake, Gill. This case is getting to all of us. We're all beginning to see ghosts.'

'I'm just curious, that's all.' She was reading the letter again. It was not the usual crank's voice, nor a crank's style. That was what worried her. And now that Rebus thought about it, the notes had seemed to appear around the time of each abduction, hadn't they? Had there been a connection of some kind staring him in the face all this time? He had been very myopic indeed, had been wearing a carthorse's blinkers. Either that or it was all a monstrous coincidence.

'It's just a coincidence, Gill.'

'So tell me when the other notes arrived.'

'I can't remember.'

She bent over him, her eyes huge behind her glasses. She said calmly, 'Are you hiding anything from me?'

'No!'

The whole ward turned to his cry, and he felt his cheeks flush.

'No,' he whispered, 'I'm not hiding anything. At least . . .' But how could he be sure? All those years of arrests, of charge-sheets, of forgettings, so many enemies made. But none would torment him like this, surely. Surely.

With pen, paper, and a lot of thought on his part, they went

over the arrival of each note: dates, contents, style of delivery.
Gill took off her glasses, rubbing between her eyes, sighing.

'It's just too big a coincidence, John.'

And he knew that she was right, way down inside him. He
knew that nothing was ever what it seemed, that nothing was
arbitrary. 'Gill,' he said at last, pulling at the bedcover, 'I've got
to get out of here.'

In the car she goaded him, spurred him on. Who could it be?
What was the connection? Why?

'What is this?' he roared at her. 'Am I a suspect now or
something?'

She studied his eyes, trying to pierce them, trying to bite right
into the truth behind them. Oh, she was a detective at heart,
and a good detective trusts nobody. She gazed at him as though
he were a scolded schoolboy, with secrets still to spill, with sins
to confess. Confess.

Gill knew that all this was only a hunch, insupportable. Yet
she could feel something there, something perhaps behind
those burning eyes. Stranger things had happened during her
time on the force. Stranger things were always happening.
Truth was always stranger than fiction, and nobody was ever
wholly innocent. Those guilty looks when you questioned
somebody, anybody. Everyone had something to hide. Mostly,
though, it was small time, and covered by the intervening
years. You would need Thought Police to get at those kinds of
crime. But if John . . . If John Rebus proved to be part of this
whole caboodle, then that . . . That was too absurd to think
about.

'Of course you're not a suspect, John,' she said. 'But it could
be important, couldn't it?'

'We'll let Anderson decide,' he said, falling silent, but
shaking.

It was then that Gill had the thought: what if he sent the
letters to himself?

18

He felt his arms ache and, looking down, saw that the girl had stopped struggling. There came that point, that sudden, blissful point, when it was useless to go on living, and when the mind and body came to accept that such was the case. That was a beautiful, peaceful moment, the most relaxed moment of one's life. He had, many years ago, tried to commit suicide, savouring that very moment. But they had done things to him in hospital and in the clinic afterwards. They had given him back the will to live, and now he was repaying them, repaying all of them. He saw this irony in his life and chuckled, peeling the tape from Helen Abbot's mouth, using the little scissors to snip away her bonds. He brought out a neat little camera from his trouser pocket and took another instant snap of her, a *memento mori* of sorts. If they ever caught him, they'd kick the shit out of him for this, but they would never be able to brand him a sex-killer. Sex had nothing to do with it; these girls were pawns, fated by their christenings. The next and last one was the one that really mattered, and he would do that one today if possible. He chuckled again. This was a better game than noughts and crosses. He was a winner at both.

19

Chief Inspector William Anderson loved the feel of the chase, the battle between instinct and plodding detection. He liked to feel, too, that he had the support of his Division behind him. Dispenser of orders, of wisdom, of strategies, he was in his element.

He would rather have caught the Strangler already – that went without saying. He was no sadist. The law had to be upheld. All the same, the longer an investigation like this went on, the greater became the feel of nearing the kill, and to relish that extended moment was one of the great perks of responsibility.

The Strangler was making an occasional slip, and that was what mattered to Anderson at this stage. The blue Ford Escort, and now the interesting theory that the killer had been or was still an Army man, suggested by the tying of a knot in the garotte. Snippets like that would culminate eventually in a name, an address, an arrest. And at that moment, Anderson would lead his officers physically as well as spiritually. There would be another interview on the television, another rather flattering photograph in the press (he was quite photogenic). Oh yes, victory would be sweet. Unless, of course, the Strangler vanished in the night as so many before him had done. That possibility was not to be considered; it made his legs turn into paper.

He did not dislike Rebus, not exactly. The man was a reasonable enough copper, a bit loud in his methods perhaps. And he understood that Rebus's personal life had experienced an upheaval. Indeed, he had been told that Rebus's ex-wife was

the woman with whom his own son was co-habiting. He tried
not to think about it. When Andy had slammed the front door
on his leaving, he had walked right out of his father's life. How
could anyone these days spend their time writing poetry? It was
ludicrous. And then moving in with Rebus's wife . . . No, he did
not dislike Rebus, but watching Rebus come towards him with
that pretty Liaison Officer, Anderson felt his stomach cough, as
though his insides suddenly wanted to become his outsides. He
leaned back on the edge of a vacant desk. The officer assigned
to it had gone off for a break.

'Nice to have you back, John. Feeling fit?'

Anderson had shot out his hand, and Rebus, stunned, was
forced to take it and return the grip. 'I'm fine, sir,' he said.

'Sir,' interrupted Gill Templer, 'can we speak to you for a
minute? There's been a new development.'

'The mere *hint* of a development, sir,' corrected Rebus,
staring at Gill.

Anderson looked from one to the other.

'You'd better come into my office then.'

Gill explained the situation as she saw it to Anderson, and he,
wise and safe behind his desk, listened, glancing occasionally
towards Rebus, who smiled apologetically at him. Sorry to be
wasting your time, Rebus's smile said.

'Well, Rebus?' said Anderson when Gill had finished. 'What
do you say to all this? Could someone have a reason for
informing you of their plans? I mean, could the Strangler *know*
you?'

Rebus shrugged his shoulders, smiling, smiling, smiling.

Jack Morton, sitting in his car, jotted down some remarks on
his report-sheet. Saw suspect. Interviewed same. Casual, help-
ful. Another dead end, he wanted to say. Another dead fucking
end. A parking warden was looking at him, trying to scare him
as she neared his car. He sighed, putting down the pen and
paper and reaching for his ID. One of those days.

*

Rhona Phillips wore her raincoat, it being the end of May, and
the rain slashing through the skyline as though painted upon
an artist's canvas. She kissed her curly-headed poet-lover
goodbye, as he watched afternoon TV, and left the house,
feeling for the car-keys in her handbag. She picked Sammy up
from school these days, though the school was only a mile and
a quarter away. She also went with her to the library at
lunchtimes, not allowing her any escape. With that maniac still
on the loose, she was taking no chances. She rushed to her car,
got in, and slammed shut the door. Edinburgh rain was like a
judgement. It soaked into the bones, into the structures of the
buildings, into the memories of the tourists. It lingered for days,
splashing up from puddles by the roadside, breaking up
marriages, chilling, killing, omnipresent. The typical postcard
home from an Edinburgh boarding-house: 'Edinburgh is lovely.
The people rather reserved. Saw the Castle yesterday, and the
Scott Monument. It's a very small city, almost a town really.
You could fit it inside New York and never notice it. Weather
could be better.'

Weather could be better. The art of euphemism. Shitty, shitty
rain. It was so typical when she had a free day. Typical, too, that
Andy and she should have argued. And now he was sulking in
his chair, legs tucked beneath him. One of those days. And she
had reports to write out this evening. Thank God the exams had
started. The kids seemed more subdued at school these days,
the older ones gripped by exam-fever or exam-apathy, and the
younger ones seeing their ineluctable future mapped out for
them in the faces of their doomed superiors. It was an
interesting time of year. Soon the fear would be Sammy's,
called Samantha to her face now that she was so nearly a
woman. There were other fears there, too, for a parent. The fear
of adolescence, of experiment.

As she reversed the car out of the driveway, he watched her
from his Escort. Perfect. He had about fifteen minutes to wait.
When her car had disappeared, he drove his car to the front of

the house and stopped. He examined the windows of the house. Her man would be in there alone. He left his car and walked to the front door.

Back in the Incident Room after the inconclusive meeting, Rebus could not know that Anderson was arranging to have him put under surveillance. The Incident Room looked like an incident itself. Paper covered every surface, a small computer was crammed into a spare corner, charts and rotas and the rest covered every available inch of wall-space.

'I've got a briefing,' said Gill. 'I'll see you later. Listen, John, I do think there's a link. Call it female intuition, call it a detective's "nose", call it what you like, but take me seriously. Think it over. Think about possible grudges. Please.'

He nodded, then watched her leave, making for her own office in her own part of the building. Rebus wasn't sure which desk was his any more. He surveyed the room. It all seemed different somehow, as though a few of the desks had been changed around or put together. A telephone rang on the desk next to him. And though there were officers and telephonists nearby, he picked it up himself, making an attempt to get back into the investigation. He prayed that he was not himself the investigation. He prayed, forgetting what prayer was.

'Incident Room,' he said. 'Detective Sergeant Rebus speaking.'

'Rebus? What a curious name that is.' The voice was old but lively, certainly well-educated. 'Rebus,' it said again, as though jotting it down onto a piece of paper. Rebus studied the telephone.

'And your name, sir?'

'Oh, I'm Michael Eiser, that's E-I-S-E-R, Professor of English Literature at the University.'

'Oh, yes, sir?' Rebus grabbed a pencil and jotted down the name. 'And what can I do for you, sir?'

'Well, Mister Rebus, it's more a case of what I *think* I can do for you, though of course I may be mistaken.' Rebus had a picture of the man, if this were not a hoax call: frizzy-haired, bow-tied, wearing crushed tweeds and old shoes, and waving his hands about as he spoke. 'I'm interested in word-play, you see. In fact I'm writing a book on the subject. It's called *Reading Exercises and Directed Exegetic Responses*. Do you see the word-play there? It's an acrostic. The first letter of each word makes up another word – *reader*, in this case. It's a game as old as literature itself. My book, however, concentrates on its manifestation in more recent works. Nabokov and Burgess and the like. Of course, acrostics are a small part of the overall set of ploys used by the author to entertain, direct or persuade his audience.' Rebus tried to interrupt the man, but it was like trying to interrupt a bull. So he was forced to listen, wondering all the time if it were a crank call, if he should – strictly against procedure – simply put down the telephone. He had more important things to think about. The back of his head ached.

'. . . and the point is, Mister Rebus, that I have noticed, quite by chance, a kind of pattern in this murderer's choice of victims.'

Rebus sat down on the edge of the desk. He clasped the pencil as though trying to crush it.

'Oh, yes?' he said.

'Yes. I have the names of the victims here in front of me on a piece of paper. Perhaps one would have noticed it sooner, but it was only today that I saw a report in one newspaper which grouped the poor girls together. I usually take *The Times*, you see, but I quite simply couldn't find one this morning, so I bought another paper, and there it was. It may be nothing at all, mere coincidence, but then again it may not. I'll leave that for you chaps to decide. I merely offer it as a proposition.'

Jack Morton, puffing smoke all around him, entered the office and, noticing Rebus, waved. Rebus jerked his head in response. Jack looked worn out. Everyone looked worn out, and here he was, fresh from a period of rest and relaxation, dealing with a lunatic on the telephone.

'Offer what exactly, Professor Eiser?'

'Well, don't you see? In order, the victims' names were Sandra Adams, Mary Andrews, Nicola Turner, and Helen Abbot.' Jack slouched towards Rebus's table. 'Taken as an acrostic,' continued the voice, 'their names make up another name – Samantha. The murderer's next victim perhaps? Or it may be simple coincidence, a game where no game really exists.'

Rebus slammed down the telephone, was off the desk in a second, and pulled Jack Morton around by his neck-tie. Morton gasped and his cigarette flew from his mouth.

'Got your car outside, Jack?'

Still choking, he nodded a reply.

Jesus Christ, Jesus Christ. It was all true then. It was all to do with *him*. Samantha. All the clues, all the killings had been meant merely as a message to *him*. Jesus Christ. Help me, oh help me.

His daughter was to be the Strangler's next victim.

Rhona Phillips saw the car parked outside her house, but thought nothing of it. All she wanted was to get out of the rain. She ran to the front door, Samantha following desultorily behind, and keyed open the door.

'It's horrible outside!' she shouted into the living-room. She shook off her raincoat and walked through to where the TV still blared. In his chair, she saw Andy. His hands were tied behind him and his mouth was taped shut with a huge piece of sticking-plaster. The length of twine still dangled from his throat.

Rhona was about to let out the most piercing scream of her life, when a heavy object came down on the back of her head and she staggered forward towards her lover, slumping across his legs as she passed out.

'Hello, Samantha,' said a voice she recognised, though his face was masked so that she could not see his smile.

Morton's car tore across town, its blue light flashing, as though it were being followed by all Hell itself. Rebus tried explaining it all as they drove, but he was too edgy to make much sense, and Jack Morton was too busy avoiding traffic to make much attempt at taking it in. They had called for assistance: one car to the school in case she were still there, and two cars to the house, with the warning that the Strangler might be there. Caution was to be exercised.

The car reached eighty-five along Queensferry Road, made an insane right turn across the oncoming traffic, and reached the bright-as-a-pin housing estate where Rhona, Samantha and Rhona's lover now lived.

'Turn right here,' shouted Rebus over the engine's roar, his mind clinging to hope. As they turned into the street they saw the two police cars already motionless in front of the house, and Rhona's car sitting like a potent symbol of futility in the driveway.

20

They wanted to give him sedatives, but he wouldn't take any of their drugs. They wanted him to go home, but he would not take their advice. How could he go home with Rhona lying somewhere above him in the hospital? With his daughter abducted, his whole life ripped apart like a worn garment being transformed into dusters? He paced the hospital waiting-room. He was fine, he told them, fine. He knew that Gill and Anderson were somewhere along the corridor. Poor Anderson. He watched from the grime of the window as nurses walked by outside, laughing in the rain, their capes blowing about them like something out of an old Dracula movie. How could they laugh? Mist was settling over the trees, and the nurses, still laughing, unaware of the world's suffering, faded into that mist as though some Edinburgh of the past had sucked them into its fiction, taking with them all the laughter in the world.

It was nearly dark now, the sun a memory behind the heavy fabric of the clouds. The religious painters of old must have known skies like this, must have lived with them each and every day, accepting the bruised colouring of the clouds as a mark of God's presence, an essence of creation's power. Rebus was no painter. His eyes beheld beauty not in reality but in the printed word. Standing in the waiting-room, he realised that in his life he had accepted secondary experience – the experience of reading someone else's thoughts – over real life. Well, he was face to face with it now all right: he was back in the Paras, he was back in the SAS, his face a sketch-pad of exhaustion, his brain aching, every muscle tensed.

He caught himself beginning to abstract everything again,

and slapped the wall with the palms of both hands as though ready to be frisked. Sammy was out there somewhere in the hands of a maniac, and he was composing eulogies, excuses and similes. It wasn't enough.

In the corridor, Gill kept a watch on William Anderson. He, too, had been told to go home. A doctor had examined him for the effects of shock, and had spoken of putting Anderson to bed for the night.

'I'm waiting right here,' Anderson had said with quiet determination. 'If this all has something to do with John Rebus, then I want to stay close to John Rebus. I'm all right, honestly.' But he was not all right. He was dazed and remorseful and a bit confused about everything. 'I can't believe it,' he told Gill. 'I can't believe that this whole thing was merely a prelude to the abduction of Rebus's daughter. It's fantastical. The man must be deranged. Surely John must have an inkling who's responsible?'

Gill Templer was wondering the same thing.

'Why hasn't he told us?' continued Anderson. Then, without warning or any show of ceremony, he became a father again and started to sob very quietly. 'Andy,' he said, 'my Andy.' He put his head in his hands and allowed Gill to put her arm around his crumpled shoulders.

John Rebus, watching darkness descend, thought about his marriage, his daughter. His daughter Sammy.

For those who read between the times

What was it he was blocking out? What was it that had been rejected by him all those years ago as he had walked the Fife shoreline, having his final fit of the breakdown and shutting out the past as securely as if he had been shutting the door on a Jehovah's Witness? It was not that easy. The unwanted caller had waited his time, deciding to break and enter into Rebus's life again. The foot in the door. The door of perception. What good was his reading doing him now? Or his faith, slender thread that it was? Samantha. Sammy, his daughter. Dear God, let her be safe. Dear God, let her live.

John, you must know who it is

But he had shaken his head, shaken his tears onto the folds of his trousers. He did not, he did not. It was Knot. It was Cross. Names meant nothing to him any more. Knots and crosses. He had been sent knots and crosses, string and matches and a load of gobbledygook, as Jack Morton had called it. That was all. Dear God.

He went out into the corridor, and confronted Anderson, who stood before him like a piece of wreckage waiting to be loaded up and shunted away. And the two men came together in a hug, squeezing life into one another; two old enemies realising in a moment that they were on the same side after all. They hugged and they wept, draining themselves of all they had been bottling up, all those years of pounding the beat, having to appear emotionless and unflappable. It was out in the open now: they were human beings, the same as everybody else.

And finally, assured that Rhona had suffered a fractured skull only, allowed into her room for a moment to watch her breathing oxygen, Rebus had let them take him home. Rhona would live. That was something. Andy Anderson, though, was cold on a slab somewhere while doctors examined his leftovers. Poor bloody Anderson. Poor man, poor father, poor copper. It was becoming very personal now, wasn't it? All of a sudden it had become bigger than they had imagined it ever could. It had become a grudge.

They had a description at last, though not a good one. A neighbour had seen the man carry the still form of the girl out to the car. A pale coloured car, she had told them. A normal looking car. A normal looking man. Not too tall, his face hard. He was hurrying. She didn't get a good look at him.

Anderson would be off the case now, and so would Rebus. Oh, it was big now. The Strangler had entered a home, had murdered there. He had gone way too far over the edge. The newspapermen and the cameras outside the hospital wanted to

know all about it. Superintendent Wallace would have organ-
ised a press conference. The newspaper-readers, the voyeurs,
needed to know all about it. It was big news. Edinburgh was the
crime capital of Europe. The son of a Chief Inspector murdered
and the daughter of a Detective Sergeant abducted, possibly
murdered already.

What could he do but sit and wait for another letter? He was
better off in his flat, no matter how dark and barren it seemed,
no matter how like a cell. Gill promised to visit him later, after
the press conference. An unmarked car would be outside his
tenement as a matter of course, for who knew how personal
the Strangler wanted this to become?

Meantime, unknown to Rebus, his file was being checked
back at HQ, his past dusted off and examined. There had to be
the Strangler in there somewhere. There had to be.

Of course there had to be. Rebus knew that he alone held the
key. But it seemed locked in a drawer to which it itself was the
key. He could only rattle that locked away history.

Gill Templer had telephoned Rebus's brother, and though John
would hate her for doing so, she had told Michael to come
across to Edinburgh at once to be with his brother. He was
Rebus's only family after all. He sounded nervous on the
phone, nervous but concerned. And now she puzzled over the
matter of the acrostic. The Professor had been correct. They
were trying to locate him this evening in order to interview
him. Again, as a matter of course. But if the Strangler had
planned this, then surely he must have been able to get his
hands on a list of people whose names would fit the bill, and
how would he have done that? A civil servant perhaps? A
teacher? Someone working away quietly at a computer-termi-
nal somewhere? There were many possibilities, and they would
go through them one by one. First, however, Gill was going to
suggest that everyone in Edinburgh called Knott or Cross be
interviewed. It was a wild card, but then everything about this
case so far had been wild.

And then there was the press conference. Held, since it was convenient, in the hospital's administration building. There was standing room only at the back of the hall. Gill Templer's face, human but unsmiling, was becoming well known to the British public, as well known, certainly, as that of any newscaster or reporter. Tonight, however, the Superintendent would be doing the talking. She hoped he would not take long. She wanted to see Rebus. And more urgently, perhaps, she wanted to talk with his brother. Someone had to know about John's past. He had never, apparently, spoken to any of his friends on the force about his Army years. Did the key lie there? Or in his marriage? Gill listened to the Super saying his piece. Cameras clicked and the large hall grew smoky.

And there was Jim Stevens, smiling from the corner of his mouth, as if he knew something. Gill grew nervous. His eyes were on her, though his pen worked away at its notepad. She recalled that disastrous evening they had spent together, and her much less disastrous evening with John Rebus. Why had none of the men in her life ever been uncomplicated? Perhaps because complications interested her. The case was not becoming more complex. It was becoming simpler.

Jim Stevens, half-listening to the police statement, thought of how complex this story was becoming. Rebus and Rebus, drugs and murder, anonymous messages followed by abduction of daughter. He needed to get behind the police's public face on this one, and knew that the best way forward lay with Gill Templer, with a little trading of knowledge. If the drugs and the abduction were linked, as they probably were, then perhaps one or other of the Rebus brothers had not been playing the game according to the set rules. Maybe Gill Templer would know.

He came up behind her as she left the building. She knew it was him, but for once she wanted to speak with him.

'Hello, Jim. Can I give you a lift somewhere?'

He decided that she could. She could drop him off at a bar, unless, of course, he could see Rebus for a moment? He could not. They drove.

'This story is becoming more and more bizarre by the second, don't you think?'

She concentrated her eyes on the road, seeming to mull over his question. Really, she was hoping he would open up a little more and that her silence would lead him to believe that she was holding back on him, that there was something there between them to swop.

'Rebus seems to be the main actor though. Interesting that.'

Gill sensed that he was about to play a card.

'I mean,' he went on, lighting a cigarette, 'don't mind if I smoke, do you?'

'No,' she said slowly, though inside she was jarring with electricity.

'Thanks. I mean, it's interesting because I've got Rebus pencilled into another story I'm working on.'

She pulled the car up at a red light, but her eyes still gazed through the windscreen.

'Would you be interested in hearing about this other story, Gill?'

Would she? Of course she would. But what in return . . .

'Yes, a very interesting man, Mister Rebus. And his brother.'

'His brother?'

'Yes, you know, Michael Rebus, the hypnotist. An interesting pair of brothers.'

'Oh?'

'Listen, Gill, let's cut the crap.'

'I was hoping you would.' She put the car into gear and started off again.

'Are you lot investigating Rebus for anything? That's what I want to know. I mean, do you really know who's behind all this but aren't saying?'

She turned to him now.

'That's not the way it works, Jim.'

He snorted.

'It may not be the way you work, Gill, but don't pretend it doesn't happen. I just wondered if you'd heard anything, any rumbles from higher up. Maybe to the effect that someone had made a botch-up in allowing things to come to this.'

Jim Stevens was watching her face very closely indeed, throwing out ideas and vague theories in the hope that one of them would catch her. But she didn't seem to be taking the bait. Very well. Maybe she didn't know anything. That didn't mean his theories were wrong necessarily. It could just mean that things started at a higher plane than that on which Gill Templer and he operated.

'Jim, what is it you *think* you know about John Rebus? It could be important, you know. We could bring you in if we thought you were withholding . . .'

Stevens began to make tutting sounds, shaking his head.

'We know that's not on, don't we though? I mean, that is just not on.'

She looked at him again.

'I could make a precedent,' she said.

He stared at her. Yes, maybe she could at that.

'This'll do just here,' he said, pointing out of the window. Some ash fell from his cigarette onto his tie. Gill stopped the car and watched him climb out. He leaned back in before shutting the door.

'A swop can be arranged if you'd like one. You know my phone number.'

Yes, she knew his phone number. He had written it down for her a very long time ago, so long ago that they were on different sides of a wall now, so that she could hardly understand him at all. What did he know about John? About Michael? As she drove off towards Rebus's flat, she hoped that she would find out there.

21

John Rebus read a few pages from his *Good News Bible*, but put it down when he realised that he was taking none of it in. He prayed instead, screwing up his eyes into tiny fists. Then he walked around the flat, touching things. This he had done before that first breakdown. He was not afraid now though. Let it come if it would, let everything come. He had no resilience left. He was passive to the will of his malevolent creator.

There was a ring at the door. He did not answer. They would go away, and he would be alone again with his grief, his impotent anger, and his undusted possessions. The bell rang again, more persistently this time. Cursing, he went to the door and pulled it open. Michael was standing there.

'John,' he said, 'I came as soon as I could.'

'Mickey, what are you doing here?' He ushered his brother into the flat.

'Somebody phoned me. She told me all about it. Terrible news, John. Just terrible.' He placed a hand on Rebus's shoulder. Rebus, tingling, realised how long it had been since he had felt the touch of a human being, a sympathetic, brotherly touch. 'I was confronted by two gorillas outside. They seem to have you under close watch here.'

'Procedure,' said Rebus.

Procedure maybe, but Michael knew how guilty he must have looked when they had pounced on him. He had wondered at the phone-call, wondered about the possibility of a trap. So he had listened to the local radio news. There had been an abduction, a killing. It was true. So he had driven over, into this lion's den, knowing that he should stay well away from his brother, knowing that they would kill him if they found out, and wondering whether the abduction could have anything to do with his own situation. Was this a warning to both brothers? He could not say. But when those two gorillas had approached him in the shadows of the tenement stairs, he had thought the game all over. Firstly, they had been gangsters, out to get him. Then, they had been police officers, about to arrest him. But no, they were 'procedure'.

'You say it was a woman who called you? Did you catch her name? No, never mind, I know who it was anyway.'

They sat in the living-room. Michael, removing his sheep-skin jacket, brought a bottle of whisky out of one of the pockets.

'Would this help?' he said.

'It won't do any harm.'

Rebus went to fetch glasses from the kitchen, while Michael inspected the living-room.

'This is a nice place,' he called.

'Well, it's a bit big for my needs,' said Rebus. A choking sound came from the kitchen. Michael walked through to discover his big brother leaning into the sink, weeping grimly but quietly.

'John,' said Michael, hugging Rebus, 'it's okay. It's going to be okay.' He felt guilt well up inside him.

Rebus was fumbling for a handkerchief and, having found it, gave his nose a good blow and wiped his eyes.

'That's easy for you to say,' he sniffed, trying out a smile, 'you're a heathen.'

They drank half of the whisky, sitting back in their chairs, silently contemplating the shadowy ceiling above. Rebus's eyes were red-rimmed, and his eye-lashes stung. He sniffed occa-sionally, rubbing at his nose with the back of his hand. To Michael, it was like being boys again, but with the roles reversed for a moment. Not that they had been that close, but sentiment would always win over reality. Certainly he remembered John fighting one or two of his playground battles for him. Guilt welled up again. He shivered slightly. He had to get out of this game, but perhaps already he was in too deep, and if he had brought John unknowingly into the game too . . . That did not bear thinking about. He had to see the Man, had to explain things to him. But how? He had no telephone number or address. It was always the Man who called him, never the other way round. It was farcical now that he thought about it. Like a nightmare.

'Did you enjoy the show the other night?'

Rebus forced himself to think back to it, to the perfumed and lonely woman, to his fingers around her throat, the scene which had signalled the beginning of his end.

'Yes, it was interesting.' He had fallen asleep had he not? Never mind.

Silence again, the broken sounds of traffic outside, a few shouts from distant drunks.

'They say it's someone with a grudge against me,' he said finally.

'Oh? And is it?'

'I don't know. It looks like it.'

'But surely you would *know*?'

Rebus shook his head.

'That's the trouble, Mickey. I can't remember.'

Michael sat up in his chair.

'You can't remember what exactly?'

'Something. I don't know. Just something. If I knew what, I *would* remember, wouldn't I? But there's a gap. I know there is. I know that there's something I should remember.'

'Something from your past?' Michael was keening now. Perhaps this had nothing at all to do with himself. Perhaps it was all to do with something else, someone else. He grew hopeful.

'From the past, yes. But I can't remember.' Rebus rubbed his forehead as though it were a crystal ball. Michael was fumbling in his pocket.

'I can help you to remember, John.'

'How?'

'Like this.' Michael was holding, between thumb and forefinger, a silver coin. 'You remember what I told you, John. I take my patients back into past lives every day. It should be easy enough to take you back into your *real* past.'

It was John Rebus's turn to sit up. He shook away the whisky fumes.

'Come on then,' he said. 'What do I do?' But inside part of him was saying: *you don't want this, you don't want to know.*

He wanted to know.

Michael came over to his chair.

'Lie back in the chair. Get comfortable. Don't touch any more of that whisky. But remember, not everyone is susceptible to hypnotism. Don't force yourself. Don't try too hard. If it's going to come, it'll come whether you will it or not. Just relax, John, relax.'

The doorbell rang.

'Ignore it,' said Rebus, but Michael had already left the room. There were voices in the hall, and when Michael reappeared he was followed into the room by Gill.

'The telephone caller, it seems,' said Michael.

'How are you, John?' Her face was angled into a portrait of concern.

'Fine, Gill. Listen, this is my brother Michael. The hypnotist. He's going to put me under – that's what you called it, wasn't it, Mickey? – to remove whatever block there might be in my memory. Maybe you should be ready to take some notes or something.'

Gill looked from one brother to the other, feeling a little out of things. An interesting pair of brothers. That's what Jim Stevens had said. She had been working for sixteen hours, and now this. But she smiled and shrugged her shoulders.

'Can a girl get a drink first?'

It was John Rebus's turn to smile. 'Help yourself,' he said. 'There's whisky or whisky and water or water. Come on, Mickey. Let's get on with this. Sammy's out there somewhere. There might still be time.'

Michael spread his legs a little, leaning down over Rebus. He seemed to be about to consume his brother, his eyes close to Rebus's eyes, his mouth working in a mirror-image. That's what it looked like to Gill, pouring whisky into a tumbler. Michael held up the coin, trying to find the angle of the room's single low-wattage bulb. Finally, the glint was reflected in John's retina, the pupils expanding and contracting. Michael felt sure that his brother would be amenable. He certainly hoped so.

'Listen carefully, John. Listen to my voice. Watch the coin, John. Watch it shine and spin. See it spinning. Can you see it spinning, John? Now relax, just listen to me. And watch the spin, watch it glow.'

For a moment it seemed that Rebus would not go under. Perhaps it was the familial tie that was making him immune to the voice, to its suggestive power. But then Michael saw the eyes change a little, imperceptibly to the uninitiated. But he was initiated. His father had taught him well. His brother was in the limbo world now, caught in the coin's light, transported to wherever Michael wanted him to go. Under his power. As ever, Michael felt a little shiver run through him: this was power, power total and irreducible. He could do anything with his patients, anything.

'Michael,' whispered Gill, 'ask him why he left the Army.'

Michael swallowed, lining his throat with saliva. Yes, that was a good question. One he had wanted to ask John himself.

'John?' he said. 'John? Why did you leave the Army, John? What happened, John? Why did you leave the Army? Tell us.'

And slowly, as though learning to use words strange or unknown to him, Rebus began to tell his story. Gill rushed to her bag for a pen and a notepad. Michael sipped his whisky. They listened.

PART FOUR

The cross

22

I had been in the Parachute Regiment since the age of eighteen. But then I decided to try for the Special Air Service. Why did I do that? Why will any soldier take a cut in pay to join the SAS? I can't answer that. All I know now is that I found myself in Herefordshire, at the SAS's training camp. I called it The Cross because I'd been told that they would try to crucify me, and there, along with the other volunteers, I went through hell, marching, training, testing, pushing. They took us to the breaking point. They taught us to be lethal.

At that time there were rumours of an imminent civil war in Ulster, of the SAS being used to root out insurrectionists. The day came for us to be badged. We were given new berets and cap-badges. We were in the SAS. But there was more. Gordon Reeve and myself were called into the Boss's office and told that we had been judged the two best trainees of the batch. There was a two-year training period in front of us before we could become regulars, but great things were predicted for us.

Later, Reeve spoke to me as we left the building.

'Listen,' he said, 'I've heard a few of the rumours. I've heard the officers talking. They've got plans for us, Johnny. *Plans*. Mark my words.'

Weeks later, we were put on a survival course, hunted by other regiments, who if they captured us would stop at nothing to prise from us information about our mission. We had to trap and hunt our food, lying low and travelling across bleak moorland by night. We seemed destined to go through these tests together, though on this occasion we were working with two others.

'They've got something special lined up for us,' Reeve kept saying. 'I can feel it in my bones.'

Lying in our bivouac, we had just slipped into our sleeping-bags for a two-hour nap when our guard put his nose into the shelter.

'I don't know how to tell you this,' he said, and then there were lights and guns everywhere, and we were half-beaten into unconsciousness as the shelter was ripped open. Foreign tongues clacked at us, their faces masked behind the torches. A rifle-butt to the kidneys told me that this was for real. *For real.*

The cell into which I was thrown was real enough, too. The cell into which I was thrown was smeared with blood, faeces, and other things. It contained a stinking mattress and a cockroach. That was all. I lay down on the damp mattress and tried to sleep, for I knew that sleep would be the first thing to be stripped from us all.

The bright lights of the cell came on suddenly and stayed on, burning into my skull. Then the noises started, noises of a beating and a questioning taking place in the cell next to me.

'Leave him alone, you bastards! I'll tear your fucking heads off!'

I slammed at the wall with fists and boots, and the noises stopped. A cell door slammed shut, a body was dragged past my metal door, there was silence. I knew my time would come.

I waited there, waited for hours and days, hungry, thirsty, and every time I closed my eyes a sound like that of a blaring radio caught between stations would sound from the walls and the ceiling. I lay with my hands over my ears.

Fuck you, fuck you, fuck you.

I was supposed to crack now, and if I cracked I would have failed everything, all the months of training. So I sang tunes loudly to myself. I scraped my nails across the walls of the cell, walls wet with fungus, and scratched my name there as an anagram: BRUSE. I played games in my head, thought up crossword-puzzle clues and little linguistic tricks. I turned survival into a game. A game, a game, a game. I had to keep reminding myself that, no matter how bad things seemed to be getting, this was all a game.

And I thought of Reeve, who had warned me of this. Big plans indeed. Reeve was the nearest thing I had to a friend in the unit. I wondered if it had been his body dragged across the floor outside my cell. I prayed for him.

And one day they sent me food and a mug of brown water. The food looked as though it had been scooped straight from the mud-crawl and pushed through the little hole which had suddenly appeared in my door and just as suddenly vanished. I willed this cold swill into becoming a steak with two veg, and then placed a spoonful of it in my mouth. Immediately, I spat it out again. The water tasted of iron. I made a show of wiping my chin on my sleeve. I felt sure I was being watched.

'My compliments to the chef,' I called.

Next thing I knew, I was falling over into sleep.

I was in the air. There could be no doubt of that. I was in a helicopter, the air blowing into my face. I came round slowly, and opened my eyes on darkness. My head was in some kind of sack, and my arms were tied behind my back. I felt the helicopter swoop and rise and swoop again.

'Awake are you?' A butt prodded me.

'Yes.'

'Good. Now give me the name of your regiment and the details of your mission. We're not going to fuck around with you, sonny. So you better do it now.'

'Get stuffed.'

'I hope you can swim, sonny. I hope you get the *chance* to swim. We're about two-hundred feet above the Irish Sea, and we're about to push you out of this fucking chopper with your hands still tied. You'll hit that water as though it was fucking concrete, do you know that? It may kill you or it may stun you. The fish will eat you alive, sonny. And your corpse will never be found, not out here. Do you understand what I'm saying?'

It was an official and businesslike voice.

'Yes.'

'Good. Now, the name of your regiment, and the details of your mission.'

'Get stuffed.' I tried to sound calm. I'd be another accident statistic, killed on training, no questions asked. I'd hit that sea like a light-bulb hitting a wall.

'Get stuffed,' I said again, intoning to myself: it's only a game, it's only a game.

'This isn't a game, you know. Not anymore. Your friends have already spilled their guts, Rebus. One of them, Reeve I think it was, spilled his guts quite literally. Okay, men, give him the heave.'

'Wait . . .'

'Enjoy your swim, Rebus.'

Hands gripped my legs and torso. In the darkness of the sack, with the wind blowing fiercely against me, I began to feel that it had all been a grave mistake.

'Wait . . .'

I could feel myself hanging in space, two-hundred feet up above the sea, with the gulls shrieking for me to be let go.

'Wait!'

'Yes, Rebus?'

'Take the fucking sack off my head at least!' I was shrieking now, desperate.

'Let the bastard drop.'

And with that they let me go. I hung in the air for a second, then I dropped, dropped like a brick. I was falling through space, trussed up like a Christmas turkey. I screamed for one second, maybe two, and then I hit the ground.

I hit solid ground.

And lay there while the helicopter landed. People were laughing all around me. The foreign voices were back. They lifted me up and dragged me along to the cell. I was glad of the sack over my head. It disguised the fact that I was crying. Inside I was a mass of quivering coils, tiny serpents of fear and adrenaline and relief which bounced through my liver, my lungs, my heart.

The door slammed behind me. Then I heard a shuffling sound at my back. Hands fumbled at the knots of my bonds. With the hood off, it took me a few seconds to regain my sight.

I stared into a face that seemed to be my own. Another twist to the game. Then I recognised Gordon Reeve, at the same time as he recognised me.

'Rebus?' he said. 'They told me you'd . . .'

'They told me the same thing about you. How are you?'

'Fine, fine. Jesus, though, I'm glad to see you.'

We hugged one another, feeling the other's weakened but still human embrace, the smells of suffering and of endurance. There were tears in his eyes.

'It *is* you,' he said. 'I'm not dreaming.'

'Let's sit down,' I said. 'My legs aren't too steady.'

What I meant was that his legs weren't too steady. He was leaning into me as if I were a crutch. He sat down thankfully.

'How has it been?' I asked.

'I kept in shape for a while.' He slapped one of his legs. 'Doing push-ups and stuff. But I soon grew too tired. They've tried feeding me with hallucinogens. I keep seeing things when I'm awake.'

'They've tried me with knockout drops.'

'Those drugs, they're something else. Then there's the power-hose. I get sprayed about once a day I suppose. Freezing cold. Can never seem to get dry.'

'How long do you suppose we've been here?' Did I look as bad to him as he looked to me? I hoped not. He hadn't mentioned the chopper drop. I decided to keep quiet about that one.

'Too long,' he was saying. 'This is fucking ridiculous.'

'You were always saying that they had something special in store for us. I didn't believe you, God forgive me.'

'This wasn't exactly what I had in mind.'

'It *is* us they're interested in though.'

'What do you mean?'

It had been only half a thought until now, but now I was sure.

'Well, when our sentry put his nose into the tent that night, there was no surprise in his eyes, and even less fear. I think they were both in on it from the start.'

'So what's this all about?'

I looked at him, sitting with his chin on his knees. We were frail creatures on the outside. Piles biting like the hungered jaws of vampire bats, mouths aching with sores and ulcers. Hair falling out, teeth loose. But there was strength in numbers. And that was what I could not understand: why had they put us together when, apart, we were both on the edge of breaking?

'So what's this all about?'

Perhaps they were trying to lull us into a false sense of security before really tightening the screws. The worst is not, so long as we can say 'this is the worst'. Shakespeare, *King Lear*. I wouldn't have known that at the time, but I know it now. Let it stand.

'I don't know,' I said. 'They'll tell us when they're good and ready, I suppose.'

'Are you scared?' he said suddenly. His eyes were staring at the raddled door of our cell.

'Maybe.'

'You should be fucking scared, Johnny. I am. I remember once when I was a kid, some of us went along a river near our housing-scheme. It was in spate. It had been pissing down for a week. It was just after the war, and there were a lot of ruined houses about. We headed upriver, and came to a sewage-pipe. I played with older kids. I don't know why. They made me the brunt of all their fucking games, but I stuck with them. I suppose I liked the idea of running about with kids who scared the shit out of all the kids of my own age. So that, though the older kids were treating me like shit, they gave me power over the younger kids. Do you see?'

I nodded, but he wasn't looking.

'This pipe wasn't very thick, but it was long, and it was high above the river. They said I was to cross it first. Christ, I was afraid. I was so fucking scared that my legs wobbled and I froze there, halfway across. And then piss started to run down my legs out of my shorts, and they noticed that and they laughed. They laughed at me, and I couldn't run, couldn't move. So they left me there and went away.'

I thought of the laughter as I had been dragged away from the helicopter.

'Did anything like that ever happen to you when you were a kid, Johnny?'

'I don't think so.'

'Then why the hell did you join up?'

'To get away from home. I didn't get along with my father, you see. He preferred my kid brother. I felt out in the cold.'

'I never had a brother.'

'Neither did I, not in the proper sense. I had an adversary.'

I'm going to bring him out

don't you dare

This isn't telling us anything

keep going

'What did your father do, Johnny?'

'He was a hypnotist. He used to make people come on stage and do stupid things.'

'You're joking!'

'It's true. My brother was going to follow in his footsteps, but I wasn't. So I got out. They weren't exactly sad to see me go.'

Reeve chuckled.

'If you put us into a sale, you'd have to say "slightly soiled" on the ticket, eh, Johnny?'

I laughed at that, laughed longer and louder than necessary, and we put an arm round one another and stayed that way, keeping warm.

We slept side by side, pissed and defecated in the presence of the other, tried to exercise together, played little mind games together, and endured together.

Reeve had a piece of string with him, and would wind it and unwind it, making up the knots we had been taught in training. This led me to explain the meaning of a Gordian knot to him. He waved a miniature reef knot at me.

'Gordian knot, reef knot. Gordian reef. It sounds just like my name, doesn't it?'

Again, there was something to laugh about.

We also played noughts and crosses, scratching the games onto the powdery walls of the cell with our fingernails. Reeve showed me a ploy which meant that the least you could achieve was a draw. We must have played about three-hundred games before then, with Reeve winning two-thirds of them. The trick was simple enough.

'Your first O goes in the top left corner, and your second diagonally across from it. It's an unbeatable position.'

'What if your opponent puts his X diagonally opposite that first O?'

'You can still win by going for the corners.'

Reeve seemed cheered by this. He danced round the cell, then stared at me, a leer on his face.

'You're just like the brother I never had, John.' There and then he took my palm and nicked the flesh open with one of his fingernails, doing the same to his own hand. We touched palms, smearing a spot of blood backwards and forwards.

'Blood brothers,' said Gordon, smiling.

I smiled back at him, knowing that he had become too dependent on me already, and that if we were separated he would not be able to cope.

And then he knelt down in front of me and gave me another hug.

Gordon grew more restless. He did fifty press-ups in any one day which, considering our diet, was phenomenal. And he hummed little tunes to himself. The effects of my company seemed to be wearing off. He was drifting again. So I began to tell him stories.

I talked about my childhood first, and about my father's tricks, but then I started to tell him proper stories, giving him the plots of my favourite books. The time came to tell him the story of Raskolnikov, that most moral of tales, *Crime and Punishment*. He listened enthralled, and I tried to spin it out as long as I could. I made bits up, invented whole dialogues and characters. And when I'd finished it, he said, 'Tell me that one again.'

So I did.

'Was it all inevitable, John?' Reeve was pushing his fingers across the floor of the cell, seated on his haunches. I was lying on the mattress.

'Yes,' I said. 'I think it was. Certainly, it's written that way. The end of the book is there before the beginning's hardly started.'

'Yes, that's the feeling I got.'

There was a long pause, then he cleared his throat.

'What's your idea of God, John? I'd really like to know.'

So I told him, and as I spoke, lacing my erroneous arguments with little stories from the Bible, Gordon Reeve lay down and stared up at me with eyes like the full moons of winter. He was concentrating like mad.

'I can't believe any of that,' he said at last as I swallowed dry saliva. 'I wish I could, but I can't. I think Raskolnikov should have relaxed and enjoyed his freedom. He should have got himself a Browning and blown the lot of them away.'

I thought about that comment. There seemed to me a little justice in it, but a great deal against it also. Reeve was like a man trapped in limbo, believing in a lack of belief, but not necessarily lacking the belief to believe.

What's all this shit?

Sshhhh.

And in between the games and the story-telling, he put his hand on my neck.

'John, we're friends, aren't we? I mean, really close friends? I've never had a close friend before.' His breath was hot, despite the chill in the cell. 'But we're friends, aren't we? I mean, I've taught you how to win at noughts and crosses, haven't I?' His eyes were no longer human. They were the eyes of a wolf. I had seen it coming, but there had been nothing I could do.

Not until now. But now I saw everything with the clear, hallucinogen eyes of one who has seen everything there is to see and more. I could see Gordon bring his face up to mine and slowly – so slowly that it might not have been happening at all – plant a breathy kiss on my cheek, trying to turn my head around so as to connect with the lips.

And I saw myself yield. No, no, this was not to happen! This was intolerable. This wasn't what we'd been building up all these weeks, was it? And if it was, then I'd been a fool throughout.

'Just a kiss,' he was saying, 'just one kiss, John. Hell, come on.' And there were tears in his eyes, because he too could see that everything had gone haywire in an instant. He too could see that something was ending. But that didn't stop him from edging his way behind me, making the two-backed beast. (Shakespeare. Let it go.) And I was trembling, but strangely immobile. I knew that this was beyond my ken, beyond my control. So I forced the tears up into my eyes, and my nose started to run.

'Just a kiss.'

All the training, all the pushing towards that final lethal goal, it had all come to this moment. In the end, love was still behind everything.

'John.'

And I could feel only pity for the two of us, stinking, besmirched, barren in our cell. I could feel only the frustration of the thing, the poor tears of a lifetime's indignation. Gordon, Gordon, Gordon.

'John . . .'

The cell-door burst open, as though it had never been locked.

A man stood there. English, not foreign, and of high rank. He looked in on the spectacle with some distaste; no doubt he had been listening to it all, if not watching it. He pointed to me.

'Rebus,' he said, 'you've passed. You're on our side now.'

I looked at his face. What did he mean? I knew full well what he meant.

'You've passed the test, Rebus. Come on. Come with me. We'll get you kitted up. You're on our side now. The interrogation of your . . . friend . . . continues. You'll be helping us with the interrogation from now on.'

Gordon jumped to his feet. He was directly behind me still. I could feel his breath on the back of my neck.

'What do you mean?' I said. My mouth and stomach were dry. Looking at this crisply starched officer, I became painfully aware of my own filth. But then it was all his fault. 'This is a trick,' I said. 'It must be. I'm not going to tell you. I'm not going *with* you. I've not given away any information. I've not cracked. You can't fail me now!' I was shouting now, delirious. Yet I knew there was truth in what he was saying. He shook his head slowly.

'I can understand your suspicion, Rebus. You've been under a lot of pressure. A hellish lot of pressure. But that's past. You've not failed, you've passed; passed with flying colours. I think we can say that with certainty. You've passed, Rebus. You're on our side now. You'll be helping us now to try to crack Reeve here. Do you understand?'

I shook my head.

'It's a trick,' I said. The officer smiled sympathetically. He'd dealt with the like of me a hundred times before.

'Look,' he said, 'just come with us and everything will be made clear.'

Gordon jumped forward at my side.

'No!' he shouted. 'He's already told you that he's not fucking well going! Now piss off out of here.' Then to me, a hand on my shoulder: 'Don't listen to him, John. It's a trick. It's always a trick with these bastards.' But I could see that he was worried.

His eyes moved rapidly, his mouth slightly open. And, feeling his hand on me, I knew that my decision had been made already, and Gordon seemed to sense as much.

'I think that's for Trooper Rebus to decide, don't you?' the officer was saying.

And then the man stared at me, his eyes friendly.

I didn't need to look back at the cell, or at Gordon. I just kept thinking to myself: it's another part of the game, just another part of the game. The decision had been made a long time ago. They were not lying to me, and of course I wanted out of the cell. It was preordained. Nothing was arbitrary. I had been told that at the start of my training. I started forwards, but Gordon held onto the tatters of my shirt.

'John,' he said, his voice full of need, 'don't let me down, John. Please.'

But I pulled away from his weak grip and left the cell.

'No! No! No!' His cries were huge, fiery things. 'Don't let me down, John! Let me out! Let me out!'

And then he screamed, and I almost crumpled on the floor. It was the scream of the mad.

After I had been cleaned up and seen by a doctor, I was taken to what they euphemistically called the debriefing-room. I'd been through hell – was still going through hell – and they were about to discuss it as though it had been nothing more than a school exercise.

There were four of them there, three captains and a psychiatrist. They told me everything then. They explained that a new, elitist group was about to be set up from within the SAS, and that its role would be the infiltration and destabilization of terrorist groups, starting with the Irish Republican Army, who were becoming more than a mere nuisance as the Irish situation deteriorated into civil war. Because of the nature of the job, only the best – the very best – would be good enough, and Reeve and I had been judged the best in our section. Therefore, we had been trapped, had been taken prisoner, and had been put through tests the like of which had never been tried in the SAS before. None of this really surprised me by now. I was thinking of the other poor bastards who were being put through this whole sick bloody thing. And all so that when we were being kneecapped, we would not let on who we were.

And then they came to Gordon.

'Our attitude towards Trooper Reeve is rather ambivalent.' This was the man in the white coat talking. 'He's a bloody fine soldier, and give him a physical job to do and he'll do it. But he has always worked as a loner in the past, so we put the two of you together to see how you would react to sharing a cell, and, more especially, to see how Reeve would cope once his friend had been taken away from him.'

Did they know of that kiss then, or did they not?

'I'm afraid,' went on the doctor, 'that the result may be negative. He's come to depend upon you, John, hasn't he? We are, of course, aware that you have not been dependent upon him.'

'What about the screams from the other cells?'

'Tape-recordings.'

I nodded, tired suddenly, uninterested.

'The whole thing was another bloody test then?'

'Of course it was.' They had a little smile between them. 'But that needn't bother you now. What matters is that you've passed.'

It did worry me, though. What was it all about? I'd exchanged friendship for this informal debriefing. I'd exchanged love for these smirks. And Gordon's screams were still in my ears. Revenge, he was crying, revenge. I laid my hands on my knees, bent forward, and started to weep.

'You bastards,' I said, 'you bastards.'

And if I'd had a Browning pistol with me at that moment, I'd have put large holes into their grinning skulls.

They had me checked again, more thoroughly this time, in a military hospital. Civil war had indeed broken out in Ulster, but

I stared past it towards Gordon Reeve. What had happened to him? Was he still in that stinking cell, alone because of me? Was he falling apart? I took it all on my shoulders and wept again. They had given me a box of tissues. That seemed to be the way of things.

Then I started to weep all day, sometimes uncontrollably, taking it all on, taking everything on my conscience. I suffered from nightmares. I volunteered my resignation. I *demanded* my resignation. It was accepted, reluctantly. I was, after all, a guinea-pig. I went to a small fishing-village in Fife and walked along the pebbled beach, recovering from my nervous break-down and putting the whole thing out of my mind stuffing the most painful episode of my life into drawers and attics in my head, locking it all away, learning to forget.

So I forgot.

And they were good to me. They gave me some compensation money and they pulled a lot of strings when I decided that I wanted to join the police force. Oh yes, I could not complain about their attitude towards me, but I wasn't allowed to find out about my friend, and I wasn't ever to get in touch with them again. I was dead, I was strictly off their records.

I was a failure.

And I'm still a failure. Broken marriage. My daughter kidnapped. But it all makes sense now. The whole thing makes sense. So at least I know that Gordon is alive, if not well, and I know that he has my little girl and that he's going to kill her.

And kill me if he can.

And to get her back, I'm going to have to kill him.

And I would do it now. God help me, I would do it now.

PART FIVE

Knots & crosses

23

When John Rebus awoke from what had seemed a particularly
deep and dream-troubled sleep, he found that he was not in
bed. He saw that Michael was standing over him, a wary smile
on his face, and that Gill was pacing to and fro, sniffing back
tears.

'What happened?' said Rebus.

'Nothing,' said Michael.

Then Rebus recalled that Michael had hypnotised him.

'Nothing?' cried Gill. 'You call that nothing?'

'John,' said Michael, 'I didn't realise that you felt that way
about the old man and me. I'm sorry we made you feel bad.'
Michael rested his hand on his brother's shoulder, *the brother he
had never known.*

Gordon, Gordon Reeve. What happened to you? You're all
torn and dirty, whirling around me like grit on a wind-swept
street. Like a brother. You've got my daughter. Where are you?

'Oh, Jesus.' Rebus let his head fall, screwing his eyes shut.
Gill's hand stroked his hair.

It was growing light outside. The birds were back into their
untiring routine. Rebus was glad that they were calling him
back into the real world. They reminded him that there might
be someone out there who was feeling happy. Perhaps lovers
awakening in each other's arms, or a man who was realising
that today was a holiday, or an elderly woman thanking God
that she was alive to see the first hints of reawakening life.

'A real dark night of the soul,' he said, beginning to shake.
'It's cold in here. The pilot-light must have blown out.'

Gill blew her nose and folded her arms.

'No, it's warm enough in here, John. Listen,' she spoke slowly, deferentially, 'we need a physical description of this man. I know that it will have to be a fifteen-year-old description, but it'll be a start. Then we need to check up on what happened to him after you des . . . after you left him.'

'That will be classified, if it exists at all.'

'And we need to tell the Chief about all of this.' Gill went on as if Rebus had said nothing. Her eyes were fixed in front of her. 'We need to find that creep.'

The room seemed very quiet to Rebus, as though a death had occurred, when really it had been a birth of sorts, the birth of his memory. Of Gordon. Of walking out of that cold, merciless cell. Of turning his back . . .

'Can you be sure that this Reeve character is your man?' Michael was pouring more whisky. Rebus shook his head at the proffered glass.

'Not for me thanks. My head feels all fuzzy. Oh yes, I think we can be pretty certain who's behind it. The messages, the knots and the crosses. It all makes sense now. It's been making sense all along. Reeve must think I'm really thick. He's been sending me clear messages for weeks, and I've failed to realise . . . I've let those girls die . . . All because I couldn't face the facts . . . the facts . . .'

Gill bent down behind him and put her hands on his shoulders. John Rebus shot out of his chair and turned to her. *Reeve.* No, Gill, Gill. He shook his head in mute apology. Then burst into tears.

Gill looked towards Michael, but Michael had lowered his eyes. She hugged Rebus hard, not allowing him to break away from her again, all the time whispering that it was she, Gill, beside him, and not any ghost from the past. Michael was wondering what he had got himself into. He had never seen John cry before. Again, the guilt flooded him. He would stop it all. He didn't need it any more. He would lie low and just let his dealer get tired of looking for him, let his clients find new people. He would do it, not for John's sake but for his own.

We treated him like shit, he thought to himself, it's true. The old man and me treated him as though he were an intruder.

Later, over coffee, Rebus seemed calm, though Gill's eyes were still on him, wondering, fearing.

'We can be sure that this Reeve is off his chump,' she said.

'Perhaps,' said Rebus. 'One thing *is* for sure, he'll be armed. He'll be ready for anything. The man was a Seaforths regular and a member of the SAS. He'll be hard as nails.'

'You were too, John.'

'That's why I'm the man to track him down. The Chief must be made to understand that, Gill. I'm back on the case.'

Gill pursed her lips.

'I'm not sure he'll go for that,' she said.

'Well, sod him then. I'll find the bastard anyway.'

'You do that, John,' said Michael. 'You do that. Don't care what any of them say.'

'Mickey,' said Rebus, 'you are absolutely the best brother I could have had. Now, is there any food on the go? I'm starved.'

'And I'm whacked,' said Michael, feeling pleased with himself. 'Do you mind if I lie down for an hour or two here before I drive back?'

'Not at all, go through to my room, Mickey.'

'Goodnight, Michael,' said Gill.

He was smiling as he left them.

Knots and crosses. Noughts and crosses. It was so blatant, really. Reeve must have taken him for a fool, and in a way he had been right. Those endless games they had played, all those tricks and manoeuvres, and their talk about Christianity, those reef knots and Gordian knots. And The Cross. God, how stupid he had been, allowing his memory into tricking him that the past was a cracked and useless vessel, emptying its spirit. How stupid.

'John, you're spilling your coffee.'

Gill was bringing in a plateful of cheese on toast from the kitchen. Rebus roused himself awake.

'Eat this. I've been on to HQ. We've to be there in two hours' time. They've already started running a check on Reeve's name. We should find him.'

'I hope so, Gill. Oh God, I hope so.'

They hugged. She suggested that they lie on the couch. They did so, tight in a warming embrace. Rebus couldn't help wondering whether his dark night had been an exorcism of sorts, whether the past would still haunt him sexually. He hoped not. Certainly, it was neither the time nor the place to try it out.

Gordon, my friend, what did I do to you?

24

Stevens was a patient man. The two policemen had been firm with him. No one could see Detective Sergeant Rebus for the moment. Stevens had returned to the newspaper office, worked on a report for the paper's three-a.m. print-run, and then had driven back to Rebus's flat. There were still lights on up there, but also there were two new gorillas by the door of the tenement. Stevens parked across the street and lit another cigarette. It was tying together nicely. The two threads were becoming one. The murders and the drug-pushing were involved in some way, and Rebus was the key by the look of things. What were his brother and he talking about at this hour? A contingency plan perhaps. God, he would have given anything to be a fly on the living-room wall just now. Anything. He knew reporters in Fleet Street who went in for sophisticated surveillance techniques – bugs, high-powered microphones, telephone-taps – and he wondered if it might not be worthwhile to invest in some of that equipment himself.

He formulated new theories in his head, theories with hundreds of permutations. If Edinburgh's drug-racketeers had gone into the abduction-and-murder business to put the frights on some poor bastards, then things were taking a very grim turn indeed, and he, Jim Stevens, would have to be even more careful in future. Yet Big Podeen had known nothing. Say, then, that a new gang had broken into the game, bringing with it new rules. That would make for a gang-war, Glasgow-style. But things, surely, were not done that way today. Maybe.

In this way, Stevens kept himself awake and alert, scribbling his thoughts into a notebook. His radio was on, and he listened to the half-hourly news reports. A policeman's daughter was the new victim of Edinburgh's child-murderer. In the most recent abduction, a man was killed, strangled in the house of the child's mother. And so on. Stevens went on formulating, went on speculating.

It had not yet been revealed that *all* the murders were linked to Rebus. The police were not about to make that public, not even to Jim Stevens.

At seven-thirty, Stevens managed to bribe a passing news-paper-boy into bringing him rolls and milk from a nearby shop. He washed the dry, powdery rolls down with the icy milk. The heating was on in his car, but he felt chilled to the marrow. He needed a shower, a shave, and some sleep. Not necessarily in that order. But he was too close to let this go now. He had the tenacity – some would call it madness, fanaticism – of every good reporter. He had watched other hacks arriving in the night and being sent away again. One or two had seen him sitting in his car and had come across for a chat and to sniff out any leads. He had hidden away his notebook then, feigning disinterest, telling them that he would be going home shortly. Lies, damned lies.

That was part of the business.

And now, finally, they were emerging from the building. A few cameras and microphones were there, of course, but nothing too tasteless, no pushing and shoving and harassing. For one thing, this was a grieving father; for another, he was a policeman. Nobody was about to harass him.

Stevens watched as Gill and Rebus were allowed to disappear into the back of an idling Rover police-car. He studied their faces. Rebus looked washed-out. That was only to be expected. But, behind that, lay a grimness of look, something about the way his mouth made a straight line. That bothered Stevens a little. It was as if the man were about to enter a war. Bloody hell. And then there was Gill Templer. She looked rough, rougher even than Rebus. Her eyes were red, but here too there was something a little out of the ordinary. Something was not quite as it should be. Any respecting reporter could see that, if he knew what he was looking for. Stevens gnawed at himself. He needed to know more. It was like a drug, his story. He needed bigger and bigger injections of it. He was a bit startled, too, to find himself admitting that the reason he needed these injections was not for the sake of his job, but for his own curiosity. Rebus intrigued him. Gill Templer, of course, interested him.

And Michael Rebus . . .

Michael Rebus had not appeared from the flat. The circus was leaving now, the Rover turning right out of the quiet Marchmont street, but the gorillas remained. New gorillas. Stevens lit a cigarette. It might be worth a try at that. He walked back to his car and locked it. Then, taking a walk round the block, formed another plan.

'Excuse me, sir. Do you live here?'

'Of course I live here! What's all this about, eh? I need to get to my bed.'

'Had a heavy night, sir?'

The bleary-eyed man shook three brown paper-bags at the policeman. The bags each contained six rolls.

'I'm a baker. Shift-work. Now if you'll . . .'

'And your name, sir?'

Making to pass the man, Stevens had just had time enough to make out a few of the names on the door-buzzer.

'Laidlaw,' he said. 'Jim Laidlaw.'

The policeman checked this against a list of names in his hand.

'All right, sir. Sorry to have bothered you.'

'What's all this about?'

'You'll find out soon enough, sir. Good night now.'

There was one more obstacle, and Stevens knew that for all his cunning, if the door was locked then the door was locked, and his game was up. He made a plausible push at the heavy door and felt it give. They had not locked it. His patron saint was smiling on him today.

In the tenement hallway, he ditched the rolls and thought of another ploy. He climbed the two flights of stairs to Rebus's door. The tenement seemed to smell exclusively of cats'-piss. At Rebus's door he paused, catching his breath. Partly, he was out of condition, but partly, also, he was excited. He had not felt anything like this on a story for years. It felt good. He decided that he could get away with anything on a day like this. He pushed the doorbell relentlessly.

The door was opened at last by a yawning, puffy-faced Michael Rebus. So at last they were face to face. Stevens flashed a card at Michael. The card identified James Stevens as a member of an Edinburgh snooker club.

'Detective Inspector Stevens, sir. Sorry to get you out of bed.' He put the card away. 'Your brother told us that you'd probably still be asleep, but I thought I'd come up anyway. May I come in? Just a few questions, sir. Won't keep you too long.'

The two policemen, their feet numb despite thermal socks and the fact that it was the beginning of summer, shuffled one foot and then the other, hoping for a reprieve. The talk was all of the abduction and the fact that a Chief Inspector's son had been murdered. The main door opened behind them.

'You lot still here? The wife told me there was bobbies at the door, but I didnae believe her. Yon wis last night though. What's the matter?'

This was an old man, still in his slippers but with a thick, winter overcoat on. He was half-shaven only, and his bottom false-teeth had been lost or forgotten about. He was attaching a cap to his bald head as he sidled out of the door.

'Nothing for you to worry about, sir. You'll be told soon enough, I'm sure.'

'Oh aye, well then. I'm just away to fetch the paper and the milk. We usually have toast for breakfast, but some bugger's gone and left about twa dozen new rolls in the lobby. Well, if they're no' wanted, they're aye welcome in my house.'

He chuckled, showing the raw red of his bottom gum.

'Can I get you twa anything at the shop?'

But the two policemen were staring at one another, alarmed, speechless.

'Get up there,' one said, finally, to the other. Then: 'And your name, sir?'

The old man preened himself; an old trooper.

'Jock Laidlaw,' he said, 'at your service.'

Stevens was drinking, thankfully, the black coffee. The first hot thing he'd had in ages. He was seated in the living-room, his eyes everywhere.

'I'm glad you woke me,' Michael Rebus was saying. 'I've got to get back home.'

I'll bet you have, thought Stevens. I'll bet you have. Rebus looked altogether more relaxed than he had foreseen. Relaxed, rested, easy with his conscience. Curiouser and curiouser.

'Just a few questions, Mister Rebus, as I said.'

Michael Rebus sat down, crossing his legs, sipping his own coffee.

'Yes?'

Stevens produced his notebook.

'Your brother has had a very great shock.'

'Yes.'

'But he'll be all right you think?'

'Yes.'

Stevens pretended to write in his book.

'Did he have a good night, by the way? Did he sleep all right?'

'Well, none of us got much sleep. I'm not sure John slept at all.' Michael's eyebrows were gathering. 'Look, what is all this?'

'Just routine, Mister Rebus. You understand. We need all the details from everyone involved if we're going to crack this case.'

'But it's cracked, isn't it?'

Stevens' heart jumped.

'Is it?' he heard himself say.

'Well, don't you know?'

'Yes, of course, but we have to get *all* the details –'

'From everyone concerned. Yes, so you said. Look, can I see your identification again? Just to be on the safe side.'

There was the sound of a key prodding at the front door.

Christ, thought Stevens, they're back already.

'Listen,' he said through his teeth, 'we know all about your little drugs-racket. Now tell us who's behind it or else we'll put you behind bars for a hundred years, sonny!'

Michael's face went light-blue, then grey. His mouth seemed ready to drop open with a word, the one word Stevens needed.

But then one of the gorillas was in the room, propelling Stevens out of his chair.

'I've not finished my coffee yet!' he protested.

'You're lucky I don't break your flaming neck, pal,' replied the policeman.

Michael Rebus stood up, too, but he was saying nothing.

'A name!' cried Stevens. 'Just give me the name! This'll be spread right across the front pages, my friend, if you don't co-operate! Give me the name!'

He kept up his cries all the way down the stairwell. Right down to the last step.

'All right, I'm going,' he said eventually, breaking free of the heavy grip on his arm. 'I'm going. You were a bit slack there, boys, weren't you? I'll keep it quiet this time, but next time you better be ready. Okay?'

'Get to fuck out of here,' said one gorilla.

Stevens got to fuck. He slid into his car, feeling more frustrated and more curious than ever. God, he'd been close. But what did the hypnotist mean by that? The case was cracked. Was it? If so, he wanted to be there with the first details. He was not used to being so far behind in the game. Usually, games were played by his rules. No, he was not used to this, and he did not like it at all.

He loved it.

But, if the case was cracked, then time was tight. And if you could not get what you wanted from one brother, then go to the other. He thought he knew where John Rebus would be. His intuition ran high today. He felt inspired.

25

'Well, John, this all seems quite fantastical, but I'm sure it's a possibility. Certainly, it's the best lead we've got, though I find it hard to conceive of a man with so much hate that he would murder four innocent girls just to give you the clues as to his ultimate victim.'

Chief Superintendent Wallace looked from Rebus to Gill Templer and back again. To Rebus's left sat Anderson. Wallace's hands lay like dead fish on his desk, a pen in front of him. The room was large and uncluttered, a self-assured oasis. Here, problems were always solved, decisions were made – always correctly.

'The problem now is finding him. If we make this thing public, then that might scare him off, endangering your daughter's life in the process. On the other hand, a public appeal would be by far the quickest way of finding him.'

'You can't possibly . . .!' It was Gill Templer who, in that quiet room, was on the verge of exploding, but Wallace silenced her with a wave of his hand.

'I am merely thinking aloud at this stage, Inspector Templer, merely casting stones into a pond.'

Anderson sat like a corpse, his eyes to the floor. He was on leave now officially and in mourning, but he had insisted on keeping in touch with the case and Superintendent Wallace had acquiesced.

'Of course, John,' Wallace was saying, 'it's impossible for you to remain on the case.'

Rebus rose to his feet.

'Sit down, John, please.' The Super's eyes were hard and

honest, the eyes of a real copper, one of the old school. Rebus sat down again. 'Now I know how you must feel, believe it or believe it not. But there's too much at stake here. Too much for all of us. You're far too involved to be of any objective use, and the public would cry out about vigilante tactics. You must see that.'

'All I see is that without me Reeve will stop at nothing. It's me he wants.'

'Exactly. And wouldn't we be stupid to hand you over to him on a plate? We'll do everything we can, as much as you could do. Leave it to us.'

'The Army won't tell you anything, you know.'

'They'll have to.' Wallace began to toy with his pen, as though it were there for that very purpose. 'Ultimately, they've got the same boss we have. They'll be made to tell.'

Rebus shook his head.

'They're a law unto themselves. The SAS is hardly even a part of the Army. If they don't want to tell you, then believe me, they won't tell you a bloody thing.' Rebus's hand came down onto the desk. 'Not a bloody thing.'

'John.' Gill's hand squeezed his shoulder, asking him to be calm. She herself looked like a fury, but she knew when to keep quiet and let looks alone transmit her anger and her displeasure. For Rebus, however, it was actions that counted. He'd been sitting outside reality for way too long.

He rose from his small chair like a pure force, no longer human, and left the room in silence. The Superintendent looked at Gill.

'He's off the case, Gill. He must be made to realise that. I believe that you,' he paused while opening and shutting a drawer, 'that you and he have an understanding. That, at least, is how we used to phrase it in my day. Perhaps you should make him aware of his position. We'll get this man, but not with Rebus hanging around intent on revenge.' Wallace looked towards Anderson, who stared drily at him. 'We don't want vigilante tactics,' he went on. 'Not in Edinburgh. What would the tourists say?' Then his face broke into a cold smile. He looked from Anderson to Gill, then rose from his chair. 'This is all becoming extremely . . .'

'Internecine?' suggested Gill.

'I was going to say incestuous. What with Chief Inspector Anderson here, his son and Rebus's wife, yourself and Rebus, Rebus and this man Reeve, Reeve and Rebus's daughter. I hope the press don't get wind of this. You'll be responsible for seeing that they don't, and for punishing any that do. Am I making myself clear?'

Gill Templer nodded, stifling a sudden yawn.

'Good.' The Super nodded across to Anderson. 'Now see that Chief Inspector Anderson gets home safely will you?'

William Anderson, seated in the back of the car, went through his mental list of informants and friends. He knew a couple of people who might know about the Special Air Service. Certainly, something like the Rebus–Reeve case could not have been hushed up totally, though it might well have been struck from the records. The soldiers would have known about it though. Grapevines existed everywhere, and especially where you would least expect them. He might need to twist a few arms and lay out a few tenners, but he would find the bastard if it was his last action on God's earth.

Or he would be there when Rebus did.

Rebus had left the HQ by a back entrance, as Stevens had hoped. He followed Rebus as the policeman, looking the worse for wear, stalked away. What was it all about? No matter. As long as he stuck to Rebus, he could be sure of getting his story, and what a story it promised to be. Stevens kept checking behind him, but there seemed to be no tail on Rebus. No police tail, that was. It seemed strange to him that they would allow Rebus to go off on his own when there was no telling what a man would do whose daughter had been abducted. Stevens was hoping for the ultimate plot: he was hoping that Rebus would lead him straight to the big boys behind this new drugs ring. If not one brother, then the other.

Like a brother to me, and I to him. What happened? He knew what was to blame at heart. The method, that was the cause of all of this. The caging and the breaking and then the patching up. The patching up had not been a success, had it? They were both broken men in their own ways. That knowledge wouldn't stop him from shearing Reeve's head from its shoulders though. Nothing would stop that. But he had to find the bastard yet, and he had no idea where to start. He could feel the city closing in on him, bringing to bear all of its historical weight, smothering him. Dissent, rationalism, enlightenment: Edinburgh had specialized in all three, and now he too would need these charms. He needed to work on his own, quickly, yet methodically, using ingenuity and every tool at his disposal. Most of all he needed instinct.

After five minutes, he knew he was being followed, and the hair stood up at the back of his neck. It was not the usual police tail. That would not have been so easy to spot. But was it . . . Could he be so close . . . At a bus-stop, he stopped and turned suddenly, as though checking to see if a bus was coming. He saw the man dodge into a doorway. It wasn't Gordon Reeve. It was that bloody reporter.

Rebus listened to his heart slow again, but the adrenaline was already pumping through him, filling him with a desire to run, to take off along this long straight road and run into the strongest head-wind imaginable. But then a bus came trundling round the corner, and he boarded that instead.

From the back window, he saw the reporter jump out of the doorway and desperately flag down a taxi-cab. Rebus had no time to be bothered with the man. He had some thinking to do, thinking about how in the world he could find Reeve. The possibility haunted him: he'll find *me*. I don't need to chase. But somehow that scared him most of all.

*

Gill Templer could not find Rebus. He had disappeared as though he had been a shadow merely and not a man at all. She telephoned and hunted and asked and did all the things a good copper should do, but she was confronted by the fact of a man who was not only a good copper himself, but had been one of the best in the SAS to boot. He might have been hiding under her feet, under her desk, in her clothes, and she would never have found him. So he stayed hidden.

He stayed hidden, she surmised, because he was on the move, swiftly and methodically moving through the streets and bars of Edinburgh in search of his prey, knowing that when found, the prey would turn hunter once more.

But Gill went on trying, shivering now and then when she thought of her lover's grim and horrific past, and of the mentality of those who decided that such things were necessary. Poor John. What would she have done? She would have walked right out of that cell and kept on walking, just as he had done. And yet she would have felt guilty, too, just as he had felt guilt, and she would have put it all behind her, scarred invisibly.

Why did the men in her life have to be such complicated, fraught, screwed-up bastards? Did she attract the soiled goods only? It might have been humorous, but then there was Samantha to think about, and that wasn't funny at all. Where did you start looking if you wanted to find a needle? She remembered Superintendent Wallace's words: *they've got the same boss we have.* That was a truth well worth contemplating in all its complexity. For if they had the same boss, then perhaps a cover-up could be arranged at this end, now that the ancient and terrible truth had surfaced again. If this got into the papers, all hell would be let loose at every level of the service. Perhaps they would want to co-operate in hushing it up. Perhaps they would want Rebus silenced. My God, what if they should want John Rebus silenced? That would mean silencing Anderson, too, and herself. It would mean bribes or a total wipe-out. She would have to be very careful indeed. One false move now might mean her dismissal from the force, and that would not do at all. Justice had to be seen to be done. There could be no cover-ups. The Boss, whoever or whatever that anonymous term was meant to imply, would not have his or its day. There had to be truth, or the whole thing was a sham, and so were its actors.

And what of her feelings towards John Rebus himself, spotlit on the reddened stage? She hardly knew what to think. The notion still niggled at her that, no matter how absurd it might appear, John was somehow behind this whole thing: no Reeve, the notes sent to himself, jealousy leading him to kill his wife's lover, his daughter now hidden somewhere – somewhere like that locked room.

It was hardly to be contemplated, which, considering the way the whole thing had gone thus far, was why Gill contemplated it very hard indeed. And rejected it, rejected it for no other reason than that John Rebus had once made love to her, once bared his soul to her, once clasped her hand beneath a hospital blanket. Would a man with something to hide have become involved with a policewoman? No, it seemed wholly unlikely.

So, again, it became a possibility, joining the others. Gill's head began to pulse. Where the hell was John? And what if Reeve found him before they found Reeve? If John Rebus was a walking beacon to his enemy, then wasn't it crazy for him to be out there on his own, wherever he was? Of course it was stupid. It had been stupid to let him walk out of the room, out of the building, vanishing like a whisper. Shit. She picked up the telephone again and dialled his flat.

26

John Rebus was moving through the jungle of the city, that jungle the tourists never saw, being too busy snapping away at the ancient golden temples, temples long since gone but still evident as shadows. This jungle closed in on the tourists relentlessly but unseen, a natural force, the force of dissipation and destruction.

Edinburgh's an easy beat, his colleagues from the west coast would say. Try Partick for a night and tell me that it's not. But Rebus knew different. He knew that Edinburgh was all appearances, which made the crime less easy to spot, but no less evident. Edinburgh was a schizophrenic city, the place of Jekyll & Hyde sure enough, the city of Deacon Brodie, of fur coats and no knickers (as they said in the west). But it was a small city, too, and that would be to Rebus's advantage.

He hunted in the hard-man's drinking dens, in the housing estates where heroin and unemployment were the totem kings, for he knew that somewhere in this anonymity a hard man could hide and could plan and could survive. He was trying to get inside Gordon Reeve's skin. It was a skin sloughed many times, and Rebus had to admit, finally, that he was further away from his insane, murderous blood-brother than ever before. If he had turned his back on Gordon Reeve, then Reeve was refusing to show himself anyway. Perhaps there would be another note, another teasing clue. Oh, Sammy, Sammy, Sammy. Please God let her live, let her live.

Gordon Reeve had levitated right out of Rebus's world. He was floating overhead, floating and gloating in his new-found power. It had taken him fifteen years to accomplish his trick, but my God what a trick. Fifteen years within which time he had probably changed his name and appearance, taken on a menial job, researched Rebus's life. How long had this man been watching him? Watching and hating and scheming? All those times that he had felt his flesh creep for no reason, that the telephone had rung without a voice behind it, that small, easily forgotten accidents had occurred. And Reeve, grinning above him, a little god over Rebus's destiny. Rebus, shivering, entered a pub for the hell of it and ordered a triple whisky.

'It's quarter-gills in here, pal. Are you sure you want a treble?'

'Sure.'

What the hell. It was all one. If God swirled in his heaven, leaning down to touch his creatures, then it was a curious touch indeed that he gave them. Looking around, Rebus stared into a heart of desperation. Old men sat with their half-pint glasses, staring emptily towards the front door. Were they wondering what was outside? Or were they just scared that whatever was out there would one day force its way in, pushing into their dark corners and cowered glances with the wrath of some Old Testament monster, some behemoth, some flood of destruction? Rebus could not see behind their eyes, just as they could not see behind his. That ability not to share the sufferings of others was all that kept the mass of humanity rolling on, concentrating on the 'me', shunning the beggars and their folded arms. Rebus, behind his eyes, was begging now, begging to that strange God of his to allow him to find Reeve, to explain himself to the madman. God did not answer. The TV blared out some banal quiz show.

'Fight Imperialism, fight Racism.'

A young girl wearing a mock-leather coat and little round glasses stood behind Rebus. He turned to her. She had a collecting tin in one hand and a pile of newspapers in the other.

'Fight Imperialism, fight Racism.'

'So you said.' Even now he could feel the alcohol working on his jaw muscles, freeing them of stiffness. 'Who are you from?'

'Workers Revolutionary Party. The only way to smash the Imperialist system is for the workers to unite and smash racism. Racism is the backbone of repression.'

'Oh? Aren't you confusing two entirely different arguments there, love?'

She bristled, but was ready to argue. They always were.

'The two are inextricable. Capitalism was built on slave labour and is maintained by slave labour.'

'You don't sound much like a slave, dear. Where did you get that accent? Cheltenham?'

'My father was a slave to capitalist ideology. He didn't know what he was doing.'

'You mean you went to an expensive school?'

She was bristling now all right. Rebus lit a cigarette. He offered her one, but she shook her head. A capitalist product, he supposed, the leaves picked by slaves in South America. She was quite pretty though. Eighteen, nineteen. Funny Victorian shoes on, tight pointed little things. A long, straight black skirt. Black, the colour of dissent. He was all for dissent.

'You're a student, I suppose?'

'That's right,' she said, shuffling uncomfortably. She knew a buyer when she saw one. This was not a buyer.

'Edinburgh University?'

'Yes.'

'Studying what?'

'English and politics.'

'English? Have you heard of a guy called Eiser? He teaches there.'

She nodded.

'He's an old fascist,' she said. 'His theory of reading is a piece of right-wing propaganda to pull the wool over the eyes of the proletariat.'

Rebus nodded.

'What was your party again?'

'Workers Revolutionary.'

'But you're a student, eh? Not a worker, not one of the

proletariat either by the sound of you.' Her face was red, her eyes burning fire. Come the revolution, Rebus would be first against the wall. But he had not yet played his trump card. 'So really, you're contravening the Trades Description Act, aren't you? And what about that tin? Do you have a licence from the proper authority to collect money in that tin?'

The tin was old, its old job-description torn from it. It was a plain, red cylinder, the kind used on poppy-day. But this was no poppy-day.

'Are you a cop?'

'Got it in one, love. *Have* you got a licence? I may have to pull you in otherwise.'

'Fucking pig!'

Feeling this a fitting exit line, she turned from Rebus and walked to the door. Rebus, chuckling, finished his whisky. Poor girl. She would change. The idealism would vanish once she saw how hypocritical the whole game was, and what luxuries lay outside university. When she left, she'd want it all: the executive job in London, the flat, car, salary, wine-bar. She would chuck it all in for a slice of pie. But she wouldn't understand that just now. Now was for the reaction against upbringing. That was what university was about. They all thought they could change the world once they got away from their parents. Rebus had thought that too. He had thought to return home from the Army with a row of medals and a list of commendations, just to show them. It had not been that way, though. Chastened, he was about to go when a voice called to him from three or four bar-stools away.

'It disnae cure anything, dis it, son?'

An aged crone offered him these few pearls of wisdom from her carious mouth. Rebus watched her tongue slopping around in that black cavern.

'Aye,' he said, paying the barman, who thanked him with green teeth. Rebus could hear the television, the jingle of the cash-register, the shouted conversations of the old men, but behind it all, behind the cacophony, lay another sound, low and pure but more real to him than any of the others.

It was the sound of Gordon Reeve screaming.

Let me out Let me out

But Rebus did not go dizzy this time, nor did he panic and run for it. He stood up to the sound and allowed it to make its point, let it wash over him until it had had its say. He would never run away from that memory again.

'Drink never cured anything, son,' continued his personal witch. 'Look at me. I wis as guid as anybody once upon a time, but when my husband died I just went tae pieces. D'ye ken whit I mean, son? The drink wis a great comfort tae me then, or so I thocht. But it tricks ye. It plays games wi ye. Ye jist sit aw day daein' nothing but drinking. And life passes ye by.'

She was right. How could he take the time to sit here guzzling whisky and sentiment when his daughter's life was balanced so finely? He must be mad; he was losing reality again. He had to hang onto that at the very least. He could pray again, but that only seemed to take him further away from the brute facts, and it was facts that he was chasing now, not dreams. He was chasing the fact that a lunatic from his cupboard of bad dreams had sneaked into this world and carried off his daughter. Did it resemble a fairy tale? All the better: there was bound to be a happy ending.

'You're right, love,' he said. Then, ready to leave, he pointed to her empty glass. 'Want another of those?'

She stared at him through rheumy eyes, then wagged her chin in a parody of compliance.

'Another of what the lady's drinking,' Rebus said to the green-toothed barman. He handed over some coins. 'And give her the change.' Then he left the bar.

'I need to talk. I think you do, too.'

Stevens was lighting a cigarette, rather melodramatically to Rebus's mind, directly outside the bar. Beneath the glare of the street-lighting, his skin seemed almost yellow, seemed hardly thick enough to cover his skull.

'Well, can we talk?' The reporter put his lighter back in his pocket. His fair hair looked greasy. He had not shaved for a day or so. He looked hungry and cold.

But inside, he felt electric.

'You've led me a merry dance, Mister Rebus. Can I call you John?'

'Look, Stevens, you know the score here. I've got enough on my plate without all this.'

Rebus made to move past the reporter, but Stevens caught his arm.

'No,' he said, 'I *don't* know the score, not the final score. I seem to have been ejected from the park at half-time.'.

'What do you mean?'

'You know exactly who's behind all this, don't you? Of course you do, and so do your superiors. Or do they? Have you told them the whole truth and nothing but the truth, John? Have you told them about Michael?'

'What about him?'

'Oh, come on.' Stevens started to shuffle his feet, looking around him at the high blocks of flats, the late-afternoon sky behind them. He chuckled, shivering. Rebus recalled seeing him make that curious shivery motion at the party. 'Where can we talk?' said the reporter now. 'What about in the pub? Or is there someone in there you'd rather I didn't see?'

'Stevens, you're off your bloody head. I'm serious. Go home, get some sleep, eat, have a bath, just get to hell away from me. Okay?'

'Or you'll do what exactly? Get your brother's heavy friend to rough me up a little? Listen, Rebus, the game's over. I *know*. But I don't know all of it. You'd be wise to have me as a friend rather than as an enemy. Don't take me for a monkey. I credit you with more sense than to do that. Don't let me down.'

Don't let me down

'After all, they've got your daughter. You need my help. I've got friends everywhere. We've got to fight this together.'

Rebus, confused, shook his head.

'I don't have a bloody clue what you're talking about, Stevens. Go home, will you?'

Jim Stevens sighed, shaking his own head ruefully. He threw his cigarette onto the pavement and stubbed it out heavily, sending little flares of burning tobacco across the concrete.

'Well, I'm sorry, John. I really am. Michael's going to be put behind bars for a very long time on the evidence I have against him.'

'Evidence? Of what?'

'His drug-pushing, of course.'

Stevens didn't see the blow coming. It wouldn't have helped if he had. It was a vicious, curving swipe, sweeping up from Rebus's side and catching him very low in the stomach. The reporter coughed out a little puff of wind, then fell to his knees.

'Liar!'

Stevens coughed and coughed. It was as if he had run a marathon. He gulped in air, staying on his knees, his arms folded in front of his belly.

'If you say so, John, but it's the truth anyway.' He looked up at Rebus. 'You mean you honestly don't know anything about it? Nothing at all?'

'You better have some good proof, Stevens, or I'm going to see you swing.'

Stevens hadn't expected this, he hadn't expected this at all.

'Well,' he said, 'this puts a different complexion on everything. Christ, I need a drink. Will you join me? I think we should talk a little now, don't you? I won't keep you long, but I think you should know.'

And, of course, thinking back, Rebus realised that he had known, but not consciously. That day, the day of the old man's death, of visiting the rain-soaked graveyard, of visiting Mickey, he had smelled that toffee-apple smell in the living-room. He knew now what it had been. He had thought of it then, but had been distracted. Jesus Christ. Rebus felt his whole world sinking into the morass of a personal madness. He hoped the break-down was not far off; he couldn't keep going on like this for much longer.

Toffee-apples, fairy-tales, Sammy, Sammy, Sammy. Some-times it was hard to hold onto reality when that reality was overpowering. The shield came to protect you. The shield of the breakdown, of forgetting. Laughter and forgetting.

'This round's on me,' said Rebus, feeling calm again.

Gill Templer knew what she had always known: there was method in the killer's choice of girls, so he must have had access to their names prior to the abductions. That meant that the four girls had to have something in common, some way that Reeve could have picked them all out. But what? They had checked up on everything. Certain hobbies the girls did have in common; netball, pop music, books.

Netball. Pop music. Books.

Netball. Pop music. Books.

That meant checking through netball-coaches (all women, so scratch that), record-shop workers and DJs, and book-shop-workers and librarians. Libraries.

Libraries.

Rebus had told stories to Reeve. Samantha used the city's main lending library. So, occasionally, had the other girls. One of the girls had been seen heading up The Mound towards the library on the day she disappeared.

But Jack Morton had checked the library already. One of the men there had owned a blue Ford Escort. The suspect had been passed over. But had that initial interview been enough? She had to speak to Morton. Then she would conduct a second interview herself. She was about to look for Morton when her telephone rang.

'Inspector Templer,' she said to the beige mouthpiece.

'The kid dies tonight,' hissed a voice on the other end.

She sat bolt upright in her chair, almost causing it to topple. 'Listen,' she said, 'if you're a crank . . .'

'Shut up, bitch. I'm no crank and you know it. I'm the real thing. Listen.' There was a muffled cry from somewhere, the sob of a young girl. Then the hiss returned. 'Tell Rebus tough luck. He can't say I never gave him a chance.'

'Listen, Reeve, I . . .'

She had not meant to say that, had not meant to let him know. But she had panicked on hearing Samantha's cry. Now she heard another cry, the banshee cry of the madman who has been discovered. It sent the hairs on her neck climbing up each other. It froze the air around her. It was the cry of Death itself in one of its many guises. It was a lost soul's final triumphant scream.

'You know,' he gasped, his voice a mixture of joy and terror, 'you know, you know, you know. Aren't you clever? And you've got a very sexy voice, too. Maybe I'll come for you sometime. Was Rebus a good lay? Was he? Tell him that I've got his baby, and she dies tonight. Got that? Tonight.'

'Listen, I . . .'

'No, no, no. No more from me, Miss Templer. You've had nearly long enough to trace this. Bye.'

Click. Brrrr.

Time to trace it. She had been stupid. She should have thought of that first; indeed, she had not thought of it at all. Perhaps Superintendent Wallace had been right. Perhaps it was not only John who was too emotionally involved in the whole affair. She felt tired and old and spent. She felt as if all the case-work was suddenly an impossible burden, all the criminals invincible. Her eyes were irritating her. She thought of putting on her glasses, her personal shield from the world.

She had to find Rebus. Or should she seek out Jack Morton first? John would have to be told of this. They had a little time, but not much. The first guess had to be the right one. Who first? Rebus or Morton? She made the decision: John Rebus.

Unnerved by Stevens' revelations, Rebus made his way back to his flat. He needed to find out about some things. Mickey could wait. He had drawn too many bad cards in the course of his afternoon's foot-slogging. He had to get in touch with his old employers, the Army. He had to make them see that a life was at stake, they who prized life so strangely. A lot of phone-calls might be necessary. So be it.

But the first call he made was to the hospital. Rhona was fine. That was a relief. Still, however, she had not been told of Sammy's abduction. Rebus swallowed hard. Had she been told of her lover's death? She had not. Of course not. He arranged for some flowers to be sent to her. He was about to pluck up the courage to telephone the first of a long list of numbers when his own telephone rang. He let it ring for a while, but the caller was not about to let him go.

'Hello?'

'John! Thank God. I've been looking for you everywhere.' It was Gill, sounding excited and nervous and yet trying to sound sympathetic, too. Her voice modulated wildly, and Rebus felt his heart – what was left of it for public consumption – go out to her.

'What is it, Gill? Has anything happened?'

'I've had a call from Reeve.'

Rebus's heart pounded against the walls of its cell. 'Tell me,' he said.

'Well, he just phoned up and said that he's got Samantha.'

'And?'

Gill swallowed hard. 'And that he's going to kill her tonight.' There was a pause at Rebus's end, strange distant sounds of movement. 'John? Hello, John?'

Rebus stopped punching the telephone-stool. 'Yes, I'm here. Jesus Christ. Did he say anything else?'

'John, you really shouldn't be on your own you know. I could –'

'Did he say anything else?' He was shouting now, his breath short like a runner's.

'Well, I . . .'

'Yes?'

'I let slip that we know who he is.'

Rebus sucked in his breath, examining his knuckles, noting that he had torn one of them open. He sucked blood, staring from his window. 'What was his reaction to that?' he said at last.

'He went wild.'

'I'll bet he did. Jesus, I hope he doesn't take it out on . . . Oh, Jesus. Why do you suppose he phoned you specifically?' He had stopped licking his wound, and now turned his attention on his dark fingernails, tearing at them with his teeth, spitting them out across the room.

'Well, I am Liaison Officer on the case. He may have seen me on the television or read my name in the newspapers.'

'Or maybe he's seen us together. He may have been following me during this whole thing.' He looked from his window as a shabbily-dressed man shuffled his way up the street, stopping to pick up a cigarette-end. Christ, he needed a cigarette. He looked around for an ashtray, source of a few re-usable butts.

'I never thought of that.'

'How the hell could you? We didn't know that any of this was to do with me until . . . it was yesterday, wasn't it? It seems like days ago. But remember, Gill, his notes were delivered by hand in the beginning.' He lit the remnants of a cigarette, sucking in the stinging smoke. 'He's been so close to me, and I didn't feel a thing, not a tingle. So much for a policeman's sixth sense.'

'Speaking of sixth senses, John, I've had a hunch.' Gill was relieved to hear how his voice had become calmer. She felt a little calmer, too, as though they were helping each other to hang on to a crowded lifeboat in a storm-torn sea.

'What's that?' Rebus slumped himself into his chair, looking around his barren room, dusty and chaotic. He saw the glass used by Michael, a plate of toast crumbs, two empty cigarette packets, and two coffee cups. He would sell this place soon, no matter how low the price. He would move well away from here. He would.

'Libraries,' Gill was saying, staring at her own office, the files and mounds of paperwork, the clutter of months and years, the electric buzz in the air. 'The one thing that all the girls, Samantha included, have in common is that they used, if irregularly, the same library, the Central Library. Reeve might have worked there once and been able to find the names he needed to fit his puzzle.'

'That's certainly a thought,' said Rebus, suddenly interested. It was too much of a coincidence, surely – or was it? How better to find out about John Rebus than to get a quiet job for a few months or a few years? How better to trap young girls than by posing as a librarian? Reeve had gone undercover all right, so well-camouflaged as to be invisible.

'It just so happens,' Gill continued, 'that your friend Jack Morton has been to the Central Library already. He checked up on a suspect there who owned a blue Escort. He gave the man a clean bill of health.'

'Yes, and they gave the Yorkshire Ripper a clean bill of health on more than one occasion, didn't they? It's worth rechecking. What was the suspect's name?'

'I've no idea. I've been trying to find Jack Morton, but he's off somewhere. John, I've been worried about you. Where have you been? I've been trying to find you.'

'I call that a waste of police time and effort, Inspector Templer. Get your nose back to the *real* grindstone. Find Jack. Find that name.'

'Yes, sir.'

'I'll be here for a while if you need me. I've got a few phone calls of my own to make.'

'I hear that Rhona is stable . . .' But Rebus had already put down his receiver. Gill sighed, rubbing at her face, desperate for some rest. She decided to arrange for someone to be sent over to John Rebus's flat. He could not be left to fester and, perhaps, explode. Then she had to find that name. She had to find Jack Morton.

Rebus made himself some coffee, thought about going out for milk, but decided in the end to have the coffee bitter and black, the taste and the colour of his thoughts. He thought over Gill's idea. Reeve as a librarian? It seemed improbable, unthinkable, but then everything that had happened to him of late had been unthinkable. Rationality could be a powerful enemy when you were faced with the irrational. Fight fire with fire. Accept that Gordon Reeve might have secured a job in the library; something innocuous yet essential to his plan. And suddenly, for John Rebus as for Gill, it all seemed to fit. 'For those who read between the times.' For those who are involved with books between one time (The Cross) and another (the present). My God, was nothing arbitrary in this life? No, nothing at all. Behind the seemingly irrational lay the clear golden path of the design. Behind this world there was another. Reeve was in the library: Rebus felt sure of that. It was five o'clock. He could reach the library just as it was closing. But would Gordon Reeve still be there, or would he have moved on now that he had his final victim?

But Rebus knew that Sammy was not Reeve's final victim. She was not a 'victim' at all. She was merely another device. There could be only one victim: Rebus himself. And for that reason Reeve would still be nearby, still within Rebus's reach. For Reeve wanted to be found, but slowly, a sort of cat-and-mouse game in reverse. Rebus thought back to the game of cat-and-mouse as played in his schooldays. Sometimes the boy being chased by a girl, or the girl being chased by a boy, would want to be caught, because he or she felt something for the chaser. And so the whole thing became something other than it seemed. That was Reeve's game. Cat and mouse, and he the mouse with the sting in his tail, the bite in his teeth, and Rebus as soft as milk, as pliant as fur and contentment. There had been no contentment for Gordon Reeve, not for many years, not since he had been betrayed by one whom he had come to call brother.

Just a kiss

The mouse caught.

The brother I never had

Poor Gordon Reeve, balancing on that slender pipe, the piss trickling down his legs, and everybody laughing at him.

And poor John Rebus, shunned by his father and his brother, a brother who had turned to crime now and who must be punished eventually.

And poor Sammy. She was the one he should be thinking of. Think only of her, John, and everything will turn out all right.

But if this was a serious game, a game of life and death, then he had to remember that it was still a game. Rebus knew now that he had Reeve. But having caught him, what would happen? The roles would switch in some way. He did not yet know all the rules. There was one way and only the one way to learn them. He left the coffee to go cold on his coffee-table, beside all the other waste. There was bitterness enough in his mouth as it was.

And out there, out in the iron-grey drizzle, there was a game to be finished.

27

From his flat in Marchmont to the library could be a delightful walk, showing the strengths of Edinburgh as a city. He passed through a verdant open area called The Meadows, and on the skyline before him stood the great grey Castle, a flag blowing in the fine rain over its ramparts. He passed the Royal Infirmary, home of discoveries and famous names, part of the University, Greyfriars Kirkyard and the tiny statue of Greyfriars Bobby. How many years had that little dog lain beside its master's grave? How many years had Gordon Reeve gone to sleep at night with burning thoughts of John Rebus on his mind? He shuddered. Sammy, Sammy, Sammy. He hoped that he would get to know his daughter better. He hoped that he would be able to tell her that she was beautiful, and that she would find great love in her life. Dear God, he hoped she was alive.

Walking along George IV Bridge, which took tourists and others over the city's Grassmarket, safely away from that area's tramps and derelicts, latter-day paupers with nowhere to turn, John Rebus's mind churned a few facts. For one, Reeve would be armed. For another, he might be in disguise. He remembered Sammy talking about the down-and-outs who sat around all day in the library. He could be one of them. He wondered what he would do if and when he met Reeve face to face. What would he say? Questions and theories began to disturb him, frightened him almost as much as did the recognition that Sammy's fate at the hands of Reeve would be painful and protracted. But she was more important to him than memory: she was the future. And so he stalked towards the Gothic façade of the library with determination, not fear, on his face.

A news vendor outside, his coat wrapped around him like damp tissue-paper, cried out the latest news, not of the Strangler today but of some disaster at sea. News did not last for long. Rebus swerved past the man, eyeing his face carefully. He noticed that his own shoes were letting in water as usual, then he entered the oak swing-doors.

At the main desk a security man flicked through a newspaper. He did not resemble Gordon Reeve, not in any way at all. Rebus breathed deeply, trying to stop himself from shaking.

'We're closing, sir,' said the guard from behind his newspaper.

'Yes, I'm sure you are.' The guard did not appear to like the sound of Rebus's voice; it was a hard, icy voice, used like a weapon. 'My name's Rebus. Detective Sergeant Rebus. I'm looking for a man called Reeve who works here. Is he around?'

Rebus hoped that he sounded calm. He did not feel calm. The guard left his newspaper on the chair and came up to face him. He studied Rebus, as though wary of him. Good: Rebus wanted it that way.

'Can I see your identification?'

Clumsily, his fingers not ready to be delicate, Rebus fished out his ID card. The guard looked at it for some time, glancing up at him.

'Reeve did you say?' He handed Rebus's card back and brought out a list of names attached to a yellow plastic clipboard. 'Reeve, Reeve, Reeve, Reeve. No, there's nobody called Reeve works here.'

'Are you sure? He may not be a librarian. He could be a cleaner or something, anything.'

'No, everybody's on my list, from the Director down to the porter. Look, that's my name there. Simpson. Everybody's on this list. He'd be on this list if he worked here. You must have made a mistake.'

Staff were beginning to leave the building, calling out their 'goodnight's' and their 'see you's'. He might lose Reeve if he didn't hurry. Always supposing that Reeve still worked here. It was such a slender straw, such a tenuous hope, that Rebus began to panic again.

'Can I see that list?' He put out his hand, making his eyes burn with authority. The guard hesitated, then handed over the clip-board. Rebus searched it furiously, looking for anagrams, clues, anything.

He didn't have to look far.

'Ian Knott,' he whispered to himself. Ian Knott. *Gordian knot.* Reef knot. Gordian reef. *It's just like my name.* He wondered if Gordon Reeve could smell him. He could smell Reeve. He was as close as a short walk, perhaps a flight of stairs. That was all.

'Where does Ian Knott work?'

'Mister Knott? He works part-time in the children's section. Nicest man you could hope to meet. Why? What's he done?'

'Is he in today?'

'I think so. I think he comes in for two hours at the end of the afternoon. Look, what's this all about?'

'The children's section, you said? That's downstairs, isn't it?'

'That's right.' The guard was really flustered now. He knew trouble when he saw it. 'I'll just phone down and let him . . .'

Rebus leaned across the desk so that his nose touched that of the guard. 'You'll do nothing, understand? If you buzz down to him, I'll come back up and kick that telephone so far up your arse that you really will be able to make internal calls. Do you get my drift?'

The guard started to nod slowly and carefully, but Rebus had already turned his back on him and was heading for the gleaming stairwell.

The library smelled of used books, of damp, of brass and polish. In Rebus's nostrils it was the smell of confrontation, a smell that would remain with him. Walking down the stairs, down into the heart of the library, it became the smell of a hosing down in the middle of the night, of wrenching a gun away from its owner, of lonely marches overland, of wash-houses, of that whole nightmare. He could smell colours and sounds and sensations. There was a word for that feeling, but he could not remember it for the moment.

He counted the steps down, using the exercise to calm himself. Twelve stairs, then around a corner, then twelve more. And he found himself at a glass door with a small painting on it: a teddy bear and a skipping-rope. The bear was laughing at something. To Rebus, it was smiling at him. Not a pleasant smile, but a gloating one. Come in, come in, whoever you are. He studied the room's interior. There was nobody about, not a soul. Quietly, he pushed open the door. No children, no librarians. But he could hear someone placing books on a shelf. The sound came from a partition behind the lending-desk. Rebus tiptoed over to the desk and pressed a little bell there.

From behind the partition, humming, brushing invisible dust from his hands, came an older, chubbier, smiling Gordon Reeve. He look a bit like a teddy bear himself. Rebus's hands were gripping the edge of the desk.

Gordon Reeve stopped humming when he saw Rebus, but the smile still played games with his face, making him seem innocent, normal, safe.

'Good to see you, John,' he said. 'So you've tracked me down at last, you old devil. How are you?' He was holding out a hand for Rebus to shake. But John Rebus knew that if he lifted his fingers from the edge of the desk, he would crumple to the floor.

He remembered Gordon Reeve now, recalled every detail of their time together. He remembered the man's gestures and his jibes and his thoughts. Blood brothers they had been, enduring together, able to read the other's mind almost. Blood brothers they would be again. Rebus could see it in the mad, clear eyes of his smiling tormentor. He felt the sea rushing through him, stinging his ears. This was it then. This was what had been expected of him.

'I want Samantha,' he enunciated. 'I want her alive and I want her now. Then we can settle this any way you like. Where is she, Gordon?'

'Do you know how long it is since anyone called me that? I've been Ian Knott for so long I can hardly bring myself to think of me as a "Gordon Reeve".' He smiled, looking behind Rebus's back. 'Where's the cavalry, John? Don't tell me you've come along here on your own? That's against procedure, isn't it?'

Rebus knew better than to tell him the truth. 'They're outside, don't worry. I've come in here to talk, but I've got plenty of friends outside. You're finished, Gordon. Now tell me where she is.'

But Gordon Reeve only shook his head, chuckling. 'Come on, John. It wouldn't be your style to bring anyone with you. You forget that I *know* you.' He looked tired suddenly. 'I know you so well.' His disguise was slipping away, piece by careful piece. 'No, you're alone all right. All alone. Just like I was, remember?'

'Where is she?'

'Not telling.'

There could be no doubt that the man was insane; perhaps he always had been. He looked the way he had looked on the days just before the bad days in their cell, on the edge of an abyss, an abyss created in his own mind. But fearful all the same, for the very reason that it was outwith any physical control. He was, smiling, surrounded by colourful posters, glossy drawings and picture-books, the most dangerous-looking man Rebus had met in his entire life.

'Why?'

Reeve looked at him as though he could not have asked a more infantile question. He shook his head, smiling still, the whore's smile, the cool, professional smile of the killer.

'You know why,' he said. 'Because of everything. Because you left me in the lurch, just as surely as if we *had* been in the hands of the enemy. You deserted, John. You deserted *me*. You know what the sentence is for that, don't you? You know what the sentence is for desertion?'

Reeve's voice had become hysterical. He chuckled again,

trying to calm himself. Rebus steadied himself for violence, pumping adrenaline through his body, knotting his fists and his muscles.

'I know your brother.'

'What?'

'Your brother Michael, I know him. Did you know that he's a drugs pusher? Well, more of a middle-man really. Anyway, he's up to his neck in trouble, John. I've been his supplier for a while. Long enough to find out about you. Michael was very keen to reassure me that he wasn't a plant, a police informer. He was keen to spill the beans about you, John, so that we'd believe him. He always thought of the set-up as a "we", but it was just little me. Wasn't that clever of me? I've already fixed your brother. His head's in a noose, isn't it? You could call it a contingency plan.'

He had John Rebus's brother, and he had his daughter. There was only one more person he wanted, and Rebus had walked straight into this trap. He needed time to think.

'How long have you been planning all this?'

'I'm not sure.' He laughed, growing in confidence. 'Ever since you deserted, I suppose. Michael was the easiest part, really. He wanted easy money. It was simple enough to persuade him that drugs were the answer. He's in it up to his neck, your brother.' The last word was spat out at Rebus as though it were venom. 'Through him I found out a little more about you, John. And that made everything easier in its turn.' Reeve shrugged his shoulders. 'So you see, if you turn me in, I'll turn him in.'

'It won't work. I want you too badly.'

'So you'll let your brother rot in jail? Fair enough. Either way, I win. Can't you see that?'

Yes, Rebus could see it, but dimly, as though it were a difficult equation in a hot classroom.

'What happened to you anyway?' he asked now, unsure why he was playing for time. He had come charging in here without a self-protective thought or a plan in his head. And now he was stuck, awaiting Reeve's move, which must surely come. 'I mean, what happened after I . . . deserted?'

'Oh, they cracked me quite quickly after that.' Reeve was nonchalant. He could afford to be. 'I was out on my ear. They put me into a hospital for a while, then let me go. I heard that you'd gone ga-ga. That cheered me up a little. But then I heard a rumour that you'd joined the police force. Well, I couldn't stand the thought of you having a cosy life of it. Not after what we'd been through and what you'd done.' His face began to jerk a little. His hands rested on the desk, and Rebus could smell the vinegary sweat coming from him. He spoke as though drifting off to sleep, but with each word Rebus knew that he was becoming more dangerous still, and yet he could not make himself move, not yet.

'It took you long enough to get to me.'

'It was worth the wait.' Reeve rubbed at his cheek. 'Sometimes I thought I might die before it was all finished, but I think I always knew that I wouldn't.' He smiled. 'Come on, John, I've got something to show you.'

'Sammy?'

'Don't be fucking stupid.' The smile disappeared again, only for a second. 'Do you think I'd keep her here? No, but I've got something else that will interest you. Come on.'

He led Rebus behind the partition. Rebus, his nerves jangling, studied Reeve's back, the muscles covered in a layer of easy living. A librarian. A *children's* librarian. And Edinburgh's own mass murderer.

Behind the partition were shelves and shelves of books, some piled haphazardly, others in neat rows, their spines matching.

'These are all waiting to be reshelved,' said Reeve, waving a custodial hand around him. 'It was you that got me interested in books, John. Do you remember?'

'Yes, I told you stories.' Rebus had started to think about Michael. Without him, Reeve might never have been found, might never have been suspected even. And now he would go to jail. Poor Mickey.

'Now where did I put it? I know it's here somewhere. I put it aside to show you, if you ever found me. God knows, it's taken you long enough. You've not been very bright, have you, John?'

It was easy to forget that the man was insane, that he had killed four girls in a game and had another at his mercy. It was so easy.

'No,' said Rebus, 'I've not been very bright.'

He could feel himself tightening. The very air around him seemed to be getting thinner. Something was about to happen. He could feel it. And to stop it from happening, all he had to do was punch Reeve in the kidneys, chop him behind the neck, restrain him and bundle him out of here.

So why didn't he do just that? He did not know himself. All he knew was that whatever would happen would happen, and that it had been set out like the plan of a building or a game of noughts and crosses many years before. Reeve had started the game. That left Rebus in a no-win situation. But he could not leave it unfinished. There had to be this rummaging in the shelves, this find.

'Ah, here it is. It's a book I've been reading . . .'

But, John Rebus realised, if Reeve had been reading it, then why was it so well hidden?

'*Crime and Punishment.* You told me the story, do you remember?'

'Yes, I remember. I told it to you more than once.'

'That's right, John, you did.'

The book was a quality leather edition, quite old. It did not seem like a library copy. Reeve handled it as though he were handling money or diamonds. It was as though he had owned nothing so precious in all his life.

'There's one illustration in here that I want you to see, John. Do you recall what I said about old Raskolnikov?'

'You said he should have shot the lot of them ...'

Rebus caught the under-meaning a second too late. He had misread this clue as he had misread so many of Reeve's clues.

Meantime, Gordon Reeve, his eyes shining, had opened the book and brought out a small snub-nosed revolver from its hollowed-out interior. The gun was being raised to meet Rebus's chest when he sprang forward and butted Reeve on the nose. Planning was one thing, but sometimes dirty inspiration was needed. Blood and mucus came crashing from the suddenly broken bones. Reeve gasped, and Rebus's hand pushed the gun-arm away from him. Reeve was screaming now, a scream from the past, from so many living nightmares. It set Rebus off balance, plunging him back into his act of betrayal. He could see the guards, the open door, and he with his back to the screams of the trapped man. The scene before him blurred, and was replaced by an explosion.

The soft thump in his shoulder turned quickly to a spreading numbness and then to an intense pain, seeming to fill his entire body. He clutched at his jacket, feeling blood soak through the padding, through the lightweight material. Jesus Christ, so that was what it was like to be shot. He felt as though he would be sick, would faint clean away, but then he felt an onrush of something, coming up from his soul. It was the blinding force of anger. He was not about to lose this one. He saw Reeve wiping the mess from his face, trying to stop his eyes from watering, the gun still wavering before him. Rebus picked up a heavy-looking book and swiped at Reeve's hand, sending the gun flying into a pile of books.

And then Reeve was gone, staggering through the shelves, pulling them down after him. Rebus ran back to the desk and telephoned for help, his eyes wary for Gordon Reeve's return. There was silence in the room. He sat down on the floor.

Suddenly the door opened and William Anderson came through it, dressed in black like some clichéd avenging angel. Rebus smiled.

'How the hell did you find me?'

'I've been following you for quite a while.' Anderson bent down to examine Rebus's arm. 'I heard the shot. I take it you've found our man?'

'He's still in here somewhere, unarmed. The gun's back there.'

Anderson tied a handkerchief around Rebus's shoulder.

'You need an ambulance, John.' But Rebus was already rising to his feet.

'Not yet. Let's get this finished. How come I didn't spot you trailing me?'

Anderson allowed himself a smile. 'It takes a very good copper to know when *I'm* trailing them, and you're not very good, John. You're just good.'

They went behind the partition and began to move carefully further and further into the shelves. Rebus had picked up the gun. He pushed it deep into his pocket. There was no sign of Gordon Reeve.

'Look.' Anderson was pointing to a half open door at the very back of the stacks. They moved towards it, slowly still, and Rebus pushed it open. He confronted a steep iron stairwell, badly lit. It seemed to twist down into the foundations of the library. There was nowhere to go but down.

'I've heard about this, I think,' whispered Anderson, his whispers echoing around the deep shaft as they descended. 'The library was built on the site of the old Sheriff Court, and the cells which used to be beneath the courthouse are still there. The library stores old books in them. A whole maze of cells and passageways, leading right under the city.'

Smooth plaster walls gave way to ancient brickwork as they descended. Rebus could smell fungus, an old bitter smell left over from a previous age.

'He could be anywhere then.'

Anderson shrugged his shoulders. They had reached the bottom of the stairs, and found themselves in a wide passageway, clear of books. But off this passageway were alcoves – the old cells presumably – in which were stacked rows of books. There seemed no order, no pattern. They were just old books.

'He could probably get out of here,' whispered Anderson.

'I think there are exits to places like the present-day court-house and Saint Giles Cathedral.'

Rebus was in awe. Here was a piece of old Edinburgh, intact and undefiled. 'It's incredible,' he said. 'I never knew about this.'

'There's more. Underneath the City Chambers there are supposed to be whole streets of the old city which the builders just built right on top of. Whole streets, shops, houses, roads. Hundreds of years old.' Anderson shook his head, realising, as was Rebus, that you could not trust your own knowledge: you could walk right over a reality without necessarily encroaching on it.

They worked their way along the passage, thankful for the dim electric lighting on the ceiling, checking each and every cell with no success.

'Who is he then?' Anderson whispered.

'He's an old friend of mine,' said Rebus, feeling a little dizzy. It seemed to him that there was very little oxygen down here. He was sweating profusely. He knew that it had to do with the loss of blood, and that he shouldn't be here at all, yet he needed to be here. He remembered that there were things he should have done. He should have found out Reeve's address from the guard and sent a police car round in case Sammy were there. Too late now.

'There he is!'

Anderson had spotted him, way ahead of them in such shadow that Rebus could not make out a shape until Reeve started to run. Anderson ran after him, with Rebus, swallowing hard, trying to keep up.

'Watch him, he's dangerous.' Rebus felt his words fall away from him. He had not the strength to shout. Suddenly everything was going wrong. Ahead, he saw Anderson catch up with Reeve, and saw Reeve lash out with a near-perfect roundhouse kick, learned all those years ago and not forgotten. Anderson's head swivelled to one side as the kick landed, and he fell against the wall. Rebus had slumped to his knees, panting hard, his eyes hardly able to focus. Sleep, he needed sleep. The cold, uneven ground felt comfortable to him, as comfortable as the best bed he could want. He wavered, ready to fall. Reeve seemed to be walking towards him, while Anderson slid down the wall. Reeve seemed massive now, still in shadow, growing larger with each step until he consumed Rebus, and Rebus could see him grinning from ear to ear.

'Now you,' Reeve roared. 'Now for you.' Rebus knew that somewhere above them traffic was probably moving effortlessly across George IV Bridge, people were probably walking smartly home to an evening of television and family comfort, while he knelt at the feet of this nightmare, a poor forked animal at the end of the chase. It would do him no good to scream, no good to fight against it. He saw a blur of Gordon Reeve bend down in front of him, its face pushed awkwardly to one side. Rebus remembered that he had broken Reeve's nose quite successfully.

So did Reeve. He stood back and swung a heaving kick at John Rebus's chin. Rebus managed to move slightly, something still working away inside him, and the blow caught him on the cheek, sending him sideways. Lying in a half-protective foetal position he heard Reeve laugh, and watched the hands as they closed around his throat. He thought of the woman and his own hands around her neck. This was justice then. So be it. And then he thought of Sammy, of Gill, of Anderson and Anderson's murdered son, of those little girls, all dead. No, he could not let Gordon Reeve win. It wouldn't be right. It wouldn't be fair. He felt his tongue and eyes bulging, straining. He slipped his hand into his pocket, as Gordon Reeve whispered to him: 'You're glad it's all over, aren't you, John? You're actually relieved.'

And then another explosion filled the passage, hurting Rebus's ears. The recoil from the gunshot tingled through his hand and his arm, and he caught the sweet smell again, something like the smell of toffee-apples. Reeve, startled, froze for a second, then folded like paper, falling across Rebus,

smothering him. Rebus, unable to move, decided it was safe to
go to sleep now . . .

EPILOGUE

They kicked down the door of Ian Knott's small bungalow, a tiny, quiet suburban house, in full view of his curious neighbours, and found Samantha Rebus there, petrified, tied to a bed, her mouth taped shut, and with pictures of the dead girls for company. Everything became very professional after that, as Samantha was led weeping from the house. The driveway was hidden from the neighbouring bungalow by a tall hedge, and so nobody had seen anything of Reeve's comings and goings. He was a quiet man, the neighbours said. He had moved into the house seven years ago, at the time when he had started work as a librarian.

Jim Stevens was happy enough with the conclusion of the case. It made for a full week's stories. But how could he have been so wrong about John Rebus? He couldn't work that one out at all. Still, his drugs story had been completed too, and Michael Rebus would go to jail. There was no doubt about that.

The London press came in search of their own versions of the truth. Stevens met one journalist in the bar of the Caledonian Hotel. The man was trying to buy Samantha Rebus's story. He patted his pocket, assuring Jim Stevens that he had his editor's cheque-book with him. This seemed to Stevens to be part of some larger malaise. It wasn't just that the media could create reality and then tamper with that creation whenever they liked. There was something beneath the surface of it all, something different to the usual dirt and squalor and mess, something much more ambiguous. He didn't like it at all, and he didn't like what it had done to him. He talked with the London journalist about vague concepts such as justice and trust and balance. They talked for hours, drinking whisky and beer, but still the same questions remained. Edinburgh had shown itself to Jim Stevens as never before, cowering beneath the shadow of the Castle Rock in hiding from something. All the tourists saw were shadows from history, while the city itself was something else entirely. He didn't like it, he didn't like the job he was doing, and he didn't like the hours. The London offers were still there. He clutched at the biggest straw and drifted south.

Deleted material

Part Four

The Cross

CUT THIS TO THE
BONE . SOLITARY,
THEN REBUS - REEVE.
BRING IN A HOMOSEXUAL
SLANT

CUT OUT PP 90 - 110 in toto .

Chapter ~~One~~.

laid

I ~~lay~~ my pack along one row of seats and myself along the other, making
sure that I would have the carriage to myself. The train shuddered its
way out of the station, picking up speed with wheezing slowness. There
was no one to wave back to, and nothing to look back for. So I rested my
head on my arms and tried to sleep.

I had joined the Parachute Regiment at the age of eighteen. Why the
Paras? Well, I had wanted to fly. I had wanted to be able to jump out of
an airplane and feel the thrill of death, the odds of landing perfectly.
And, for different reasons, I had volunteered five years later to join
the Specail Air Service, the SAS. The train which lulled me to sleep also
took me closer and closer to my new home, the SAS's special training camp
in Wiltshire. I dreamt of Fife, of my boyhood, of all the games of soldiers
and the tales of glory in combat. And when I awoke, thirsty, hungry, I found
that the train was stopping, that I had slept for several hours, and that I
had arrived.

I threw my pack down onto the platform and leapt from my carriage. My
head felt groggy and I craved tea. I wondered if I would have time to eat
a snack before they came to pick me up.

'Trooper Rebus!'

He was a big bastard, sweating under the armpits. It was summer, and in
this neverending countryside the bees floated past and smells of wild flowers
hung in the air. These things made him seem out of place, his bulk somehow
obscene. He strode towards me, waiting until the train had picked up steam
again before speaking. He had been badged, wearing his insignia with a
certain nonchalance as if there were nothing easier than gaining that tiny
badge with its dagger and its motto. I wanted it.

'There's a jeep waiting. Come on.'

He walked away without further introductions. And I followed him, past

the empty waiting-room and the clock that had stopped ticking. I cannot
recall the name of the station. But I remember the name of the camp where
I was to be taken. It was called The Cross.

Sure enough, a jeep stood outside. The air was thick with heat, and I
was looking forward to feeling the breeze from the back of the jeep. A
driver started ~~it~~ the engine up as the segeant jumped into the passenger
seat. I swung my bags into the back.

'What the fuck are you doing?' roared the sergeant. 'Get your shit out of
my jeep. Now, the camp's six miles this way. Just you follow us. If you lose
sight of the jeep, then you lose your way. If you lose your way, then you
retrace your steps and catch the next train home to mummy. Alright?'

With that he banged the fascia, and the jeep took off, screeching around
a tree-lined corner. There was no time to think, no time to reflect. I just
hitched my pack onto my back and started jogging.

When I rounded that first bend, I saw the jeep waiting for me up ahead.
Then, with a roar more of laughter and derision than of gasoline, it screeched
away around another corner and was lost to sight.

This was the first of the sickeners, a sickener being that which is devised
to rid the SAS of time-wasters and no-hopers. With the pack beginning to feel
like a mountain on my back and my arms, only the thought of shame kept me
from jacking it in right there. I could see the faces of my friends in the
Paras if I returned to camp the same day I'd left. That would have been
intolerable. So I jogged, walked, and finally crawled through the afternoon
sun, losing all sight and all hearing of the jeep, but plodding on anyway,
hoping to find the camp without it. After an hour, I knelt in the road and
considered whether failure would not be better than this. Just then, a roaring
from behind became a screech of brakes. The sergeant stood over me, his
shadow huge in the failing sun.

'Well,' he said, 'in all my years of army life, you are the slowest
fucking snail I can say I've ever encountered. You really are pathetic.
This is no life for you, sonny. Tell you what — ' He leaned down over me,
grinning, his eyes dark. 'Let's drive you back to the station, eh? There's
a train due in thirty minutes. We could just make it. You put your feet up
in the jeep and I'll drive you back there myself. Sod this for a lark, eh?
You go back to your regiment where you belong.'

I had, of course, heard rumours about this sort of treatment.

'No, sir,' I said. 'I'm fine. I'll make it.'

'Sir!' He rose to his full height, looking like a rogue missile. 'You
don't ever call me sir!' He leant close to me again. 'Do I look like a sir?
Do I act like a sir? No, I look like a bastard, I act like a bastard, and I
am a bastard. You call me "bastard", okay? Not Mister Bastard or Sir Bastard,
just bastard. Understand?'

'Yes, bastard.'

I saw his foot draw back but could not avoid it. It arched high, then low,
a real pendulum of a kick which caught me dead in the gut and had me rolling
on the ground.

'Don't you ever call me a bastard,' he said, wagging a finger. 'Not ever.
You call me Boss. Do you understand? I could have you out on your ear, laddie,
for calling me a bastard. Do you understand?'

'Yes, boss.'

'Again!'

'Yes, boss.'

'Again!'

'Yes, boss!'

'Good boy. That's a good little boy.' He rubbed my hair. 'Now, are you
going to lie there all day, or are you going to get to your feet and follow

the jeep?' He rubbed his chin. 'I miscalculated back there. I'm afraid we've
taken you the wrong road. There's still seven or eight miles to go. At the
rate you run, soldier, it'll take you all fucking night to get there. Are
you sure about this? Are you sure you don't want to go back?'

'I'm sure, boss.' I rose to my feet. The kick still thrummed in my
stomach, but it had been a playful tap to him. He slapped my back.

'Come on then, sonny. Follow us.'

And I followed, staggering like a drunk man. I was not small, you must
understand. I weighed ~~about~~ 164 pounds, and none of it was excess luggage.
You don't last long in the Paras by being a 'sonny', a 'laddie', or even
a 'snail'. But I knew the rules of the game here; roughly, I admit, but I
knew them. I could not hope to comfort myself with the thought that things could
only get better. I knew that all they would get was worse.

As twilight settled upon the lanscape, and the birds began to sound the
end of their day, I pulled myself around bend after bend, eventually coming
upon the jeep again. I approached it slowly, expecting it to draw away again.
It did not. The sergeant was smoking a cigarette.

'Get in,' he said, his voice level, unconcerned.

I stared at him, then at the impassive driver, then at him again.
'No tricks,' he said. 'How's the stomach?'

'Fine. I'm fine. How far are we from the base?' I stood by the jeep, my
pack on the ground, my arms aching.

'Only half a mile. That's why I decided to give you a lift. Hop in.'

'Thanks, boss. But if it's that close, I'd like to run the rest of the
way.'

He studied my face.

'You look like a fucking ghost, son. No bullshit, now. Get in.'

'Will you take my pack and my jacket?'

He shook his head, then nodded. I stripped to the waist, threw everything
~~into the jeep,~~

into the jeep, and slapped on the fascia. The sergeant gave me a wisp of a
smile as the jeep roared away, and I began to follow it, enjoying the sweat
drying in the cool air, enjoying not having the pack to carry, enjoying the
run and the feeling that I was not about to let my regiment down.

Not yet anyway.

There were six of us in the room, which comprised three bunk-beds, three
chairs, a window and a small table. Home for the duration of the training.
I slept in a lower bunk, while above me lay the wiry figure of Terry Lomax,
an Australian who had been sent across to Britian to train with the SAS. In
another bunk were Mike Scully and Jim Brady (Scots Guards), while in the
last bunk lay Gordon Reeve and Paul McNab (Seaforth Highlanders, Black Watch).
Why they had put all the Scots together I could not guess.

'Up you get, you lazy sods.'

It was six in the morning, the start of my first full day of training.
While we washed, the talk was of the Middle East. The SAS were being deployed
there, and things were looking as though they could get nasty.

'Time for chat, eh?' The sergeant was peering in at us through the wash-
room door. 'Soon put a stop to that. You'll soon be so tired you'll hardly
have the power to breathe, never mind gibber on about nothing that bloody
well concerns you.' He stepped into the room. We were standing to attention.
'Get on and wash. Breakfast's in five minutes.' He began to pace up and down
while we washed. 'Do you know why you've been put together? It's not an
arbitrary arrangement, you know. Nothing's arbitrary here. No, you've been
put together because, in plain language, you are the men least likely to. Do
you understand what I'm saying? You six, and I'm including you especially,
Lomax, have, in our minds, got not a hope in hell of completing this training.
Not the faintest fart of a hope. Just thought you'd like to know that. Put

your minds at rest about the stresses and strains of passing. You have no
chance of passing. We've got your return tickets all ready and waiting for
you in our files. You're shoddy, you see. We've been checking up on you with
your regiments and you are all shoddy, falling apart even. Scully and Brady
are the real pushy bastards. We just love pushy bastards here, Scully and
Brady. Lomax is a total no-hoper, like everyone else in the Australian armed
forces.....'

'Don't push it, mate.' Lomax had shaving-foam around his lips, but he was
doing his best not to look ridiculous. Veins stood out on his neck like coils.
He was pointing his safety razor at the sergeant.

'Mate! Don't you ever call me your mate again, Lomax. I'd be angry with
you if it weren't for the fact that I know you'll be leaving us so very very
soon.' The sergeant, turning away from Lomax, who cut the air before him with
his razor, continued his roll-call. 'McNab, a has-been. Getting too old for
all this, aren't you, McNab?'

Paul McNab was maybe thirty to thirty-three. He looked fitter than the
rest of us put together, and he looked angry.

'You see,' the sergent continued,' McNab has something to prove, or thinks
he has. That's why he's here. He wants to prove to himself and to everyone
else that he's Peter Pan, the boy who never grows old. But you are old, McNab.
Your reaction times are shot to hell, and that's what you'll be if you ever
find yourself in the field. And that's why we'll fail you, no matter how good
you are. You're a liability, just as you stand.'

McNab dried his face, smiling at his tormentor, saying nothing. So the
Sergeant passed on to me.

'Snail-pace Rebus of the Parachute Regiment. Men who choose to jump because
they can do bugger all else. Can't run, can't fight back when down, and can't
stay the distance.'

'With due respect, boss, I think I can stay the distance.'

His face was suddenly in front of me, an inch from my eyeballs so that I could not bring him into focus.

'And I say that you can't. Bad luck, sonny.'

His breath smelled of caries, of dying organisms. He had death on his hands and death in his eyes. He could have put me out of action in about ten seconds dead, literally. I wanted to be like him.

'Now who have I missed out? Oh, Reeve, are you still here? Good God, I thought you'd packed your bags last night. Why didn't you? You're just wasting my fucking time here, Reeve. You're wasting everyone's time. You're a nobody, a shadow. I don't think I like the thought of having to order you about even. You're just a waste of my breath. Get your stuff together after breakfast. I'll fetch your travel vouchers from the office. Okay?'

'Fine,' said Reeve, smiling at the sergeant.

That got him. For a slight moment, almost imperceptible, he was startled. He marched up to Reeve and did the eyeball treatment on him.

'What did you say, Reeve?'

'I said "fine", boss. You fetch me my ticket and I'll shove it up your arse.'

I didn't see the fist flying towards Reeve's stomach, but Reeve did. He skewered sideways, caught the arm and twisted it around towards the sergeant's back. It was quick and it was clever. But not clever enough. The sergeant drove his elbow hard into Reeve's ribs, at the same time stamping down heavily on his bare foot with a regular issue boot. As Reeve gasped and crumpled, the sergeant caught his head between his arms and forced his fingers, fingers as thick as pork sausages, into Reeve's winpipe.

'I think I'm beginning to like you, Reeve. You're easier than I thought you'd be.' With that, the sergeant pushed Reeve away onto the tiled floor, where he lay, gasping for air.

'Breakfast's ready,' the Boss said, leaving the room.

'Jesus Christ!' We crouched over Reeve, helping him to his feet, throwing some water on him.

'Anything broken?'

'I'm fine.' He seemed embarrassed more than hurt. 'Fuck off, will you? I'm not a baby.'

'Maybe not, but that bastard made you look like one.'

Reeve turned on Terry Lomax, who was drying under his arms with his towel. The Australian was grinning, but Reeve looked fiery mad still, spoiling for a fight.

'You better watch yourself, Aussie.'

'Says who?'

'Hold it,' said Paul McNab, holding up one of his huge shovel-like hands. 'We're all tense. It's not our fault. It's that bastard's. So let's calm down and get to breakfast before there's any more aggro. Okay? This is the first day remember. There's a lot more aggravation to come. Keep your head on, whatever. That's the only way to get through.'

'I'll bear that in mind, Professor.' Reeve picked up his towel and washbag and left the room.

Chapter Two

My first six weeks at The Cross were the hardest six weeks of my life, bar
none. For the first ten days we did nothing, it seemed, but march and do
weight-training, ~~and~~ march and do press-ups, march and survive the numerous
sickeners, sickeners which quickly did away with a dozen of us troopers.
(Everyone who comes to the SAS is demoted to the rank of trooper until they
can prove themselves. I had been a corporal in the Paras, like many of the
other men, I'd taken a cut in pay to come here.)

The sickeners were inevitable, yet they always managed to catch us on
the hop. After a fifteen or twenty mile march (with pack), we would arrive at
our destination only to watch the lorries gathered there drive away as we
approached. The Boss would come over and inform us that we had another
ten miles to do for being so slow. One trooper gave up at that point, throwing
his pack and his uniform down onto the muddy ground (the SAS having contrived
some rain from somewhere), bawling out the Boss, who stood, arms on his hips,
smiling contentedly and glancing at us: look, he was saying, you'll be like this
soon. And some of us started to believe him. But we all started marching
again (all save that one), and when we'd covered a mile or two we found the
trucks waiting for us after all.

That was a sickener.

Another sickener, the one that finally did for Jim Brady, was the
mud crawl. During a march, with our packs still on, we would be told to
crawl under some tarpaulin. The tarpaulin was tight, so that our faces were
pushed down into the mud, and in the mud there would be little delights such
as sheeps' entrails, the corpse of a maggoty dog, blood and leeches and God
knows what. Brady came screaming from beneath the tarpaulin like a man
possessed. His face ruddy and his chest dripping coils of ~~li~~ dead matter,
he bawled out the Boss, and the Boss smiled and patted his shoulder. He liked

nothing better than to gloat on failure. That drove some of us on; others, it drove mad.

We usually had six or seven hours of sleep, but several nights we would be wakened in the middle of the night and told that we had thirty seconds to assemble some weapon that was lying in bits before us, some weapon we would never have seen before. Heads thumping and groggy, we would set to the task with fingers that seemed as pliable as dead meat. Then the Boss would leave us, informing us that we had only another hour's sleep left.

'Sleep tight,' he would say, 'another one of you is destined for the chop tomorrow.'

He wasn't always right, but usually he was. Lomax was shipped back to his regiment one morning without our knowledge. We were told that he had asked, in the middle of the night, to be sent home. In the morning his bunk was tidy and no note had been left.

We were also, in that first training-period, taught map-reading. This was straightforward enough. Each trooper, having gone through an elementary course, was taken into the wilderness at night and told to find his way back to camp by morning. Map references were given to us, but were never to be written down. That was the first law: memorise. The enemy would then be forced to torture you if they wanted to learn anything. As a corollary to this, later there would be training in interrogation and counter-interrogation techniques. They taught us map-reading in the Paras, so I was well-prepared for that particular test, and the elementary parachute course was easy enough, though we lost another man there. He was afraid of heights, and had not told anyone. The officers shook their heads. No one could believe that he had asked to join the SAS when he was scared of heights above twelve feet.

After a few lonely cross-country marches, accompanied by my map and compass (maps had always to be folded a certain way so that the enemy could not discover your destination from them), the day came for the big march:

forty miles to be completed within twenty hours, with a fifty-five pound
pack on your back and a ten-pounds rifle on your shoulder. Even the Boss
came along, showing us on a set of scales that the bricks in his rucksack
came to the necessary weight. He grinned at me as we readied ourselves for
the start.

'This is where we lose you, snail-pace. This is where we sort out the
men from the boys.'

A whistle blew, and he started running. There was a five-minute lapse
between us, just as in a complicated race. But the objective here was not
gold or glory; it was survival.

I spoke quietly with McNab and Reeve before the off. We had had precious
little free time in which to create friendships, but there was a sense of
barrack-room solidarity amongst us, and that was enough to be going on with.
McNab, I saw, was nervous about this latest venture. Perhaps, I thought, the
Boss had been right about the older man. Perhaps McNab was doing this for all
the wrong reasons.

But, just at that moment, I was damned if I could think of any right
reasons. We all had to be mad.

The whistle blew, and I jogged away from the officer with the watch.

'Best of luck!' called Reeve. Breathing regularly, I said my own little
prayer.

In the distance, I could see the Boss beginning to climb a rise. There
were two hills to cross on our intended route, and I made a wager with myself
that I would catch up with him before the first of them. In fact, however, I
caught him much earlier than that. He was breathing hard, too hard it seemed,
and his face was a dark, vein-scarred red.

'Cheerio, Boss,' I said as I passed him. He did not reply, and I did not
look back.

The intensive fitness training had paid off in gold. I could feel myself

fitter than I had ever been. Also, my senses were sharp, including that sense
which matters most: common-sense. I knew when to take it easy, and when to
cut corners from the route. They had picked a bastard of a day. Raining, a
fine drizzle that soaked and cooled the body down while inside the combat-
jacket I sweated profusely. The rain became like little needles, and my hands
began to turn numb, like lumps of wood ~~curled~~ carved around the straps of
my pack. The countryside may have been beautiful beneath that bruised-looking
sky, but I was in no position to admire it. My eyes were on the terrain beneath
me, and my mind was on pot-holes, heart-rate, dehydration, night-fall. Once
darkness fell, it would be like Hell out on this plain. Thank God the training
had prepared us for Hell.

A couple of tough and leathal-looking troopers ~~from~~ passed me before night
had fallen, but for a snail I thought I was going very well indeed. I rested
once, drinking a little water from a stream. There would be food only at the
end of the march, if I completed it. Luckily, as night fell, the rain ceased
and a large, bright moon came up, shining out from behind a slight veiling of
clouds. The countryside was lit up for miles around, and I remembered that it
was the ~~longest~~ shortest night of the year. That made my spirits rise a little, and I
plodded on towards the second hill.

'How are you doing?' Gordon Reeve was at my back.

'Christ, you're making good time.'

'So far so good,' he said, his mouth dry with gluey saliva. He attempted
to spit it out, but a long starnd of spittle merely gripped to his chin and
to the front of his jacket. He did not move his hands to wipe it away.

'The Boss is in a bad way,' he said. 'I passed him about five miles back.
He looked well and truly fucked. He was all over the place, nearly veering
off the route. Silly bastard.'

'Serves him right.'

We slowed to a walk, taking in cool air in silence. I was becoming a
little dizzy and was afraid that it would show in my walking. As I concentrated
on making every footstep level and linear, I thought of McNab and The Boss,
men older than us and perhaps, just perhaps, not so strong as us. It made me
feel a bit better. Every tiny victory like this over my consciousness was
something to celebrate, for every such victory stopped me from crashing to
the ground, the soft, inviting ground, to sleep and to admit final and
irremediable defeat.

'What about McNab?' I asked.

'I don't know. He left after me, and he hasn't passed me. He'll be alright.'

'Yes, he'll be fine.'

There was another long pause as we walked, then lifted our pace to a
slow jog.

'Go on ahead if you like,' I said. 'I'm alright.'

'No, it's nice to have a little company.' Reeve looked across to me and
grinned, his face a ghostly yellow covered in a sheen of sweat. 'But we better
stop yapping and concentrate on the task in hand.'

'Fine by me.'

And that was that. We jogged and walked, jogged and walked, and watched
the earth beneath us move from dull grey to dull blue to brown as the sun
rose and the birds started to squawk. I thought I could see an eagle
gliding overhead at one point, but I stumbled and was reminded to keep my eyes
on the track and the road ahead. My hands, arms, back and chest had gone
numb some time ago, and the pack on my back felt like a living thing, but
we had broken through the crucial barrier, beyond pain now and beyond words,
just machines to lift our legs and pound them down a few inches in front of
where they had been before, and to go on doing that until Kingdom Come.

I checked the map every now and then, never nedding to resort to the torch in
my jacket, but I did not have to tell Reeve that we were going the right way.
The path was clear enough, and we passed a few stragglers, some of them
in need of help, who told us by their presence that we had not strayed from
the course. Those poor men. But to stop would have been fatal now, to do
anything would have been fatal, anything except go on. My legs began to
chaff (?) against the material of my trousers, my thighs were cut by my
underpants, and my back seemed raw from rubbing, my shoulders seemed open
wounds. But none of that meant anything; pain had lost its meaning, its
reality. It was hard to imagine that there was a real world away from this
bleak landscape, a real world where people would be rising from their
musty beds and having breakfast, getting into their cars for the morning's
drive to work, cramming into trains and tubes to spew out into a million
offices all over the country. While we pushed ourselves beyond limits none
of those people would ever know about, would never have to fear or overcome.
It made the whole thing seem at once ridiculous and meaningful.

'I'm going to push on now, Rebus. See you at the dinner-table.'

And with that, as if someone had pushed him in the back, Reeve was off
and running. It seemed impossible, and so I refused to accept it. A few
minutes later I looked up again, and sure enough he was away in the distance,
pounding across the soft ground, pushing up the final hill. I knew that I
would be just within or just without the expected time, and so I refused to
be drawn into heroics. I slowed thankfully to a walk, a slow, staggering
drunk's walk, and admired the morning with its gossamers and its plants.
Then I stumbled again and fell, and as I pushed against the ground I felt my
pack pressing back down onto me, stopping me from rising.

'Shit.'

Slowly, agonizingly, I slipped the straps from off my shoulders, which
immediately began to rage with fire. Then, my pack on the ground, I was able

to get to my feet. My legs felt airy, weightless. My whole being was aching, but rejoicing also. I stared hard at the pack. Could I put it on again? Did I want to put it on again? The answer was no, but I put it on anyway. I heaved it from the ground and swung one arm into a strap. Then I arched to one side, swinging the whole pack onto my back and pushing my other arm into the gaping arc of the strap. I stumbled again, but righted myself. I was frozen now, a still centre. I looked behind me. There was no one in sight. I needed a push, needed someone to start the stubborn motor again. But no one was there, and I stood, wavering as though standing in water, thinking to myself that I was destined to be one of the poor sods whom I'd passed in the night.

No, that would not do. I pushed one foot ahead of me, then the other. I began slowly, like a clockwork mechanism, but picked up speed, each step hurting like glass splinters ripping through me. A wind was blowing now, and the sky was again the colour of a bruise, the colour of violence. There was violence inside me as I trod the stone-strewn path, but all around was quiet, the quiet before some vehement storm, the quiet of the other world. Even the birds had stopped their noise, leaving the wind to do its business and the clouds to churn and churn their way over me. The first drops of rain, goaded by the gusts of wind, came lashing horizontally into my face. I would take it, I would take everything that was coming and more.

'Come on, you bastards,' I cried, 'give me more!'

And then I was stumbling into the arms of one of the medical crew. I tried to push past him, but he kept on shouting into my ear:

'You're finished! You're finished!'

No, I was not finished yet. I would complete the march. They couldn't stop me now. But then someone pulled my head up and forced me to look around,

and I saw the lorries and the tents and the cooking food, the men milling
around those who had already finished the course. Gordon Reeve waved to me
from behind his mess tin. I had made it. I tried to wave back, but it was as
if my hands were glued to the straps of the rucksack, and when I looked at
them I found that they were bleeding.

'This one's a bit of a mess.'

'Get him some tea. Are you okay? Trooper Rebus? Are you okay?'

'Rebus is it? Twenty hours and fifty minutes dead. Well done.'

'Get him into the medical tent.'

Later, as they were bandaging my hands and my legs, and I was sitting up
to drink some sugary tea, Reeve came in.

'Have you heard?' he said. 'Have you heard? They've found McNab carrying
the Boss. Carrying him! He'd been carrying him for about five miles, they
reckon. McNab's suffering from exhaustion, but the Boss is in a really bad
way. Christ. He might die.'

But the Boss ~~was already dead~~
refused to die.

Chapter Three

No, the Boss refused to die, but we did not see him for a few weeks, a period
during which some of us thought we would die. There was no rest after the
endurance march. We still had to learn combat survival training (including
how to escape from the enemy and how to withstand torture; also how to give
torture). There were also field first-aid training and written tests to be
suffered, and the tests were by no means a soft option. The senior officers
would be there to watch us mutter and stumble our way through some presentation
or other, shaking their heads in disbelief at our inaptitude.

At this time there were rumours ~~about~~ of an imminent civil war in Ulster,
of the army being used to keep the peace and to root out insurrectionists.
We knew, too, that some of the SAS regulars were in Oman. As stories flew,
the day came for us to be badged. McNab, though drawn, looked proudest of
all. There was a special commendation for him, for having aided a comrade in
the face of adversity, but when it came to the citation for best trainee, I
was thunderstruck to hear my own name called. With my new beret and cap-
badge, I accepted the citation and the handshake. They had told me I was the
best of the bunch, and I could not help but feel elated.

There was a bit of a celebration in the mess that night. Crates of beer,
whisky and champagne were soon depleted, and some girls were brought in from
God knows where to dance with us. The officers were there, too, imploring
us to call them by their first names. I sat with Reeve and another trooper
from the Seaforths. We knew, I think, that this moment of glory was to be
short-lived. For a start, none of the regulars would think of us as SAS men
until we had proved ourselves way beyond this initial testing-ground, and there
was also the knowledge that only a few of us would survive the rest of the
two-years' training to become regular and long-term SAS soldiers. In a sense,

none of us had scratched more than the surface of what it meant to be a member
of the Special Air Squadron.

'Top of the class, eh?' Gordon Reeve slapped my shoulder, squeezing it
and raising himself to his feet. 'A toast! To John Rebus, a snail no longer,
but a bloody fine bugger all the same!'

'I'll drink to that.'

'Here, listen,' Reeve urged me to come close to his ear, 'I've heard a
few rumours, heard a few of the officers talking. They've got plans for us,
Johnny. Plans. Mark my words.'

Reeve slumped back into his chair, singing a plaintive chant of the
Highlands of Scotland, while I, feeling slightly woozy my, stood up to
get some fresh air. One of the dancing girls was outside doing the same.
She seemed surprised to see me.

'You're not Archie,' she said. 'Oh, well, it doesn't matter, I suppose.'
She reached for my hand, but I brushed her away.
'I only want some fresh air,' I said.

'Suit yourself.'
'We always do.' I smiled, but in studying the woman I found her more
attractive than I had imagined. No one seemed about to leave the mess.
'Okay,' I said at last. 'Come on.'

We had to decide which skill we wanted to specialise in. Reeve and I both
chose CQC - Close Quarters Combat - which entailed the use of aikido, ju-jitsu
and a plain old Browning automatic (13 rounds, 9 millimetre) in an enclosed
space. At first, we were beaten to a pulp by our instructors (some of whom
came from the Army School of Physical Training, while others were boot-tough
SAS regulars), and we found ourselves having to become acrobats as well as

everything else.

'You must enter the room,' I'd be told, 'and disarm the enemy by all means
possible while leaving the kidnapped diplomat unharmed. Intelligence believes
there to be four kidnappers, three armed with shotguns and one with a knife.'

This conversation would take place outside a mock set-up of just such a
situation. With the Browning, all two-pounds and seven-ounces of it, in my
hand, I would be told to get on with it. I had thirty seconds to complete my
attack.

There would, of course, be five kidnappers, not four. Our intelligence (known as
The Kremlin) would have got it wrong. I would duck and
weave after my crashing entrance, rolling and firing (blanks), seeking the
diplomat and the one with the knife. Then the whole thing would be played back
on a television set and I would have to go through my mistakes time and time
again. On more than one occasion, Reeve and I, together with two others (the
typical four-man unit) would have to carry out a raid on a mock-up of an
embassy or a warehouse or some installation. At first, we were shot to hell
inside twenty seconds, but we soon learned. Even our aikido instructors came
to be wary of us as opponents.

There were other things to learn. We knew how to kill men in unarmed and
armed combat, but we had to learn how to kill from a distance, and that meant
bomb-making, from simple booby-traps right down to the most sophisticated
timing and trigger devices. We were shown the favourite IRA bombs, cans of
nails with a little gelignite, alarm clocks used as timers, clothes-pegs
and solder-wire as triggers. It became apparent to me that we were being
trained almost as terrorists, so that we could appreciate how their minds
worked. To defeat them, we were becoming them.

And then there was the survival course. Carried out under combat conditions,
and run by a Joint Services Interrogation Unit, this was the real bastard in
the apple-barrel. Hunted by other regiments who, if they captured us, would

stop at almost nothing to prise from us information about our mission, we had
to trap and hunt for food, lying low and travelling across bleak moors and
hillsides by night. Aware that we were to be treated as enemy by our comrades,
aware of the stories of broken limbs and mental disorders suffered by those
captured in previous exercises.

Reeve and I, working with two others, seemed destined to go through these
sorts of test together.

'They've got something special lined up for us,' Reeve kept saying. 'I can
feel it in my bones.'

The other two men in our hideaway could feel it too, perhaps, for they
kept to themselves and darted us suspicious glances from time to time as if
we were a dangerous element - dangerous to them, that is. We had several tasks
to fulfil. These were reasonably straightforward jobs such as assassinating
a general, blowing up a power-station, handing documents over to a resistance
force at a pre-arranged location. We were behind enemy lines, working without
contact with our base (any base) and without reassurances that anything we did
was right or wrong. Trucks of men would hurtle past our undergrowth, dogs
would be heard barking up the wrong tree while we snuck away downriver, and
helicopters with searchlights would prod the night-sky as though pricking at
a haystack. But we survived, feeling good, feeling like the SAS, we survived
one week, then two. I spent time thinking back to my childhood, and to the
week's R & R which I had spent wandering aimlessly around London, putting in
time until I could return to the unit. Perhaps this feeling of ease had something
to do with it. Perhaps we were becoming too confident.

Anyway, no excuses offered, we were caught.

Lying in our bivouac, we had just slipped into our sleeping-bags for
a two-hour nap when our guard put his nose into the shelter.

'I don't know how to tell you this,' he said, and then there were lights and guns everywhere, and we were half-beaten into unconsciousness as the shelter was ripped open. Foreign tongues clacked at us, their faces masked behind the torches. Christ, this was for real. I tried to awake from the dream, but a rifle-butt in my kidneys told me that this was no dream. We had been captured by foreign soldiers, by men whose language we could not understand, despite our linguistic training. This was for real.

Acknowledgements

The writing of this novel was aided hugely by the help given to me by the Leith CID in Edinburgh, who were patient about my many questions and my ignorance of police procedures. And although this is a work of fiction, with all the faults of such, I was aided in my research into the Special Air Service by Tony Geraghty's excellent book *Who Dares Wins* (Fontana, 1983).

Rebus left the station at four o'clock. Birds were doing their best nearby to persuade everyone that it was dawn, but in reality it was still dark. Rebus decided to walk home, a distance of two and a half miles. It was a cool morning, the air damp with the expectancy of a day's rain. Rebus breathed deeply, relaxing now, but his mind was too full of those files, and little pieces of recollected fact & figure haunted his otherwise pleasant walk.

Near his flat, he passed a little grocer's shop outside of which were stacked crates of milk and morning rolls. The shop was silent, dead, as was the street, only the distant rumble of a taxi and the hesitant dawn chorus disturbing the solitude. Rebus looked around him, examining curtained windows. Then he swiftly tore six rolls from a layer and stuffed them into his pockets, walking briskly away. A moment later he hesitated, and walked on tiptoe back to the shop.

He lifted a pint of milk out of its crate and made his getaway, whistling silently to himself.

Nothing in the world tasted as good for breakfast as stolen rolls with some butter and jam and a mug of milky coffee.

———┤├———

~~Description of Flat.~~

~~He sleeps.~~

~~Wakes up. letter waiting (unstamped).~~

FOR THOSE WHO READ BETWEEN THE TIMES.

Bring in anecdotes of police life
  (eg. the head in the abbatoir's
  mouth, etc.) . . . .
    ALSO EDINBURGH'S SEAMY SIDE.